The Moanin' After

The Moanin' After

A novel by

L.M. ROSS

Q-Boro Books
WWW.QBOROBOOKS.COM

An Urban Entertainment Company

Published by Q-Boro Books

ISBN-13: 978-1-933967-35-6
ISBN-10: 1-933967-35-8
LCCN: 2007923275

First Printing APRIL 2008
Printed in the United States of America

10 9 8 7 6 5 4 3 2 1

Cover layout/design by Candace K. Cottrell; Photo by Jose Guerra
Editors: Candace K. Cottrell, Latoya Smith

Q-BORO BOOKS
Jamaica, Queens NY 11434
WWW.QBOROBOOKS.COM

Acknowledgments:

I owe a sincere debt of gratitude to every artist, every writer, every poet, every singer, every player, every musician who ever stroked the keys, the strings, and the skin of my soul.

It may indeed take a village to raise a child, and it takes a small, yet faithful army to feed the spirit of a writer. And so, I must thank my loyal troops: Candace, Sunshine, Linus, Lois, Ronnie, Joycelyn, Carolanne, Tim, Randi, Odessa, Lee, C.C., and Grady.

Dedication:

Rest in peace, Brotha Anthony Howard, who, like me, believed in dreaming in color.

The Moanin' After is a character study about people you will know, recognize and feel from the inside out. With themes of success, love, loss, deep loneliness, anger and hard-edged rage, ***The Moanin' After*** is about choices and their sometime brutal consequences. It's about secrets and lies and the way they can so slyly determine the shape of the future.

INTRODUCTION

Once, they *were* the party, baby. They were the freaks, and the dance, the music, and the whistles, the holler, the sweat, and the heat of the grind. They were the cool fools, hyped up on speed and booze and tripping on ecstasy. They were the high-pitched sirens and the manic screams of the city.

They made the streets, the clubs, the backrooms, and the alleys all moan and holler and freak beneath the indigo night. They were the sex, and the light, the smoke, and the furtive cigarette. They were the weed, and the high, and the ridiculous giggle after it. They were the hot sigh, the wild grunt, and the primitive sweat of the hard luck, transitory fuck.

They were this city's rogue Romeos and its sorrowful addicts, its oxygen thieves, and its dying poets.

And then, all at once, they were gone.

And now, on Saturday nights in New York City, some eight million people still exist to live and breathe, to date and dine, to drink and smoke, to party and get high. Some still live to dance, to freak, to kiss, and to fall in lust with a body that glows as it sweats in the dark. Some still pray and some will still dream. Some will aspire, some will scheme, and some will sadly quit.

Some will still find the energy to create and some will only destroy. Some will bitch and whine and kick and curse and scream at God. And some will get their hearts broken, and dwell in the loneliness of their own private hell . . .

And the city still blinks and strobes and winks and laughs its steely cold laughter at them.

New York City, 1978

They called themselves "Da Elixir." It was just two hours before their first live show at the Apollo Theatre. Tyrone Hunter, David Richmond, Pascal "Face" Depina, and Faison "Browny" Brown were teenage boys, sitting on the train, high on dreams, and envisioning a future so bright, they'd all have to resort to sporting Wayfarer shades.

Browny imagined his own exotic Paradise.

"When my career jumps off, I'ma be like, fuck y'all! For real, yo. Fuck you bastards! I'ma build me a mansion on a beach in Bali, and just cool the fuck out, eatin' peaches with some freaks in bikinis, yo!"

"Hell, you losers can eat the dust from my crush, fat-ass, fully laid-out, mint-green Mercedes. Yeah, I'll probably go to Hollyrock, make a few pics, and marry a couple starlets. Then, I'll just get fat and bald and talk about what hot gold shit I *used* to be," Face Depina predicted, high on weed, Hennessy, and dreams.

"Hmmm. 'Marry a couple starlets,' Facey? Somehow, I just don't see *that* in the cards for you," David teased.

Face gave David a smirk and shot him the middle finger.

"Now, as for me, well, I see myself giving a Royal Command Performance," David predicted. "And after my bold and daring *pas de deux* with some hopefully Nubian Nureyev, everyone will be agog. But I'll still be a rebel dancer, so I'll wear a bloody, bawdy, blooming jock to tea," David joked in veddy proper English.

Then Ty chimed in, as only Tyrone Hunter would.

"Well, later for the Brits, boss rides, and Bali. If any of you future egomaniacs even think about trippin' around me, I'll just have to write a nasty tell-all about your rich, sad, pathetic asses," he promised.

It becomes a running theme in life how memory floats in and out of shadow, then burns with a light so bright that it stifles the present. You see a face or you hear a song. It triggers something *warm* in your mind. It resonates in your heart, it radiates in your soul, and suddenly you are drawn into this whole other place. It is some calmer, more beautiful space; a deeper dimension, more valid than reality could ever be. The memory is so vivid, that for a few fresh moments, you are free to exist inside this time and place again. You are with someone, some well-loved face, and they are with you. The aura, the vibe, the memory is alive inside this golden hue of light. You are suddenly imbued by this light, and the feeling inside it becomes so intense. You can *smell* the air around you. You can feel this person's presence, see them, hear them as clearly as you experience the music. You are *there*. It feels just right. You love and *need* this place so much, you long to close your eyes and drift away inside the sheer reverie of it.

You want to reside there, to stay fixed in that place until the other side of forever.

But then suddenly, the song ends, the mood, and the face, it drifts away. And you're back here again, stuck inside the less sacred, less authentic, less *real* present place.

Perhaps we should thank God that memories can sometimes stifle the present.

CHAPTER ONE

SPIRITS IN THE MATERIAL WORLD

New York City, December 1994

A part of Harlem was still in mourning. The spirit of Tyrone Hunter had left the brownstone building. For some, it is indeed a sad time whenever an artist dies. Another of their minions had left them, vacated that heady world of their own re-invention: a world of creativity, of music, of dance, and of loud and quietly tragic beauty. Never again would he walk these city streets of lovers and losers, nor step side by side with the deeply fabulous and forlorn. There would be no more sightings of his long thin shadow rubbing and cavorting with the neon-lit poseurs. The angel of fate had selfishly taken him. Now, his *absence* was a palpable thing. He would not be among those veteran eccentrics who'd strut and fret under garish city lights. He would never again speak to the plight of the homeless, or write with cryptic disdain for the terminally chic. He was gone, and with his death, so went his dream of love, his vision of coupling and of transcendent sex with *meaning*. *Gone* . . . was his impression of long blue moans manifesting in sighs that came, and left, but never saw the fortune in this prize he'd offered.

Ironically, it was he, Tyrone Hunter who had once said to his best friend:

"Sometimes, when you're happy, you think: Hey! I've got the world by its big ole nappy balls. Then that world twists, and it all slides away so quickly. Someone you *love* with all your heart is suddenly . . . gone. Just gone. And it's so fucking hard to contemplate: *that* was the last time I'd ever see his face. Nobody warns you, everything good and right and gay would be suddenly just vanish, with nothing and no one to ever take their place. No one smiles, and says, 'Please, baby boy. See this *crazy* look? *Remember* this crazy look, because tomorrow it will be stolen right from your eyes.' "

Tyrone Hunter held on to things like souvenirs from a sad and finite little fair called: Life. David Richmond was inside that haunted apartment; the one Ty had long considered *home*. He was going over papers and clearing out the myriad of Tyrone's earthly possessions. This was both an emotional and tedious undertaking. As anal and meticulous as Tyrone could be, everything held its own precious space and memory. It only made David even more unsure of what he should keep, and just what he should toss. David was gingerly placing a pile of manuscripts inside a cardboard box, and as he did, a large stack of leather bound tablets fell to the floor.

"Mmmm . . . what's this? *More* literary junk, Ty? When did you ever *not* write? Damn you, and your fuckin' writing! Maybe you should've tried *living* a little bit more, ya dead, half-beautiful bastard!" David hollered those words in a scuff of a voice. It was the only voice he could muster. He was surprised that his anger at Tyrone for dying that way he did hadn't made him buckle and dissolve into tears.

Something in David, some years-long curiosity, some need to reconnect with Ty made him spring into action. Quickly, he removed and unknotted the twine holding that first stack of tablets together. He blew away the light trace of dust, and opened the tablet.

The very first page read:

WARNING! WARNING! DANGER! DANGER! David! Davy! Duch! STOP! NOW!

Please! Mind Your Damn Business! If you are currently in possession of this journal, it can only mean one intrusive thing: you've been rummaging through my personal belongings! Damn you! Damn you! Damn you to Hell! Damn you with the patented-five-time-Esther Rolle-as-Florida Evans-version of the word: Damn!

David, where is your sense of decency? Where the HELL is your respect? Please, man! I know, somewhere way down deep inside you, you're better than this, so don't you dare disappoint me! I am begging you to please put this book away!

If you go any further, and you read beyond this first page, trust me—I will know it! Please remember, I've made a decent livelihood out of being a keen observer. So, if you read this, even on the sly, and then try to be slick about it, I will SEE right through you. I'll decipher it in your attitude. I will clock it, and feel it in our silences. Trust me. I *will* know. So BEWARE! If you dare read this, regardless of your so-called boxing expertise, I swear—on everything holy—I will kick your no-good, wicked little ass all up and through these mean streets of Harlem ! Do you hear me? You got that, punk? Please, put this damn book down! NOW—David! These words were not meant for your eyes. Well, at least not while I'm alive.

You have exactly five seconds to put this book back where you found it, starting now: 1. 2. 3. 4. 5!"

But David had not violated any strict moral code of ethics. He had not intruded upon his friend's privacy. The time for threats and the occasion for warnings had come to pass. Now, those journals, those mysterious writings were truly *meant* for him. Those words, those memories, those painful truths were intended for *his* eyes only now. They were to be Tyrone's final conversations with him.

David took a step backward. The creak of the floorboard resounded in a slow, kind of whining moan. It was a ghostly, almost otherworldly sound rising from the silence of that room. Suddenly, he was overtaken by a most naked sensation. This moment was what he'd always dreaded and tried his hardest to avoid: a feeling of being profoundly deserted, left all *alone* in the world. He looked to the heavens. Defying tears that gathered like impulsive rain clouds in his eyes, David turned the page.

To The Best Friend, I, Or Can Any Man Could Ever Have On This Entire Planet, David:

Well, Duch, these are my most precious journals. You know, the ones I was forever recording the experience of being me, Tyrone Hunter. I never have had the balls to publish them. I always realized their content could, and most probably would hurt people. Please, let me state, right here and now: I have always, always tried my best to be a good person, and an honest cat—especially with you, Duch.

But, let's face it, I'm human, and thus, I'm flawed and fucked up. The person revealed in these writings is still very much me. Only here, he doesn't have an editor, and no filter or a censor to pretty-up the sometimes ugly reality. Consider this . . . me . . . Tyrone . Unfiltered. Uncut. Unplugged.

Some of what you'll read—I can guarantee—it will most likely piss you off, Davy. So be it. You just need to know this: never once did I ever stop loving you, or being your friend. Today and always, you are my Best Friend.

What you will discover here will inform you, enlighten you, and yes, sometimes hurt you. The only possible reason you are in possession of these journals now is because fate somehow slipped up, and yours truly must've kicked that proverbial bucket before your little wild ass did. Now, ain't that something? Me, the always wannabe righteous one, the one who played it safe, who never left home without a condom, who warned and stressed and worried about you!

But, sometimes, strange shit happens.

Hey, remember that night just before Face Depina's fated shooting? Remember, when you'd showed up at the club, in drag. You'd just come back from attending Rue DeDay's untimely funeral. I was saddened, but mostly shocked because I'd no idea Rue was 'sick.' Remember? You said:

"She wasn't sick. Good queen. Horrible ba-a-ad judge of traffic. Glitter all over the place."

And I thought about it, and I replied: "Isn't it queer? I'd almost forgotten, there were *other ways* for us to die."

Yes. David remembered Ty saying that, exactly. At the time, David was high, damn near wasted on X, but he remembered it. He wiped the slowest tears from his eyes. He closed the book, and he exhaled a long and anguished sigh.

Why . . . why had Tyrone done this to him?

David recalled how, at the height of the crisis, when people were falling by the wayside, the tragic reality and the hollowness of those deaths had affected Tyrone's very soul.

But David had no time for the grief, nor the morose pity parties Ty would hold so close to his heart.

David said to him back then: "Ain't *you* the one who told me, 'never let the motherfuckers steal your joy'? Well, where that joy boy at? I *liked* him. Is he even in the building? Ty, I know you got dreams. You lettin' it steal all your fuckin' dreams, Baby-Boy. Don't you *want* to be *happy*?"

But Tyrone just stared out his window at the twilight activity of the metro, and he didn't speak. He couldn't seem to find the words nor the strength it took to speak them. He did *that thing* he so often did with his dreads, running his hands through them until they stood on end, like antennae, picking up the gist of his deepest thoughts. Finally, through slow and crazy tears, he managed to turn to his best friend in the whole world, and he said:

"I . . . I wannabe . . . something . . . some . . . thing . . . *radical* . . . something . . . fuckin' epic. I . . . wanna be . . . a happy . . . black . . . gay senior citizen."

The irony was, Ty didn't die of a big disease with a little name that was stealing all the lives and the breaths and the dreams of his friends. He died on another continent trying to save the world, one African child, and one hunger at a time. The small plane he'd boarded, suddenly, inexplicably fell from flight.

But David thought just maybe Tyrone Hunter might've died from a tragic disease called: Loneliness.

A Black gay senior citizen? It was a broad and epic dream, especially for certain urban black men in the 1990s. Everything—all those ironic words and lessons from years ago, they were flooding to the surface now.

David heard himself speaking out loud in that room:

"I was just tryna find the right place to put you, Tyrone. You dead bastard! I know you were tired. You'd told me as much. Are you still so tired now that you can't even muster up enough fuckin' energy for a decent afterlife? C'mon! Tyrone, *show yourself*, damn it! I've got about of 550 miles of hot words for you. I had hoped I'd come here, and you'd *appear* . . . just for me. I *need* you to show me the way, now, like always. Tell me everything is gonna be all right. Let me know how *fly* life is on the other side. Please. Just tell me, something! But all I got is this *nothingness!* I guess I don't deserve any Miracles.

"So, there's just these freakin' words in your journals now? That's *it?* Is this your weak little way of being my ghost? You and *your fuckin' words*! You always did *talk* too damn much!"

David threw the thick journal onto a daybed. He was unsure, uncertain if he had the strength to ever read it or any of its passages. This was only the first of many journals, and it was already breaking his heart.

New York City, Three Months Later

Some eight million people lived and breathed, walked or rode, ran or shuffled, prayed or got high, struggled or thrived, dreamed and worked, made love and fucked, laugh and cried, were born, and then, died here. But the irony of New York was, sometimes it became a small global town. Often you kept running into the same familiar friends and fools, cons and clowns, freaks and felons, paupers and poets, and even the occasional ghost. That night, for David, the ghosts and the fools of yesterday had taken to making their rounds.

The cool spring breeze flowed through his long evening coat, and for a while, it felt so refreshing for him. It was good to reclaim his tempo amongst the sexy people again. He was swinging his thing and bobbing along with this syntax of singing. He had his memories of Ty, and a little piece of music with him, and so, like Miss Nina Simone, David was **"Feeling Good,"** feeling strong, even feeling just a little high. He stepped with a certain artistry in his cadence, as if his every move was animated to coincide with the beat and the rhythm of his trademark strut. When David walked, it was all sauntering peacock and spontaneous bop, and people would recognize him from blocks away.

Someone had already recognized him.

Like everyone, David had a past. Due to this, and his well-earned reputation for the notorious Art of Being Outrageous, people would always think of him as "*That Wi-i-i-i-i-ild-ass boi David!*" But, in truth, David Richmond was no longer a *boi*, and he was not so wi-i-i-i-ild anymore.

In those days and months following the death of his best friend, David wasn't so sure if he was even *real* anymore. Sometimes he thought, maybe he wasn't real. Maybe some of us only *really exist* inside the eyes of others. Maybe some of us live lives, stranded inside a glorious past where there is music and light and laughter, and our friends and the people we hold closest to our hearts never really die.

Perhaps now, David was just a memory, a vision only some people could see. There were times on strange days and stranger nights, when he felt like he was nothing more than an urban apparition. Maybe, he too was just a ghost now, sleepwalking in the dark of the city, patrolling its dead and dying streets.

Many people do not believe in ghosts. David Richmond didn't always . . . but then suddenly life played its series supernatural tricks, and he slowly *began* to believe. If he squinted his eyes, just so, he could almost *see* those lost spirits. They were swaying and singing songs on Manhattan street corners. They were swinging from rooftops, and dropping down to the alleyways in the heart of the bowery.

David could have sworn he had seen them floating down

and skulking around the aisles of bookstores. It was as if they were calling him, yearning for him to *see* them, and to read their stories.

And if you don't believe in ghosts, if you never seen any evidence of their existence, then maybe only ***The Sensitives*** are truly meant see them, and to feel their cold breath on the skin. Maybe only a sensitive few can hear the tremor of their heartbeats rolling by. And even fewer will detect this long blue moan in their cries.

Sometimes David wanted to scream: "Tyrone Hunter! Can you see me? Ty, are *you* one of those ghosts now?"

It wasn't such a far-fetched notion. David had imagined he'd saw remnants of his departed friend in most every place he went. Ty was always alone, always roaming the city, his long-legged stride moving in and out of the face parade. David would catch sly glimpses of him in the strut of silhouettes filtering down Lexington. Ty was in the eyes, the arms, and the legs of a man wheeling a pushcart down Seventh Avenue. David could see faint pieces of him in the bobbing knees of hipsters, and in the bowed legs of a Harlem ball-player. Tyrone was even in those darker aspects of that sad-faced Brooklyn kid who never smiled in public.

More than once, David thought he'd saw Ty's spirit shifting against the race, the swoosh and the pulse of subways. It would drift and loiter like some past-life vagabond who'd rise and release his moan along the loneliest of streets. And at night, it would flit through the scuttling traffic and leave its homeless shadow against a firelight's flicker.

Sometimes and some days, Ty seemed to be everywhere, watching David with a sentinel's attention. Those quick and vigilant Hunter eyes were taking everything in while glimpsing his friend's progress. Those eyes were keeping score and keeping tabs on the pulse of David's lifeline . . . and measuring the weight of his failures.

If Ty had indeed become one of those lonely ghosts, then he was caught in between Heaven and that Special Purgatory; a waiting station comprised of black men who loved black men, and who died with their dreams and their stories unfinished. These were men who had perished with their joy and their utter bliss, sadly unrealized.

For David, it didn't seem possible that a spirit as vital and consequential as Tyrone could ever go away so abruptly. It didn't make sense that Ty would abandon him, without leaving some eloquent ghost around. Sometimes all David could do was wonder. But then sometimes, he didn't have to wonder at all.

Times Square was buzzing, and so he was, his body alive with its own fly-boy electricity. David Richmond was walking quickly beside a vision, a Tyrone memory. And Ty, for once, was keeping time with him.

As he passed the building where Xenon had once been, his mind shifted back to younger days when those vibrating floors and walls had become his makeshift sanctuary. He recalled how some of the best nights in his life were spent dancing that sly, inventive way he did. Back then, he was a slave to the rhythm of men with flames in their legs and groins as hot and erect as their dreams. You could find him, deep in that scenery, hopped up on speed, and bouncing to the echo and the energy of Techno. Other nights he affected the hard-core b-boy, hyped on weed and the street beat of Hip-hop. Still others, he became that tequila-wasted chico with a quick-smart mambo in his hips, sampling the hotness of Salsa.

David's whole life had been a series of fast nights, and fast dances with naked torsos, and sweat-drenched faces, when the music ignited his inner freak, and neon would bathe his skin.

But he was younger, and beautiful, and effortlessly more limber then.

Though, he'd once been King of those fabulously nocturnal creatures who'd put the ART in "PARRR-Tay!" this night on the town had become a rare occasion for David. He'd said goodbye to that *other* life. It was another world, another time, and for David Donatello Richmond, many disco balls, lost dancers, and several hundred T cells ago.

In the blink of a swift and attentive eye, David thought he'd seen someone he *didn't want* to see.

Maybe it was, and maybe it wasn't, but just in case it was, he began to walk more briskly.

The streets and their numbers seemed to fly by like concrete speed demons. Forty-ninth became Fiftieth and Fiftieth became Fifty-first all in the velocity of an urban blur. Soon, he was at the crosswalk of Fifty-second Street. And as he waited for the light to change, a grimy hand from his yesterday touched the elegant sleeve of his evening coat, and at the same time, David heard his name being ***screamed:***

"YO! DAAAAAAVID?"

David turned. It was him. *Oh Gawd! Dammit! Faison Brown!*

CHAPTER TWO

THE GREAT UNSUNG & MISERABLE PRICKS

"Yo, yo, YOOOOOOOOOOOOO! DAVID RICHMOND UP IN THIS MOFO!"

David's shoulders stiffened, and he thought:, *Oh. God! Please! Not this charismatically-challenged bastard with a terminal jones to be rich and famous! Browny? Oh, no. Say it ain't so, "YO!"*

But it *was* so. Browny was all up in David's face. It was indeed Browny, in the flesh, wearing an absurdly loud plaid clown coat ensemble, his tilted green applejack cap standing high, like some unsightly exclamation point. Browny was rolling his eyes all comically at him . . . grinning, as if things were chill, all groovy and peachy keen between them, when we they both knew, they weren't.

"Browny. Daaaaaamn! Could ya speak up? I don't think ***every*** Negro up in Harlem heard you, bruh!" David snapped. Browny and that mouth! David used to joke: ***"If you can't be handsome, at least be noticed."***

And Browny, being Browny, he'd taken that phrase to a whole new plateau.

The light changed, as he proclaimed, "Davy the Dancer.

Ain't tryna dance *away* from me now, are you? C'mon . . . walk with me, talk with me, yo."

And so, that night just kept getting better.

"Yo, been a l-o-o-o-o-ong time, chief. Glad I ran into you, though, 'cause me and you need to rap about a few things," he said.

David's mind was screaming and then howling a most disgusted, "*Uuurrrrrrrrrrghhh! Freakin' oxygen thief!*" But he played it off, as only a former Performing Arts High student could.

"Really, darling?" he said.

Performing was what David did best, and it was the one link between he and Browny.

As a part of a long-ago assignment, they'd formed a group and called themselves, "Da Elixir." This was all back in that special school they'd attended. As a talented group of soul-singers, Da Elixir was the sum of four parts:

Tyrone Hunter, the writer, who was as persistent in his search for Love as he was in the poignancy of never quite reaching it.

Pascal "Face" Depina was the beautifully glorious teenaged Adonis with something a little broken inside of him.

Faison "Browny" Brown was the ghetto-bred thug with the chime of a Better Angel in his voice.

And David Donatello Richmond was the flamboyant dancer who was bound for Hollywood, and all places east of Babylon.

It was David who'd said back then: "Maybe the world ain't quite ready for us. Well, what the fuck! Guess what, world? We're here. We matter. We manifest. We're young. We're the shit. We're wild. We're a success. Got the whole fuckin freakin' R&B world at our feet! Ain't much stopping us now. Hell, we're the kings and *queens* of New York!"

And in less than twenty years time, two of them were gone.

Now the two surviving members were in midtown Manhattan, walking, as Browny kept talking. Yes, he was off and running with that mad swift and LOUD riff of his. He talked a LOT. So much of it was gibberish, and it reminded David that Browny could be a most tedious and verbal cat, indeed. Browny was always "'YO"'-ing and yapping, and riffing so rapidly, always fracturing English with a vociferous vapidness, and forever being his most annoying and most contemptuous *Browny*. There was some mention of his wife, Juanita, who had several children by various men, and their wanting and failing to conceive their own a little *Brownling*.

On his best day, Faison Brown stood a good five-six, and Juanita was a statuesque, five-ten. Browny weighed 160 pounds, dripping wet, and she tipped the scales at a solid 257. Together, they were a physical hilarity, a ridiculous unisex Muff and Jeff joke. People wondered about them. No one really *got* the connection. No one, including, David.

David thought, *Wow! Imagine that! Sometimes fate actually does gets it right . . . because the idea of Browny and Juanita reproducing is a wild and scurry concept, indeed.*

There was more talk, mind-numbing talk; something about a job he claimed he'd lost or just quit, which, he was most probably fired from, *if* that job had even existed.

To David's ear, it was the same shit, a different day, a different month, a different year. Everything he said was LOUD, as if he were talking to some piss-poor creature with a severe hearing loss.

David's mind drifted, as if often did, back to Tyrone. David and Ty would sometimes contemplate on just what made Browny so damned LOUD, so contentious, so *urrrgggh* . . . and so got-damn . . . *Browny!*

Tyrone Hunter, ever the amateur analyst said, "Davy. Be easy on the brotha! If you look at him, and listen to him, it's so obvious."

"What's so obvious, Brotha Freud?" he asked.

"Genetics, it fucked him in the ass. There's this talented, scared, desperate monsta living inside that little stubby body. In a six six-foot world of people being noticed, Browny represents that whole five-six, *Napoleonic* complex bullshit, personified. When you realize this, and where it all comes from, you have to allow him to just *be* Browny . . . though you still always hope someday, he'll *work it o-u-u-u-u-t*!"

But David never bought it because David was maybe a half-inch taller than Browny . . . and Emperor Napoleon was never a factor in his own complex complexity.

To David's mind, *the cause* went much deeper. It was a pure untreated case of D. C. D. (Dark Child's Disease). Years of being endlessly taunted and teased by those viciously creative Harlem kids had done a real number on Browny's fragile psyche. Eventually, he internalized it all, until it became his very own suit of self-hatred.

In some ways, David could relate. It wasn't so much different than being called a "faggot" as a kid, and hating the word, hating the meaning of faggot *in* you.

And so, for Browny being little and being dark, being what some called "too black," this was treated like some kind of terrible defect. Over time and agonies, it would grow into a handicap.

Some people go through life using their disappointments as some perpetual crutch to lean upon, like the saddest of all possible cripples. In the worst-case scenarios, it becomes a crippling of the soul.

"So Nita's keeps talkin bout wantin' a baby, and I'm out here without a decent gig, and like all this shit is tryna wear a brotha down, yo. But I ain't stressin' it. Got sum'm *big* brewin', Chief. And it's about to *get crackin'*, yo." Browny said this rather cryptically, and left his pregnant pause to float the inside the Times Square scenery.

Was David supposed to have *asked* what that "*sum'm big*"

was? He didn't dare, because he knew it would only invite more buster, more bullshit, and more Brownyisms.

"Yo! Can't get over' seein' *you*, man. Nobody told me your *stankin'*, scandalous azz would be rollin' though here tonight, yo!" he announced, so LOUDLY to all of midtown Manhattan.

My scandalous ass? Hell, my scandalous ass surely don't stink any worse than that stank fume wafting from your own.

He, and that mouth were *murdering* David right there, in public, and Browny didn't know it.

Or did he?

It was hard to tolerate people like that, on the regular, but tolerated his ass, David did. He had for years. Some might ask, why? Well, David could be quite saintly, that way. He tried, sincerely ***tried*** to take people as they were, no matter how loud or uncouth, no matter how fucked-up, and regardless of how foul, or how downright ***unfashionable*** they were. He was all for makeovers, but he stopped short at trying to *change* anyone. David had have been guilty of that behavior, in a past life, but in his old age, he'd found it just didn't work out, especially if those people weren't invested in trying to change themselves.

So, he'd breathe deeply . . . and he'd tolerate. That's just what David tended to do. This *toleration thing* did not mean he wanted to spend much *time* around tedious people and their "stupid, life-wasting asses!" Everyone had every right to their own misery. However, he wasn't about to sit idly by and listen to them bitch, wail, wallow, and dwell in their sobbing schools of victim-hood. No. Not David! Not anymore. Time was too damn short, and that was *not* the way David Richmond chose to roll.

So, he just let Browny talk. Hell! Who could've *stopped* him? He wondered if Browny had even noticed that it wasn't really a conversation . . . only him, delivering yet another of his ghetto blue soliloquies.

Frankly, David could not have been any less interested in engaging in a *tete-a-tete* with the likes of Faison Brown. They rarely ever ended pleasantly. Though neither one of them had come too close to being physically, *cut* . . . sometimes their conversations ended abruptly, and even violently.

Faison had his problems since God was a tot. But there was one particular behavior David Richmond *had* to correct in him: If you were not a part of David's family, not gay-friendly, or not one of ***"the children"*** of the tribe, then you did best not to disrespect him *or* his sexuality. There would be no calling him out of his name. And you didn't dare lay a hand on David Richmond, or anyone you ***presumed*** to be gay, at least not around David. He simply wasn't having it. And if you did, then David would check you. He would correct you. He would *deck* you, if he had to. And with Browny, well, David HAD to take it to the deck.

Yes, it was eons before, as high school boys, but some things endure and some moments are eternal. They play on a reel, and strobe light inside your memory, and their internal alarm can sound deep within the psyche.

Pretty boy Pascal "'Face'" Depina was a witness to that clocking and was amazed by the surprising viciousness of it. Seeing this provided some years years-long fodder for him to cackle at Browny. Depina watched the furious speed in that lethal left- hook when David tapped "The Brown Bastard," and Depina held his stomach, leaned against his locker, and cried out loud with laughter. Face Depina howled at the sight of Browny going down in a slow, fractured thug-boy ballet. He'd actually seen the lights go dark in Browny's eyes when the hook landed squarely and hard on the chin.

"Oh shit! Oh shit! Yo, David. Give me five! Man, you just knocked his thick, insecure Black ass out, yo! Cold-cocked him—HOARD!"

Being seen as *heroic* in Face Depina's eyes was a milestone for David Richmond. David felt all warm and self-assured deep inside, and he *lovingly* slapped Face Depina five.

As Face Depina would tell it, "Da-a-a-a-a-mn, kid! You should be *embarrassed* as HELL, Browny! Little *gay* David just laid you the fuck out . . . like KA- BAM! And you hit the floor all *HOARD*! Like, SPLAT!" Depina nearly died, laughing hysterically at him. It was legend.

It was also an *early* reason for what would soon become Browny's life-long, full-on hatred of Face Depina.

The lesson from Browny's messy little hallway encounter: Beware of small gay boys who also happen to be *trained boxers!* They ***don't*** play. Straight-up!

David didn't feel that Browny was necessarily *afraid* of him. But: "he respected what's left of his tattered li'l rep enough to *not* to fuck with me. Ever!"

And now, many years and many cried tears later, there Browny was, vampin and rappin', spinning and be-bopping, and in between, he was grinnin', just cheesin' like he was actually *glad* to see David . . . or something. David was keen, and when he whiffed, he smelled *a rat* under all that cheese.

But eight city blocks of Browny was all David could endure. And if Browny wasn't going to be *man* enough to address those foul things he'd said about Tyrone at the funeral, then there wasn't point in going any further.

As they'd reached West Sixtieth Street, David thought it best to put an end to the charade, that mockery of a conversation.

"Wish I'd time to continue this rap, girlfriend," he said. David had an annoying tendency of calling people "girlfriend" who were neither girls, nor a friend. "But I'm really just passing through on my way to Carnegie Hall," he fibbed.

"Oh? Fo real, Davy? You *are* lookin' kinda fab tonight,

yo," Browny said, checking David's style with an envious once-over. Of course, he *did* look fly . . . as David was, his usually elegant self. But that was clearly beside the point. He'd always dressed well, and for every situation. That night he rocked a self-creation: a long, indigo duster coat, with matching trousers, topping the ensemble with a rather natty pearl-gray silk ascot. Yes, David was, indeed, looking kinda low-key fly, that night. But this *wasn't* about his fashionable wizardry.

"Don't nobody ever see you 'round this place no more, yo. You a hermit, now? Gettin' to be like your boy Tyrone—rest his lonely soul. Hey, c'mon! Lemme buy you a drinky, for ol' times sake, yo."

A drinky? That sneaky little jab at Tyrone aside, you can't be serious. You couldn't possibly be. You? Browny, picking up a tab? That would be like one of the signs of the Apocalypse. Or some such shit. .

It was an historical fact. Browny never pulled jack but matches and remnants of lint from his own pocket . . . and David almost wanted to clown him, remind him of his notoriously Jack Benny ways. But fact or not, in David Richmond's ongoing journey in Becoming a Better Person, he swiftly chilled and kept his inner insult comedian at bay.

"Actually Browny, I don't drink anymore. Haven't, in almost two years. But you wouldn't know that," David said. It was the truth, his honest truth—straight, no chaser.

However, being Browny, he'd detected David's unwillingness to imbibe with him as an abrupt slight. It wasn't. David noticed that Browny looked somewhat discarded. He hadn't been, not entirely. If he *had* been coldly dismissed by David, surely Browny would have *known* it.

Trust. The Good Lord must be testing me tonight. I mean what else could this shit be? And yet, my quick, hip-smart fag wit button remains on edit. Imagine that!

David Richmond always had 90-11 ways to tell a bastard

to: get lost; suck my dick; kiss my azz; drop-dead, mother-fucka; eat shit and die, bitch; etc, etc. And 169 of them were non-verbal.

And so, on this night, David hadn't back-slid into the land of the seethingly scatological, and for *that* little victory of mind over matter, he was personally proud of himself. He'd kindly kept his tongue. Still, he witnessed that patented famous dark dark-child grimace of Browny's, and it had claimed his forehead in that most vile of ways. David knew him well enough to be aware of his hyper-sensitivities. He was always beyond poor, severely po, just plain ole broke-dick Browny. But he didn't look particularly junkie-shabby that night, ill-fitting, lime-plaid sport-coat ensemble notwithstanding. To David, Browny looked, *aiight*, if now not quite *all right*.

Was he clean? Had he finally sworn off that damned pipe? David couldn't tell . . . not really . . . but he did hope so. Like Ty, David *wanted* to believe in Browny. He'd always been a sucker for fools and busted-up dreamers. He held secret wishes for busted-up people. He always hoped they'd finally see and recognize their own potential.

"So, why don't you step into a bar with me? People need to *see* you, out here lookin' all fancy, yo," Browny asked in a tone caught between flirting and almost begging.

With you? In that clown coat, and matching chapeau? Negro, please!

"Thanks," David said. "You know me. I do *try* to keep up appearances in this li'l dive of a city."

"Yo, you *sure* you ain't drinkin' tonight? Or you just ain't drinkin, with *me*?" he asked, styling his cheap jacket and that hurt-up look again. Maybe he really hadn't *quit* the pipe, and a bit o' liquor would suffice until that next hit. He looked hungry, a tad sad, and perhaps just a little mad at David.

"Chill on all that! I quit, I told you."

Standing there that night, with the city racing around them, David didn't want to leave him, in mid-grimace, with that hurt feeling that he was being dismissed.

What would Tyrone do? David wondered. He thought for a moment, and then, the inspiration hit.

"So, Browny, you know I have my own salon on Seventh, right? The fashions are very fly, and we do some very exclusive designs. Why don't you drop by sometime? Yeah, come by, and I'll fit you into a *nice* li'l suit. The shirt, the tie, the whole magilla. Here. Here's my card."

"Yeah right!" he scoffed. "Yo, like I could really *afford* any of that ritzy shit *you* be designin'." He frowned.

"Browny. Can it! You can drop by, all right? Just call before you come, and let *me* worry about the rest." David winked.

"Fo real, yo?" he asked. His voice suddenly lifted and its pitch rose into something resembling a short yet beautiful song. It felt to him like a song of friendship.

"Fo real, yo," David said.

And for some reason, unbeknownst to even him, David found himself kissing Browny on the cheek. And for some stranger reason, unbeknownst to Browny, he didn't blanch or twitch at the touch of it. It was a moment when they were just *cool*.

"See you around, Faison Brown."

"Probably will, 'cause I'll be around, yo."

Little did David know then, Browny did have *sum'm big* . . . bordering on HUGE under the grimy sleeve of his cheap-ass sports sport coat. That night, maybe he'd wanted to drink with David, to pick his brain or to soften him up for the terrible blow.

If so, and if that indeed was the case, Browny could have just as easily had said, "Yo! I really need to talk to you,

David. It concerns you, me, Ty, and Facey, and it's important, yo."

But he didn't say it, which would later lead David to believe "The Brown Bastard" was trying to purposely be slick and secretive with the bullshit he was brewing. And *bullshit* was exactly what it was.

CHAPTER THREE

BEWARE OF BLUES SINGERS ON THE SKIDS

David would live to curse the night that one of those "fools" had come out to play; a fool determined to make madness and a mockery inside his old stomping grounds.

Say what you will about Faison Brown (and people usually did). He was a crack-head, a user, a felon, a class-free attitudinal bastard and a low-down and dirty, nasty, drunken boozer. He'd been an irritant, a hemorrhoid, and a thorn in almost everyone's side. All that and more was Faison "Browny" Brown, on a *good* day. But the one thing that kept Browny most alive was the fact that he could sing. He was a damn good singer. In his prime, he was a divine vocalist. No one with a working pair of ears would deny him his due, at least in that department. Faison Brown could sing. More than this, like a cockroach in a nuclear war, he possessed an inbred mechanism for survival.

He'd managed to outlive many of his loved ones, his few friends and acquaintances, and even his enemies. He was still here, decades after the death of his brother Trick Brown. He'd even lived to see Trick's murderer dead and buried, if long after the fact. Yes, as others dropped dead around him, Faison "Browny" Brown was still on the planet, still raising hell, still turning the word "YO!" into his own ghetto art form. He was still here, making that loud Browny noise, and still trying *to raise the dead*.

In Browny's mind, he believed just maybe there was a reason why he'd outlived the others in his long long-ago singing group. A reason and a cause that he'd outlasted the glossy likes of face depina, and even the high-minded Tyrone Hunter. '*Hell,*' he thought. *I'll probably outlive that little queer David, too.*

When he considered all he'd seen and been through, Faison Brown was not above swinging his own longevity like a big black dick in the faces of his oppressors.

In the spring of that year, he'd exhausted all other resources, but still, Browny was, "a man of ideas, yo!" It had always been Browny who'd tried time and again to get the guys in the group to reunite.

But as Browny remembered it:

Back in the day, those mugfuckers turned me down every fuckin' time. They all just dropped me like I was too damn hot! Even when I wanted to help my boy Jon, God rest his soul, with his medical bills . . . that damn Pass-cow "Face" Depina just laughed at me, yo. I remember that one night in Zebra Den. Depina was high and full of his self, as usual. When I came to talk to him about getting the boys back to together for a benefit, that motherfucker dismissed me, then tried to clown me in front of his fancy model friends. I wanted to kick his conceited ass right then and there. The nerve of junkie- bastard laughin' at me! And he wondered why he got *shot* in his high-yellow ass, that same damn night?

Karma is a bitch, yo.

Now he's gone, and Tyrone's gone, and David's not *interested*, so gettin' the group together, well, that's pretty much impossible. But there's always *another way* to score, yo. After all, I did have me a story to tell. Now MY story is the stuff of those bestsellers, a tale of my teenage bout with fame. I mean a story about greed, sex, and deception, secret homos, tricks, and the trickers and trickery of being famous. Yeah, ya damn right. I gots me a story to tell, yo!

Once, long ago, someone had told Faison Brown that he could never write is own story, much less a book about those days of long ago.

He didn't have the talent, or the clarity. He didn't possess the sober mind, the true details, nor the needed *perspective* to write a tell-all.

Apparently they were wrong.

While Faison Brown didn't actually sit down to pen his own autobiography, by himself, he had a ghostwriter do it for him. The following was the treatment to the World According to Browny:

> Once upon a time there were four boys in New York City. Three of those boys were very talented at what they did, and what they did was dance and sing like stars. They did it so well, they became famous, all while they were very young. The other boy wasn't so talented. But that didn't seem to matter, because his name was Face Depina, and when people looked at him, they thought they saw a Star Quality! While they were still teenagers, those four boys recorded a hit record together. That record made it to number one, and stayed there for three consecutive weeks. And for a short time, those four boys were golden.
>
> But then, one of them, the one who had Star Quality, and who thought he was SOMEBODY, suddenly up and

left the group. And then, because he decided to leave, another one soon followed.

That was the end of those teenagers, who were once so golden. But it wasn't the end of the story. No. The story was only beginning. The one who thought he was SOMEBODY became very famous just for having Star Quality. He stood in front of a camera, and he looked good.

That was it. That was all. And yet, for this, he became a very, very rich man. But was this famous-for-looking-good man ever really happy?

No. Why? Well, there were so many demons he needed to keep quiet. Too many memories were screaming in his head, and he tried like hell to kill the noise of them.

He'd developed a liking for sniffing that fine, thin, white girl up his nose. This was considered fashionable in the '80s, and I'd seen him snorting it many, many times. Hell, back in the day, I even did it with him, when he couldn't find someone richer, or prettier, or whiter than me. Some people are just born to be junkies. I believe Face Depina was one of those people. Nothing really worked, though. Not until the time he found his cure. Heroin was the drug of *his choice.* Sure he'd done the others, but inside a hotel room, one lonely, foggy night in London, when he stuck that first needle into his arm, Face Depina thought he'd found God.

Well, Depina lived and worked and played with his god for many years. Most people didn't even know. Then, suddenly, and very mysteriously, Pascal "Face" Depina dies of an O. D. ?

Question: How does somebody who had been a professional junkie, on the sly, for fifteen fuckin' years suddenly just O. D.? Riddle me that.

Suicide?

Oh, hell no! Not Face Depina! Never that! He was too crazy filthy *stinking rich. He was very good-looking, or so everybody thought. He was mad famous. He loved that limelight. Hell, he adored just being Famous Good-looking Face Depina too much to ever kill himself.*

So, I ask the question no one else seems to want to ask:

Who gave him that overdose? Who really killed Face Depina?

This is the true story of just the way it all went down."

New York City, Spring 1995
DAVID:

My shrink and I would sit inside a pale blue room. And there he'd be, studying me, with those intense blue eyes, as I'd recite my blues and my moans.

Bet I know what you're thinking. I do. You're thinking: so what he hell is a ***Black*** man doing sitting inside a shrink's office? What he dun done? What holy Hell did he raise, and how many fires did he set? Black men don't do psychiatrists. When we're in crises crisis mode, some of us tend to do drugs, or drink, or God. So, for *my* black Black ass to be there in that chair, surely it had to be an act of sheer buck-wild madness, right? As you sit with this book in your hand, and judgment racing at the curve of your lips, are you wondering how many innocent people did I, slaughter? Did I just go off one day, and shoot every motherfucker on the subway?

Well, I'm not violent, nor am I a ***merciless*** killer. Despite my slightly wicked ways, I'd always been a man with a deep and profound sense of grace. And so, by nature, or some capricious trick of fate, I'd always remained crime-free. But

I was sitting in a shrink's office for a damn good reason. You see, there was something seriously *wrong* with me.

Pssst . . . Can you keep a secret? Come closer. My secret is this: I am not a ***well*** man. Hell, I may already be dead by the time you read these words. If so, whatever you believe in, please, without getting all Dionne Warwick about it . . . please, say a little ***prayer*** for me.

David Richmond had been suffering from a chronic loneliness. For him, loneliness was a kind of disease; a syndrome so deep, so friendless, and desolate, that sometimes it even *moaned*.

He wanted to rid himself of that disease and its symptoms. He wanted to extinguish those haunting sounds in his ear, but he was beginning to hear them everywhere, like Muzak inside the closed elevator doors of his psyche.

In the time since the death of Tyrone, Doctor Horowitz had become, by proxy, David's semi-confessor. David trusted no one entirely, not anymore, so Horowitz had to settle for the demi-truth and the partial stories. But with this latest foul step of Faison Brown's, it behooved David to let go, to release some much needed steam and histronics.

"I'm telling you, Doc, the timing could not have been more perfectly sinister. Two of the main protagonists, the two people he held the most disdain and animosity for, were gone . . . and the dead can't fight back, can they?"

"Is that a rhetorical question, David?"

"Yes, Baby-Doc.," David exhaled. "See? After Facey passed, followed *only months* later by my sweet Ty, the memory of our group 'Da Elixir' has been fresh in some people's minds. The sales of our old single were suddenly renewed, and there's even been talk of finally releasing that previously unreleased LP on CD."

"So, are you about to become a celebrity again?"

"Me? Not hardly. That dance has been done to death. And that's not what I'm seeking anymore. But Browny? Please! It's all that Brown Bastard ever lived for."

"Do you resent him for having that desire . . . to be famous, I mean?"

"No. Hell, no. It was a dream we *all* had once upon a hit record. But the rest of us grew the hell up and got over it. And he can be as famous as his destiny allows, if he did so with his *talent*. He *can* sing. At least he used to sing. Hell, there was a time even *I* wanted to DO him when he sang. So let his hungry ass *sing* for his supper! But when he rakes *my* friends through this bullshit he's concocted and wants the public to think it's fact, yes, I do resent the HELL outta that!"

"Ok. That's understandable."

"See, when Ty passed, this greedy bastard saw opportunity. I guess he thought maybe, just maybe the turntables were finally spinning a new rhythm for his chronically hard-luck ass."

"How so?"

"Doc, ever since the day of Ty's funeral, after he unleashed all this foul, false, fucked-up shit to the media, I kept my distance from him. Sure, I *did* have a major bitch to pitch at Browny's ass that day. Trust me! But with all the hurt and stress I was under at the time, I'd decided to just let the bitch slide by, un-bitched at. To make matters worse, that last performance of his Irrational Black Madman Act occurred when I had *no voice* left. Fortunately for him, I was afflicted, and so I couldn't form the choice words to curse his monkey ass out!"

"Yes. You suffered from a form of aphasia. The emotional stress of Tyrone's death, it left you temporarily mute. And I've been meaning to get into that with you, David."

"Easy, Doc! One sickness, one *pathology* at a time, ok? I'm telling you, this was a *sick* and twisted thing he did. Browny waited until he was just outside the freakin' church to strike with the foulness. In one of those lucky-for-HIS-desperate-ass moments, a local *Eyewitness News* reporter interviewed him immediately after Ty's funeral. When that camera light went on, Browny went into his own self-promotion, fuck-my-departed-friend mode. Of course, this fool's display was broadcast at eleven. I saw it. I sighed. I hated everything he had to say. But he'd said it . . . fine! I thought that would be the end of it. Big mistake. Huge motherfuckin' mistake!"

Truth be told, Faison Brown was more than ready for his close-up that day. He'd been waiting his whole lifetime for it. On that solemn occasion, he did not freeze- up and suddenly become the dumbstruck, tongue-tied wannabe-a-thug of his old high school talent show days.

That day, Browny had *things* to say. Too much had been eating away at his confused and jealous gut. So, with his wife Juanita by his side, he told the intrepid reporter:

"I had to come . . . known him almost all my life. I was in the group, too. Ty mighta wrote the songs, but I was the *real voice* of Da Elixir. You can ask anybody, yo. We was just about to fly to the west coast to do *Soul Train*, when 'Passcow'—well you remember him as 'Face' Depina—he quit on us. And then that little David Richmond followed him. I wanted Tyrone to keep the group together. Yo! I almost begged him! I told him we could just find us two new members, yo. No! But he had *other* selfish plans. There was a whole lotta sides to Tyrone Hunter."

When asked what he would most remember about Tyrone, Browny paused, looked into the camera and said, "Yo, I didn't hate him or nothin. Fo real, I didn't. But if you want the truth: he stole the food that shoulda been in *my* mouth. And besides all that, my only brother was murdered one night, while hangin' out with Tyrone Hunter. That's right, I said murdered! And Tyrone didn't even catch a scratch! But how can you call somebody your boi, and friend, and when they in trouble, and you act like a coward, and you just turn and run?"

His wife Juanita tugged on his jacket. "Honey Bear, now's not the time for all of that."

"Baby, I'm just tellin' the man the truth. Yo. The truth shall set you free, right?"

It was the perfect sound-bite for a vulture-hungry media. Ironically enough, Browny had served as his own press agent. Suddenly reporters wanted to know more. And didn't Browny always yearn for his chance to shine?

Soon after, an enterprising agent who saw more than a little interest in a sensational story of tawdry and tantalizing proportions contacted him. Though Faison Brown's name had no marquee value, the players in his little saga did: Pascal "Face" Depina was once a world famous model/actor. And Tyrone Hunter's reputation as a successful writer and humanitarian was among one of the most respected within the community. Browny's darker portrayal of them would surely shake up readers, change some perceptions, and rock the rafters of others.

The agent assigned a writer to ghost for him. Contracts were signed, and then a hefty advance was provided.

And Browny asked, "Yo! Do I need readin' glasses? Are all those zeroes on this check, correct, yo?"

DAVID:

"To be real, Baby-Doc, I pride myself on being fairly sensitive. I've always been a cat who possessed several talents. One of those talents was that I *understood* people. I mean I understood them in a way others never could. This was a gift. But, the radar was *way off* when it came down to Browny's true heart. I had no idea of what went on in the man's viscera. After all those years, I never knew . . . I mean I had no fuckin' clue that Browny *hated* us all so much. I almost wanna weep for him. But to be honest, a part of my soul hurts behind this shit."

But what good were David's tears and against Browny's live grenade? What's a prayer against a shotgun's blaze?

David's voice drew quiet with emotion, as he confessed, "It's a real kick to the solar plexus to think: I know this person, and this person knows me. And maybe he's not and has never been my *favorite* person—but I never once wished him any ill will. It's really kind of creepy to walk around thinking you *know* a person—when in fact, beneath it all, there lived this sick and twisted individual—some emotional assassin, lying in wait to strike and kill you dead, at any given moment."

"Well, we can never know the true heart of another person, no matter who we are, or what face they wear," the doctor informed him. "But what do you think is his true motive, David?"

"It's too easy to blame it on liquor or crack, or the things that anger and grief make you say. If I had to name the *real* culprit, I'd say it's *naked greed*! Dollar, dollar bills, yo!"

The sad truth is . . . for The Love of *Money*, some people will kill and re-kill their own brothers. Money was always Number One with a Bullet in the life and hard-times of Faison Brown. This excursion into the seedy world of tabloid lit offered him more cabbage than he'd ever seen in his whole cabbage-free existence, and for the very first time, with *his* name on the check.

Juiced on that heady initiative, Browny riffed. He spit, he spat, he spilled, he guessed, he embellished, and he straight straight-up lied.

Summer 1996

The tales within his manuscript were inflaming and incendiary, to say the least:

Browny systematically dressed-down each member of the group. First and foremost, there was Pascal "Face" Depina. Having twice lived under the same roof as Face, Browny had indeed been privy to several of Depina's peccadilloes.

Face Depina was portrayed as a talent-free pretty-boy, hustler, bisexual junkie, with a coward streak as dark as a skid mark, and about a hundred miles long. Browny's hatred of him was apparent in every line dedicated to Face. But his descriptions of Depina's sexual proclivities were, at times, downright sickening.

Nothing and no detail was left spared, from Face's being an S&M devotee, to the special room he'd built for his more deviant activities.

Beyond its long and sordid trail of lies and deceptions, the book more than hinted that Face Depina's death may not have been the *accidental* junkie's overdose it was always believed to be. Just perhaps there was something far more *ominous* afoot. When one read carefully between the lines, one might have gotten the distinct impression that *Bliss* Santana, Depina's former flame, may have had her manicured hand in the deed.

However, the book didn't stop at the demoralizing of Face Depina. Tyrone Hunter was painted as little more than a lucky opportunist and a shyster who'd gypped them all, but most especially Browny, out of his rightful royalties. Ty, under Browny's treatment, was a tortured homosexual who lead a hermetic existence, who gave and donated most of his monies to charities because he was deathly afraid of dying from AIDS, and going to Hell for his deviant ways. Tyrone, at his best, was given to fits of playing God. To make matters worse, Tyrone was portrayed as a "coward."

And those were among the kindest things Browny would say about him.

No one was given a free ride on the paper trail of blame.

David, in Browny's version, was a fey and flaming queer, given to fits of blatant promiscuity, all in vain, because the one he truly loved, Face Depina, would have nothing to do with David's "faggot ass." Browny even suggested that none other than Face Depina had most probably *orchestrated* the near fatal gay-bashing incident David suffered on the mean streets of the Village.

No one came out of this nauseating tale smelling like a pristine rose in Spanish Harlem, except, of course, for Faison "Browny" Brown.

Yes, he managed to tell a few unpleasant truths on himself: his bout with alcohol, his cruise into crack cocaine abuse, and his time spent behind bars, yet he dismissed the fact that he'd become someone's jailhouse "bitch." But Browny's unique perspective was beyond hurtful and libelous. It was just plain wrong. His take on the life and times of Face, Tyrone, and David, simply put, reached the stellar heights of inaccuracy.

Was it all a case of bad juju? After reading Faison's version of the not-so-fabulous life, who in their right mind would possibly blame little Browny? The poor, unfortunate fool was a supremely talented lug who was mistreated, used, and abused by most everyone he'd ever met. He was chronically cheated, lied to, and left to kiss the concrete while the others within his group went on to live such fabulously decadent lives.

With the publication of Faison Brown's mendacious and moronic memoirs, David was absolutely enraged. He could not have cared less about the lies and half-truths Browny's tome divulged about him. But how dare Faison Brown *besmirch* Tyrone Hunter's good name, especially after all Ty had done for him! What of all those loans Tyrone extended that Browny never repaid, and all those coldest of times when most everyone in New York City had given up on the shabby likes of Faison Brown?

Just *who* would magically appear inside his dark and lonely corner? Absolutely no one cared, not a soul, except Tyrone Hunter.

Ty did so, because the greatest truth was that Tyrone deeply loved Browny's brother, Theodore "Trick" Brown.

Trick's untimely death remained a bitterly sad and tortured memory with the deepest regions of Tyrone's heart. So, for Browny to even *suggest* that Tyrone could have STOPPED Trick's murder, and he just didn't bother, this ugly accusation alone was surely enough to have made both Tyrone and Trick rage, and spin in their uneasy graves.

But David Richmond was still alive, still vivid and livid! And so, it became his job to do the raging, the spinning, and the fighting for the dead.

DAVID:

I had read quite enough of all that talk, thank you. Through the years, despite Browny's penchant for being this crude, greedy, and endlessly uncouth bastard, and even despite his homo-hating ways, I thought I'd forged a *pleasant-enough* relationship with him.

People can surprise you sometimes. People, even the dark and miserable one's can show you . . . the God in them.

Once, Tyrone called me back in November of '91. He was all upset and worried, because it was the night Magic Johnson announced his HIV status to the world.

"Did you hear? Did you hear about Magic?"

But I was still living and swinging in the swirl of my own

self-denial. Tyrone was adamant. Damn it! *Magic had it!* Wasn't that enough evidence that *no one* was safe?

Maybe what I said seemed jovial, and trite:

"Well, it's true, I did spend some time in LA. But Ty, I swear we never once knocked Nikes . . . or in *his* case, clacked Converse."

Tyrone became all appalled, all offended and shit. He virtually called me a "serial-killer" for running around NYC having indiscriminate sex, without getting tested for HIV. His attitude absolutely reeked. It was another of his little morality manifestos from atop his little white horse in Harlem. It sounded wholly judgmental, and this was not the first time, I might add. Self-righteous moral-policing bastard! I'd had about enough of him! So, I'd promptly hung up on his pompous ass.

Those were my wild days. I was being David, on nine. The Wild Stage David was in an entirely different league. I was busy exercising the demons of my God-given *Davidness*, the sexual dynamo, without much thought or conscience. I was being *me*, and how dare my so-called *best friend* pass judgment on me? I'd had it with him! My attitude was like, "Fuck Tyrone Hunter!"

Consider me divorced from that friendship.

Well, *months* passed.

Ty would call me, sounding all pitiful and pathetic and leave these deeply apologetic messages on my machine. But I was pissed, hurt, and deeply into being the stubborn bitch, so I never once answered him.

Then, in the spring of 1992, Ty's father passed. I'd no idea. Tyrone and I were still not on speaking terms.

Enter Browny. Faison Brown, of all fuckin' people on the planet! With Mr. Hunter's funeral looming, Faison somehow found his *most righteous shred of manhood*. He called me to deliver the terrible news, and mostly to guilt me and remind me into recognizing what a treasure I had in Tyrone:

"Yo, David. You got yourself a friend in Tyrone. Ya ain't gon' find no better. Shit! Let's face it, ya don't deserve none. Ain't sayin' he's perfect, yo. But he's good people. You know his father died, right? Well, he did, and the funeral's Wednesday. So, is you gon' be a bitch, or is you gon' be his BOY? Huh?"

This was *last* person in the freakin' solar system I would ever had expect to show any concern. But he did, and Browny's rare and sober fit of concern, well . . . it worked.

I attended Mr. Hunter's funeral. It marked my reunion with Ty, after several months of bitter silence. Browny's act of utter selflessness convinced me that beneath the gruff dark-child scowl, beyond the drinking, drugging, and the rank, stank, foul attitude, and Lord knows beyond the bad *clothes*, Faison Brown did indeed have a *heart*.

So, where the fuck was that *heart* now? I was determined to find it, if the motherfucker still existed.

And thus, in quest of finding the heart of Faison Brown, I thought I'd make a little appearance at the book signing for this vile 345-page creation of his dark and pissed-off delusion.

CHAPTER FOUR

IS *MS. MAYA ANGELOU* IN THE BUILDING?

Midtown Manhattan*, *Summer 1996
Barnes and Noble Bookstore, Chelsea

DAVID:

It was some event. This little in-store soiree was damn near, but not quite, fabulous. A rather large crowd of misfits, gossips, and various media types covered the proceedings. I couldn't even remember the last time I'd seen Browny smiling so widely, but low and behold, captured in a glossy black and white photograph, there he was: Faison Brown, enlarged and cheesin' like some well-fed idiot. This self-serving likeness was parked in the main front window, along with a tasteful display of his hideous book of lies. I stared at the photo for a moment. I couldn't believe my eyes. Was *this* the tormented Browny of old? He looked—well—hell . . . almost handsome!

I thought to myself, *Those fat advance checks must've worked wonders for this Brown Bastard's complexion.*

As I stepped inside the store, I was determined to mind my manners. I did not want to make a scene. Repeat, I did NOT want to make a scene. I'd promised myself I wouldn't revert to stereotype; freak-the-hell-out and *read* Faison "Browny" Brown's ass out loud in that public setting. Instead, what I did was purchase the cheap-ass book and I waited patiently in line with the rest of the huddled masses yearning to read freakish fuckin' lies.

As I drew closer to the head of this line, I saw a scrubbed-up Browny sitting, a king about his court, signing, cheesin' for the press, smiling and having his picture taken with a few of his new fans.

It was a warm summer day, and yet, Juanita Brown stood in the background, close by the table, in a fully let-out mink coat. I mean, a *big-assed* coat, at that! The woman was lookin' like a thick-ass *ghetto* Loretta Young! And she was just a-smiling and oh so proud of her li'l man's time in the sun.

I stood waiting, praying that the right words would come to me. I was indomitable now. I would *not* be the mad fag or fly into some a foul fairy's flight of fury. This joint was a respectable establishment. An unwelcome scene from one of this *renowned* author's disgruntled, highly pissed-off characters would've been tres uncivilized. No. I would deliver my message in a slow and succinct fashion.

Unlike Browny, I never lacked for social graces. The line thinned. Suddenly, it was showtime:

"My, my . . . so much activity!" I looked around and inquired, "Is Ms. Maya Angelou in the building? Oh no. It's only *you*. The great scribe, who sits and breathes and lies for a fee. How are you, today, my *friend*?"

When I'd said "my friend," the phrase wore an edgy shade of sarcasm. I wore black. My mood wore red. Even his dense ass *had* to surely notice it.

"David! My li'l homey-sexual. How you doin'? You want that signed, yo?"

I tossed the book of vile and hurtful fabrications onto the table before him.

"I just came here to say, as an author of a *supposed* biography, you write an elaborate fiction. And as someone who I once considered a demi-*friend*, you sadden that shit outta me, Browny. I hope you were paid enough to buy a piece of that island on Bali you always dreamed of. Maybe there you'll rest there, and sleep content on your little beach of lies."

"Now David. Don't be like that, baby. Yo. Everybody's gotta make a livin', don't they?"

"And I'm sure . . . many people do. I hear some actually acquire humble gigs with inadequate little paychecks, and they muddle through this shit-house we call life. But some others, they just can't seem to *hack it*, can they? So *they* choose to make a livin' off the dead, right? Never thought I'd say this, but: Today, I'm actually *glad* Ty and Facey are gone. At least now they can't see the little heartless, hustling, Black, green-eyed monster you've turned into."

"Come now. Let's not get ugly up in here," Browny said nervously, looking around for security.

"Get ugly? Oh, it's w-a-a-a-y too late for that, baby. Tell me something, Browny: WHY did you do it?"

"It's like I said, I had me a story to tell, and yo, a brotha's got bills. Besides, David, this ain't the place for no showdown, yo," he said between his clenched teeth. He was beginning to sweat a little too.

"See, I almost *get* why you'd want to re-assassinate Face. I know you always did have your little hater issues with him."

"Ya damn right. Ain't never liked him."

"Roger that. But I also think it would be wise to expect

the actress, Miss Bliss Santana to be filing a libel suit very soon."

"Hmmp!" he grumbled. "Let her stank ass try."

"So I get the Face Depina hatred, sort of . . . because you always did have some mysterious axe to grind with him. But why *Ty*, huh? If I live well into old-age queendom, I will *never* get that one."

"Oh, so I guess you didn't *read* the damn book, yo!"

"Oh, I read plenty. But the fact remains, whether you believe it or not, Tyrone actually held some loyalty and even some fuckin' *love* for you. And trust me, that's a concept you've always made ve-r-r-rry difficult for the world at large. But he had the heart to *care* about you, Browny. Even when no one else gave a dry shit, he gave a half-a-damn about what happened to you. And if you can look in your mirror, knowing you've *disgraced* his honor, then more power to you, *bruh*."

The others in line were beginning to grow restless. Well, fuck 'em!

"So what I really came to say to you is this: God don't like ugly, and you've been giving Him nothing but black and ugly for years. There will be Hell to pay for that, trust. And oh yeah: Stop blaming people for the fucked up way your life turned out, 'kay? Stop being the eternal bruised and severely burned-black victim! That show is tired. It's been running for too many fuckin' years . . . but it ain't bangin' in New York. Besides, the audience is bored with it, and with you."

"Do you see this crowd, man? Yo, my audience ain't hardly bored."

"Yeah. Funny thing about crowds—they tend to gather in droves around the most ugly and grizzly of accidents."

I could tell he was getting mad. I could see it by the building fire in his eyes. He was damning me to Hell. This was Faison Brown's Finest Hour. The last thing he wanted or *needed* was a furious scene starring the likes of me all up in his face. Well, my attitude was simply: fuck it . . . and fuck him!

He whispered to some tall, chesty, bricked-up Black man, whom I supposed was his handler. Imagine that shit. Browny actually had PEOPLE now! I heard him say, "I need me a five minute break, yo."

He got up from the table, grabbed me by my elbow, mumbling "you little fuck," as he lead me outside. Juanita and her big-ass fur followed us. I guess he had to make sure his big bad brontosaurus of a bitch was in tow. If I was provoked into some physical shit (and I wasn't far from it—trust!), I guess, maybe he thought, *Nita's kinda thick, so she'll be my back-up, yo.*

Suddenly it felt like a scene from a B movie, a Bonnie and Clyde thing—très ghetto style, of course.

"Now, what you gotta say to me, David?" he asked, arms folded, head cocked to the right, fronting that old high school bully-pose of his.

I was deeply tempted to knock him the fuck out!

"What do I have to say? Only that you make me . . . sad. Only that you sicken the shit outta me, and maybe I shouldn't be surprised, but I really did *think* you were *better* than this."

"Hey, don't knock nobody's hustle, yo! Your hands ain't exactly clean or hustle-free, David. And you *know* I know it, too!"

"So where the fuck is your robe and your gavel, huh?"

"What?"

"Who, in God's name, appointed YOU as anybody's judge?

"Yo . . . my publisher! That's who!"

"Well, maybe you'll both burn in Hades."

"Then we won't be alone, will we? I'll be sure to say hey to your boy Face for you, yo."

"Well, if he's there, I'm sure he's waiting for your foul ass."

"Look. Let's don't do this. We got a lot of history, Davy. We been through a whole lotta shit together. And I ain't tryna make you my enemy now. You need to go home, yo."

"And I suppose you're gonna make me, Browny, you little punk motherfucka?" I didn't mean to call him out, least not in front of the wifey and the coat and all . . . but to know Faison Brown was to *want* to kick his ass, hard—and often.

"If I have to *make* you leave, then I will, yo!" Browny issued his pitiful threat. Of course, it fell on deaf ears. I was hardly scared of him. Never been.

I chuckled a little. I couldn't help it. If he *had* to? Jigga, please! Him, and what army of fuckin' stank, cracked-out drunks? Oh, I was so ready to take him on, and that big chunky Bogart bitch with him. And I *used* to *like* her!

"Now that's a little too rich," I said. "Seems like I remember you thinking I was some soft piece of Swiss cheese way back in high school, didn't you? Huh? Yo, Browny! Yo, why you so quiet, yo?" I mocked him. "Yo, Juanita, did yo MAN ever tell you how I PUNKED his little thick, frontin' ass back in the day, yo? Funny. I didn't see *that episode* mentioned in his book."

"What you talkin' 'bout, David?" Juanita asked.

"You mean he never told you, how this soft little fag actually knocked him flat unconscious?"

Juanita's entire mouth went ajar in total disbelief. Lawd! Somebody catch her, before she falls and wrecks the concrete!

"Well, I'm that same cat who kicked your thick ass then, Browny, and I'm quite sure I can still dust off those gloves and deliver another beat-down. Need we repeat old history? So what you NEED to be askin' yo-self is, do you *really* wanna be embarrassed on the day of your big debut, baby?"

"Is he tellin' the truth, Honey Bear?" a dubious Juanita whispered in Browny's ear.

"You are *really* expecting HIM to tell you the *truth*? Please. Just how deluded are you, Black woman?"

"Hey, watch it now!" Juanita warned.

Okay. Granted. I won't lie. The sista did look a li'l ominous. Juanita was a straight-up, hard-core Harlem hell-raiser from way back. I'd heard stories. They weren't pretty. I half-expected her next move would be to drop that big-ass mink, rip off those cheap-ass bargain store earrings, break out the Vaseline, and go all grizzly on me!

"Yo, David, me and my co-writer wrote my book the way *I* saw things," Browny claimed.

"Oh, so you're Mike "Browny" Wallace, the galloping truth-slinger, now? Hello? Is this *60* fuckin' *Minutes*? And where are those damn hidden cameras? You say it, so it all must be *true* then. Lawd knows you always were about as clear-headed and sober as an Eagle Scout through the years."

"My baby acknowledged his own problems in that book," Juanita added. "Did you even read those parts?"

"Well, that's what an *auto*-biography is supposed to be about, Juanita. *His* life! Not the lies and fabrications of someone else's! And that's what you did, Browny. This so-called biography is a scandal sheet full of the foulest bull-shit. It's damn shame that innocent trees had to be murdered for this shit. It's vile. All you did was recite a ton of hurtful lies and spoke on things you have no fuckin' clue about. And now you wanna try to pass it off as the gospel truth? That's just wrong! You're wrong, and you damn-well *know* it!"

"Oh. I get it now. You mad 'cause I didn't kiss Tyrone's rich, stuck-up ass in my book, yo? Well, you can save all that bullshit for *your* novel, 'cause maybe he was yours, but Tyrone Hunter never was MY hero."

"He was the best man I, or you, will never know," I said, my voice cracking.

"Bullshit!"

"Baby, Tyrone fed you more fuckin' bread than the Eighth Street soup kitchen. He could've listed you as a fuckin' dependent on his taxes! But I guess you forgot all about that. He bailed your ass out jail too, didn't he? Hmmm . . . that must've slipped your memory, too. He treated your thick, uncouth, ungrateful ass better than a casual millionaire treats his trust-fund baby. And . . . *this* is what you do? This is how you *thank* him?"

"Maybe he did all that 'cause he felt *guilty*. Ever think of that, yo?" Browny snapped.

"Guilty? For what? Please, tell me this isn't about Trick!"

"You know it!" Browny quipped.

"Faison. When the fuck will ever you face reality? Newsflash! He couldn't *be* there to play Superman for Trick. Tyrone was many things, but he wasn't perfect. He wasn't cut out to be some avenging angel. Damn it! He was a seventeen-year-old KID on a dance floor . . . that's all. Your brother was messin' with straight-up-to-the-core dangerous motherfuckas, and you *know* this! But somehow you've twisted Ty into the absentee savior. He could *never* be that. *You* couldn't be that either. No one could. But why not blame Ty, right? Blaming Ty is easier than blaming Trick for fuckin' up, for dealin' with thugs and cutthroat hoodlums, isn't it? Have you ever dealt with the sad fact that the way he lived was what caused your brother's end? He lived by the sword . . . and he died by a cheap knife."

"Watch it now!"

"Face it! Accept it, and get on with fuckin' life, man! All you're doing is wasting so much precious *time*, HATING someone for something you'll never understand."

"See, baby. I told you *not* to put that stuff in there! It wasn't right. But, n-o-o-o-o! You let that damn check blind you. You know it's true, Honey Bear," Juanita added. She was beginning to regain my favor, *a little*. "David, just so you know,

I had nothing but love for Tyrone. He *was* a good man, a decent man. But what's done is done. It's too late to change it, now."

Browny's puny troops were withdrawing, and their numbers dwindling. Faison contorted his mug as if he were taking a particularly difficult shit.

"Baby. Don't do this now! I ain't tryna hear it, yo."

"I'm just sayin', Tyrone wasn't no devil. But that Face Depina boy—that's a whole other story!"

I knew that if I'd only milked it, I'd have the two of them fighting like mad dogs in the street, and *my money* was on the bitch Juanita. Surely there'd be some hot words and perhaps *fists* exchanged once they were back to their Harlem digs. But igniting the flames of marital discord was *not* my mission. It was only a bonus.

"I just don't have it in me to forgive you for this. You crucified my best friend. And you did it for no fuckin' reason, other than the all-almighty green. And for that, and few other things, you truly do deserve a swift and thorough ass-kickin'. But that's not my job, ANYMORE. I'll leave your cosmic reckoning to Karma."

"Stop talkin' *crazy*, David!" he said, all annoyed and shit.

"You'll always be Browny . . . livin' proof that you can take some Negroes out of the ghetto, but you can't make 'em wash they ass!"

"What's that supposed to mean?"

"It means you'll never change . . . and beyond your needless attack on Ty's character, and pissing all over Facey's grave, that's just about the worse thing of all. The fuckin' fact that you'll never be any better than what you are now . . . it's tragic and sad, really."

"Fuck you, yo! Li'l faggot!"

"Baby, stop!" Juanita gasped, as if it was the *first time* she'd ever heard him say that, about me.

"Didn't I already TEACH you, once, to watch that

fuckin' word around me?" I was ready start swinging on him again. And it wasn't because he'd *said* it. It was because he *thought* he could *hurt* me by saying it.

"Baby. Don't go there. This is David . . . *DAVID*, Honey Bear!"

"Didn't *he* just insult and disrespect *me*, yo? Callin me 'sad' and shit. I ain't no sadder than you, David."

"Oh, I have my sad days . . . that's true. But I'm not alone. Everyone I know has some shit with them. But the ones with any sense, any decency left; at least they *try* to change. Oh, but not you. Never that, Browny! No, and the tragic fact that you'll NEVER fuckin' change is the *saddest* piece of bullshit of all."

"Yeah, well maybe *I'm* not the one who needs to change, yo!" he cracked, holding his wrist limply.

"Juanita, I might holla at *you* again. Browny, you can eat shit and die, motherfucka!" I spat.

And with that said, I took my copy of his so-called autobiography, and hurled that cheap motherfucker across the street.

That day, I resigned myself to walk away from him and his bullshit. Forever.

CHAPTER FIVE

MEMORY STIFLES THE PRESENT

When you look deeply into the eyes of someone who is dying, you carry *that look* with you always. It was sacred.

To this day, I can still see that look.

A quick upward motion, followed by this sharp and rattling breath, and I knew I'd be the last person they'd see on this earth. That breath, that final inhalation, it froze there inside the space between us, as if they welcomed the idea of what would come after it.

Death. Maybe it was beautiful. I hoped so.

And then, there was just . . . That Look. When I reflect back to that expression, I think maybe it was . . . gratitude. The days, the nights, the years of raging were all over then. Finally, all of the pain and silent suffering was finished. It was done. They were free of it. And me? What about me? When would I be free?

I'd like to believe when someone passes on, when their soul leaves this earthly plane, it sighs, and there comes this Long Blue Moan.

And then, slowly, they leave us.

He was gone.

It was me . . . I'd helped him on that journey into the life beyond. I'd done what he'd first, asked, and then begged me to do. You can judge me if you want to, but what I did was nothing less than a naked act of *Love.* The proof was in my actions. I try to tell anyone who'll listen: Love is a *verb*, damn it! It's a motherfuckin' verb! So, this thing I did for him, it was my verb personified . . . Now . . . ain't that Love?

"I love you."

People say it all the time, but how many of us actually do one damn thing to *prove* it? I *did* my best to love until the very last breath. This was my final present to him.

Now, ain't that Love?

And *that's* the way I wanted to be remembered: as someone who didn't just spew those three overused words, but as action, a verb, *and the* one person on this crazy, beautiful, hideous earth who put an end to his suffering forever.

I took one final look at him . . . peaceful at last.

Peaceful, dammit! Now, ain't that Love!

Back then, I didn't feel as if I'd sinned some terrible sin. And I still don't, even now. I guess when the end comes for me, The Creator will be my judge.

BLISS

She thought of him often. She thought of that night, and the beauty of his face under the soft blue light of her bathroom. She remembered his hands, how large and long his fingers were as he stroked the soft nape of her neck. His liquid green eyes didn't look so sickly then. His kisses wore no trace of the poison resting, nesting, and brewing inside him.

He was still so irresistible, then. The sex itself was not the best for either of them, but something in her—some weak and remembered part of her heart—still *wanted* him . . . and he wanted and he *needed* to be wanted again.

She wondered now, if *it* happened in a single stroke, in the flutter of his eyes as he arrived inside of her. Strange, how *close* she felt to him in the moment of unity, of two souls touching. Strange how her eyes widened and she shivered that moment when his disease had found a new home inside of her.

She didn't talk about Face Depina much anymore. It wasn't that she hated him for what he'd done to her. It was just too painful a place to visit. Besides, she *saw him* daily in her their daughter's face. Tyra, with the same liquid green eyes as her father, and the same mischievous smile that could so easily break a mother's heart. No, she didn't have to talk about Face Depina to feel his presence in her days and nights, or to know of the hold he still had upon her, and his aching grip upon her life.

As she checked her reflection in the mirror, she noticed two new wrinkles under her eyes. She could have sworn they weren't there the week before or even two days before. But they were there now, softly mocking her with curse of a beautiful woman who was slowly aging.

It was enough to piss her off. She was trying to make a comeback in New York, in a career that worshiped youth and looked upon aging with a not so quiet disdain.

She thought maybe the stress and strain of recent events had caused the invasion of those damnable new lines etched in her face.

Upon reading a serialized excerpt of Browny's ghostwritten tome in The New York Post, all was not light and blissful in La Casa Del Santana.

"Who is this slimy motherfuckin' cocker-roach! Whoever he is, I'ma kill him! I swear fo' God, I will kill this so-called *anonymous* bastard, dead!" Bliss Santana screamed.

Vases flew!

Tyrone Hunter had once told her that if sadness wore a color, it would be a profoundly deep shade of blue. But if anger were a color, it would have been that sharp shade of icy-green threatening to burst through the gaze of Bliss Santana's irises.

That green came into the softness of hereeyes and set flames there when she'd read those hideous lies about Ty, and Face, and then about her. How dare this stranger (or so she thought at the time) write such terrible, hurtful lies!

True to her hood-rat Jersey roots, Bliss Santana was not above fighting a man, *like* a man! Yes, she'd been a well-respected actress, but she'd never lost her fire, and never was above going -ballistic whenever the moment suited her.

"Lies! Lies! LIES! All of it! This mangy bastard can lick my cat! How can some motherfuckin' stranger dictate something as truth, when he knew nothing about it? And sure-as-shit doesn't know me! Dammit! This is libel! Straight up fuckin libel," she told her lawyer.

"And, why all the mystery? Huh? I'm sure it's gotta be one of those dead-beat, ghetto-bred bastards; another one of those fuckin' hangers-on, and trust me, Pascal Depina had far too many. And now, the vultures are descending, in droves! Reporters are blowing up my line asking for a comment. Well, fuck them! Read between my fuckin' fingers! Those sons of bitches can lick my motherfuckin' cat! No! I told you, I don't know this slimy motherfucker! Pascal had plenty of bottom-feeders over at that loft. I'm sure that's the connection. What? Friend? Really? Well, even IF he was, what kind of friend does that to someone? Huh? I'll tell you who: only the lowest of the low! When Pascal died, people came to me, offering me six figures to write about my life with him. Sure, I could've used the money, but I refused every one of them. I loved Pascal. I'm raising his only child, for Christ sake! One day, when she's old enough, she would read it, and it would destroy her. And why would I want to my daughter exposed to any more ugliness? Why would any mother want to see her child hurt any more than she's already been?

"And who the fuck is this vile- low-grade motherfuckin' vulture to slander him? No. Yes, I know I can't stop someone else from writing about him. But I'll be damned if I'll let some cheap motherfuckin' hack soil MY name in the process. No, I haven't read the whole book. I'm sure I would fuckin' vomit! Violently! You DO know they practically placed ME at the scene, that night? Please, read between the lines, Harold. Well, that's what I PAY you for, dammit! Where does this person, this sub-being, this polluted piece of *shit* get off writing about things—personal conversations I had with Pascal, when no one else was there? It's a fuckin' fiction, Harold! You're my lawyer, damn it! I want this madness stopped! Yes, I'm serious! Serious as murda! Damn it, he may not know me. But trust me, he's about to!"

Bliss slammed down the phone.

She saw that lamp, that lovely Tiffany lamp that Pascal "Face" Depina once gave her, when she'd discovered he cheated on her, again. Bliss Santana howled a primitive cry, grabbed that exquisite lamp, and she hurled it violently against the wall.

Browny's book had a devastating effect on her. Those tales of she and that whirlwind known as Face Depina haunted her now. Face. Oh, Face. She'd never forgotten him.

Her mind swept back to that day, in the fall of 1986.

He was Adonis, and Venus too. She looked at him, and her molecules hummed. Such was his initial effect. After some people met Face Depina, their molecules never quite stopped humming.

The first time Bliss saw him, he was standing on the set, illuminated from behind by a spot. He was six-five and beyond merely beautiful. She noticed how tall he was. Men such as him, men like her father who were with mixed with Latino blood, they lead with their chins. They seemed to stand more erect, taller than the rest. She reasoned that was how a man stood when he was out to prove something.

Pascal "Face" Depina *was* out to prove something. He moved in a slow sway toward her. The light left his wide shoulder, and another settled on his face. And she thought, *Oh, my God!*

A cool Savannah breeze swirled over her arms and every part of her skin became a city of raised goose bumps. Ice-green eyes cut over the room and landed like warm emerald-and-bronze butterflies all over Bliss Santana.

Hers was the rarified world of soap operas. She'd worked with scores of men, handsome men, pretty men, stunningly beautiful men. But Pascal Depina was light-years outside being just another beautiful manchild back then.

Who was he, anyway? she wondered. *Was he a scared little boy, or a cocky son of the streets? A sly fox, or a sad and shelter-less puppy?*

Strange, how the things we find ourselves attracted to . . . wind up being the very things that make us cry.

They met, they sparked, they laughed, they sexed. Yes, Pascal "Face" Depina was out to prove something. Perhaps it was that he could make long and convincing-enough *love* to a woman. Perhaps that a famously fabulous woman, could, in fact, be made to fall in love with him. Bliss Santana was the prize, the physical manifestation of success, and the gaudy arm-candy that would signal his arrival. For Face Depina, she represented something more than sex, his greed or his undying passion to succeed at any cost. She was the fast-food rescue for his hunger, personified. Such was Face Depina's starvation for something *better* than the life he knew.

He saw her at first as just another hustle, another body,

another orifice, and by then he'd known plenty of those. Yes, this hustle came nicely furnished, in a softer package, but it was a no less *complex* situation.

The Naked Rules of Manhood
A Gospel, According to Face Depina:

"Having a big dick can make you rich, once you know how to work it. Hell, I musta been like fifteen or so when I learned this shit. Lemme tell ya 'bout my first teacher.

"She was this young chica from the neighborhood. She wasn't my first, but this was my last proper and religious one . . . a good girl, ya know? I knew she was a virgin, and I wanted to break that shit in. I'd been kissin' on her for a few weeks, fingerin' her for days, and she finally decided she'd give me a piece of that precious, unfucked pussy.

"Well, when I dropped my draws, her eyes went all bugged-out. She said something in Spanish, and that damn bitch crossed herself, three times! Oh, I tore that coochie up, pa! Worked it like a champ. Had her ass so strung out on the dick, she wanted to give me shit for free, just to keep me and . . . it . . . around!

"So, her daddy owned this used car lot, right? And by the end of that summer, I was cruising the block in a hot used Chevy Nova. But I didn't pay shit for it. Well, that's not true. Let's say, I paid, in trade. It's a real sweet deal, when you fuck the right poon-tang. The cash and prizes can be pretty damn fly. But I gave as good as I got. And wherever she is now, she's prolly still walking bowlegged, and I'm sure she ain't never forgot me.

"See? Those were the *good dick days*. Trust me, I was happy to be Blessed. But, with a big one, comes big responsibility. Seriously, man! I mean, you fuck around and tap the wrong one, and suddenly you got some half-insane motherfuckin' bitch goin all crazy over your shit. You think I'm playin? Well, I'm not. You wanna know the truth?"

He grabbed his crotch for emphasis.

"See, the truth is: this motherfucka here is my meal ticket. It was my moneymaker when I was a dead-broke kid. Once I learned I could *trade* it for cool cash and prizes . . . sheeeeeit, it was on and poppin', then! It got me off the streets, and had me eatin' peaches on a sunny beach in The Hamptons. See?

"I found out that my dick pushin' in and out the right fag's ass could get me enrolled in a special school for . . . ummm . . . special fags. So, the truth is, I ain't never been mad at being Blessed.

"The way I see it is: Big Dick, Big Future. Hey, I didn't make the rules . . . I just recognize 'em! Oh, no doubt, I'm a pretty motherfucker . . . but this dick? Now that's my real my power. Trust me, Claude."

His male model quasi-confidant Claudio Conte laughed "You are a wild, big-dick muthafucka, no doubt."

In the mind of Face Depina, his prodigious penis had succeeded in determining, not only his physical worth, but his spiritual profit in modern society. Sometimes, in the darkness of a sexing room, it even determined his value as a human being. He sought to be the best he could be in bed . . . and his erect penis had become, for some, a vivid carnal entertainment . . . and for Face Depina, a moral compass.

Let us not even venture into the size of his balls.

And so, Bliss Santana and Face Depina would become a couple. Face, the soon-to-be red-hot model, and Bliss, the award-winning soap actress were as pretty as any *Vogue* cover. But in reality, without the airbrushing, their story was not a very picture-perfect one.

Years later, Bliss Santana threw herself on her sofa, and

the memories sped by as fast and as furious as that runaway Jaguar of yesteryear. . . .

Mid-January 1991

After reading a blind item in the *New York Post* with obvious homosexual undertones, about a once red-hot male model who'd gotten caught in a melee with his famously always-there bodyguard, she had easily figured out just who the main character was in the ongoing satire that had become her life.

Bliss Santana was not a woman to be played with or preyed upon.

And then suddenly, she discovered herself in rather delicate and decadent condition. That's when Bliss went on a mission to find and *kill* Face Depina.

She waited in a rented Jaguar in the West Village, and when he finally bopped home fresh from a long day's journey through another abusive night, she called him over to the car, and made him get inside. The two took off onto the Westside Highway for a harrowing ride Face Depina would never forget.

With eyes blurred with tears, Bliss announced, "I'm pregnant. It's yours. Do we abort or what?"

"Awww. You pregnant, for real?" he asked, in that bored voice he usually reserved for people with vaginas.

"For real," she said, taking his shaky hand and placing it on her belly. "Wanna feel?"

But all he could feel was ill.

"Seriously? You pregnant, and it's mine? Not Claudio's or Julio's or maybe Tyrone's?"

"Sorry. I'm not half the whore you take me for."

He held his head in his hands, and wanted to make it all go away.

"Bliss, you *know* how I feel about kids. I don't want none.

Never did, and you knew that. Trust—I know—nothin' worse in this fuckin' world than some unwanted kid! Are you stupid? Did ya think you'd *keep* me this way? No. No babies. Not now, not ever! Damn you! You shoulda been more careful."

He looked wired and nervous. He was starting to tic inside his skin. By then, that creeping familiar gnaw settled in his belly. He knew what it was.

"Pull over! I'm sick. Pull the fuck over!" His voice was shrill as a siren.

It wasn't an easy trick, pulling over on the Westside Highway, but Bliss found the skinniest of shoulders. Face got out and vomited all that was left inside him.

"She's pregnant? A baby? And it's mine? Fuck, fuck, fuck, FUCK!"

He opened the door, got back inside, and with green eyes weighed down by a sickly seriousness he said, simply, "Get rid of it!"

"So, we abort," she said coldly, staring at the white lines of the highway exploding beneath the wheels of the now speeding Jag as she applied more pressure to the gas pedal.

"And you need to slow the fuck down! You too emotional. Don't fuck with my head. I'm sick, damn it!"

"Yes. I know you're *sick*. And except for that one time, three and half months ago, I'd long stopped fucking with you, and your sickness!"

She looked at him and wondered in that moment if his beautiful pitifulness had succeeded in driving her crazy, and if she *was* crazy, would she *know?* And could she stop *being* crazy if she just simply said or screamed, "NO"?

"Pascal. You said to get rid of it. So I'm about to, right here and now."

It was that first yellow shout of dawn. The road was dotted by delivery trucks and 18-wheelers, lots of them, zooming by. The speedometer glided from 70 to 75, pushed up on 80.

"See, now I know you're crazy. You better stop fuckin' around, Bliss! Slow down!"

Eighty became 85, then 90.

"Slow down, Bliss! Baby, slow the hell down! See? See that, you just missed that last exit. What you doin'? Take your foot off the gas, you fuckin' crazy, pregnant, stupid bitch!"

Nothing he said registered. Even if it had, *she* was feeling sick now. Sick of his voice. Sick of his promiscuity, his moods, his friends, his jiggling Lolitas, his excuses . . . the whores, the boys in leather, the groupies. She was sick of how he and the rest of it made her *feel*. Most of all, she was sick of loving him.

But she couldn't stop even though she wanted to. She wished there wasn't a baby in her womb. And she wished it wasn't his. She wished it was Tyrone's. Maybe then it would be kinder, gentler, loving, and *healthy*.

"Oh God! I'm so sorry, baby!" Face said out of fear. "I'm sorry. Sorry for everything. Everything, you hear me?"

He'd said "everything" as if he *knew* he had *it*, and had given it to her and possibly their *baby*.

"I never meant to hurt you Bliss. I don't know why I do shit sometimes. I'm sorry. I mean it. Now, *please* slow the *fuck* down!"

"Slow. The fuckin'. Car down, Bliss. Please! Slow down, before you kill innocent people!"

"Nobody's innocent anymore," she said.

"Yo! Bliss! Look out for that truck! Get away from the fuckin' truck, Bliss! Please, slow down!"

"You afraid of trucks, Pascal? There's still *so much* I don't know about you. But I know you *used* me! I was a perfect beard for you, wasn't I?"

This mad-crazy bitch is doin' 100 mph on the fuckin' Westside Highway!

"That's why I'm naked under this coat. Your public will think we were two insatiable lovers who just couldn't keep our hot hands off each other, and that we were fuckin' our brains out when we reached our wailing, bloody-red climax. See? Even after everything, *all the madness and shit* you've put me though, I'm still trying to protect *my* man! Now ain't that Love?"

She swerved around one 18-wheeler into the lane of another. Horns blew.

God, not like this! Not with this crazy bitch! Do something to stop this shit right now. Say something!

"Bliss, this is stupid! Look. Let's don't be stupid, let's be crazy. Let's do completely nuts. Let's get *married*. I'll . . . I'll marry your ass if you want! You hear? We can do this. Bliss, we could raise the kid, together. Bliss, slow down! Bliss, baby, you hear? You my *boo*. Bliss, there's a kid in this shit. Slow the fuck down, baby! Slow . . . the . . . fuck . . . down, baby . . . " He finished in a whisper. And the "*baby*" in that whisper had somehow reached her. She eased off the gas, and she did slow the fuck down. A baby was worth more than this. A baby, even sick, was worth more than him or her or them together. *A baby. My baby! This is my baby!*

Her truest sanity, the part she only let herself see, came back into focus. She'd make it alone. Fuck that tortured pretty-boy junkie crying and begging beside her!

This was still *her* baby.

And so, for a while, she used her guile to seduce Ty Hunter, and she worked her wiles on the most sensitive areas of Tyrone's sensitivity. She had a fit of lukewarm sex with him, and she *almost* convinced him the baby was his . . .

In the end, Bliss Santana gave birth to a baby she would

name Tyra. But the baby was the spitting image of her beige-skinned, tumultuous, green-eyed junkie lover. And together she and her infant lived with a time clock ticking within them. . . . And its mechanism was triggered by Pascal "Face" Depina.

CHAPTER SIX

LANCING A HEMORRHOID

Bliss Santana was not about to be someone's punk-bitch. Nor would she allow herself to be scandalized for very long. In a city as big, strong, rich, and powerful as NYC, it helped to know a few big, rich, and powerful people. Being as an actress of some renown, Bliss had known her share of them.

One of those powerful men was a man named Zaire Monk, Esq. Monk was a Wall Street power broker of sorts. Monk had also known Tyrone Hunter, intimately. What had began as a friendship would in time become an affair of the heart. And while their relationship didn't stand the slings, arrows, and tests of the upcoming millennium, Zaire Monk had never stopped liking Ty, nor had he ceased respecting the spirit of him. And so, when Monk got wind of that book, and the terrible things it alleged about his friend Tyrone Hunter, it didn't take much persuasion from Bliss to win him over to the righteous side.

With Zaire Monk's resources, along with her own, Bliss Santana managed to put the kibosh on Browny's poison tome. While there were already twenty thousand copies in circulation, Zaire Monk bought the surplus and, burned them. He purchased all the rights from the publisher, and there would not be any more sold, anywhere.

This was the last thing Browny ever expected. With that unpredicted turn of events, the anticipated fortune of Faison Brown was suddenly, once again in dire jeopardy.

Browny, being Browny, was instantly enraged and beside himself with fury. This was his fabled brass ring, and the quick ticket to notoriety. Finally, it was about to happen for him. Finally, people would know *his* name. It felt like a bad, bad, horrible bad dream. How and why did these terrible things keep happening to *him*? He wanted to shake someone, to hit someone, to kill someone. He wanted to make someone pay!

"Honey Bear, you still made some money from the deal. Now, listen to me. If we put some of that in escrow, we might have a nice piece of change for the future," Juanita reasoned.

"The future? The future?! Shit! Don't you *get it*, woman? I waited too fuckin' long! I waited all my got-damn life, yo! Shit! I wanna be paid in full, now!"

Faison Brown saw this as yet another roadblock on the highway of his perpetually stalled career. One more time, just when he could almost *taste* his piece of fame cake, someone had overturned the banquet table. For so long his life's trek had been on terminal stall, and then finally the journey was getting back on the fast track. Only this time, a boulder was thrown onto the highway of his approaching fame.

For this, he erroneously blamed the wrong culprit.

Though his publisher would remain mum on the details of his book's not receiving a second, more lucrative printing, Browny's piss-poor arithmetic skills quickly put two and two together . . . and he got six. *David!*

David had most of Tyrone's money now. Davy *hated* that book. David hated the things Browny thought to include as well as what he'd excluded from it. Yes, it *had* to be David. He possessed the means and the mind to do it. Hadn't David had been against him and his quest to succeed since they were teens? Yes, in Browny's estimation, David had.

And didn't David show up at that book signing, spewing venom?

"I know who it was. It had to be him . . . that little fuckin' faggot bitch David, yo!"

And for this, in Browny's mind, David had to pay . . . and pay *big*!

Browny's dome went into a deeply dark place, a place of memory and back-biting, pettiness, and jealousy. It was a selfish, self-serving, self-congratulatory place where he was never allowed entry. It all came sweeping back: Face Depina left that group, only to have achieved a bigger, almost instant fame as a model. David became a dancer, and was in his own way, for a moment, living out his balletic dreams. Tyrone made out the best of all, and for something that didn't take years of crawling or struggle to achieve. They, the three of them had made a reality of their teenage dreams, and Browny was busy making license plates, and fashioning crack pipes out of aluminum foil.

And now, *David* possessed the bulk of Tyrone's money, his estate, his future earnings; income. David had a freaking fortune! David, not *him*! David Richmond was "livin' all high on duh hog," while Browny and Juanita had to settle for *hog maws*. David, the failed "crippled-up" dancer, was tripping the light fantastic on what Ty had amassed from writing that one fucking hit song way back in school.

Yes, Ty'd invested wisely, and he had an uncanny beginner's luck. But wasn't it stupid, wasteful and blind to *will* all those riches to *David's* dubious behind? David was living under a doubtful prognosis, at best. The last time Browny looked at him, he could almost *hear* that clock tick-tocking. And when David did finally kick, what the hell would become of all that money, that beautiful unspent cabbage then? Would it go to some of Ty's mindless charities? Shit! Why should some people who didn't sing on the record, and had nothing to do with its success reap the "bennies" from it? Shouldn't he, Browny, finally see some enduring residue from that flight with teenaged fame?

Wasn't he, as a singer, "the best singer in that whole damned group," entitled to some proceeds of it? It had all been germinating in Browny's psyche for years . . . *but how could it be done?* What could he possibly say or do (or undo) to make his lifelong dream of fame and fortune a reality?

Needing a hit of faux inspiration, Browny slipped into his old ways:

He had almost two grams of coke. He was sure, as much as Juanita *loved* to cook, there had to be some baking soda in the crib. He got some bottled water. He took a cookie sheet and sprinkled a light covering of coke on the bottom. He took a tablespoon of the baking soda, and sprinkled it on top. He began to add the water evenly. He'd planned to cook it for fifteen minutes. A long long-time addict, he could already see himself baking it some more and letting it sit overnight, freezing it, and then entering the fast-food world of crack nirvana . . . Only, he hadn't counted on Juanita showing up early.

She entered. She whiffed. She sniffed, and *she knew*. She smelled it, and something bigger than crack began to cook then brew violently inside her. She charged into that kitchen, and Juanita Ruby Mae Lewis-Brown promptly went full-barrel ballistic on his ass.

"Oh NO, you won't! Not in *MY* house! Not this shit again! Fuck no! The Hell you will, motherfucka!" she roared. Trying to take possession of the pan, she violently struggled with her husband. "No! Give it here, dammit!

Faison! You hear me? Give it here! This ain't the way, baby!"

They struggled. They fought. They heaved and pulled. Juanita was possessed with more strength, more anger, and she was far more determined. Browny wanted to hit her. Draw back and HIT her hit her HARD! Hit her hard enough to knock her violently-opposed ass out! But he knew if he hit her, and she didn't go completely unconscious, it would only make her madder and stronger than she already was, and then, all kinds and violent varieties of HELL would surely break loose in Harlem.

He was very much afraid of the wrath of Juanita Ruby Mae Lewis-Brown. He was even more fearful of losing her, and his own life . . . and so that he let go of the pan.

With most of her fearsome might, Juanita hauled off and smacked him hard across the face. It stunned him. It embarrassed him. It was a blow to his already diminishing manhood. Then, she ran. She ran into the bathroom. And she did the unthinkable. She flushed Browny's prize, his sanctuary, his shit-colored escape route, down the toilet.

He felt like crying.

"You's a weak, bitch-ass motherfucka! I told you when we jumped that motherfuckin' broom that I wasn't about to stay hitched to some weak-ass motherfucka!"

"Fuck you, yo!" he spat. And with wild tears streaming from his eyes, Browny stormed out of the apartment.

As he headed down the hall, Juanita hollered at the top of her pissed and frustrated lungs, for all the neighbors and *God* to hear.

"If you plan on smokin' that shit, then don't even bother to bring yo' Black ass back here, ya worthless motherfucka! Ya heard? 'Cause I *will* kick your weak, Black, motherfuckin' ass out, for good, this time!" she promised.

She meant it.

He wondered if she'd change the locks as she'd done before. He wondered if she'd file divorce papers, as she'd threatened before. He wondered if, after all the time they'd been together, in the end, if she too, was only after the money. But, his broke ass never had made much money, and he wondered if she was tired it. Was she were finally through with him, finally exhausted with his dreams of singing, and his get-rich-quick bullshit schemes, which had always, always failed? And then, he wondered what he'd do without her.

He wondered a lot of things.

Just when all looked hopeless . . . fortune or something like a serendipitous twist in destiny suddenly paid a visit to one Faison Brown.

That night, he was sitting at the bar of the Lennox Lounge, his favorite Harlem watering hole. He was hurt and angry, and desperately sloshing down his shit tide of troubles. Nothing seemed right. Nothing was ever fair. The future, whatever *that* meant for him, was nothing but a dark, dismally disturbing blur. It had gotten to the point where his hours were *afraid* of his days.

Gazing in the mirror behind the bar, he didn't like the image glimpsing back at him. Drugs and prison, life and its dizzying series of disappointments had *aged* him in a way that could break any mother's or an old friend's heart. Browny never started out as handsome boy, though there was once a compelling magnetism to him, especially when he opened his mouth and sang. But then, life happened, and some men retire those dreams, those wishes, those things that made them special, and revealed their uniqueness. When they do, it begins to show in their aspect. It is then that they get the faces they deserve.

Faison Brown always felt that he deserved more than the banquet table of his life offered him. He was becoming less a man and more a ridiculous urban stereotype. He hated it. He hated his life. He hated that everyone else had in some way received their Miracles, and he tired of wondering where the Hell was *his* Miracle.

And then, oh then, as he continued gazing in that smoky mirror, something rare occurred. It was if The Creator has had been listening to Fasion Brown's deepest thoughts, heard the misery song he'd sung for so long, and decided enough was enough. It was then that The Creator delivered a Very Special Miracle just for him—just for Browny.

Oh, my God! He gasped. He swallowed. He gasped again. He blinked his eyes. It wouldn't go away. He closed his eyes. He shook his head. He opened his eyes again. And that *Miracle* was still there, and it was staring back at him.

Browny knew he was a little drunk, but he wasn't quite so hallucinatory in his drunkenness. He was high, yes, but not flying . . . just tipsy, at best. And that Miracle was the most *beautiful-est* thing he could've ever imagined. And when he stared at it, he could *see* the future, and that future was no longer so embedded in the past. He saw his future with dollars signs written all over it. Oh! That night, on that bar stool inside of the Lennox Lounge, the darkness had finally, finally lifted. Browny's whole dismal, dizzy world began to catch a whole new brilliantly rich and beautiful light!

Hours later

"Juanita? Nita . . . baby? You up?" he whispered excitedly, in a rush of breaths.

"You high?" she asked, half-wake, and half dreaming of something better than ache he was causing her.

"No! Hell no, woman!"

"Look at me, dammit!" she demanded.

"I just had a coupla drinks, but that's all, yo," he promised.

She turned the lamp on, got a good, well-informed look

at him, and decided she believed him. "Yo, you think it's right what David did to me? Huh? For real, yo? You think that li'l smug bitch deserves *all* Ty's money?"

"Honey Bear, please, just let it go!" an exasperated Juanita rolled her eyes, and laid her head back down to sleep.

"No! Fuck all that let-it-go shit! I got something that'll rock that li'l fagateer's world, yo. I mean fuck him up . . . once and for all!"

"Baby, I know you got beef with David now, but I don't want you hurting him. That ain't right."

"See? Yo, that's the *beauty* of this, baby. I ain't gotta hurt him at all. In fact, *I* ain't even gotta raise a finger in his direction, yo. I tell you, this shit is perfect! I'ma give David what he thinks he wants, and then, after he gets it, I'ma get—no, bump that—*we* gon' get paid, yo!"

"What kinda craziness you talkin, baby?" Juanita asked wearily.

"Yeah. Crazy. That might just be the right word, yo."

He gazed at this woman he called his wife . . . the Bonnie to his Clyde, the Ethel to his Fred. Though she was several dress sizes plumper than Ethel Mertz, she was a thick woman, full of earthy elements, and for Browny, there was a beauty in the voluptuous roundness of her. Her complexion was a deep shade of good chocolate. Whether standing, sitting or lying down, her larger than life breasts announced her womanhood. There was a pride and purpose in every large and assured step she took . Yes, she was a bit "big faced-did," some people in Harlem called her . . . but never, ever in her presence. She used her mouth to broadcast who she was, and it gained attention, and it demanded your respect.

Browny gazed at her and he thought just perhaps, his woman, his wife, should know of his plan, and become his partner in a little crime called: *Gotcha!*

"I got somethin' I gots to show you. I was gonna keep it

on lock . . . but you my wife, my woman, my other half, yo. So, I'ma trust you to keep this shit just between us, yo. I *can* trust you, right?"

"What? What is it, Honey Bear?"

"Yo, just answer the damn question, baby."

"Honey Bear, after all we been through, you know you can trust me, fool!"

"Good."

With that reassurance, Browny left their living room. He went into their bedroom closet. He retrieved a small metal box from the top shelf. He used to keep his drug stash in that box. There was a time when that small metal box was Browny's feeble little treasure trove. He then took a small silver box into the living room, all the while grinning at his own newly perceived brilliance.

Producing a small key from his pocket, he proceeded to open the box there in Juanita's presence.

When he showed his wife the contents of that box, she drew an astonished breath. Her hand trembled slightly as she took the article from the box and she stared at it a long time.

It made her happy, at first, then sad, and then, all at once, afraid. Afraid of what Browny was going to *do* with it . . . and she was just a little afraid for David.

"No. No it ain't what you think, baby. But this here is my new weapon, yo. This is the money-shot!" Browny smiled the most cunning of grin in his smile arsenal.

Juanita Brown did not grin, nor did she smile back.

"I know. I know. This is our future. This right here is our gold, yo."

CHAPTER *SEVEN*

Bliss Blooms Again!

Can a rumored bad girl and once sizzling Latina actress recapture her glow, let alone her near-legendary sizzle at age forty-one? If that once sizzling Latina in question happened to be Bliss Santana, the answer would be indubitably, “Hell yeah!”

Bliss was actually a few years and experiences older than forty-one. Her age was a sheer pretense of vanity; a woman’s gentle lie. It really didn’t matter in the scheme of things because she looked utterly lovely, and to some, even sensational.

Bliss Santana was nothing, if not a Phoenix. She’d risen from Jersey girl, smoldered as a sexy Salsa instructor, and flamed into an awarding-winning soap actress. A *Blacktress*, Face called her. The trip she’d made was not an easy one. This was a woman who had been burned numerous times while walking through fire, but Bliss Santana was indeed a fire-walker. She’d been seared and scarred, and still she had survived her life, even her life with Face Depina.

And so it was written.

David Richmond saw the feature on her in the *Daily*

News. It both elated and amused him. He and Bliss were never been what one would call "friends," but they did share one thing; a once shining, but tarnished thing in common: they both were in love with Face Depina.

Strange, that they hadn't meet, in the flesh, until the sad day of Face's funeral. On that occasion, even through his grief, David was feeling extraordinarily generous, insightful and complimentary. Bliss never forgot it. She was impressed by the cute little copper-colored man-child in the sedate black suit. She thought his eulogy to Face was the most telling.

DAVID had spoken with the voice of his inner philospher, of his love and understanding of Pascal "Face" Depina:

"Once there was this gorgeous, gorgeous time when we where all living our dreams. I loved that boy . . . And the cherry on the cake of my outrage, is that the world gets so judgmental of behavior, when it's only *human*. The way we are, and how we got there, it's called the survival of human beings, baby."

"No matter what kind of love, friendship or solace we offered, he'd take it like a hungry, desperate thief, and maybe he silently resented us for being chumps. Whatever we gave him, it was never enough. He didn't trust love. When a child is never given the keys to love, the possibility of being able to accept love dies a little more every day. So maybe we should take comfort in what he was able to give."

David really did seem to understand Face Depina in ways that those who pretended to never did and never could. It was, indeed, a devastating day for him.

Later, as the people who knew fragments of Face and pieces of Pascal gathered outside in the street, Tyrone was trying to convince David to spend the night with him, and not go out and fling himself into something or *someone* risky. For David, often promiscuity was the physical antidote for his grief.

It was then that Bliss Santana joined the two of them on the street. Oddly enough, considering the people they'd loved and had in common, it was her very first time being in David's inimitable company.

"Well, hello, Miss Bliss. At last we meet."

"So you're David," she said, managing the slowest of smiles.

"I need to tell you something," David began.

All at once, both Ty and Bliss held their breath.

"Once I had a crush. So many of my stories start out that way. He was a muy *gaupo* Puerto Rican chico from Newark. But he couldn't Salsa to save his pointy-toe-shoe-wearin' life. So, cute as he was, I had to drop-dip him. But, as a goof, we once tipped into a dance school. The point of this little review is, I watched you once. Remember working at Arthur Murray's, teaching those Latin steps to them old, rhythm-free people?"

"Yes. Another lifetime ago."

"Well, you were something to see in that lifetime. You reigned supreme in that tight yellow dress with the feathers on the side. I thought, 'Aye Caramba, mami! Wow! Look at her!' You were way too pretty for that place. It was a waste of time and talent. But every now and then, one of those rhythm-free men got a step right. When that happened, something in your face brightened, and you just let loose. Suddenly, you were Rita Moreno in *West Side Story*, hair flying, dress gliding, so free and sexy. You were a spirit. We should all be so free and sexy," he finished sadly.

"Free? Isn't it sexy to think so?" Bliss asked back then.

At that time, her reply wore the shade of a riddle. David had no idea of the ticking time-clock Face Depina had given her.

"I'm going to hug you now, Bliss," David announced. "Now don't get skurred. It'll be very short and sweet, but sincere. Are you ready?"

She planted both feet firmly. "Yes, I think I am."

David's hug was very much like him: short and sweet and most of all, sincere. And he said, "God bless, Bliss. Goodbye, Ty. We'll talk." He kissed his best friend's cheek, and then he walked away.

After that tragic day, Bliss headed back to her home in Atlanta, and occasionally David thought if her, but they hadn't laid eyes or hands or hugs on each other since.

It was a time for reunions.

It was autumn, and the city skies wore periwinkle, and the air, a different hint of blue. David became very wistful in autumn. It was his most reflective of seasons. The death of summer can do that to a man's spirit. And so, David decided he would go to see the new and improved *Broadway* Bliss.

The headlines read: BLISS BLOOMS AGAIN!

After an extended period spent out of the all-perusing glare of the spotlight, after raising her daughter Tyra, suddenly Bliss Santana was back, and, as a theatre critic phrased it, "The boys of Broadway bow at her feet, and the stage becomes a place of Bliss once she inhabits it."

"Could you possibly *rephrase* that last line, please? 'The boys of Broadway bow at her feet' makes me sound like The Fag-hag Supreme! I've never been half the whore some people have taken me for . . . hey, that rhymed," she giggled. Her laugh was actually more ballsy than a girlish giggle. It was a deliciously broad and bawdy guffaw, full of sexy smoke with undertones of risqué thoughts.

"Is that David Richmond in my door? Oh. My. God!" she exclaimed. David wasn't sure if she were being *genuine* or just the exaggeration of an actress putting on a show. But she rose from her seat in her dressing room, and dashed forth to embrace him tightly.

"Oh! You just don't know. I have wondered what ever happened to you, Sweet Boy. You sweet, sweet boy! Let me look at you. Damn! You're lookin' kinda elegant, *papi*. Is there some hideously aging portrait you keep in an attic somewhere?"

"No, *cute* doesn't age, it only ripens. And you, my dear, are lookin' more fabulous than those big ole bouquets of roses up in here. Please don't get it twisted, but IF I were so *inclined*, I just might be tempted to do a little bump and grind with ya, mami," David joked.

"Boy! Don't be startin' nothin' you can't finish up in here! You've no idea. A few spins with me, and I'll put that *dancer* back in your spine!"

"Oh really? So you got skills like *dat*?"

"Honey please. I thought you knew. I'll have ya movin' like Alvin Ailey did, back in his prime," she teased.

David chuckled sadly, and yet softly at the thought of him *dancing* again. She seemed to know what to say to him, and in just which way to say it.:

"Hey, I'm just testifying, things are so dry here in Blissville, that I'm seriously considering switching teams. Hell, this *is* Broadway. I might have to become a *Friend of The Carpet*!"

"You? A lesbian? Really? Well, I wouldn't hate it if you were. I happen to *love* my lesbian sisters. They are the last *cool women* on the planet who give me NO me competition for . . . ummm . . . the penis."

"The penis? What a concept! Are you becoming *proper*, now? Penis? What ever happened to that good ole dependable '*dick*?' "

Hmmmm . . . So this is the same Bliss who somehow garnered my Facey; the same chick that even Ty had fallen in homo-love with, back in the day. David, all at once *got* it. The Bliss standing before him was sexy and charming and lewd and well . . . damn it, even . . . *likable!* This Bliss Santana—as Ty had once told him him—was, "One of the last great New York broads, by way of Jersey City."

David studied her as he was beginning to embrace the idea of her in his mind. If there could ever be a female version of Face Depina, Bliss's aspect came closest to it. Tall and infinitely gorgeous, her high and vibrant bones offset her light caramel skin, and her eyes had these soft green lights inside of them. Like all great women, she was a stunning cacophony of likable qualities and wide and varying emotions. It seemed to him, she had a city within her skin, a multi-cultural energy that was strong and soft, harsh and lovely, refined and yet bawdy. Like Face and Tyrone before him, he too, was drawn into that vast and feminine complexity. In Bliss there lived a duality, which was sometimes electric as The Empire State, juxtaposed against the sadness of the bowery.

Over dinner at B. Smith's, Bliss displayed a little of what made her such a delight to be around. But along with the fun, she also emitted a bit of a mystery.

"Have you seen that *Brown* creature lately. . . is he still crawling around the streets of Harlem, whining and lying about the past?" she asked David, her face changing as her eyes narrowed with some seething scorn.

"Honestly, Bliss, Browny is not someone I care to associate with anymore. And I'm actually quite content to be far away from his little isle of resentment and misery. That so-called biography, it was hurtful, mean-spirited. And it was wrong . . . just plain bullshit."

"Oh, I KNOW, honey! Though, at the time, I didn't know HE was the teller of the lies. And it was a book of *lies*, let there be no mistaking that rancid shit. Very slick of him to have used a ghostwriter to hide behind, like a little cowardly punk. That part of the mystery had me stumped for a while. But not long."

"Oh, so I guess you never *attended* any book-signings?" David chuckled at the memory.

"Excuse me?" Bliss asked, sipping from her water glass.

"Oh, sure it was all wrapped in some kind of cheap, synthetic secrecy at the beginning. But once the book came out, so did he, so-to-speak." David chuckled again, only that time, a bit reflective as he said, "Any chance at the spotlight is and will always be for him, like a case of flies to feces."

"Book-signing? No. I never attended jack-shit of his. Though I might make an exception for his funeral."

"Funeral? Well, I would wish *that* on him or anyone."

"Nor would I. And I'm not some cold-blooded bitch. But I *do* think Karma has a very good memory . . . and it takes pages of notes on the bitches and bastards still crawling this earth."

"Interesting concept," David allowed. But he thought: that wouldn't explain why Ty is gone.

Bliss played with her spinach salad and continued, "Once I discovered it was *him* behind it, it didn't matter. I barely *knew* him. I don't ever recall being in his company for very long. So for him, or *it*, to run around telling these wild and vicious stories where *I* was being quoted, *falsely*, well, I just wasn't having it! Lies and liars! I'm so *done* with them. Besides, nothing remains a lie for very long. And that's why *I* put an end to that *mockery* of a manuscript."

"What?" David did a spit-take, expelling his water across the table in Bliss's direction. "Get outta town, woman!"

"No. I like it here! When it isn't *raining*!" she said, wiping her blouse.

"Sorry," David said, dabbing his mouth with one of B.'s fine napkins. "But just when I think I'm no longer capable of being shocked, you do! SO that was YOU?"

"Yes. I still do *know* people, David. And I do have *some* power left, yanno?" She winked.

"Oh, I don't doubt it, Bliss-ness. And I'm very sure he might be about three different shades of *pissed* over it."

"Well, remind me to send him a picture of me, yawning."

David chuckled and thought, *Yes, she's definitely an interesting woman, this one.*

"To hear *him* tell it, everyone he knew was so full of viciousness and backdoor treacheries. I wasn't, until I was *pushed* to be."

"But that's the story of his life, and he's sticking to it. Everyone has always been out to get him."

"Please! It ain't all *that* Shakespearean, baby. Maybe he's just got bad luck! Or else, he's his own worst enemy."

"Exactly! See that? You know him, and you didn't even have to go to school with him or sing beside his little foul ass."

"Oh. I *got* him. Trust me. Some people embrace their misery as if it paid them some hefty check to keep holding tight to it. But just maybe *none* of that energy is the *real* reality. Maybe they just *suck* at being human beings," Bliss allowed.

And David thought, *Yes! That's it. Bliss does GET it! Maybe some people DO suck at being human beings. Maybe they're just born fucked up. Maybe they live for those childish outbursts, because that's all they had have left. Maybe they need an excuse to exercise their fucked-upness. Maybe, just maybe, the naked truth in this is: they ain't all dat, and never were all that important in the scheme of things.*

He wondered if just by him *thinking* this way made him a *cold* person.

But then, he considered his and Browny's long and sordid history. Browny had always been one those folks who'd refused to let go of the past . . . or rather *his* hazy tripped–out version of it.

That little proclivity *irked* David even more than Browny's lack of fashion sense, even more than his loudness—and that, David felt, was plenty damn irksome enough.

"Fuckin' Browny!" David shook his head.

He realized he had to cleanse Browny out of his mindset, and flush his bloodstream of the residue, because he knew that sometimes you could think and think, until you *think* a thing *into being*. Browny was a negative force, full of nothing but negative energy, and David was sincerely *trying* to think positive thoughts and to live a positive life of change for the better. It was crucial. It was necessary. His doctors told him so.

Bliss chipped in, "Yes. Browny. I've a poignant phrase for people like him: 'Fuck 'em.' Now, please, pass the butter," Bliss said in a huff. "Well, enough about insects! Let's talk about ME, shall we?"

"Yes, let's . . ."

"Last night, I took my damn self, by my lonesome to a party down on Houston. Baby, I wish I had me a decent dance partner to show my best stuff on that floor—someone like *you*! I arrived at about one, sans posse, stage crew or the tedious but necessary people who comprise my glam squad. I swear to God, David, sometimes I just want to be *me* again. Me, before the acting career took off, before the awards, the men, the jewels, the fools, the downward spiral, and the big comeback. Me, before the nose-candy, and all that drama and shit. I wanna be Bliss again, before pregnancy, stretch marks, and motherhood. Just *me*, damn it! Me," she paused. "Before *him*!"

DAVID:

I knew *who* she meant, and she *knew* that I knew it. We had this crazy kind of shorthand when it came to him.

Maybe she chose to call him "Pascal," and he was always and forever "Facey" to me, but whenever Bliss and I were together, there *he* would be, all six-foot-five-inches of beautiful gorgeousness, right in between us. He was the bond and the glue and the space that intruded into our silences. He was a part of our best and most beautiful memories . . . and yet, he was the enemy too.

We forged this strange thing some might call a *friendship*. Yes, Bliss and I. Grasp the pearls! We shared a little semi, demi-weird vibe here and there, most usually at a table in B. Smith's. This lovely little bourgie paradise was just down the street from her show, and she still so loved being recognized.

This one night in particular, we were in B.'s, chillin', and as always, Facey was sitting with us, gazing at the menu, as calm and cool as any apparition could be. Yes, Facey, or so I imagined him, resplendent in this full-length leather trenchcoat, looking oh so *notorious* in his sway. Maybe he'd even laugh to see Bliss and me fast becoming what we had never been before: friendly, on the way to being friends.

Bliss was so full of stories, and had a way of telling them that put you right there in her skin. But the story she revealed that night seemed designed and composed with more layers than an onion.

"Last night I was this single New York City girl, on the prowl. Since you're a hard-core fashion-forward cat , ya know I've gotta give you details: I went very classy. Wild-ass diva hot, fitted, just above the knee black skirt, black fishnet stockings, black stiletto pointed-toe Jimmy pumps, with crisscrossing ankle straps. Baby Cakes, the Jimmy's were fierce! I wore my hair loose and free, just like I tried to be, if just for one night only. Topping this ensemble, I rocked a pink knee length, kid-leather coat. It reminds me of an Easter coat I had as a girl—very soft and feminine-looking."

"In other words, you were red hot-tah," I chipped in.

"Red hot, mami hot! Mad hot, hot hot-to- trot, hot hot-like- fire hot," she said. "So as I walk in, there's this rather mature-lookin' brother sitting there. He sees me . . . and his face lights up like Christmas in Hollis Queens. I think, oh damn, he *recognizes* me! Urrrggh! I don't really mind a little recognition, but this one was in no way shape, form or fashion, *my type*! You know the ones, a little too old and inactive looking. So he says, 'I been sittin' here *waitin'* for you, so you make sure you save me a dance! I'm thinking, *Okay. He doesn't know me. He's just another deluded basket case.* So I say, 'A dance? Ok. Sure, hon. We'll do that.' And I proceed to walk inside, thinking nothing more of it. Only, here he comes right behind me, in typical basket-casebasket case stride, talkin' 'bout: 'Naw , girl, I'm comin' right now! I'm gon' be wit' you all night. You ain't gettin' rid of me.'

"Wow! Look at all these hot menz you attract! You sly fox, you!" I chuckled.

"Yeah. Whatevuh! All my brain is screaming is: '*Oh my Gawd! No, he did'n! Am I gonna have to do it? Am I gonna havtuh come out of my rich trick bitch bag and cuss this fool out before my freakin' night out even gets started?*' I mean, what the fuck was his problem? My plan was to ignore him, give him the quick slick Jaguar pass. I've handled my share of stalkers before, and this one, he was just small change."

"Ok. Handle yours."

"So the place is thick with people and music. The DJ's playing 'Rock Creek Park.' Do you know it? By the Blackbyrds?"

"Girl, please! Know it? That was one of my early theme songs. I made 'doin it in the park, doin it after dark,' my lifestyle for a while. I was *such* a literal boy," I confessed.

"Oka-a-a-a-ay. So yanno . . . instantly, I'm *loving* it. I wanted to dance. I needed to dance. Trust me, baby, a dance was *necessary!* But an oh-so so-casual glance over my shoulder reveals, DAMN! He's still there, watching my every move! I breathe, try to stay cool, and I say to my basket case stalker in a cheap suit, 'Arruh, bruh, aww . . . that's our jam. But I just gotta check my coat first.' So, he proceeds to *follow* me down the stairs. Waits, while I check my coat, doesn't even help me take it off, doesn't even offer to *pay* the coat-check chick. *Strike Two*! Plus, I'm thinkin, *If all these semi-gorgeous men see me walkin' in here with this fool, they'll think I'm with him. Shit! I'm Bliss Santana in a public revue!*"

"Can't have that!" I offered.

"Exactly! So I go up stairs, the song's still on, I'm thinking, yes, I can still dance to the last minute or so of it, and be done."

"Cool. Dance, and then drop-dip him. That's the move," I said.

"Well, yes, that *was* the plan. But as I'm walking to the dance floor, basket case says, 'Wait a minute' he's 'just gotta go to the bathroom, real quick.' I'm thinkin', what *What the fuck?! I ain't yo' date, fool!* 'Wait?' Wait, my ass! So I keep struttin' toward the dance floor, and thank God, someone steps in my path! I mean he just falls there, as if from disco heaven, and he asks me to dance. Yes! Oh God, yes! We danced a few songs. I mean DJ Felix Hernandez played those jams from my wild days, baby, so you *know* I got stupid on that dance floor. And as we finished, another man, this one a handsome young papi, takes my hand and there we are, making Latin smoke on that floor. And that's the way it was for like the next ninety minutes. One brother or papi or the rare White man with rhythm came along, one after another as if there was a race to dip my magnificently sexy ass!" she giggled. "Don't mean to sound vain, but that shit felt s-o-o-o-o-o good!"

"Well, I relate. You were the hotness. Hotness attracts hotness. It's practically one of the club commandments, or some such shit."

"Yeah, and I was droppin' like it was hot-tah."

It was then that she became ghetto; the Jersey girl in full; her essential Bliss.

"So there I was, dancin', eyes closed, hair all bouncy and shit, wigglin' and shakin' errthang, even some imaginary shit . . . but I was graceful wit' it though. Yes, crazy and sensuous . . . that stuff these young prostit-tot heffas ain't old enough to know about. You know, if I was watchin' myself spinnin', twirlin', dippin', windin' grindin', I woulda said, 'Girlfriend ain't been out dancin' in a long-ass time!'

"Well, it was your night out . . . the best time to unleash your freak."

"And ya know this! Because my damn freak had been in a state of deep hibernation, baby. Anyway, so then, when the DJ Felix slowed the pace. I went upstairs, just walkin', checkin' out prospects, and guess who shows up?"

"Ummm . . . Bruh Man, the basket case?" I surmised.

"Ya damn skippy! 'There you go,' he yells. 'I been lookin' all over for you, girl'! Talkin 'bout his shoes hurt, and why don't I sit with him until his 'feets got get right.' So now *ya know* he's bout half-a-sec from bein' cussed the fuck out. He couldn't be serious. *Life* was happening all around us. People were dancing, sweating, and having mad fun. And he wants me to sit, while he nursed his bad feet? Madman, please! Life was right there, spinning and twirling and laughing and . . .

She paused just long enough to make me curious. And then she said, "Old-ass bastard, wastin' my time on this motherfuckin' planet! I'm serious. It *pissed* me the fuck off! Who really knows how many nights we get to dance away all our constrictions. So my attitude is: don't you fuckin' DARE waste my fuckin' time, if you can't fuckin' find your fuckin' rhythm! Bastard!"

And I thought, *Oh God! Was she trying to tell me something? Was there something real and essential and part of her core she was trying to telegraph to me?*

I wondered about this for the rest of the evening.

I never liked it when people felt the need to speak in riddles to me. I'd much preferred they made things plain. I was never stupid or by any means, slow. There was no li'l yellow bus parked out outside my door. I just liked it when you come at me *real* and un-riddled. I'm good at figuring out men, some men—Hell most men, because, in truth, the majority of us really ain't all that complicated. But women? Strange fish, indeed. Even a dumb woman is usually *smarter* than a fairly intelligent man will ever be. God gave them that guile gene, along with their ability to reproduce. They can *work* you, and even when you're paying close attention, you won't even notice that you're *being* worked. That's their gift. It's a strange mechanism . . . fascinating, really. Many times, they'll take you into their confidence, and you begin to relax in it. Bliss was doing this to me. You think you can trust then, know them much better than men, until they do something, or *say* something, that reveals that you can't, and you never will know them.

What was she really saying to me? What did she, or didn't she want me to know?

Bliss Santana keep kept talking and spinning her web of words, reciting this fiercely feline and endlessly feminine yang in my ear. There *had* to be a reason, a *purpose* for it all. She didn't appear to be the kind of woman-chick inclined to small talk or mindless chatter and shit. I didn't know her well. I just *sensed* this about her. So, just what was her *story?* Did she, would she, trust me enough to *tell* me? As I watched her mouth, I began to wonder about Facey. Then, ever so temporarily, I pondered just where else that lush red mouth had been, with who, and when, and for how long. Most of all, I wondered about the *story* behind her words.

"This fool just keeps following me," she prattled on. "And being a so-called 'true playa fo' real,' he proceeds to try to *mack* me."

"Oh no, he did-n!" I said, all faux-interested and shit. And all the while I wondered: what was up with this suddenly *ghettofied* Bliss. Hadn't she ditched the urban tongue for something decidedly more *Mid-western*?

"Oh yes, he did," she continued, working her Afro-Latina head side-to-side in 'round-the-way girl-style. "But I gotta give the brother credit. He grew on me like an old school classic. Had me crackin' the hell up, talkin 'bout, 'Now see, years from now, when the keeids is grown, and we're two old geezers, we gon' sit back in our rockers, look back on this moment and laugh . . .'"

When Bliss said *that*, when she repeated that phrase old geezers, I sensed some sad premise, some utter impossibility behind that phrase.

Okay. So she she's was finished, I thought. *Mindless New York club story*, I thought. *Had no real hidden agenda*, I thought. But there we were together, an odder couple than Felix and Oscar, and therefore, I thought then and still believed there was a *reason* for it.

If I sound as if I didn't quite *get* her or *trust* her actressy ass, make no mistake: It's only because, I didn't, back then.

This had little to do with her association with Facey, and more to do with instinct. Truthfully, I could never hate or dislike her or anyone who truly had love for Facey. Not to get all Minnie Riperton about it but, Lovin' him was easy, because outwardly, he was beautiful. But I also knew the ugly inside of him, and I loved him anyway. Bliss and I were never rivals in that sense. Besides, if I added up the time I'd spent alone in his presence, *my time* would've kicked her time's ass, by several naked years. If I were to calculate the meaningful words passed between Facey and me, again, I'm quite sure, I'd win. Facey loved me in his own quiet way, no matter what he said or how he'd said it. When he was so cruel to me, and that shit-tide of vile words would break my face, it was usually the *narcotics* talking, not his heart. Not his true heart. So, my mistrust of Miss Bliss Santana, stunning approaching-upper-middle-age *Blacktress*, was not, repeat NOT Facey-based. It was centered partly on my wickedly keen sense of gaydar (which, in itself is a sixth sense) and my primal gut instinct.

I went to Performing Arts High School, damn it! Dance was my major, but I did know a little something about acting. I could *act* interested with the best of them. I could act friendly, concerned, curious—Hell, even loving—and most folks would not see or pay any attention to the little man behind my curtain, pulling all the strings.

So Bliss was back, and Broadway had her. But what I had was a mystery.

That night David dreamed and everyone he ever loved made an appearance in it. His mother was complaining that his dance shoes didn't fit. Rico, his first lover, was telling him he'd forever be a "damn faggot!" Carlos, the last lover he'd known who'd died from AIDS, he'd kept quoting his favorite Spanish poet. Victor, his current squeeze, appeared to whisper, "Puppy, you're dancing to too fast. Please, quit it!"

Ty emerged from behind a blue curtain, telling him "I've never seen or known a more extraordinary talent!" David blinked and Ty was still there, with his arm around a smiling boy. But David didn't recognize him from any of Ty's past lovers. And the more he studied the face in the dream, the more it appeared that Ty was embracing his own self, his *younger* self.

As the dream moved on, Face Depina appeared with a large piece of tape fixed to his beautiful lips. Then Bliss stepped out from behind his shadow. There were purple sores all over her.

David awakened quickly in a cold sweat. He *knew* the secret now. Bliss Santana was sick!

CHAPTER EIGHT

A COLLECTION OF BONES AND REGRETS

The sickness. While some young men were beginning to feel somewhat at ease, that sprawling disease continued to grow and flex its muscle within the community. It was still present, still clinching its relentless fist and taking on *new* prisoners of color.

New York was still David's city—a magnificent, multitudinous, maniacal, and monotonous bitch, speaking in its multi-culti sensory language. Yet as familiar as dreadlocks in Harlem, and Hip-hop in the South Bronx, common as plastic Adonis gods in Chelsea, and Arab men manning newsstands, there remained, a rhythm.

New York City was David Richmond's favorite ho, and through the rumbling and swishing, banging and clashing he, like everyone, had come to depend most upon that whore's rhythm.

But now, was it really the city, or just David steadily losing rhythm?

The Center

He'd heard it all inside that place. He'd sit and listen like a haunted student to the testimonies of young men. It was there they relayed the tales of their lives to him and the rest who'd gathered for comfort, for solace and for fellowship. There, inside those walls, they revealed their truth, they could say it all, without shame or judgment or moral indictment. They recalled the ignorance, the mistakes, the lies or the foolhardiness in the acts which led to how they'd contracted the disease. Some of their stories were hot and reminiscent of David's own notorious past. Others bordered on the incredibly tragic. David would sit and listen to them all, his mind open, and with his whole heart devoid of judgment.

This was the Community Center—the place where David gave back. He didn't have a master's degree in sociology, nor a doctorate in psychology. But David had lived The Life, in full. What he could offer now, were his own experiences, some good, a few glorious, and others quite self-destructive.

David heard the horror stories of young people who had been disowned and banished by their families, and he could relate. These were the families that swore eternal love and commitment until the day their gay, lesbian, bi, or transgendered sons and daughters spoke the truth of their sexual orientation.

There were times when David held court during those group discussions, certain faces within the assemblage would shift and change. Once, in the beginning, he saw the faces of old lovers, losers, and beautiful suspects, some of them dead, others of them sick. Any one among them in that room just may just had have been That One who'd given him his own death sentence.

* * *

Even though David reasoned these phantoms were there to either applaud or berate him, he knew in his heart, he was doing the best he could do to make a small but valuable difference. When he looked around at those faces, and heard their stories, he thought these those young black and brown men could have been his younger twins from another decade. So many of their lives and their choices mirrored David's own.

Nassir was twenty-six, and a buyer for a large department store:

"I'm a born fag, a hyper-fag. Always been attracted to a wide variety of men; Black, Brown, Yellow, Puerto Rican or Haitian, Norse, Irish, American Indian, Polish, French, those hunky Italians, and masculine Asians. It was just a matter of time before this thing bit me in the ass. But you wanna know something? I had my fun. I'm twenty-six fuckin' years old, and I regret nothing. I never felt it was *cool* to insist on using condoms. The few times I did, I'd ruined the moment. Some men would get insulted. If I liked them, I didn't wanna piss them off. So . . . if they looked good, and seemed hot and healthy enough, I'd just say, 'fuck it!'

"But they had to be masculine, macho even. It didn't matter what age or race they were. If they liked me, and looked and acted like men, I'd let them do anything they wanted. Everybody wants to be wanted, right? And it's even better when the type you want, wants you. I think I probably got this thing in the gym. I was working out constantly, trying to get the body other men admired. Well, I got the muscle, and the attention of beautiful machos. . So, gradually, locker room orgies became my scene. Y'know: Line 'em up, fellas. Show me how much you *want* me!"

Quincy was small, brown, petite, and doomed:

"I always knew I liked boys. I knew it in the third grade. There was this very cute boy with a shy thing for me. We'd kiss after school, and hold hands on the way home. But one day, his father saw us, just holding hands, and he cursed me, and beat him son all the way into the house. After that, we didn't kiss or hold hands anymore. In fact, he wouldn't even look at me. I felt so ashamed, and I didn't even know why."

"Yeah, shame. I know that song by heart," Nassir added. "But then, when I finally found someone who wasn't so ashamed of liking me, it turns out he wasn't strong enough to leave his wife. Married gay men. What a sad and delusional life that must be."

"I was never attracted to married men, or any man over forty," Quincy said. "But the first man I'd I was ever been with was my neighbor. His wife was my mother's best friend. His oldest daughter used to even babysit me. I'd known him most of my life. But I never thought of him *that* way. But then, one day, when I was fifteen, I was sick, really sick with the flu. This man, he dropped by, when no one else was home. He claimed *his wife* told him to bring me some chicken soup. Chicken soup? Can you believe it? Well, I did. I was so weak and so sick, I couldn't even move. He knew that. He sat on my bed and he talked to me. I noticed him rubbing my thigh as he talked, and it made me a little uncomfortable. He asked me if I could get up and walk. I told him I'd tried, but I felt too weak. Those were the last words I said, before . . . he, he. . . . God! He put his sweaty hand over my mouth, and he . . . *raped* me! I was so ashamed. I never told my mother, or even my best friend. I never told another soul. Two years later, that same man died, from AIDS."

The room fell silent after Quincy's testimony. Some looked at him with shame, pity and even disgust. Some others simply looked at the floor.

Damon, a once handsome Latino, was a seasoned player, at twenty-eight:

"Sad. I think the married ones can be kinda sexy. I always liked the challenge. I dug that they been with women before, and that their semen had made babies. It was an odd kinda turn-on for me. I figured if I turn a married man out, I must be pretty good with my shit. It depended on the guy, of course, but if he was married and had kids, I *wanted* to seduce him, just to see if I could work him into sucking me, fucking me. Okay. I admit it. I'm a sick little fuck. I'm a very *sick* little fuck. Funny, isn't it . . . how *sick* a little fuck can make you?"

Damon said, "I wish I could tell you—it happened on this night, at this club, or that this gym, with *that* guy. But I can't. After a while, I became this submissive pig. Names, didn't count and faces didn't mean shit. None of that matters, when you're a stone whore slut, like me. I guess HIV is my punishment."

"No! Please, stop that! This isn't a punishment. Was contracting it from a rapist some form of punishment for being too *weak* to fight? Hell, NO!" David protested.

Jose, a lean, delicate-looking Blatino, was twenty-four and a former hustler:

"I tricked from the time I was fifteen. Some did it because they were poor and needed the cold cash. Some did to make enough money to help out their mothers. Some did it to buy the latest sneakers, or something pretty for their girlfriends, or take 'em to the movies or dinner or some shit. Me? I did it because I was gay, and cute, and men liked me enough to *pay* for it. It's a trip, to have some rich son of an old wealthy bitch in a brand new Mercedes pull up in front of you, and practically *beg* for sex. That was pure petro for my fuckin' ego, man! After a while, I did some real kinky shit strictly for the coin. I was am ambitious fuck. Hell, if I had the right connections, I could've gone into porn or something. I was a fuckin' celeb on the docks."

"A celeb on the docks? Wow! Lucky you. Do they give Oscars for that shit?" Quincy asked sarcastically.

"Yo, you gotta a prob with me, Quincy?"

"I'm just sayin', I'm here because I'm sick. And I didn't do anything like whore myself out. I didn't know it then, but the first time I ever had sex, it wasn't even my choosing, and I got this fuckin' disease. I was always pretty careful about who I had sex with after that, but it didn't even matter, because I'd already gotten IT. And *you* sit here, like you're all proud. Like you did something great! A 'celeb on the docks'? Man, that's not something you need to be braggin' about. That's just sick!"

"No. You wanna know what *sick* is, Quincy?" Jose snapped. "Sick is being somebody's fuckin' victim. And that's what *you* are, sweetheart! At least, I took control of my own body, most times. And nobody took shit from me I didn't *want* taken!"

Quincy quickly got up, grabbed his jacket, and prepared to leave. David halted him.

"Quincy, don't you dare walk out that door! Believe me, you're *nobody's* victim. I thought I told all of you long ago to leave that victim mentality at the door, along with your shattered or puffed-up egos. People, I don't like this judgment aroma wafting around here like some *other* kind of *plague*. We *don't* judge here. We talk, we listen, and we learn we're not alone. So, please, *be* men! Stop the bullshit! Sit down, Quincy! Jose, you think you can manage to tell us your story, *without* the braggadocio?"

"Hey, I'm not tryin' to brag. Is it braggin to say: this fag could do a dozen johns in a hour, and still be home by midnight? No! That's the truth."

"Oh, and I'm sure it was all mad fabu. And you were walking around like Sheila E. in your full-length mink, humming all about 'The Glamorous Life.' Please, don't play a player, kid," David said.

"I'm not sayin' it was *all* good. Yeah, sure, sometimes it got rough. I've had my ass kicked a few times, been robbed, ripped off, and *half*-took," he said, looking smugly at Quincy when it said it. "I've even been stabbed twice. See this scar on my neck? It ain't there for effect. It's real, and it's got its own story. Like everything else, there's a poz and neg, but trickin' was my life.

"I'm realistic. I know it I ain't got no future. And I ain't so cute anymore." He boldly ripped open his shirt and showed them all the souvenirs from his exploits. "See these lesions on my chest? KS ain't such a turn-on to those some rich sons of an old wealthy bitches, in brand new Mercedeses," Jose finished, he quickly closed his shirt, and looked down at the floor.

"Wow. So you don't trick anyone. You wanna fuckin' parade? Try givin' up sex! That's what I've done. I gave it up. Did it, cold turkey, baby! I just don't feel *safe* being out there. And I don't even wanna deal with the chance of givin' this thing to somebody else. But the saddest part is, I'm still horny. I'm still tempted. Sometimes I'll see some young, sexy, cool-as-shit teenager, zipping around on a skateboard . . . and I'll think: '*Whoa! Can I have a little piece of that, please?*' But all those thoughts and what ifs end up inside the bed of my head now. And in my head is just where they'll stay," Damon said.

Nassir added, "I know people still fuck with no protection They suck and fuck and get fucked like madmen fuck when they finally break free of the fuckin' asylum, man. And they KNOW this disease exists, and don't even bother getting tested. Shit! They already KNOW they have it! Hell, that's just wrong on so many levels. I ain't sayin' I'm perfect, but at least I'm tryin' to do the right thing!"

"Oh, we ALL know those fools. And they're around, baby. Probably waxin' ass or gettin' waxed in a dark bathhouse even as we speak," Jose replied.

David's thoughts kept shifting back to Quincy. In some ways he reminded David of Ty. Not that they resembled each other in the least, or even lead similar lives. There were like night and day in those aspects. However, gazing at him was like gazing at a dying poet. There was a quietly romantic expectation that both Quincy and Tyrone sought and wanted from the world. And the world always told them: NO!

CHAPTER NINE

Funeral for a Poet

After leaving that session, David remained haunted by young Quincy. Mentally, he was inside his own private funk, and his mind revisited that painful day, the day he wanted to wipe clean from the blackboard he called his life, forever.

December, 1994

It had been raining for three straight days and nights—a Nor'easter the weathermen called it. Through howling winds and ceaseless rains, David could not sleep. More than the raging elements, it was the constant noise and racket of his thoughts, the years what-ifs which haunted him now. He looked, that day, like one of those hungry children Tyrone Tyrone had gone off to Africa to try to save. Ty was forever playing the rescuer. But it was David who needed rescuing now.

Dressed in his natty blue suit, his lover Victor called out, "Mirror check." And so David did.

He'd glanced only once in the mirror, before he and Victor were to leave for the service.

Just a week before that day, he didn't have to look very hard to see the dancer there. It informed his posture and made him taller than his physical dimensions allowed. There was sill a pronounced youthfulness, a cuteness to him, which never made that manly shift into handsome, and this kept a part of him eternally a boy.

But after Ty's death, when David saw his own reflection, he hardly even recognized himself anymore. His amber eyes were clouded by the cataracts of a grief, so large, and so intense, it hurt to gaze at them. Seeing what *this thing* had done to his face that day literally hurt his senses, the way it ached to peer at a starving Somalian baby. Anyone with clear vision could glimpse that hunger and see it had *overwhelmed* him.

But by then, grief had overtaken most everyone who'd known and loved Tyrone Hunter. Tyrone, who had a Sensitive's way of taking on your misery, harnessing your pain, extracting your loneliness, and absorbing it all *for you* inside his tightest embrace. Now, he was gone. Others felt it too. That utter hunger for consolation, it was not David's hunger alone.

David pressed his face against the cold, wet glass of the limousine window as it took its own sweet time arriving at Abyssinian Baptist Church.

Even as his Papi, Victor Medina, stood strong and tall by David's side, that brawny presence didn't seem quite enough. Though, at just a little over five-six, David had always been somewhat vertically challenged. Yet, for years, there was something like a stalwart *tree*—a mighty *oak* holding up the ladder of his spine. This quality had long been a part of his posture, and now it had sadly withered.

Strange the things you notice. That day, one could see how grief eats away at the carriage of even the best dancers.

If David was once a mighty oak, suddenly that oak had diminished into—a smaller thing—a weeping willow in need of sustenance, of sun again.

But the willow that wouldn't weep, had at least, made it there.

As he stood outside the church he felt the weight of his legs grow heavier.

The weather seemed to announce the day. Someone—maybe the meteorologists—perhaps even God Himself had thought enough of Ty Hunter to deliver him more clouds. Clouds for Ty's funeral . . . what self-respecting corpse could ask for more?

Though the rain had ceased, the sky sat attentive in its own dismal gray haze. Gloom had moved in, dropped its heavy baggage, and made its home in New York City. It was so custom-tucked for the likes of Tyrone that this day would fit his demeanor like a dark, well-tailored overcoat; a coat, like the one David last saw him wearing.

It was closing in on eleven AM. The rain began to fall again as it pounded down on the city's streets of rogue Romeos and sorrowful addicts, its oxygen thieves, and its dying poets.

The East and West Village hipsters, a few has-beens and a sprinkling of never-weres had gathered alongside Ty's stoic mother. There, in that a room of jazzmen, balladeers, and mystic hooligans had assembled to get their grief in order.

Before the pulpit stood an old gray man with the posture of a makeshift Satchmo. He clutched his horn and began to blow. Beside him, a zaftig woman with a voice as big as Mahalia Jackson's cleared her mighty throat. Together, in a robust and moving gospel crescendo, they played and crooned their song of love, transference, and sympathy, "Come Ye Disconsolate."

It was indeed a disconsolate day for many. Ty was gone, and with him, so went his dream of love and coupling and transcendent sex with meaning . . . of Long Blue Moans manifesting in sighs, that came, and left, but never saw the fortune in this prize he'd offered.

While some may have felt a physical void, the sad truth was the city would go on being the same tough, rhythmic and steely bitch as it always was. It seemed nothing had really changed. New York would continue to scream and freak in its in concrete skin. People would still seek shelter, still hover and covet the glaring haven of a life lived inside taller erections, still have sex anonymously without stress, worry or concern or latex. People would throw come-hither glances, sip their apple martinis, still laugh high and bawdily while smoking their furtive alley cigarettes, and like the city itself, people would continue to break other people's faces, spirits, and hearts apart, at a rate of about a million, daily.

After all, this was New York City, with its rogue Romeos and its sorrowful addicts, its oxygen thieves, and its dying poets.

As David climbed the steps to the church, he wondered: *Why do my legs feel so heavy*? Just then, it hit. Soon as he stepped inside those doors, for a moment, everything went a little bleary. The world, its objects, the mourning people in it, everything surrounding him began to spin. Feeling dizzy, all senses whirling—overwhelmed by it all, David found himself collapsing against Victor's chest.

What's wrong with me? he wondered. This was not scheduled.

"David's Faint" was not written into the carefully printed program, the one those polished brown ushers handed out to everyone. Clutching the stereotypical linen hanky and catching the vapors was much too cliché a behavior. Ty deserved far better than that—better than a cheap fag's imitation of a fag. David couldn't have that either—at least *not* on this day. And so, weak, dehydrated, lost or not, he somehow found the will to rally himself back into that painful world, back into consciousness.

Victor touched his face lovingly. "You all right, Puppy? See? You should've eaten something."

David didn't speak. He still couldn't speak. It hurt to even *try* to speak. He buried his head in Victor's chest, and though he'd determined he wouldn't cry, his guard broke down. He clutched his lover's lapels, and silently, he wept.

David used to do so much *better* at funerals.

He had the distinct feeling Ty would've approved of this ceremony. It was a sedate affair, which featured just the appropriate amount of tears and whimpers, remembrance and song; along with a modest display of calla lilies. Yes, the occasional wails rose to accompany the well-worded tributes, but for all those who'd attended, it appeared to be almost funeral-perfect.

There were lighter sounds and words of comedic recollections of Ty's stiff posture and his patented bowlegged walk. A few nodded when an old professor recalled the furrow of Ty's disapproving brow, and how even when he laughed, a part of him still appeared somewhat distressed.

People had naturally expected David would be called to deliver the eulogy. But for obvious reasons, he could not. And so, the choice, by proxy, fell to Imani, *Ty's African*. Imani rose to the challenge quite nicely. With Nigerian-accent intact, he summed up the essence of Ty most definitively when he said, "This life was gentle, and the elements so mixed within him, that nature would stand and say to all the world, 'This Was A Man.' Shakespeare must have known Tyrone in another life."

Ty's sad but lovely mother Ms. Laura Hunter sat in the first pew beside David , her warm toffee face shielded by the shade of a sedate hat of smooth black feathers. David always liked "Ms. Laura," and that day she looked as sturdy and sanctified as ever.

Victor Medina was on David's left, clutching his hand. The eternally gorgeous Bliss Santana was there as well, along with her young daughter Tyra. But something in Bliss's face and in her bearing appeared inconsolable. David never quite *got* the oddly shared affinity she and Ty had forged together—but actress or not, her tears seemed genuine. Faison Brown looked ever-so-slightly contrite, and beside him sat his faithfully plump wife, Juanita. There were all sorts of people with little or nothing in common, except, they'd lead lives in which Tyrone Hunter had helped to make a difference. The rich and the poor, the homeless, and the glorified, the hungry and the overfed had all shown up to pay their respects. There were old lovers, new friends, and people Tyrone had worked with, helped, touched, loved, or consoled. It was all just a little too much for David.

Ms. Laura had asked if he'd like to be a pallbearer. And suddenly David wondered, *Has grief made her silly*? There was just no way on God's green earth that David could have hacked that responsibility. The thought of carrying Ty's death inside *a physical box* would have demolished him completely.

Woman, please get a grip! I am not about to fall the fuck out in the middle of that long aisle, carrying Tyrone, and all those memories.

Besides and beyond the public embarrassment, his fainting spell would only serve to hog all the attention, and even in the after-life, Ty would have never forgiven him. Still, Ms. Hunter had proposed it, and so, as well-meaning as the offer was intended, David shook his head no, and gently refused her. She seemed to understand. She *appeared* to be a very sweet and agreeable woman. It made David all the more curious, as to why Ty had so rarely spoken of her.

There was a balloon in David Richmond's chest, and it kept expanding as it threatened to swell, to well up and burst with blood and tears inside his throat. At least, that's what it *felt* like, watching that closed box. A part him seriously doubted if Ty was even in there, reposing in that metal box. David had not *seen* him in there. Whatever his remains, they must have been too gruesome for communal display.

Yet for David, it was better to think lovelier thoughts, to imagine himself into believing that Ty *was not really there*. No! Tyrone was still in Africa. He was happy, and that furrow had finally left his brow, at last. Ty was madly happy, amid the sound of tribal drums and Nubian dancers and beautiful black faces. Ty was lying safe and content in the arms of the most handsome a Nubian warrior of all—a man called Imani.

It was such a lovely reverie.

Only, Imani was there, in that church, grieving with all the rest of them. Life was beyond unfair. It was cruel and viciously hideous, and for some, it always seemed to end so badly.

Once the service was done, a random cool possessed the limbs of the fashionable Black men who wore crisp black suits and matching black shades as they walked the silver coffin down the aisle, out the door, and to the waiting black hearse.

Ty's passing had so emotionally trounced David's spirit. Even that breezy jazz bounce so inherent in his walk had abandoned him now. He stood among the rest who'd gathered on the wind-driven street to say their final good-byes. He watched this whole surreal scene through sleep-deprived eyes and thought, *This ain't no funeral. Not really!* It appeared to be more like some tragic ballet; a doomed and fractured dance, performed in painfully slow motion.

Just then the sober drag queen locked deep inside David wanted to resurrect her self. She wanted to ditch her Jimmy Choo's, wanted to run, wanted to scream, wanted to hurtle *her* mess of hysterical wreckage toward that closed coffin. It seemed so wrong; some appalling travesty that this silver box could possibly hold the remains of his bestest friend.

He wanted to run and jump and dive upon it, and he wanted to howl from the top of his anguished lungs:

Lawd, no. Not Ty! ! NO-O-O-O-O! Lawd! Please don't take him! I'm not ready to let him go yet. It's a mistake, you fools! It has to be! Ty wouldn't do this—not to me! Y'all don't understand! He wouldn't leave me like this! Lawd, please! Take me! Not him! His work wasn't through here!

Could anyone understand that when, in pain, even the best-intentioned queens sometimes lose themselves to drama and angst? Yet, he was being David, on three, instead of his usual nine. He was David, dressed in his tastefully constricting little black suit, with not a wig or a Jimmy Choo in sight. Ironically, Ty would have surely saw seen the humor and pathos in a little after-service episode from him. But the hysterics were abruptly cancelled, due to misery. David didn't have an ounce of humor left.

As the hearse slowly drove away, a brighter light gradually intruded inside the day's looming gray. A small hint of bright orange sun emerged from the clouds and into a piece of periwinkle sky. David watched this small but meaningful feat of God in hopeless astonishment.

DAVID:

There was still so much I'd wanted . . . *needed* to say. But I had no words. Grief had kidnapped the motherfuckers. The sheer heartache of Ty leaving, like this, without any warning—it had left me . . . mute. It seemed as if my world was full of nothing but brutish betrayals. Even my freakin' larynx had betrayed me—taking away my speech, my words, and my screams. If you *knew* me, surely you'd see the fuckin' irony: Yes. Pain can and will do such strange and terrible things to even eloquently cute and aging boys like me.

That odd kidnapping of my vocal apparatus, my core

strength, my voice—it occurred the day I'd received the tragic news. I wanted to scream then. God, I wanted to SCREAM! I'd tried my hardest to, but no scream ever came to the surface. Three days later, I still could *not* scream. I could not even whisper. I'd all these feelings, these cries and hollers, and years of emotions stored up in me. They were bottled up to the freakin' rafters, and I'd no sane place tall or broad or wide enough to vent them. But my true voice, that screaming voice remained active inside his my skull. And that voice was crying now:

WHY! Why, Tyrone! Somebody please make sense of this senseless shit! God help me! Somebody explain this shit to me! Why him? Lord, why him!

Victor drew his arm tight around David's shoulder. Everyone should have at least one rock. Victor, more than ever, in those last past few days, had proven to be David's Gibraltar. David loved that man. He still did. It was not a madly, young, and foolish love, but sometimes we get a little less than we deserve. And for his part, David felt blessed to deserve even a *piece* of him.

"It'll be okay, Puppy. You'll see. You'll survive this. Look at me!" he grabbed David by my collar." I believe in you!"

The Gift That Keeps Giving
January, 1995

It was the dawn of the New Year. David was deep into that transitional period of questioning everything from his future, to the loss of his faith, from his capacity to forgive, to his ability to *love* in full. Most of all, he was questioning his own resilience.

He'd gone to three specialists, seeking the cure. They all said the same thing: there was nothing physically *wrong* with him. They all claimed it was psychosomatic, a case of "selective aphasia," and that his voice would come back as soon as *he* let it.

"*Aphasia?* Whatever! It sounds like some old drag queen, wearing cheap-ass perfume!"

Then, just as strangely as it disappeared, David's voice just as magically returned. It was like wearing a tight turtleneck made of sandpaper. It still hurt for him to speak, but at least he *could* speak again. The first words from his mouth were shameful ones:

"*Fuck you, Tyrone Hunter! I fuckin' hate you!*"

David knew Ty would *understand* his anger, because it came from a place of love, and desertion. David loved Tyrone deeply, and he always knew Tyrone loved him, no matter what was said or done in the interim. Even in death, their love would be forever.

They never spoken of certain things—things like money. Ty was not one who'd placed much worth in material possessions. It was almost *funny* to him how the money kept coming his way for something he'd done as a teenager. Yes, he'd written that hit song, but Tyrone did not feel particularly *worthy* of the continuing fortunes it had garnered him, and so he was always willing to share it.

When David was a dancer, he had his own coin, unreliable as it sometimes became. He'd made, at best, a meager living—but David Richmond was in no form, shape, or fashion, *rich*. Still, he had an issue taking things from people, even Tyrone, no matter the how many times Ty had generously offered, and no matter how desperately David could've sorely used the assistance.

There were others in line to become Tyrone's *trust fund babies*, especially after their freakishly successful stab at singing fame. David was too proud to ask for money. Pascal "Facey" Depina made too much of his own coin as a top model to care about Tyrone's windfall. But Ms. Laura Hunter was an anxious beneficiary to the richness of those funds, as was Browny, who never had any problem whatsoever, taking or asking for the copious handout.

But that was a friendship of a vastly different color; and Ty and Browny's love song was written in a whole *other* key.

Ty had made a vow many years ago that, he'd share his royalties with each member of our the singing group, Da Elixir. He'd always contended he couldn't have gone on to have a hit record without the other three contributing their talents. That was a kind, but gentle *lie*.

Now years later, that sense of *sharing* continued.

David didn't know if Tyrone's intent was to piss him off, or just to show his undying love and reverence, but he soon discovered Tyrone had gone and done this most miraculous thing. In his will, Tt Ty had decided, years before, how his possessions would be divvied up upon his death.

He thought of death a lot. The way David thought about going crazy, in between bouts of sizzling sex with red-hot-chili papis, Ty thought about death and dying. He considered it even more than most gay men his age. And to that end, Tyrone, that gentle, *long-faced beautiful bastard*, divided his loyalties between various charities; Hale House in Harlem, of famine relief in Africa, several homeless in NYC shelters, and then one David Donatello Richmond.

He's trying to make me cry, again.

It was miles outside of sweet, and light-years above thoughtful. It was incredibly over-generous, downright otherworldly so. Because of this, David Richmond would never again *want* for another physical thing—except for the only thing he truly wanted, and that was to have Tyrone, breathing air beside him again.

Ty's worldly treasures, his bounty, his interests included a portfolio containing blue-chip stocks, twenty-five percent of his future song royalties, a treasure trove of photographs and manuscripts, *and* the ownership of his Harlem apartment.

David was under the distinctly uneasy impression that the apartment held memories and lost spirits in its walls. Tyrone had become acquainted with one particular haunting, and for David there was a quiet kind of madness in that belief. Yet, it was in that where David had regained his voice. It was another of those eerie coincidences and strange turns-of-events, replete with the things that could not be explained.

This was the very same apartment Tyrone swore he'd shared part-time with the ghost of his love, *Trick Brown*. For years, Tyrone would hold marathon conversations with Trick, as if he was completely oblivious to Trick's violent end. Ty was not a whimsical person, but he did wholeheartedly believe he and Trick shared a love, a union that defied the rules of their separate earthly planes. Quite frankly, this place and its unseen spirits freaked David out.

However, beyond the occasional moan or the groan of floor-beds settling, David Richmond had never once felt a Trick's presence there.

But much of what made Tyrone Hunter who and what he was, remained, like his journals, like the furniture, and the photographs, and the paintings, and the fixtures. These things made this place feel *alive* as if he still *lived* there.

And it was then that David finally found the strength to begin reading those journals, because he realized by doing so, it would be like having Ty with him, and truly alive again.

David commenced to read them like a freshman student; a student of the person he'd *always thought* he knew.

Excerpt From Journal Number Two:

Can you understand how you can love and admire someone so much, and yet never want to be them? That's how I feel about David. He is, without question, the most talented, loving, crazy, beautiful person I know. And yet, I always felt just a little sad for him. He uses his sex as a lure to draw and attract the most *unworthy* people to him. It's like he doesn't even know what a prize he is, and that he should be and deserves to be cherished. David doesn't cherish himself. I don't know if he ever will.

Just reading those words angered David. He was back to hating Tyrone's judgmental ass again! David violently threw the thick journal onto a chair.

David couldn't take it. Not that day! So he tossed it. But when he did, the book landed in a *peculiar* way. It flipped open to another page, and photograph loosened from its spine. And he thought, *Well, isn't that queer?*

David felt compelled to walk over to it. It was as if Ty was *calling him back*. He picked up the picture, and a smile broke across his face, like a low tide forming a wave that sparkled with a radiant sun.

Wow! There we were. Teenagers. Weren't we a couple of beautiful kids? Well, at least one of us. I always was the Adorable One.

The picture was one of those taken by Tyrone, the budding photographer, when he was sixteen, and David, fifteen. The smiles they wore could have easily blinded their onlookers. This was what *Happy* looked like—at fifteen and sixteen:

Tyrone had his arm around David's shoulder. He was a gangly 150 pounds, but one could still see Ty's his coltish allure even then. That Hunter face was long and thin with its toffee skin and curious features all trying at once to be handsome. His crowning glory—a bank of pomade-assisted curls—adapted from old Sal Mineo movies. His almond eyes were a deep, dramatic shade of sable with a haunted gaze of directness. His most bewitching feature, though, was his puffy, heart-shaped lips that at times seemed almost begging to be kissed. But that day, those lips appeared the happiest David had ever seen. Then David glanced at himself, at fifteen, smiling from his eyes outward. His grin was infectious.

When had have I ever been THAT fuckin' happy? he wondered. But that photograph provided substantial evidence that he was, at least once, in 1977.

Though David's eyes were lined in mascara, the photo revealed their soft, light-hazel overcast. Ty once said of David's eyes, "they always looked as if he'd just awakened from a pleasant dream. But still, there is this private little comedy act going on behind that strange gold curtain." Ty seemed to know the shape of David's soul, even then.

Both those boys in the picture looked so crazy, so free, with no edge of tragedy and no anticipation of what the years would bring.

Ah! Youth! David suddenly wished he could bottle it.

Gazing at that picture gave him a certain strain of happiness.

Suddenly, he remembered a turning point in their friendship. But even more than remembering it, Tyrone, the writer, had thought to record it—even the parts of which David had never been privy to, back then.

David could not put the journals away now. He began to read and discover and grieve and laugh and gasp and giggle and get pissed. The subject was Tyrone Hunter: the best friend, he never truly knew.

Tyrone's Journal Entry
Late November, 1977

Ever since Mr. Raines assigned us to do a project together, I wondered just how I could work through all this craziness. I am *hating* this thing! All I want to do is get a decent grade, pass this damn class, and be done with it.

I could just strangle the hell out of that little David Richmond! This was HIS wise-ass idea. He suggested to Raines that we form a group, it was his idea that we perform an original song. MY SONG! David is a trip. But why a group? I've never been much of a group person. I know this is only happening because David's all hot in his tutu for that freak Face Depina. It's all he ever talks about. Face said this and Face did that! Face! Face, forever Face! It's sickening. Like David's got a chance in hell of ever getting some pretty boy who calls himself "Face." Please. Get a grip, David! Most of all, I sit here wondering, what the hell am I doing with the likes of these cats? Faison Brown, and Face Depina?

Faison Brown is strictly ghetto. Yes, he can sing. But he's also a bully, with no work ethic, whatsoever! Oddly enough, he does have the makings of a true artiste: profound talent dwelling inside a miserable human being.

And Pascal "Face" Depina, please! He's been strutting around school, telling people he's Paul Newman's "lovechild." What a joke! The biggest joke is that some fools actually do believe him. But I'm not one of them. Sure, he does sort of, kind of look like Newman, if Newman was half-black. But doesn't Paul Newman have real talent? Face Depina is all surface. He's six-five, with curly, brown, half-white-boy hair and so-called 'pretty' green eyes. That's all cool, but this cat has absolutely no substance. Plus, he's got zero skills on vocals. And he dances like a white girl, from Long Island. Can't move worth a shit. But David was quick to say he'd teach him. Good luck!

I've spent weeks working on just the right melody, the lyrics, the arrangements, the song itself. Finally, I feel like it's tight and right. Now that I'm finished, I really need David to see it. Strange, I know. But it seems like I've developed this freakish respect for David. He is one of the crazy and deeply talented. His honest assessment of my skill means a lot to me.

And so, feeling very much like a musical genius, tonight I invited this crazy-talented boy over for the big debut.

David is into this theatrical thing. The heavy eyeliner and blush makes him pretty, but kind of freaky-looking, too. One gaze, and needless-to-say, the Moms and Pops were not amused. The Pops was on his way to yet another card game. Gambling is still his bitch on the side. The bitch must have been particularly horny tonight, and so Pops was out of the door real early. But he did stop to shoot Davy a stoned-faced, "Hey." It was so cold and so disrespectful. It was like he was saying in a single look: "*I ain't got no love for faggots*."

David laughed out loud when he read that part "So, Ty, was keeping secrets, yet again. He'd never once mentioned the Pops had no love for me!" *I guess my utter butta charm was completely lost on him*.

Suddenly Tyrone's early writings were a bit more intriguing. David just *had* to continue reading now.

TY:

Once Pops left, the Moms gave David the sanctified fish-eye. She grabbed my sleeve to ask in her patented whisper, "Tyrone? Just what's going on with you two?"

"Nothing, Ma," I told her. "David's a little crazy . . . but he's also the most talented person I know."

Just as I said that, I realized some little *crazy* part of me . . . *Loved* . . . David.

Ever since this past summer, she's been different with me. I guess a boy can only hide his pain, anxiety, and queer magazines under the mattress for so long, before something clicks . . . *Aha*!

Moms' way of confronting me was to place the offending magazine wide open on top of my desk, all wrinkled and stained, in front of God and Judgment and everything. When I came home, and I saw it there—wide-opened . . . OH, MY GOD! It shocked the absolute secretive shit out of me!

I was utterly mortified. But then, this whole other thing rolled up inside me, and it was this deep sense of invasion. It began to well and rage in my chest. I was not nervous or scared anymore. No. Hell! I was hot and bold and so enraged at the nerve this woman. So, I marched straight into the kitchen to confront her. This was something I'd never dreamed of doing before. Not to my mother!

" 'Are you a crazy person? Huh? God! Don't believe you did this! Don't I deserve any privacy at all? Why was *this* on my desk, huh?" I demanded to know. I was wild and so angry I even shook that rolled up porn mag at her.

But instead of her coming back equally bold, or even being shocked at my confrontation, my moms simply said,

"Now I *know*, Tyrone. I know," she'd repeated, calm as a guru in mid-meditation. She continued to peel her potatoes with her back turned to me—as I imagine it will always be from that day on.

"Okay. Well, you know, and it's no big deal. Now you know, and nothing's changed, Ma. Don't you see? I'm still Tyrone. I'm still your son!"

What would follow was too ugly and too painful, too personal for David to read just then. He skipped over key sections, making a mental to note to read them when he could take it. He flipped to another part of the same section.

I just stared at my mother, as if everything good and right inside our relationship seemed to drain like rusted water clean out of her body, her eyes, her mind, and her heart.

"And for God's sake, whatever you do, don't ever tell your daddy!" she warned.

David had to stop reading in that moment. He could feel the elements around him suddenly stand silent and still. Everything opened up to the abrupt arrival of an epiphany.

"Damn Ty. You never told me that, Baby-Boy. How tragically, utterly, stupidly sad! You were *out* to me, and all the rest, but you were never respected, forget about *accepted* by your own damn people."

Is that why you wrote, and gave, and lived the way you did? Was it all for her? Were you trying to pay some cosmic mea culpa for being a disappointment in your mother's eyes? Damn it! It was your life! It was your fuckin' life, and you wasted it, Ty! You fool! You fuckin' wasted it tryna make somebody else proud of you!

Ty's Journal Entry:

And now, a few short months later, David, The Artist Soon To Be Known As "The Duchess," stood in our doorway. My Moms obviously thought he and I were *doing it*. ICK! That idea was so far from ever being true, that I secretly found some humor in it. The Moms vanished into her thinking room to ponder the vices of the men in her life. David sat on the sofa. I cleared my throat, hit my best second-tenor and played my song on the family's Spinet piano. I never claimed to be the greatest singer. I'm not. I can carry a decent tune and give lyrics a little color. Well, I found my voice, and sang from my soul that day. As my fingers stroked the last keys, I looked at Davy, and saw these crazy tears in his eyes. Was it Love?

"It's, it's wonderful! No, bump that! It's the *shit*, Baby-Boy! I mean, daaaaammnnn . . . I'd buy it, dance to it, and play it at my wedding. Well, *somebody's* wedding. C'mon on. Let me hear it again . . . ," he asked.

David's enthusiasm was like my gold . . . so I sang and played it again. David stood and began working his wicked little body into a kind-of-jazz-dance motion around the music. It was inventive and sexy, but not too suggestive. The Moms caught his act, and even *she* dug it. She positively *liked* her some David, and invited him to eat with us. Of course, by the end of that visit, the Moms stopped liking him and had fallen in love!

"He's so talented! Such a little gentleman and cute as a copper button."

David was on his best behavior. He didn't freak a fairy's flight inside our family room. He was courteous, observant, and boyishly flirtatious. He complimented Mom's on her roast beef, her hair, her complexion, her choice of new furniture (thanks to one of the Pops' rare paydays at the races).

By night's end, she was kissing Davy's cheek, and helping him with his cape. Suddenly, she too was his fan. Even I was amazed at how quickly he'd worked her. I figured it must've been the line about her complexion being "spun brown-gold velveteen."

Later that night, as I was walking David to the corner to catch his train, he became very quiet along the way. I wondered if something was wrong, but I didn't say anything.

Then, a few blocks later, as we stopped at the light, and in front of traffic, with the city racing around us, David embraced me very tightly. And inside that weirdly uncomfortable display, he said, "Your mother's so cool. I like her. Your song's the shit. See you Monday. And you know what? I love you, man."

Then, he kissed my cheek.

I was stunned by that kiss. But even more, I was shocked by his NAKED declaration of LOVE for me! And he said it like he *meant* it. It sounded pure, not fake, frothy, or full of fucky intentions. But it really didn't matter *how* he said it, because the little fool opened his damn mouth, Love came out—and it totally freaked my world!

Upon reading that, David had to laugh out loud. Laughing was a must as he thought, Trust me, Ty, my young naïve high school girl—your world needed more than a little freakin'!

CHAPTER TEN

Do The Sanctified Witches Ride Brooms?

In the time since Ty's passing, David had not been in touch with Ms. Laura Hunter very much. He was suddenly more ill at ease about even the thought of this woman, knowing now, from Ty's journals, how his mother had emotionally distanced herself from her son. But there was nothing David could do to change their relationship, and it saddened him that Ms. Laura Hunter was little more than a Bible-toting, self-righteous phony.

Thus, when his phone rang and Ms. Laura was on the other end, David was mildly surprised to hear from her. But he decided to remain *cordial.*

"Hey Ms. Laura. How you doin', girl?"

"Well, I'm fine, David. Just fine . . . though I do get a little troubled sometimes," she added.

"Well. I do understand that, Ms. Laura. I do. I know it's not easy. I miss him, too. More every day. Not one hour goes by that I don't think of him. But my doctor tells me, that's healthy."

"Your doctor? So *you* sick now?"

Whether he was or wasn't sick was none of her damn business as far as David was concerned. But he thought it best to *clarify*.

"I mean, Baby-Doc. Doc Horowitz. You know, my shrink," David confided in an off-the-cuff fashion.

"Oh."

There was something inside of that "oh" and in the silence that followed, and it troubled David a little. Had he said too much? As he heard Ms. Laura breathing on the phone, he sensed a hint of disapproval.

"Well," she said tentatively "I don't believe in 'shrinks,' as you call them. I firmly believe we should take our troubles to the Good Lord. There ain't a problem in this life The Almighty can't fix," she paused. "You DO believe in the Good Lord, don't you, David?"

David rolled his eyes. "Uh, yes. Of course. My father was a minister, you know. I *believe*. Always did. I'm just a little *pissed* off at Him right now."

"It don't do you know no good being mad at *your father*, David. I'm sure, he *tried* his best . . ." Even that last sentence from her was veiled in something that felt, more than a little like, judgment.

"No." David chuckled for a short, polite length. "I mean, The Lord. I'm pissed off at The Lord, Ms. Laura. I mean, He took away by best friend, and He ain't gave me a reason why."

Now . . . what did David have to go and say *that* for?

"Lord. Boy, don't make me have to come over there and *smack* you silly!"

"Ma'am?"

"Don't you *evuh* fix your mouth to say you're pissed off at The Lord! That's *crazy* talk!"

"No, Ms. Laura—that's real. I try to keep it *real* with the Lord. He knows me. I'm His *boy*, David, and he He knows all about me. So even if I didn't say it, He would *know* that He's made me damned angry."

The phone was silent for the longest time.

"Hello? Ms. Laura. You still there?"

"I didn't realize you were such a heathen, David Richmond."

"A *what*?"

"Well, I *knew* you were a *homosexual*, but I liked you anyway. I've always prayed for you, and of course, for my Tyrone. I've always prayed one day, you'd *both* see The Light."

"Oh. I'm seeing the Light, Ms. Laura. In fact, sometimes the very same people who *claim* to see it best, be actually wanderin' around in the darkness."

"Now what's *that* supposed to mean, young man?"

David knew this conversation was beginning to get out-of-hand, and was, in fact, starting to turn a few shades of ugly. But damn it, now the woman was getting on the frayed end of his *last damned nerve*. He tried to choose his words carefully, and yet still he didn't quite *know* what would fly from his mouth.

"Ms. Laura. Maybe it's this phone connection, but to my ear, it sounds like you're *judging* me. And that ain't right. I don't believe in throwing stones. That's one good Christian lesson my dead daddy taught me, and it stuck." He slowly exhaled.

"David. I'm not judging you, no more than I judged my own son. I just hate the sad fact that unless you repent for your *sinful* ways, you'll never see the Gates of Heaven."

"Oh. But I will. Trust, I *will*. And no matter what kinda *head trip* you did on *your son*, he was a good and *decent* person, and an upstanding *man*. I don't believe *who* he loved . . . matters too much to God. It only matters *that* he loved. And Ty, he loved with his *whole* heart. So, as far as Heaven goes—

trust me—Ty's already there. And maybe, Ms. Laura, you need to be worried about whether or not *you'll* be seeing those Pearly Gates!"

Damn it! I done said it now. I don't believe that shit just flew from my mouth!

But fly, it did. And just as quickly, Ms. Laura Hunter slammed her phone down.

"Hello? Hellllooooooow? Oh no she did'n!"

But she *had*, indeed. The dial tone in David's ear was *not* a friend.

Little did David Richmond know, his tongue, his honesty, and even his sanity would soon be called into question. Ms. Laura Hunter's crusade was no longer invested in trying to right the wrongs she'd perceived in other people's sex lives. David had just gone and made himself another holy and sanctified *enemy*.

Within a week, a rather legal looking letter arrived at David's door. The gist of it was that now Ms. Laura Hunter was contesting the will of Tyrone Hunter. Point of fact, she was contesting David's rights to *any* inheritance, thereof.

"Oh *no* she did'n. What the fuck? Is this her idea of good *Christian* etiquette on display for the Free World and all the New York State court system to see? So, this heifer wants to fight with me, now? And just what are the grounds, exactly? That I happened to be personally *pissed-off* at God? Damn, Ty! I do understand now, Baby-Boy. This woman is a piece of work!"

It was never about the *money* to David. Though it was a nice luxury, he hadn't exactly been going on mad shopping sprees, purchasing mad cars, madder jewels, and going plumb mad with power. But if Ms. Laura Hunter wanted a fight, then she would surely get one. Tyrone's money provided well, and thus David could

afford the best civil, criminal, and probate lawyers in the state.

This was bigger than family, bigger than pride, and bigger than sexuality. This was about, Ty's wishes, **Ty's allegiance. This was about *Love*.**

CHAPTER ELEVEN

I'm Okay, You're Fucked Up

Dr. Horowitz's Office:

"Sometimes, I wonder, *Am I going crazy? Can people actually feel their selves going crazy?* Maybe what I was feeling, what I was hearing, maybe it was the prelude to my own insanity . . . just . . . before that final flip.

"The more I think about it . . . just maybe the real-deal insanity is a feeling that comes on like a storm—all dark and quiet at first.

"Then suddenly, something in nature moans. It rains and the wind begins whip and howl. You're stuck inside of it, and you can't see any clearing. And then, from somewhere inside that storm, you *realize* it isn't the downpour, or that furious wind that's howling. It's *you*, FOOL!

"You, *raining*.

"Everybody rains, sometimes, right? But maybe *crazy* is the hard-core deluge. Maybe it's the whipping rain, the howling winds, that stinging wail of hail where everything comes down all at once.

"I saw him again."

"You saw *who* again?"

"*Ty's ghost.*"

The doctor released a silent, almost indiscernible sigh and scratched his wrist. This was something he did when he detected the air, the whiff of a patient's bullshit.

"I saw him, Baby-Doc. Just as clear as the congested day. I was walking down Seventh Avenue, at dusk. It was rush hour. Mad crowds of people everywhere were scrambling. Then, this tall, thin, almost handsome brother moved with his own flow towards me. He looked me right in the eyes, and then he just walked right past me. It's the strangest shit, but these days, I *keep seeing* him. It's like Tyrone is *still here*, in the City, but for some ungodly reason, he's mad and he's not speaking to me. I've been seeing this so often now, that I've taken to calling him, this person or this vision: '*Ty's ghost*.' And I'm not even afraid of it. But I really do hope it's a ghost . . . because, if it's not . . ." David's voice trailed off to a faraway village full of fog, and it felt like that place where crazy people go. He shook his head "If it's not, then I've really gone *off*, man. I mean full-tilt, fetch-the-straight-jacket-time out-of-mind. I mean, really fucking . . . insane! And I can't afford to go crazy right now. Not now. I've got way too much *sane* work to do."

"Maybe it's the ghost of guilt . . . or the spirit of unfinished business. Maybe we should talk about the *unfinished* things, David."

"You keep saying I should talk about it. Well, I'm here, ain't I? But what the hell is ever gets fixed here, huh? Why should I even *be* here, talking about anything real? Huh? Will it bring back the best friend I ever had, Doc? There's a question for you. Are you mystical or something? You deep into reincarnation, this week?"

"Well, for starters, there was a period when you couldn't talk. You couldn't speak about anything. You had no voice.

You were struck *mysteriously* mute. But there was nothing *physically* wrong with you. Was there? That's not *natural*, David. We lose people all the time, and we grieve for them. We get angry, and bitter, and we may even curse them, or God. But how many of us *lose* our ability to speak?"

"Maybe I had nothing to say," David snapped back defiantly.

"Interesting. Your so-called 'best friend' dies in a tragic plane crash in another part of the world, and you had nothing to say?"

"I see what you're doing. You're trying to make me cry. Sorry, Doc. Won't work."

"Much like your tongue which wouldn't work, right?"

Was the doctor being flippant or merely searching? Whatever his intent, that comment caused a small incision under David Richmond's skin.

"Oh. So, you wanna *see* my tongue work, huh? Is that it? Well listen to this: Fuck you, old man! You don't *know* me! You think I can sit here for an hour, twice a week, give you little tidbits and bullshit pieces of me—and suddenly you have *me all figured out*? Wrong!"

"I wouldn't suggest such a notion. Is that how you see me, David? Do you see me as all-knowing?"

"Oh. I see plenty. I see that the problem, especially with you so-called educated people, is y'all *think* you have all the answers, the secrets, and all the creature comforts to living a more mentally stable life. That's the joke, and the trip of you. And what are *we*? We're just your little amusements, right? Puppets with your hand up our asses, right? No, here's a better metaphor: we're the sad marionettes whose strings you pull, when you're bored. Well, news flash: I'm a *Black faggot*. That makes me *doubly* complicated. You don't get to know all the stuff inside me, and you *never* will. See, as dumb and uninformed as *you'd* like to *think* we are, we're smart enough to keep our core shit to ourselves—because it's ours, and we *own* it. You might rule the world, but damn sure don't own our psyches! Sitting there thinkin' you *know* me. Trust! You don't even have a fuckin' clue! So get over yourself, Doctor."

"David, maybe you can help me. Somehow I sit here and I'm baffled as to how your *anger* and my supposed superiority have suddenly played into our relationship."

"Good. I'm glad *your* ass is baffled now. Must be that time for you to see *your* shrink. Are we through here?"

"No. Actually we're not. I've been contacted by a Nathan Darby Brice, Attorney at Law. It has something with a case being filed against you."

Suddenly, even above that quick and certain erection of anger, David laughed. He laughed good and hard and full.

"Oh. I see. So now, she's questioning my fuckin' sanity? That fuckin' religious freak of a woman! I don't believe the balls on her. What does she really want? This woman won't be happy until she sees me, and every other butt-lover on the east coast in a fucking straight-jacket! The sanctimonious bitch!"

"David. Relax. You haven't *murdered* anyone."

David became deeply, painfully, historically reflective. The word" "murder" had brought him to a dark and hidden place; a place he could not afford to share with the doctor, or Victor, or with anyone, now.

Horowitz repeated, "Don't let it stress you too much. You haven't murdered anyone, David."

"No. I haven't," David said, in a vacant, almost foggy voice of defense. "Well, not yet. But the day is young." David placed his head in his hands and sighed from the far reaches of his soul. "That said, no one's privy to the things we discuss here. However, I may be called to testify on your state of mind. Strictly for legal purposes, I assure you." Dr.

Horowitz said. "Oh, really?" David exhaled as he looked to the heavens. "This day just keeps gettin' fuckin' better!"

A man can never feel more *alone* than at night, in the city. It was The Bewitching Hour. This was that time Tyrone loved best. It was that time when everything between the twilight and sunrise became more active, more alive. An effervescent New York would shimmer in its blue and sensuous skin. You could detect its resonance. You could hear its music echoing from the halls of some lively Jazz emporium. For Ty, those sounds swung inside the stereophonic juke joint in his mind. The bottom of a booming bass line would rumble against the mood of a piano's fretful poetry. His feet would tap. The cry of the horns combined inside his private reverie. It was Jazz, man! That hip and esoteric kind of music, and Tyrone Hunter would be digging it, digging it madly.

Jazz was the only pure thing left. It was the sound and the Spirit of The City. Riding shotgun with the cries and screams and the whooshing traffic, it filled the urban air like a mild intoxicant. Sometimes, he could almost taste it on his palate. Jazz had this bittersweet flavor. And when the elements were just right, its players would conspire to take him away to a lush and much more dazzling place. Inside those clubs, Ty would close his eyes and let lewdness of the sax become like a lover; blowing ever so sweetly between his long, thin thighs. He could ride on a note until it became a slow and wistful glide into euphoria. This alone was his Blue Moaning Moment, when the whole damn City ignited in flames of magnificent sapphire light.

Tyrone lived his blues by day, and he loved his Jazz at night. He was a romantic that way. Beyond the enchanting echo of a new soul's first sweet "hello," nothing thrilled his laconic spirit more than copping moonsets to that melodic rhythm place. He'd let loose inside that neon-lit abandon with its sex and its surrender, and even the chance of love's bold and reckless possibility. It was all there, swirling inside the night's air, in the music, in that shining blue glare of light, in the rhythm, in the meeting of lonely eyes . . . and even inside that unspoken promise of . . . What If. Some nights, Ty would just live and breathe for it.

And now, David Richmond had grown to love this blue-hued hour, too. He was walking through the tedious beauty of Times Square with the city flashing its neon wares like a gaudy diamond necklace around him. His mind was on Tyrone, again.

As he turned down Seventh Avenue only a block away from his salon, a shift in his aura began to brighten. Strange, the mood that came over him then. Not sad, not so lonely anymore . . . instead he was buoyed by a reflective optimism which had begun to claim his stride. He saw something, or rather some one, and he found himself walking faster, almost rushing toward that figure. He nearly called out in a piercing cry,

"Ty? Ty! Hey Ty, wait up!"

But then he realized, it couldn't be Ty. *Ty was dead*. With each new stranger and every faux sighting, which, always resulted in nothing more than a ridiculous trick of the mind, Tyrone seemed to *die . . . just a little more* each time..

Maybe he was dead . . . but never in David's mind. And David had to get his *mind* right. He *needed* his mind right, now more than ever before.

He took the train home. Home? That too was beginning to feel less real.

Strange men with eternally beeping beepers had come to invade his space again. Was it really *his* space, Ty's space, or Laura Hunter's future space?

These men, this small parade of them had come to eyeball him, to investigate his home, and more to the point: his sanity. It was enough to most the most sanest person crazy with anger. But David was on his best behavior. He had to be. He could always fake it when he had to project an air of calm and serenity.

He could shape-shift, straighten up his spine and do the damn sanity dance to its utmost effect. His words would be carefully chosen, his posture erect. Thank God for an earlier career in things theatrical! Because of this, he could masterfully succeed in convincing his critics and his onlookers that things were indeed, A-ok.

He knew Laura Hunter was behind this invasion, or more precisely, Laura Hunter's greed. If something incriminating were found there, then it would only booster her case against him.

There were pills, loads of pills, but each of them were prescribed by his physicians. He hated the idea that strangers, and especially Laura Hunter would know of his *condition*, and his health status now. But even this didn't cause him to trip, flip or lose his composure.

Later, the night before the start of the proceedings, David sat down and wrote himself a letter to his Creator.

Hey God,

How You doin'? You aiight, my Father? This is Your boy, David. You know, that wild-ass one, David Richmond? I know You're watching me, and so You must know there are some things going on around me, and I don't, and I won't even pretend to understand them. And maybe I'm not supposed to, but it would sure be nice if You would smile down on me, Father. Maybe pat my head, or tap my shoulder and lead me down a more Righteous Path.

Please, don't give up on me. I'm trying very hard to be

better . . . even here in the wilds of New York City, I AM TRYIN' to be Better!

I hope You're not too pissed at me for the sins of the past, because You know, like all the rest of Your children, I'm very much a work in progress.

That's it. That's all.

Peace-out.

David

CHAPTER TWELVE

LADIES AND GENTLEMAN OF THE JURY

Day One in the Court Case: ***The State of New York Vs. David Donatello Richmond***

DAVID:

Oh, it was on and poppin' that day. On and poppin' like poppity-poppity-pop-pop popcorn. The plaintiff, Ms. Hunter, was most properly attired in her two-piece light blue suit of indignity. Had her fancy white lawyer represent her, too. A very siddity type, in his sensible Brooks Brothers gray, and crisp white buttoned-down veneer, my dear. Oh, he came to play. But hell, so did I. My attorney, Miguel Augusto Del Los Rios, a most pleasing papi, in and out of his briefs, and he came to rep me, in full. Actually, he headed the *team*, representing me, and Tyrone's estate.

I sat there and listened to this character assassination of me, and my friends, my lifestyle, and my beliefs, and I wanted jump from my seat and strangle that mofo in the Brooks Brothers suit. He knew nothing about me, yet he read off this falsified litany of my so-called prior acts and antics.

It became very clear to me that Ms. Hunter was a mind-fuckin' witch, in good standing. A so-called "Christian" witch at that. She brought out the big guns. Me, I just brought the truth.

Tyrone was of clear and sober mind and *halfway-decent-gay*-body when he made out his will. There were no hidden deathtraps or clauses or codicils enclosed to contest or punish me for speaking my mind or for being myself. Ty didn't play that shit. And what had I'd *done* anyway, besides question and stand up to the Queen Bee, that witch's religious fervor and her judgment of Ty and me?

According to the statement given to HER attorneys, Ms. Laura Hunter was "extremely close" to her beloved son, Ty.

I wanted so bad to scream, "Objection, your Your Honor! This witch is sitting here committing blatant perjury! Please scratch that last comment from the records. She *never* accepted him. Never! She hated that he was what he was, *and* that he made no apologies for *being* what he was. Please recognize, this *heffa* is a liar!"

Oh, but Ty's diaries and journal didn't lie. And just maybe Ty's voice could save me, even from the grave.

Day Two:

The lies continued. Ty supposedly promised her a home in Miami, a ridiculously high monthly allowance, a new Mercedes every two years, and a generally lovely life of luxury and leisure. Please. Ty never promised her a rose garden! He was a good son, but not, repeat NOT, a forgetful one.

Though she'd never accepted him, she'd no problem at

all accepting his generosity, or taking the money he offered. And Ty had taken good care of his mother, this witch, who was now turning all shades of puce green and ugly. Trust. Miss Margaret Hamilton's Wicked Witch of the West had *nothin'* on Ms. Laura Hunter!

As she sat on that stand, I halfway expected to see her nose start growing. Oh, I stared that witch down . . . especially when she recalled the reason why she'd brought me to court.

According to *her* tedious testimony, I:

"David Richmond was a spendthrift and the most hedonistic of heathens." I'd capriciously "taken numerous trips to Europe and to the wilds of Africa, all on Ty's dime."

Ladies and gentlemen of the jury, let the record show: I *did* go to Europa strictly for the business purpose of extending my fashion line. That was NOT on "Ty's dime." And yes, I also went to Africa. I did so on Ty's behalf to continue his support of the clinic he wanted built in Rhodesia. If the witch had only *asked* me, she'd have *known* that shit. But her good Christian head was so far up the ass of her dead rejected son's bank account, she never even noticed the *foulness* of the act.

When I took the stand, swore before God and everyone to tell the truth the whole truth and nothing but . . . the cruelest cut of all for me was her lawyer dredging up the state of my sanity.

This bastard with a law degree grilled me relentlessly.

"Mr. Richmond, are you not currently under psychiatric care?"

"Yes. I didn't realize that was a crime, sir."

"And just how long have you been under this care?"

"It's an ongoing process, much like life."

"Would you put it in weeks, months . . . years?"

"Four years and counting. I'm not ashamed. In fact, I

highly recommend it, for *some* people," I said plainly, aiming my gaze directly at the Hunter witch.

"And wasn't the reason you initially went into, urruh, therapy because you liked to dress in women's clothes?"

"Urruh, no. I'd been doing *that* for years."

Ms. Laura looked so damn repulsed, I thought the woman would seriously up-chuck and vomit all up and through the courtroom.

"I went into therapy, because I'd been severely beaten, nearly to death . . . by a tribe of people with a vicious hate for homosexuals."

"But were you not wearing *women's* clothes, at the time?"

"Yes. At the time I was dressed as a Holly Golightly, so, considering *that* fit of lunacy, I guess I musta had it coming to me. I *deserved* to beaten to near-death, right?"

"Mr. Richmond, as a witness you're simply required to answer the question."

"Yes, I was wearing women's clothes at the time I was savagely beaten by a group of thugs and blatant gay bashers. But I'm dressed in *men's* clothes, today, as I have been for several years. And still, the beatdowns continue comin'," I quipped, again staring holes through that witch of a woman.

"Your Honor, please!" the attorney implored.

"Please, answer the questions, simply and succinctly," the judge duly admonished me.

But hopefully, I'd made my fuckin' point.

"So, you dressed in women's clothes, for years, and you've been under a doctor's care, for *years*, and you still feel YOU are the most qualified candidate to manage such an immense estate?"

"Tyrone Hunter obviously thought so. I'm not here for the money. I'm here to protect Mr. Tyrone Hunter's last wishes."

"Again, Mr. Richmond, knowing your own *peculiar* past,

do you honestly feel that *you*, more than my client, the deceased's own *mother*, *you* are better qualified to be the executor of Mr. Hunter's estate?"

"Yes. Indeed. I do."

"Are you currently under medication, sir?"

I didn't answer right away. I had to think of what I'd taken, when I'd taken it, and what I'd taken it for.

"There's a certain regimen I must adhere to, strictly for health, *not recreational* purposes."

"Oh, and what *regimen* would that be?"

"Objection your Your Honor," my attorney yelled "My client's physical health is not on trial here. I'd like to call a sidebar."

And so the attorneys and the judge spoke in animated hushed tones as I looked on, knowing that witch actually wanted my HIV status made public. Talk about cold-blooded.

After three minutes or so, though he was clearly disappointed, her attorney rephrased his original question to me: .

"Are you currently under any kind of psycho-active drugs, Mr. Richmond?"

"No sir. Sober as a judge. No offense, Your Honor."

The judge smiled at me. I think she was falling a little *in love* with me, despite herself.

"I have no further questions at this time, but reserve the right to question the witness again."

I left the stand, and this bastard then called Baby-Doc as a witness. Oh, Lawd! My heart was racing in a crazy rhythm. What the hell was *he* gonna say?

I watched him being sworn in, and noticed how he refused to look at me. That was *not* a good sign!

"Dr. Horowitz, how long have you be treating the defendant?"

"Close to three years, give or take a month or so."

"Is that common?"

"That depends upon the patient, and what it is they seek from the therapy itself."

"In David Richmond's case, do you find anything unusual in his actions?"

"Unusual? Well, Mr. Richmond is an unusual person. But having spent time with him, I think *unique* might be a better word."

"Could you be more specific?"

"Well, he's a lively, *theatrical* person."

"Would that be *a nice* way of saying you find him deeply troubled?"

There was a long pause after that question. It was much too long of a pause. Was *he* going to betray me now?

"When Mr. Richmond first came to me, yes, he was troubled, to a degree. However, I wouldn't say deeply."

"Perhaps confused, then?"

"How so?

"Confused . . . about his sexuality?"

"Umm . . . no. Mr. Richmond knew then and still knows who he is, sexually. I don't think that's ever been issue for him. It just manifested in a way that was self-destructive for him, at the time we first met."

"Was he? Self-destructive? How so?" the witch's attorney asked. He was clearly on some vicious fishing expedition, and I, of course, was ALL ears.

"Yes, in that he'd placed himself in situations that were not safe or healthy for his well-being."

"Well, wouldn't that alone be the act of an *unstable mind*?"

"No. Not necessarily. For example: people who smoke are clearly aware that it's *unhealthy* to do so, and yet they still do it. That doesn't make them *mentally* unstable."

Good answer, Baby-Doc! I was starting to *like* him again, lookin all spiffy in his li'l gray flannel suit.

"Let me ask you this, Doctor, and I need to remind you

that you're under oath: Has Mr. Richmond ever displayed any behavior that made you, as a mental health professional, think he was, ummm . . . not well?"

Again . . . with the long pause. But by then, I too was going over my history with Baby-Doc. And it had been a tumultuous one. I'd cussed him out, numerous times. Hell! I'd even told him I'd seen Ty's ghost! But there were some things I *didn't tell* him, and never would. And if I had, surely those things might've had me *committed*.

Baby-Doc took a sip of water, and the whole damn courtroom sat on pins and needles.

"Mr. Richmond is a very spirited patient, and spiritual man. His behavior can be, at times, erratic, then placid, high-strung and then morose. But he knows there are limits to behavior. And while he's pushed the envelope a few times, and he's never stepped over the line. Stepping over the line of socially acceptable behavior is how *I'd define* an *unhinged* person. In my professional opinion, I would not define Mr. Richmond in such a way. If I did, I would no longer be equipped to treat him."

I wanted to run, just jet-speed up to that stand and lay a big-ass kiss on this man's balding forehead. Yes. I truly wanted to embrace this small Jewish man in the John Lennon glasses, I so affectionately called "Baby-Doc."

A defeated attorney said, "No further questions, Your Honor."

Then, just when I *thought I* was winning this sucka, those witches and warlocks went into my past, swept out the closet of old relations and produced: "Tah-dah! Adeva, daahling!"

Adeva? My drag queen confidant from back in the day? What the motherfuck? I would've been *so* glad to see the old girl, still alive and kicking, BUT not like *this*! She'd chosen to rock a mad ridic ensemble into that courtroom. I mean m-a-a-ad for even Adeva's frocks! This was *not*, *repeat NOT* the appropriate drag for daywear! This was a little something from the Josephine Baker collection, all see-through and complete with its strategically placed feathers. There was this audible gasp, and then a fit of wild laughter in the courtroom. Yes, Adeva was wearing the feathers, but *I* was the one who just knew *MY* goose was cooked!

She told these stories of the wild times, and of how "craaaay-zeee!" I was in the old days. How I once had this vicious blood-letting fight with Imona Lotta, a certifiable and, yes, psychotically jealous queen. How I, and my gang in drag, showed up Facey's fashion show, which I'd ruined unintentionally, by wearing something like Miss Joan Crawford would've styled in Mildred Pierce! But . . . in my defense, I was *fierce!*

Oh, the courtroom screamed, and I was duly mortified by that drunken picture of us, flashed on a screen, all drag-out, tore the fuck up, and high on ecstasy.

"Observe. This, is the *person* placed in charge of a multimillion dollar estate, your honor. The state rests."

I wanted to crawl under the fuckin' table, and just disappear in a soft pink cloud of dust.

CHAPTER THIRTEEN

Dead Sons Tell No Tales

I know old Willie Shakes, as Ty called Shakespeare, once wrote, "First, kill all the lawyers!" But, to that, I must say, please, spare Miguel Augusto Del Los Rios! That man was a prince, a royal fuckin' prince, and his kingdom was the courtroom.

Without getting all Stevie Wonder about it, He told me, "David , don't you worry about thing." He has a way, a mad lovely way of placing a firm, hairy hand on my delicate shoulder, and reassuring me. "The truth is on your side."

Then, he broke out the big gun! No! Not *that* gun! Though, truthfully, I did muse a fantasy or two about him and his fine Latin ass. Papi musta spent some time in the gym! But anyway, the "big guns" of which I speak were those journals Ty had so copiously written in, and they were like a harsh spray of Raid on a cocker-roach.

My attorney was going enter into the proceedings, Exhibits A, B, C, and dammit, D!

Maybe those journals really were Ty's lifeline to me. I remember thinking, *Wouldn't be ironic, if Ty's voice could save me once again, if even from the grave?*

I mean, the thing I had in my corner were his own words he'd written about his dear *mumsy*. It was all there in black and white; all the forced child-star blues, the strain on their relationship, the discovery of his sexuality, the raised hand to him, the rejection, and even the "day when the balloon floated away."

It was time for MY defense. Much of the same subject matter was addressed and readdressed ad nauseam. Dr. Horowitz, who'd proven to be a better witness for *the State*, retook the stand to declare me to be of sound mind and *hotty* body.

Adeva, reappeared in a more *sedate*, but the no less out-there form of dress. This time, it was a knock-off of that little short white number Sharon Stone wore as she was *shooting beaver* to Michael Douglas and a room full of police detectives in *Basic Instinct*.

God! What can I say about Adeva? Good queen, lousy femme hygiene! And the legs, Adeva! Oh my God! Couldn't you had have at least *shaved* those nappy motherfuckers!"

Things were looking rather bleak for my defense.

Still, he noticed how the judge kept studying him in a way that wasn't entirely *judgmental*. She was a sista, in her mid-fifties, with a sensible bob, and had a certain unmistakable motherly quality. It had gotten to the point where David wondered whether she had a *crush*, or a *bachelor* son who she felt was perfect for him.

When he was called to the stand again, David answered the questions directed at him with a calm ease of spirit. Whatever was said of him, had already been said. He couldn't deny his past, nor would he apologize for it.

"May I please address the court, Your Honor?" David asked.

The judge, David's *secret sweetheart*, granted him permission to speak. And it was then that he let it rip.

"You happen to be meeting me while deeply ensconced in my *Stage Three*. Yes, this is my third act, people. Unfortunately, for the true-blue party freaks, just beneath your starched collars, I've changed. I'm not half the fag, excuse me, the *homosexual* I used to be. I sought therapy to get some answers, some clarity and resolution to my past behavior. Please notice, I said resolution, *not* absolution. I regret nothing I've done. My only real regret now is that Ty, my best friend, is not here to see this travesty.

"And just for the record, I'm here for *him*, Ms. Hunter. I'm not the David you once thought you knew. You know, that merry queen? That queen is dead. Long live the *new* and steely queen. I'm here for him, fighting for him, and *his* wishes, not yours."

DAVID:

She would not even look at me. The woman stared straight ahead, just past me, even when I spoke directly to her. Talk about disrespect. Thank God, Tyrone, was *nothing* like her.

Oh, when she took the stand on cross-examination, we tore her freakin so-called case in two. Miguel Augusto Del Los Rios, Esquire, asked, "Mrs. Hunter, when was the last time you were in the company of your son Tyrone? And by that, I don't mean the last time you received or cashed one of his checks. I mean *physically saw* your son?"

She paused for a long time, trying to compute it. Finally,

with something like fake tears and faux emotion trembling in his voice, she answered,

"I believe it was at his father's funeral."

"I see. And what year would that have been?"

Again she paused. "1992."

"Interesting. But you lived in the same city, a mere subway ride away. And you hadn't laid eyes on your *own son*, in the last two years before his death in 1994?"

Good question, papi!

I watched her fidget in that chair. I watched her shaking hand gently smooth back an errant weave hair. And in effect, watched her case very slowly crumble.

"Ty was a writer. A photojournalist, so, he was away a lot. But, but he called me. He, he called me often. And he never, ever forgot a single holiday," she boasted.

"Yes. I see," my attorney stated dubiously. "Actually, I have his phone records here. And I've taken the liberty of highlighting the calls HE made to you. Not the numerous ones *you* made to him, requesting, ummm . . . More money."

And then, in a great dramatic flourish, a slide projector appeared. The lights dimmed, and there before us were the records depicting two years worth of phone calls. There only *three* measly lines which highlighted Tyrone's phone calls to his dearly beloved mother. And hadn't she'd just testified that he called her "often?" Well, I, and the courtroom begged to differ.

Her own words provided the kindling for the fire, which burned down her lying house of cards.

Finally, my most excellent attorney asked the *fated* question:

"Ms. Hunter, how did you *feel* about your son being a young gay man?"

The very question itself seemed to *shock* her. Surely it was a normal question, and most necessary inquiry, considering the situation at hand. I, like everyone else present sat alert in our seats, awaiting her answer.

"Well . . ." she hedged. "Tyrone had his own life. And while it wasn't my personal choice for him, I was . . . supportive. I just wanted my son to be happy."

Damn lie.

"Do you recall how you *discovered* your son was gay?"

"I . . . ummm . . . I believe I found something in his room, when he was a teenager. Your Honor, I really *don't* understand why any of these questions are necessary. This all happened so long ago."

But my attorney simply said, "Ms. Hunter, the past so often informs and dictates the present."

And with that statement, he walked over to defense table, gave me a wink, and produced a very telling entry from Tyrone's journal.

"You say, you discovered something in his room. It was a magazine, was it not?"

She sighed, ran her hand across her neck, and replied,", "Yes."

"Your Honor, I would like to enter into the court record, Exhibit H. But before I do, Ms. Hunter, would you please take a look at this material and verify it to be in your son's handwriting?"

She glanced it and said,

"Well, it *looks* something like his writing. But I wouldn't swear on it."

"Let the records show that I have numerous samples of Mr. Hunter's handwriting, and an *expert witness* on board willing to testify to its legitimacy, Your Honor."

"So be it, Counselor," the judge said.

"Ms. Hunter, I asked you how you *felt* about your son being gay, and now I'd like you to read, *out loud*, what your son, Tyrone Hunter, had to say about this subject."

She looked directly at me as if she wanted to shoot a poison arrow through my forehead. With a shaky hand, she took the journal, cleared her throat, and began to read Ty's words:

"Now I *know*, Tyrone. I know," my mother repeated, calm as a guru in mid-meditation. She continued to peel her potatoes with her back turned to me—as I imagine it will always be from that day on.

And I said to her, "Okay. Well, you know, and it's no big deal. Now you know, and nothing's changed, Ma. Don't you see? I'm still Tyrone. I'm still your son!"

"That filth ain't what I want for my son. It ain't *right*," she declared, sounding all holy and sanctified. "You've read The Bible. I *know* you have. It's abomination, Tyrone! Great God in Heaven, why *my son*! ? I want you to take the Bible to bed with you tonight. I want you to read it, and you *know* just what chapter and verses I mean."

"Ma, a whole lot of things in *your* Bible make no sense to me."

Suddenly, Laura Hunter stopped reading. She must've known what was coming. Once again, she feigned some deep emotional distress, and so, my attorney took the journal from her shaking hand, and HE read the rest.

Just then, my mother did something she'd never done before. She quickly swung around, with eyes on fire, and she raised her hand, high, so high in anger. I turned my cheek and prepared myself for the sting of a lifetime, and I closed my eyes for the blow of it. But only, the sting never came. She stopped just short of swinging that open hand down on me.

"*My Bible*? Makes no *sense?* Boy! If you *ever* say anything like that in my presence again, I swore 'fore God, I will smack your sinful ass clear into next week's Bible class! It's wrong. And *you* wrong. If you don't have to believe me, just look at your Uncle Jerome. If you don't change, I'll just feel *sad* for you. You'll live a very lonely and very sad life. You always was a sad child. No matter what I did, or tried to make of you, you always did it sadly. Now this. I'll always worry that you ain't livin' right, in God's sight.

"No, you'll be just be livin' sad. I got too much love for you to hate you. But if this continues . . . I'll forever hate what you choose to do. You hear me?"

I just stared at my mother, as if everything good and right inside our relationship seemed to drain like rusted water clean out of her body, her eyes, her mind, and her heart.

"And for God's sake, whatever you do, don't ever tell your daddy!" she warned.

"She didn't understand me, and she never would. I could see that now. I suddenly felt like everything was dissolving, disappearing all around me. I saw my image of our family picture on top of the TV set, and I watched it slowly liquefy. It was taken when I was a sad-faced seven-year-old kid.

My mother had bought me a balloon in an effort to soothe me because I'd just been rejected for my last commercial. I guess I wasn't so cute anymore.

Well, after the photograph was taken, soon as we stepped outside, the gust of Harlem wind snatched that balloon from my grasp. It flew away like some last yellow puff of hope high inside the air. Maybe our love was like that yellow balloon. Maybe sometimes it escapes our grasp, and it just floats away.

And now my mother knows I'm gay, and I feel just like I did that day, when the balloon escaped. My truth had become this barrier between my mother and I. My sexuality, my discovered *freakishness* was never to be spoken of again. Not ever again. I hadn't changed, but my mother had. Whatever feelings she had for me, they shifted into something cold and unresponsive. *Was it still Love*? Sometimes I wonder.

DAVID:

She just sat on that stand looking all holy and sanctified foolish.

Score 50 big points for my side.

A slow tear ran down Ms. Laura Hunter's softly indignant cheek.

Greed is a very ugly thing. Greed, it is succeeded, only by those surface-lovely mothers who refuse to accept their gay or bi sons, but who would so gladly, *take* their money.

It was she who'd begun that unnecessarily ugly battle, and she who started that hurtful fire. And in the end, it was *Ty's own words* that set the inferno, which burned down her little house of lies.

Miguel Augusto Del Los Rios, Esquire, truly did his damn thing! Thank you, papi!

I wish I could say I felt sorry for her. Truth was, I really, truly, deeply, *didn't*.

CHAPTER FOURTEEN

Maybe The Devil Has Green Eyes

On the last day of testimony, Faison Brown sat discreetly in the courtroom as the final judgment had been read. And now it was official. David had won, and he would retain all of Tyrone Hunter's money. Browny could not stomach it. He wanted to vomit inside his own mouth. There would be no "congrats, yo!" coming from him.

Once again, it was David: ten, and Browny: zero, on Da Elixir fairness count. How could Tyrone not have shown *Browny* any love in the end?

Browny recalled years before, and that fated day Tyrone had come to see him in prison. He remembered *that look* of pity Tyrone had given him from behind the glass partition. Drug possession had landed Browny there, and he'd plenty of time to twist and stew in all his boiling resentments. Browny had very few visitors, but Tyrone, ever the true-blue, pushed through to see him.

Browny had so many secrets cluttered within the madness of his own head and the wilderness of his heart. That day, he was really to tell Tyrone one of them. But the deepest, darkest secret of all, he'd kept all to his himself. He had to. It was way too much for Ty or anyone to understand. If he told someone, they would only see him as the ultimate sucker, supreme!

How do you tell a friend that you decided to cop to the criminal changes of another? How do you form the words to say: *I'm the asshole who took the drug rap for Face Depina?*

When he'd visited him, Ty looked well. But Browny felt that anyone would look good if they were sitting on a wad of *unspent* money.

"So . . . talk to me, Ty. Tell me, what's been shakin'? You still writin'?"

"Yep. When I can. You know me, always observing."

He still held resentment for Ty, making all that cash, writing that hit song, living large on the royalties from it. He feigned interest in Ty's projects, and David's career in dance, but it was all a ploy to finally getting around to the subject of Face Depina.

Ty wanted to know, "How are you doing, Browny? Seriously, man?"

"Hey, look around . I'm just chillin' like a villain. My life's on hold. Hell, my whole damn show's on lockdown." He chuckled sadly. "But a wise man once said, 'this too shall pass,' right?" He jerked his shoulder if to shrug his own reality away. And then it was back to Pass-cow.

Beyond all the other shitty things, Pascal Depina's success had been irking Browny in a most particular way. Face was living a crazy fabulous life, and Browny was rotting in jail. He wanted to indoctrinate Tyrone into his personal, if unofficial, Face Depina Hater's Club.

"Remember that night, after we cut that hit single?" Browny asked.

"Yeah. I remember. It was only like a thousand years ago," Ty said.

"But do you remember *that* night, yo?" Browny kept

stressing. "It was a mad cold December night, crazy windy and shit. And then *you* suggested, since your folks were away, we drop by your crib to celebrate. We had wine, and liquor, and cheeb, and shit."

"Yes, Browny. I remember," Ty reiterated. Tyrone tried not to show it, but he felt *sad* for Browny, still holding so tightly to their teenaged past, as if life would never become any better for him than that time long ago.

"See, yo, the way I remember it, we all got blitz-blasted. We talked and laughed, then, one by one we all fell asleep. But maybe we *all* didn't sleep," Browny suggested.

Just then, Ty recalled the aftermath of that evening. It was a bit of a drunken puzzle, and Tyrone had never quite put it together. But suddenly, a jailbird with an angel's voice was about sing his aria.

"The next day, Face came up to me on the street and he flashed me this piece. He was all smiles and braggin' about liftin' some 'bourgie jewelry' the night before."

"What?"

A certain bloat of uneasiness came into Tyrone's belly and it grew with every word Browny spoke. It expanded, until it formed a sickening feeling in his gut. Ty felt woozy. He held his stomach. He thought was going to spew.

"Browny? What, what did it look like?"

"It was old. Some old gold pin, with pearls circlin' it. It looked like a piece of old money to me."

And Ty recalled, that particular article all too well.

His mother's prized possession had mysteriously gone missing. Its disappearance was the cause of *much* tumult in the Hunter household. Ty's gambling father had always been presumed the thief. This theif left Laura Hunter's heart crushed, broken, and never to be mended. She'd run all out of forgiveness for this man she'd called her husband. Of course, Mr. Hunter denied it repeatedly, but to no avail. There were arguments and kneeled prayers at the altar. This was followed by even more arguments, and more fevered accusations, and more church, and more denials. And finally Ty's mother, no longer able to stand her husband's "deception" put his father out on the street. They separated, and later divorced.

There hung inside their apartment, an odor no amount of Lysol could eliminate. It was the death of love and the stink of mistrust pervading their home. Now, after all those years, Ty discovered it was *not* because a lying father, but a lying, sleazy thief of a bastard named Face Depina.

"Man, Ty. Pass-cow is so foul, yo. He even *laughed* about the shit when he was tryna figure how much cash he'd get for it. He was a guest in your people's house, and he stole from y'all, yo."

"Shut up! Don't say no more! You knew? You could've said something . . . But you didn't say or do shit!"

With all the rage boiling inside him, Tyrone punched the plexiglass separating them. Browny jumped.

"Damn, you! You fuckin' coward!"

"You act like *I* stole it, yo! I just kept my mouth shut. That's all."

"Yeah. You're good at keeping your fuckin' mouth shut!"

"What you mean?"

"You, and your history. Just like that night on stage, how you keep saying you *should've hit that note* and people would've known *you* were the talented one. But you didn't, did you, coward? You didn't do shit, and look at you now!"

"Yo. Don't go there, Ty! It wasn't mine to tell. Don't go shootin' the messenger, Chief!"

"For once, you could've stepped up. But you didn't. Fuck it. Just be you, Browny. It's workin' out just fine for your ass. I'm out."

Strange how that one jailhouse visit, so many years ago, had come back to haunt Faison Brown now.

People had always said what a *righteous* man Tyrone Hunter was. Well, maybe that was the side he wanted them or *needed* them to see. That wasn't such a righteous thing he'd said to Browny. Though Faison Brown had averted his eyes, and tried not to show it, those words, coming from Ty, had cut him deeply. It was so easy to judge him, when Tyrone was on the other side of the glass. He could spew his harsh and toxic accusations, and then just get up and leave. That was what Tyrone did. But for Browny, the prison memory of it would continue.

BROWNY:

What if Tyrone was right? What if I'd opened my damn mouth and sung when everyone was so damn focused and on pretty boy Depina? Maybe that producer would've let *me* sing solo. Yo! Maybe I woulda got me a contract and had a string of hits, made mad cash and been a bigger name than Pass-cow Depina ever was! Damn! Ty was right. I coulda been BIG, if I'd just opened my damn mouth!

Yet, hadn't Browny sealed his own fate the day he copped to that drug possession charge? Sure, it was Face Depina's stash, and Face should had stepped up and spoken up like man. But no! Never Face. He was too damn pretty for prison. He was pretty and popular and hot and in-demand. He had his grand film career all mapped out, and hard time was never in the Grand Depina plan. For Face, a *hard time* was something he presented to *other* people, or the hot thing he pulled so recklessly from his sleek designer pants.

No one, not even Browny himself, would quite understand why he'd decided to take the rap. It had something to do with honor, and the repayment of a mortal debt.

One time in his miserable existence, Face Depina had indeed risen to the occasion. He'd pulled Browny out from the path of a viciously speeding bus. The bus had a proper name, and it was called Razor Morrisey.

Razor threatened to stick a deadly blade deep into the chest of Browny's ambitions. Browny knew this was not an idle threat. Razor Morrisey (or one of his flunkies) had already taken the life of Browny's older brother.

Just when all seemed lost, and it appeared Browny would suffer the same bloody fate, in walked Pascal "Face" Depina with the missing cash. Face had to literally *sell himself* to amass the amount needed, and he never told Browny, or anyone, the price he had to pay to obtain it. But Face paid that price, and that payment had saved Browny's piss-poor life.

And so, some sleeping decency crouched deep within Faison "Browny" Brown was suddenly awakened years later, detained by the police on a cold New York City pavement, where he lay, face down, alongside Face Depina. It was then that Depina called in his favor.

"Pssst! You owe me, Browny. Tell 'em the stash in *yours*, and you'll never want for anything else, ever again," he'd whispered in a hiss.

Prison was its own private Hell, and just a little worse. Still Faison Brown had served the time that rightfully should have been Depina's sentence. Browny served it buoyed by a shaky promise that his life would become golden once he was back on the outside.

Of course that all proved to be a lie.

Browny recalled how smug Face Depina was when he finally was able to *find* him. Face had assumed that whatever the lingering after-effects of prison, Browny could drink or smoke them away. But Browny was not going away.

Finally, Face decided it was time to take him upstairs to

his tres fancy digs and buy his pathetic ass off, for one and for fucking all!

Browny couldn't help but be impressed by the lifestyle of newly rich and consistently devious.

Once inside, Depina sat at his desk and he wrote a check, a nice check. But for Browny, cash alone was not sufficient. He saw Face for the punk he always knew him to be. Browny's behavior, on crack, was usually enough to put the "hy" in hyper. But surprisingly, once granted an audience with the famous Duke of his Disaster, Browny's tone was placid, even measured . . . at first.

"Just 'cause I'm calm, don't mean I ain't walkin' around on fire, man. See me, I'm a firewalker. That's the kind of man I be. But, yo! What kinda man you be, huh? You tryna *buy* me? Is that it? Nah. I ain't goin' out like that. A few bills for three *years* in Hell? And it *was* Hell, Pass-cow. Maybe a little worse. Look at you, standin' there, all tall and proud in this place. And look at me, all small in mine. I ain't the same big tall strappin' buck as you, Mr. *Face* Depina. So, why was *you* shittin' bricks, anyway? Huh? Was ya scared of the sound of them steel doors closin' you inside? Did ya figga you was way too *pretty* for that shit? Scared ya wouldna survived, huh? That's the thing about you arrogant pretty motherfuckas. Bet ya thought they'd line up, hold ya down, and take turns raping yo pretty ass . . . Well, guess what? It don't matter if you pretty."

"Look, it's too bad you had to go through that shit. That's rough. I never meant for—"

"SHUT THE FUCK UP, AND PAY ATTENTION! Somewhere between them poundin' fists red with your blood and them kicks to your insides—something clicks, man. You realize, I'm gonna *die* like *this*. And for what? 'Cause some crazy motherfucker wants my ass?"

Browny paused just long enough to wipe his mouth, but never the ugly memories.

"Men in prison, they ain't into that warm, fuzzy shit. Foreplay don't exist, except for you suckin' his dick." Browny fought back a tear. "That first time hurt, man! And it never did stop hurt'n."

Perhaps Browny would've been very surprised to know, Pascal really *did understand* that feeling.

Pascal "Face" Depina had been taken against his will, and on his sixteenth birthday. That violent taking of Depina's manhood had shattered something in him; some thing inside his being that never healed. That event, that violent night, it had shifted the soul inside of in Pascal Depina. It made him colder, meaner, less concerned about another human being.

So, you think some bad shit's happened to you, Browny? Well guess what? Fuck you!

"But you wanna know what kept me *sane and alive*, yo? You, Pass-cow Depina. You, and the future beyond that big beast of a motherfucka drummin' down on me. I had me a future on the other side of that razor wire. So, was all I needed to do was keep breathin'. I've seen a young boy, even prettier than you, hangin' from his own sheet because he just couldn't take another beatin', another pair of women's panties, another man, another diseased dick rammed up his cryin', helpless ass. That boy coulda been me! Yo! Now you wanna offer me a check, and say we even? I don't think so, Pass-cow! You just don't get it, do you? It ain't about the money, fuckin' asshole. I want a life. A career."

Silence filled the loft.

"You a fan of The Godfather of Soul, huh?" Browny, the true singer and truth slinger, sang most ominously: "I don't want nobody, to give nothin', open up the door, and I'll get it myself!"

"I ain't God, Browny! I can't just snap my fuckin' fingers, and presto, you get a motherfuckin' life!"

"I don't see why not. Yo! Ya played God before when ya guilted me into sayin' those four little *please-fuck-my-ass* words: 'The stash is mine'!"

Depina had seen this scenario coming. It was supposed to be a brother-to-brother agreement. Of course, Browny was too weak, too pitiful, too needy to follow through. Depina almost wanted to laugh. Browny was the ultimate sucker.

Stupid, stupid motherfucker! Yeah, you copped to it. You got in the damn car, and shit happened. Didn't take much beggin', did it? Yeah, I said I'd hook you up. I was desperate, you crazy fuck! All that time on the street, you still don't know when you bein played. Fuckin' hemorrhoid—that's all you are!

"Know what, Pass-cow? Once, when I was tryna build myself up into a big, strong man like you, I ordered the Charles Atlas kit from the back of a comic book."

"Yeah-yeah. What's your point?" Face asked, his buffed arms folded, his long legs spread wide in defensive stance.

"Of course, Pass-cow. Yo! Wouldn't wanna waste yo time, you bein' one of them in-demand type motherfuckas. See, I got the kit, but it was just a lotta pictures of a half-naked Atlas workin' out, and some instructions and shit. I felt ripped the fuck off! But they kept sendin' me more shit. Same shit. So I quit. Stopped payin' through the ass for some dumb-ass photos. Yo! Now, you pay attention! This is the good part: Mr. Charles Atlas, or somebody in his muscle camp, wrote me a letter 'bout debts. They was tryna shame me, sayin' how a real man pays his debts. Then they went all Oriental on my ass. They got this ancient Chinese sayin' that the worse thing any real man could do was to lose his honor. Without that, a man ain't nothin'. They called it 'Losing Face'!"

"Yeah, so, and . . ."

"Don't you get it, fool? You don't attend yo debts, boy. Ya ain't got no honor! You ain't no man! You, Pass-cow Scared Punk-ass Depina done LOST FACE, motherfucka!"

Depina eyeballed Browny, and wished he possessed the supernatural power to make him disappear, forever. Just make the world forget there ever was a Browny.

Still, that term *Losing Face* buzzed like an annoying black fly in Depina's aggravated ear. A fly he couldn't shoo away.

He felt as if his back, his well-paid, artistically photographed back was against the wall. There was a need for quick damage control. Depina got on the phone and placed a call to his Agent. As he to tried to *and make things happen*, Browny walked around the place. He gazed at all the new, fancy shit that could've, should've, would've probably been his: the big screen TV, the top-of-the-line stereo system, the plush Italian leather furniture, and that fly-ass view of Manhattan staring back in its steely majesty.

Depina hung up the phone, took a deep breath, wrung his long, elegant hands, and hit Browny with his latest plan.

Face told him of an independent film he was workin' on, which had a got a nightclub scene and needed a singer. Browny began to see very real stars in the corner of his eyes. Every feature in his face lit up brighter than the Rockefeller Center Christmas tree.

"Yo! An open door. That's all I want."

But that door never opened for him . . . at least not completely.

He'd only know the sound of closing doors, and some distant cackle that would sometimes awaken him at night. It was the ghost sound of Face Depina's laughter.

But, even when he allowed himself the onus of at least part of the blame, he could not escape the part Face Depina had played in the sticky little theatre of his destiny. Face, that pretty-boy, bronze, Paul Newman wannabe, that "lucky piece of shit," that model/actor/junkie cat, he was dead now.

Ty Hunter was dead, too.

But the money and all the rich and shiny potential of what it could do for him, wasn't dead. The answer lay with David.

CHAPTER FIFTEEN

ATTENTION SHOULD BE PAID

When it rained like this, relentless like this, David Richmond hated the city. Ubiquitous rhythms gave way to the clacking, drumming, and swinging of storms, and the city no longer held its authentic syncopation. The song of New York was gone. Its lively vibratos, its uproar and crescendos had diminished into a long and listless moan.

The streets and landmarks were shrouded, blemished by cloud and neglect, as the fog-laced towers stretched for want of sun. It seemed as if God Himself were weeping over these ruins.

David wanted the New York City in his head again, the one that moved and blinked and twitched and flowed in its own fluid rhythm. He wanted the New York Technicolor portrait, and that day, and that night, the city was a dark and listless still life.

Where was his urban demi-paradise? The humming Harlem one; the platinum Fifth Avenue one; the weirdly hip, black-clothed bohemian one; and the one with a million dazzling lights that seemed to dance beneath the high-rise balconies.

But *that* City is as dead to him as his best friend. It was beginning to feel like some cosmic conspiracy.

This was supposed had to have been a *special* day, but nothing about it had felt special. Was he the *only one* who remembered?

Walking those streets, David wanted—*needed*—to see that mythic picture postcard again, that sun-drenched plaza of modernism, which held his people in the squeeze of its asphalt palm. Where was that steely strut and stare of people with purpose, marching like troops of determined soldiers, moving, shifting, rudely, stealthily to reach their core New York objective? David wanted the machinery of *that* City again; the one with the cars racing and the subways rumbling and the disrespectful taxis. . Anything would be better than the sight and sound of New York, on that particular morning.

It would have been Tyrone's thirty-sixth birthday.

Ty's Journal entry written on his thirty-first earth day, read:

The other day, it rained, and I saw this babbling man standing there, hypnotized by a trash can fire. A mumbling woman joined him, her hands outstretched in a makeshift attempt to know the glow, the feel of warmth again. Together, they were trying to keep from freezing; to keep this city's cold from infiltrating their posture. I see people like that all the time. But this place hardly ever pays attention to homeless people, and that constant fight they wage with winter and gravity. Most days, like this day, no one pays attention.

Tomorrow, I'll be serving up turkey dinner in a soup kitchen.

Happy Thanksgiving.

One Love.

Ty always paid attention. Tyrone Hunter cared about the babbling men, and the mumbling women and all the rest of those who go through their days picking up handfuls of nothing and throwing it, hurling it everywhere.

For this day, Tyrone's birthday, David wanted more than sadness, more than just to think of Ty and remember him fondly. He wanted to *see* Tyrone. But since he knew he couldn't, David wanted to acknowledge that day. He thought perhaps he and Victor could have a quiet celebration in memory of Ty.

Strange how two vastly different people can somehow fit. David and Victor were very different souls.

Raised a strict catholic, Victor was the son of immigrants. He was a serious man, and a deeply internal one. He'd done all the *right* things, married the right girl, who just happened to be the wrong sex. Together they produced two sons, moved to Queens, and lived a life that appeared to be a sweet Latino version of The American Dream.

But he had a few secrets he didn't share with anyone, not even himself. His attraction for men was a thing in which had silently tortured him for years. He could make convincing love to his wife Patricia, as long as his mind held tight to masculine imagery. He'd dealt with his secrets as many men did, in his quietly masturbatory way.

He was winning that war with his private sexuality, until one inescapable drunken night. It was there at the little El Barrio bar he co-owned, when his eyes slowly drowned in the ojos of a handsome busboy he'd hired. Victor thought this boy was beautiful, and he'd employed him just so he could look at him and imagine. But what transpired that night would gradually change Victor perception's of his proud Latino manhood. And as it continued to happen, their coupling began to change the sham he'd called his life. He'd fallen in lust with a handsome twenty-year-old busboy. His name was Miguel. For Victor it was a part-time Hell, and one he sought the need to end. But when Victor tried to end it, the Miguel went a little unhinged. Last night calls to Victor's home became the norm. The boy had developed a growing obsession with him. At first he was threatening blackmail, and then he was threatening suicide. Victor was beside himself with guilt and worry. Yes, a man can keep many things away from his wife, but he can't keep his wife from being curious.

With Patricia Medina, curiosity became concern and concern became suspicion. Suspecting another woman, she followed Victor to the club one night. She watched her husband get into his car, and then open the door to a young man, a young man nearly close to the age of their oldest son. She watched with even deeper curiosity until she saw that young man kiss her husband, and she saw the boy's head descend, and she watched with painful awe as that boy went down on the man she loved.

And having seen her heart, and her dreams, and her life began to crumble as she bitterly whispered, "Maricon!"

Victor arrived home to find his wife and his two sons gone.

Years later . . .

Victor didn't speak much. He was man of action and of verbs. He' had steadied and held David up countless times, and he listened to him better than most anyone, except Tyrone. But Ty always provided an answer or a comment, or he would volunteer something that made you feel you weren't alone. David wished Victor possessed the same quality. He didn't. David once thought it was because English wasn't Victor's native language. But while his English had improved in the time they'd known each other, the quiet nature of the man had not.

All throughout the trial, Victor had his restaurant and his downtown lounge to run. That lounge, Cool Relax, was going through a transition and a decline in business as newer, hipper establishments flooded the area. Ever mindful of the flightiness of customers and in the club scene in general, Victor went on trips to Venezuela, and then to the Florida Keys eyeing new properties in which to invest. As such, he wasn't always there in the way David needed him to be, and David didn't blame him one bit. It was a sign that, no matter happened to him, Victor had a life outside of David Richmond-ville, and that would have to sustain him once David was gone.

When David showed up at Cool Relax, he was hoping to do just that—to cool out and relax. He sat at the bar watching the people flowing about and settling into booths to lounge, to eat and sip their apple martinis, and to enjoy the fest that was New York nightlife.

Victor had a small crisis in the back, and so David patiently waited, though his patience for waiting was beginning to wear thin.

He saw Victor's son, Raul, the older one, the one who held an unhidden disdain for him. David nodded casually, and Raul as always, promptly cut his eyes and ignored him. Some boys did not take kindly to the men for whom their fathers had forsaken their mother's and their families to be with. Though, David was never a part of the equation that caused the rift, he was the face, the body, the presence in Raul's father's life now. This was an unforgivable offense.

It occurred to David that since Victor and Raul had tried to forge this a new beginning, another attempt to build a bridge of communication, perhaps his presence there would make things uncomfortable. This was an afterthought, though, and now David was there, and no matter how much Raul despised him, David couldn't just suddenly vaporize and disappear.

With Raul working at the lounge now, David had the distinct impression that Victor was purposely *staying away* from him . . . at least, in public situations.

Raul said to his father, just loud enough for David to hear him say it, "Your little *fag's* here."

When Victor finally emerged from the back, he wore a strange expression. He hadn't *expected* David. And yes, Raul was pissed that David just showed the fuck up.

And now Victor was trying to sooth the spirits of both these people who he loved.

"Hey. Puppy? Everything ok?"

David wanted to tell him things were *not* ok. He wanted to tell him, he was lonely, and it was Ty's birthday, and maybe they, just the two of them, could spend some quality time together. He wanted to say it, but Raul appeared behind his father's shoulder, glaring menacingly at David. Raul was expecting a new crisis, a new reason for David to occupy his father's time.

"Everything's fine. I just wanted to say hello, papi."

"You sure?" Victor asked.

"Yup," David answered, finishing his club soda. "Have a good night. See ya later. Goodbye Raul."

Again, Raul said nothing.

And as David was leaving and heading out the door, he mumbled to himself, "Grow the fuck up, Raul! Your father likes dick. And he always did. So, get over it!"

As he headed home in the rain, David heard that voice. Sometimes, it came in a shout, and sometimes in whisper. Always it was his own voice hissing in his ear: *Your gonna die! You're gonna die! You're gonna die!*

He wondered now, if this was what *Ty* felt like? If so, why didn't David *get it* then? Tyrone had so often spoken of the loneliness, without ever saying he was lonely. He must have been. David was starting to feel it . . . to know the taste of lonely now.

Did it serve to remind us that life is short, the angels are watching and clocking us, and this is our last hurrah to fall in love, or trip into lust, go crazy and just fuck a stranger? Should we make love, fuck something, hug someone, anyone to let them know . . . we're still alive? Or should we be simply manufacturing new tears?

Life was far more precious now. David didn't know how much time, how many days or months he had left, but he was determined that his time would *not* be allowed to slide by, unacknowledged or un-cherished.

People would no longer escape his words of love or even the fire of his wrath when it was necessary. Sure. He was still David, and still a human being, so he would not in any way, shape or form be leading an angel's life, only a *realer* life of honesty, and of more integrity.

This became very, very taxing at times. He may have to be mean and assume the role of cold and heartless bitch-bastard. But even that would be necessary. Time is too precious for bullshit!

As David waited for the light to change at Fourteenth Street and Third Avenue, a yellow cab splashed him as it pulled over quickly to the corner. David was duly upset, and it was also indicative of his day, this lack of attention, this absence of respect.

"Ruthless motherfucka!" he hollered.

Just then, a tall, distinguished black man exited the same taxicab which had just splashed him.

"Damn! Sorry about that, ace," the man said.

"Not your fault! I blame that freakin' go Speed-racer Racer bastard in a turban!" David hollered, flipping the offending driver the high, indignant middle finger. David's furious *bird* notwithstanding, the offending driver sped thoughtlessly away.

But the man who'd just apologized to him had a familiar face. And that face seemed to recognize him as well.

"David? You're David. Ty's friend, right?"

"Yes. And you're. . . no, don't tell me. I remember . . . It's a country . . . your name . . . It's an African country. Niger . . . ria. No. Ummm. Seriously, I do remember," David said, wiping the wetness from his rain coat.

"It begins with a Z," the handsome brotha hinted, glancing back at David, amused.

"Zaire! Yes! Zaire Monk, dammit!" David conjured, proud that the meds hadn't totally flushed his memory for people he vaguely knew from the past .

"Ri-i-i-ght." The two clasped hands "How the hell are you, David?"

"You don't even wanna know. Trust. How you been, Zaire?"

"I'm good. Good. Funny, I should run into you, because I was just thinking that today is Ty's . . ."

"Birthday! Yes! Thank GOD! *Someone* else remembered!"

David smiled sadly.

"Man, please. Tyrone was truly one of the *unforgettables*! Maybe not everyone recalls his birth date, but they'll always remember the size and shape of his heart."

"Yeah. That's nice. I hope so."

"I was supposed to be meeting someone. But I'm late. Business as usual, and I guess he lost his patience."

"His loss," David said.

"So, where are you heading? Did you eat yet? If not, you wanna grab something?"

"Not really hungry, man. But there's a Starbucks just up the street."

Over coffee and mocha lattes' the two of them reminisced about old places, well-loved faces and how the city didn't seem the same without them.

And David wondered, *Wow! Zaire! Did Tyrone send you here to meet me on this street, on the evening of this particular day?*

David noticed that time had been very kind to Zaire

Monk, Esq. It was so easy to see in him that which has had so attracted Tyrone: The full, questioning lips and liquid eyes. Zaire was a lovely chocolate-skinned brother, and he carried sex on his face, his lips, and his legs like a stallion that never slept.

Coffee soon turned into a later dinner scene, in an Italian restaurant. Zaire so spoke fondly of Ty, and was just what David needed:

Someone who knew him, loved him, and missed him almost as terribly as David did.

Scene from an Italian Restaurant:

"I've gotten a few my shareholders together, and I twisted a few well-cuff-linked arms, and the plan is to send a large donation to Ty's African Children's Fund. I feel like he was onto something, necessary."

"Ah, Zy. That's wonderful. Thank you, *so much* for that."

And though he was pleased, David mentally speculated if it was simply an act of charity, or if Zaire still held a private culpability for the way he and Ty had ended.

Zaire, as strong, secure, mature, and professional as he may have been to the unknowing eye was very much a Mama's Boy. And after nearly nine months together, Zy had invited Ty to dinner at his parents' home. For some strange reason, unbeknownst to David, Zy's parents didn't *take* to Ty—Zaire's mother especially. These were surface differences: Ty wasn't from the Islands. Ty didn't belong to the right fraternity, and frankly, they didn't feel Ty's decidedly bohemian ways was were a good fit for their enterprisingly Black Wall Street son.

And so, days later, Zaire ended that relationship. But he'd never had forgotten the vibe, the sex, or the meeting of the minds he and Ty once manifested.

"And you know who I saw recently? A brotha named Faison Brown. 'Browny' is what they call him. Your former brotha in song." Zaire laughed a little.

"Please, stop the madness! He's *no brotha* of mine."

"Yes. Madness would be a good word for him. The context of the visit was that he wanted *me to buy* enough shares in a little recording company to gain controlling interest in it."

"And why would he ask of that of *you*? Hold up! Don't tell me. Lemme guess. I had something to do with Da Elixir, our old singing group, right?"

"Yes, exactly! He desperately wanted the music in the marketplace, so he'd receive his royalties. When I questioned him about this, turns out, it was some old album you guys recorded way back in the day. Music, he claimed was being 'held hostage by the suits, yo.' But the kicker was, according to *him*, that this was something *Tyrone* would've wanted done."

David abruptly spat out his salad. Grabbed his glass, took a guzzle of water, and asked, "What?"

"The Tyrone, *I knew* was never about wanting a music career and he didn't live for the almighty dollar," Zaire said.

"Then *you knew* him well."

"Though we were very different in that way, that was something I really respected in him. But this Browny character, he's bad news. I got a very foul vibe from that little man."

"Trust me on this, Zy . . . the vibe you picked up on was on-point, and nothing more than selfish greed. Damn him! Damn him to hell! He just *never* stops! You know, I actually used to worry about him. Those sob-sad motherfuckin' people, like Browny, they would occupy my mind in the worse way. Hell, there was even a time when I used to worry about folks—people I didn't even know—people like Liza, little Michael, and yes, lawd he'p her, Miss Diana Ross."

Zaire chuckled a good, hardy laugh.

"David . . . You can't be that serious, or *that* gay!"

"I *am* serious. And I *was, that gay*! I used to worry about these dizzy bitches, like they were family, like my favorite misunderstood auntie's or some such shit. Yes. I used to be just *that ridic*. Well, no more. You hear me? If these damn bitches can't manage to get their shit together, well shame on their rich and sorry asses! And the same goes for *Browny*, my once so-called *friend*. If he, and the rest wanna be all about bitchin' and expending some full-of-shit negative energy my way, then, bub-bye! I'll see ya next lifetime. I am not wasting any more of *this one* on you fools and your sob-sad asses!"

"The sob-sad have their stories, I'm sure. Doesn't mean we should have to endure them," Zaire hinted.

What Zaire didn't tell David and what David would never know was of Zaire's handiwork, along with Bliss Santana's to squelch that book of lies Browny helped to pen. Though David would have been mad grateful for it, Zaire was not the kind of a man to pat himself on the back.

"So, are you seeing anyone now?" David asked.

"I'm starting to stick the big toe into the dating pool again. I met a cat. A younger one. A little different than what usually attracts me."

"How so?"

"Well," Zaire hedged. "I've never really been interested in anyone who wasn't Black, whether they be Jamaican, Haitian, or African-American. And . . . well, he's not. He's such a beautiful-looking boy. But being young and Latino, he's got a few issues with his sexuality. To be truthful, he's pretty much a closet case. Bad family history, and all that. But it's my hope that being with me, maybe he'll open up and just let himself love and be loved. It's a process. In fact, I was supposed to meet him when I ran into you. But as I said, I was late, and I guess his impatient, young ass, stepped, or else, he turned chicken-shit."

"Hey, it happens. But I hope it works out for you, Zy."

"And what about you, David?"

"I've been with the same man for quite a while . . . pushing into record book territory for me. His name is Victor. And like yours, he's Latin, but unlike yours, he's *older* than me. I've always been a lost boy, searching for his daddy."

Victor Zaire laughed. "So, considering your theory, I guess I'm currently in search for my lost boyhood."

"Hey, we've *all* got our issues." David winked. "The cool thing is, Victor's a wonderful man. Not perfect, but a supportive gato, and I'm at the stage in my journey where I need that in a man. Pretty as some of them can be, a *boy* just wouldn't do."

"You say, he's supportive. How does that manifest for you?"

David thought about this, and he said, "Last week, Victor and I decided to go to the movies. Victor, bless his heart, is not half the cinemaphile that I am, but sometimes he humors me, and he supports my love of the arts.

"Well, that flick was *so* damn boring, and completely uninspired. I realized, hell, I'm not being entertained here. So, I got up, shook Victor awake, and we walked out of that motherfuckin' snore-fest with a sure and certain quickness, baby!"

"That bad, eh?" Zaire laughed.

"Terrible. But the point is: why the Hell waste two whole precious fuckin' hours out of my life, being *bored?* Maybe other people do. But I've no time for it. Not anymore! And Victor completely understands this in me."

"That's a good attitude, actually. You know, I had this teacher in my eighth grade science class. Didn't like her much, but once she made a point, and I'll always remember it. See, I was a brain in that class, and the work came easy for me, so I usually finished before everyone else. One day, I'd handed my test to her, and asked if I could leave, because, frankly, I was bored as hell, and I told her, "This class is boring to me."

"Whoa! You were a verbal *and* bold one, especially for a freakin' brainiac."

"Yes. I guess I was. But she told me to sit back down. And then she said, 'If you're bored, then you're a *boring* person, with a boring mind.' "

"Whoa! She came back *heavy* with hers!"

"Yes, but I think she said it to make me think bigger and broader than my limited scope of things."

"What do you mean?" David asked.

"Well, it means, it's no one else's job to *save you* from being bored, or to entertain you. That on us, it's on *you*. In other words, if you, in the vast wilderness of your own mind, can't *think* of something worthwhile to do with your time and your place here, then damn it, *you're boring!*"

"Wow!" David said. "Just wow! I *get* it! Thank you for that. And thank *her!*"

"Well, it's getting late. And I should be leaving. Dinner's on me, Davy. Let's call it a little celebration for Ty," Zaire said with a warm smile.

It was a nice time, a reflective time, for both David and Zaire. David felt they'd somehow *honored* Tyrone that night, because they'd spoken his name; because they had remembered him fondly, and it had made them smile.

Zaire gazed out the window next to the table he and David shared. His eyes suddenly widened. "Damn! There he *is*, across the street!" Zaire uttered in happy amazement.

"There who is?" David almost wanted to ask, *Who? Tyrone?*

"My date. The one I was supposed to meet earlier."

"Oh? Cool. So this night is looking up for you, Zy!" David winked.

"Well, I guess we'll see," Zaire said, kissing David's cheek.

"Take care, my friend. Wonderful to see you again," he offered, before rushing out the restaurant in a horny, heated rush.

And being slightly curious, David glanced out the window.

He saw the young, beautiful-looking boy. The one with "a few issues with his sexuality." The one was who was "pretty much a closet case with a bad family history."

David watched as they embraced quickly, and then he saw his face. *Oh, my God!* The beautiful Latino was Raul Medina. Victor's son.

The air rushed out of his mouth for a moment. *Raul? What the . . .*

And just as Patricia Medina had whispered years before, that night when she'd caught wind and vision of her husband's secret, suddenly David Richmond too, whispered, "*Maricon*!"

CHAPTER SIXTEEN

THE STUFF OF FIRE AND FAKERY

Harlem's morning light spilled through the blinds, just enough for David could see Victor's head resting peacefully beside him.

The night before, David was made love to . . . not fucked, not taken, not turned out, but made pure and ecstatic LOVE to. Victor was, as usual: *Magnificent!*

His physical love was a knowing waltz of hands moving, descending, then gliding to David's glands. His strong masculine coaxing, his deliberate stroking made something in David's very viscera dance! His kisses came slow and soft and smooth as cocoa butter . . . and made David's skin glow from under its sores. The way Victor loved him, it made his insides flutter. David's eyeballs spun as his heartbeat quickened. That long long-ago dancer came alive inside of his limbs again! His breath began to sputter as the wildest of contortions wrecked his face. That wildness seemed to spread downward to the might of Victor's shaking thighs.

Like something fierce and untamed, a howl came as the

sweat broke upon their skin. Both of them were swept inside a soul-satisfying passion. It had overtaken the rhythm of their glide. David rocked and Victor rolled, their hips collided, and something like a Scream in David dissipated into a sigh.

"Aye . . . Aye . . . I . . . Papi!"

Victor was breaking and sliding and careening inside that fire in David's body. And soon, he was a body full of spasms and pelting his seed into the latex between them, as David soon began erupting from the ride.

They were thrashing as their atoms came clashing together, and for a moment, all of nature cried.

Outide, it was raining, and the weather had gone insane. The sky filled with thunder, lightning and a wild rain . . . and that stirring of the elements, it made David feel whole and wanted, desired and *loved.*

But when it was over, some envious thing came into his head, that once he was gone, someone else would know of this magnificent love that Victor made.

He would be dead, and Victor would be alive, and someone else would know the lovesick feel of the Earth moving woozily upon its axis.

And now, he stared at Victor's beauty, and for a long time, he was silent. Gently, his hands traced him in an effort to form a touch-memory, in an attempt to never forget the firm, brown contours of Victor's body. He let his fingers run gently over the slopes of his arms and into the brush of Victor's chest.

David held his breath, as his lover's eyes slowly opened in a glance that met inside his own. His eyes locked in a soulful gaze. Victor's arm pulled David closer in a quick, almost violent movement.

"Hey you. Good mornin', Puppy."

Victor's thick, brutish hands ran down David's frail shoulders, as he kissed the left one. Victor's hand then sailed across the lean sinews of his biceps, and gradually to the small of his back. Though he felt a minute tremor inside, David didn't say a word. Victor ignored those blue and purple bruises dotting David's back. To him these were only David's beauty marks, reminders that he was human, and fragile and real.

He detected David drawing a sharp breath as he nuzzled him below his neck. It was the softest of moans David released as he exhaled with from deep within. He didn't say anything. He didn't need to. Words would've dissolved into ashes inside that shadow-soaked room. Words would've diminished The Moment. Words would have destroyed something sacred as soon as they'd fallen off their loving tongues.

David was trying to make certain changes in his life. Among them, he wanted and he needed to do something valiant and set Victor free. He didn't want to be free *of* Victor's love. He simply wanted to release Victor from the obligation of caring for him. This was a difficult maneuver. David couldn't simply say:,

"Papa . . . it's not working . . . I need you to leave. Go find yourself someone young and *healthy*; someone you can plan a future with! Go with God, my beloved! Go, with my blessing, papi!"

For David to have actually said those words, it would have had the opposite effect. Victor would have only attached himself even closer, harder, deeper to David. Thus, when the time came, and David would become really, deathly, terminally sick, Victor would only be crushed. Crushed even more. David had the roughest time of most anyone on the planet, seeing someone he loved be crushed.

It was this reason that he didn't tell Victor what he now knew about Raul. But what good would it do to tell the father, that the son not only hated him for what he was, but now hated himself for being *the same*?

Something strange and emotional was going on David's his head and in his body. As his T cells were dwindling, he didn't want the added stress nor sympathetic weight of Victor caring too much, only to witness the slow yet inevitable breaking of his heart.

Dr. Ted Horowitz's Office:

"I've been thinking quite a bit about the men I've been in love with. There was always some kind of sickness attached to love for me."

"Well, you've heard the expression, 'we're only as sick as our secrets,' haven't you, David?"

"Heard it? I've lived it. And just maybe, some of us are only as sick as our choices," David said, as his mind harkened back to the sight of Zaire and Raul's embrace.

"What do you think your choices say about you?" the doctor questioned him.

"Well, my first choice was Rico. He took my cherry at fifteen, and had me dreaming some sick dream that we were both in love. But what was true love for me, was only some sick, secretive, kid-greedy lust for him.

"Then there was Facey, God, I just knew I loved me some Face Depina. Perhaps it was the love of my life. Though the sad truth is, I was never Facey's love. Real love can't exist without reciprocation. In my head, I know this now.

"Then there was Carlos. Ah, Carlos. I deeply loved me some him. Everything about him was romantic, warm, and so sensuous. He read me poetry in Españnol. He made loved to my nipples . . . and just my nipples alone, for hours. He made me feel wanted, needed, adored. And oh, how I adored me some him. I wonder sometimes if my adoration stemmed from knowing his time was short. We did things at warp speed. We traveled, went places we'd always dreamed of going: Mexico, Puerto Rico, Disney World. We never put things off, or delayed them till next year, next month, next week. We didn't speak of the future. The *Now* of Carlos was exciting.

"And when this thing, this disease had gotten the best of his spirit, cheating on him was far too easy. Carlos *depended* on me. He trusted me wholeheartedly. That beautiful sick, and trusting man! Still, even my considering stepping out of the dance and finding a more risqué partner became a risk I was afraid to take.

"And yet shit happens . . .

"And now I've convinced myself into believing that Victor was The One. Trust me, I've known my share of prized specimens and sweet poetic men. For a time, I *thought* each of them was The One. But Victor, see, he wants the other David back. He wants his 'Puppy.' In his heart of hearts, he wants the David he met two years ago, when life was just another party, another dance, another freaky hand down my pants. He wants the David I've either outgrown, or I'm too damn tired to manifest."

"Ah, you mean, 'The Fun David?' Yes. I was wondering what ever happened to him. Tell me, does that David still exist?"

"In bits and pieces, I guess. I still try my damndest to get a sufficient giggle on, because, well, it's expected. But I used to be always so full of fun, that it became my *role*. Ya know, this year, the part of the happy-go-lucky queer will be portrayed by: David Donatello Richmond. And yes, I enjoyed being the bawdy, flamboyant one who lived for big fun and bigger men. That cat was a mad trip, and I liked being ridiculous."

DAVID:

Something happened in that instance, as I was speaking to Baby-Doc. For some reason, I had to pause, and be very still. I literally *had to* because This Thing had come over me. I could *feel* it, whatever it was. It was on my face, and in my chest. It felt like the space I was in had changed and darkened, like a shadow across the sun. Or more like a storm cloud had just moved in and hovered above the pale blue room. I knew, somewhere in me, I was being *listened* to, and by more than just that degreed man with the John Lennon granny glasses staring back at me.

Something or someone else was *listening*. Was it human or beast or spirit? Was it *God?*

Whatever it was, it was compelling me to speak only the truth.

"I liked being ridiculous. I liked being that cat who danced better and harder and freer than the rest. Even after the accident, and even after the career was over, I remained very much a dancer in my soul. You don't easily surrender the thing that makes you most alive.

"And then, I lost some good and decent people and I never thought I'd survive with them being gone. I lost my mama when I was ten, and no kid should ever lose their mother, when they're ten! I thought on the day she died, 'I will never get over this.' And I never did. Not really. But I *survived* it.

"Then, I lost Facey. I lost Carlos. And then, as if that wasn't enough, I lost my Tyrone. I *loved* those cats, man. You'll *never* even know how much. But even *they* weren't my whole reason for being. Dancing was. It was my comfort and my smile. It was my pleasure, my work, my bestest friend, my sex, my God! Even when my legs betrayed me, the dance didn't. It had been there too long. Not being able to dance again, it had become like, my amputation, the separation between David and the rest of the world. I think I know now what it's like to be an amputee. You have a vivid memory of that missing limb. But the spirit and feel of it still itches, still twitches, still screams—and still begs—for attention."

"I understand, David. Though, at times, when I approached the subject, you've shut down. I gathered it was too painful to share it fully. But I *get* it," Doc said.

But he didn't *get* it. Not really. Here he was asking me if I missed the "old David," and he didn't even know who that David was . . . only the fun, silly-ass one I'd shown him. Sure, he'd come through for me at the trial, and I was more than thankful that he did. But I still didn't know what he'd *thought* of me. I never did. But then, in that moment, more than anything, I needed him to *get* me. Why? Maybe because the only ones who ever did . . . they were no longer breathing air.

"They say everything happens for a reason. Was God trying to tell me something? I have been so pissed at Him for taking my legs, and then taking my friends away. Through all the things that followed, the drinking, the doping, the sleeping around, I never found that one drug, narcotic or stimulant, strong enough to numb me from the reality. I even had this trick, this thug who I used *let* beat up on me, because, more than being punished or hurt, I needed to *feel* something again. Dancing is painful. I needed *that pain* again. "'Hit me! Punch me in my legs! Brutalize my hamstrings, damn it! No! Harder, there! C'mon, punk! Is that all you've got? Stomp on my feet! Do anything to make me feel that sweet brutal pain again!'

"Does that sound *sick* to you, Doc? Well, for me it was very sane. Need I remind you, must I explain why I'm sitting here right now? I'm sitting in this chair, because three years ago, a group of Black and Puerto Rican thugs tried to beat me to death with a fuckin' tire iron. Maybe, that's all they were . . . just heartless, homo-hating thugs. Or maybe, just maybe, they were *angels*," I cried.

Didn't that fool with a master's degree, *get* it? Hadn't he been *listening* to me? I have been trying to *feel* my fuckin' *life* for years!

"So . . . to answer your question, yes. I miss the old David Donatello Richmond. But *you* never knew him. He was a natural-born dancer, and he did his dance to death. He was fun, and he was free. And he liked to frolic and fuck and be fabulous. Then, in one free and frolicking fuck of a moment, it all went away. He doesn't dance so free anymore."

"I get that, David. I do. But are you speaking literally, or in figurative sense?" the good, if dense, Dr. Horowitz asked.

This man was truly pissing me the fuck off! My time was too *precious*. Why the hell was I wasting it with him, this fool? Wasn't my hour upon his stage over yet?

"I mean, there are many ways to dance, aren't there? You've often used dance metaphors with me, and in some cases I've taken them to mean 'sex.' So, in some ways, your dance isn't over, yet. Life is a dance," the doctor discerned.

Oh, this bastard *really* fought dirty, using my own damn metaphors against me! It was the time for me to *read* him, in full! I looked at my watch. It read 3:25. Good. I've five minutes left.

"I believe your original question was, if I missed the 'fun' David Richmond. Well, for a man with so many impressive degrees, you are decidedly astute-free these days, Doc. I thought you knew. I got tired of him. I gave *him* up for Lent. I gave him up for Ty. I gave him up because, frankly, he wasn't working for me any more. So, that David has died. Grieve if you must, but the queen is dead. Long live the *new* and steely queen. If it makes you feel better, more accomplished, you can just hold a little funeral in your head. I'm steel now, resistant now. You'll get no 'Life-is-too-hard-and-I-just-can't-take-it it-anymore,' dramatics from me.

That sympathetic, shrinking violet variety of fag, well, he don't live here no more, my dear! Are we clear? I hope so."

I was feeling like: *Yes! I guess I just told this bastard with a degree!*

Then, I stood, grabbed my ever-so-stylish pork pie, and set it on my head at a most dangerous tip. I grabbed my ever-so-elegant black leather trench, swung it, Sinatra-style, over my shoulder and prepared to make my exit with a most debonair-like flair.

But Horowitz stood. The Princeton-bred wisdom in his keen blue eyes turned into a certain strain of sadness as he countered me.

"I know it's unprofessional to say so, but what the Hell, report me if you must: You really disappoint me, David Richmond. I once saw so much *potential* in you. You'd grown by leaps and bounds. And through it all, you used your humor like a sword. Whoever that David was, he was ready to stab, joust, and take on the world, one heart at a time. He was a natural natural-born *fighter*! Oh well. It seems the thieves of life have stolen yet another of the truly fun ones."

"Please. Where did fun ever get *that* David? What did it bring? I'll tell you what: a marathon of fists, real and figurative fists, flurries of furious fists punching, hitting, cutting, jabbing, stabbing, thrusting, landing, stunning, and dizzying me. And I always came back on shaky legs, with wobbling knees, both eyes blackened, face swollen the size of Texas, and I have fought back and won, dammit! Recognize! I *am* a fighter! Realize that beneath this deceptive exterior beats the heart of a serious ass-kickin' warrior. I've had to be. It was necessary. So don't fuck with me, because chances are, these days, I won't be in the mood to be fucked with. Got it? See you, Thursday."

I left then, more pissed-off than ever.

Next on my hit list was Victor.

Sometimes, no matter how hard you try to perfect a dance, a pas-du-duex, your partner steps on your fucking toes. Shit gets shabby. What is supposed to look graceful and effortless, instead, looks ugly. The dance, it doesn't work. It becomes amateurish . . . and I hated amateurism. It made a mockery of my sense of aesthetic.

Victor Medina could move quite well. Being older than me, he was a more seasoned dancer at life. He'd even learned a few new moves and innovative steps in an effort to stay in touch, to remain in the groove. But still, sometimes I just wasn't satisfied.

If Ty were here, I know, for sure he'd ask me that inevitable question: Is this Victor Medina, The One? Does He he make you Feel *The Long Blue Moan*?

Ah, Victor. He didn't make it easy, that sweet, sexy infinitely foolish man.

I hadn't been eating well. I'd too much on my mind. But being a former chef, on his night off, he'd cooked me up a feast. The table was set with fresh paella, mushroom salsa, chicken tostados in his famous chocolate and chili sauce. It was all quite remarkable.

The room was filled with candles, and Ray Baretto's music serenaded the place. He looked especially handsome in his crisp white guaybera shirt. So much hope burned within those dark Spanish ojos, as if the future, our future together was brighter than all the beaches of Puerto Rico.

This, this moment was the worst thing about being sick: the good-bye. You choke on the implications of it. You try *not* to remember how alive and affirming your time was with them, because then the words all seem impossible. And so, I lied.

"Baby, this is all so-o-o-o-o sweet. You, next to Ty, are sweetest

man I'll ever know. But let's don't do sweet. Not now. I'm not feeling very sweet, and I hadn't been acting very sweet lately."

"Puppy?"

I knew the best way to piss off a man, especially a Latin man who prides himself on his utter machsimo was to suggest that they lacked the skills, the know-how, the utter *cojones* needed to keep their lovers *faithful*.

"Victor, we're *sweet* together. But let's be real. There's just no *fire* left in us, not anymore. Me, you know I live to feel the fire."

"Puppy. No. What are you sayin? I give you fire, every time. Sometime it's quiet, but it's still fire, no?"

"No. Victor, it isn't. I'm fond of you, and I like the things you do, but there's no flame there. And it hasn't been there for a while. And you *know* that it's been lacking. It was lacking so much, that I had to go . . . and . . . try to . . . find it . . . elsewhere."

I saw my baby's face fall. I watched it just free fall into a bottomless pit of fear and surprise and hurt.

"'Well, I've found it. And it makes me so happy."

I lied trough my tears.

"NO! Impossible! I love you! You love me! This, no . . . this, this is crazy! Stop it, Puppy!"

"Please, don't hate me, baby. It's just that I don't want to *waste* whatever time I've left in this *lukewarm* place, with this nice, sweet love we make. It feels wrong. *I need more*. I've finally found someone who gives me more, who gives me *fire*. Please, be happy for me."

I did love him. How could I not love a man as good and kind and beautiful and patient as Victor? But he wasn't Facey. And he wasn't Carlos. He didn't read me poetry in bed. Yet still, he was a *poem of man.* And for that reason and a thousand others, I had to let him go. I had to let him BE *the poem* in someone else's life. Someone who could give him a future of love and happiness . . . and a sense of what . . . *normal* was.

It occurred to me that Victor was my *second* act. He came so soon, just two months after losing Carlos . . . that I began to think he was *my gift*; a gift for the pain and the loss of Carlos and for all the hurt that came before him. See, I believe God looks out for all of His fools and His damaged children, too.

But this wasn't working out the way I'd planned. He was hurt by my words, but he was still *standing* there, as if waiting for me to tell him it was all some cruel, dark joke. But I wasn't joking. I was aiming to give him his freedom from the likes of me. This was to be MY gift back to him! Didn't he see that? Didn't he, somewhere inside him, even secretly want it?

I saw him staring at me, like I'd kicked him somewhere, someplace deep beyond the balls, or the heart, but in the far reaches of his beautiful foreign soul. I hated myself for it. Didn't he know I was doing it *for* him. Didn't he understand I was *freeing* him from the burden of me, and this fuckin' disease? He looked at me, thunderstruck. But his eyes, they never turned cold, just defeated . . . just so, so unbelievably *sad.*

"And now you know, I haven't been faithful. Don't be all surprised or hurt. Sooner or later we whores, we *punta bitches* always do revert back to form."

"Fuck you!" He balled up his fist mightily. "You liar. You fuckin' liar!"

Was he going to hit me? If so, if he did . . . I felt as if I *deserved* it.

"Liar! That's what you are. That's all you are! I loved you, and you do this to me, to us? Fuck you!"

He slammed that fist against the wall, mere inches from my head.

"Yes. Fuck me. Now, if you'd grab a bag, pack of a few belongings and leave, I'll give my new lover a call, so *he* can do just that. Fuck me!"

I never wanted to see his eyes that way, and I never wanted to be the one who'd placed that look inside of them. I resigned myself into believing I'd never see that look, or those sad Spanish eyes again.

CHAPTER SEVENTEEN

Sorry Seems To Be The Hardest Word

The following Thursday's session:

"Well, it seems I'm now auditioning for the role of Joan of Arc, Doc. And trust me, I would give even the glorious Miss Ingrid Bergman a cinematic run for her money. You see, last week, because of my belief, and my sense of wanting to do the *right thing*, I chose to burn at the stake."

"Excuse me. David? What do you mean? Your metaphor somehow eludes me."

"Please, *read* the subtitles under my chin. I've ended things with Victor. It's over. Finished. Finis. Kaput. Fade to black. I'm Joan of Arc, dammit! And now my heart is all charred and shit. I'm sure I must look hideous."

"Sad. But I'm sure you had your reasons. And, David, I didn't like the way we ended things last week," Horowitz began sternly, "and whether you meant it or not, you ended our session with what could be read as a threat—a threat of bodily harm."

By then, David had some time to think and marinate in

all that had been said. He felt just a little contrite. He felt like he was hurting all these people, good people left and right. The man deserved an apology.

"Look. I'm sorry if things turned ugly. These sessions are very, very *hoard* on me sometimes, Doc. But I didn't mean what I said as a threat—not a physical one. You know I would never lay a hand on you, man. Really. That's not how I roll. I was just angry. That's all."

David thought that was sweet enough. But no. Now *the doctor* needed to read *David* his rather sedate riot act.

"It's becoming a habit with you, David, to leave here angry. I ask a question, and you reply with spite, with mockery or anger. What do we really accomplish by this, David?"

"Well, my life is a whole lot more angry these days, Doc."

"It doesn't have to be. Sometimes we can use humor, and laugh in the face of our own adversity. You used to be such a kick. I actually enjoyed our past sessions when you applied the kind levity and light in your responses. Yes, we've sparred plenty, and you've tried it to get my goat, but most times, you displayed that the core of your personality was one of humor. You lose this, David, and the fight becomes so much harder."

"I used to laugh, incessantly. I still have my humor. And still I love to laugh, I do. But it just seems like I lose my humor a little more every day. God! I'm even starting to *sound* like him!" David shook his head in irony.

"Like who?"

"TYRONE! Tyrone, damn it! That fool missed out on so much fuckin' life, and light and laughter being so-o-o-o serious, forever holding on and holding out, relentlessly looking for his *Long Blue Moan*! And I don't think he ever *really* found it!" David shouted.

"Hold on! Wait a minute, David. You're losing me here. What exactly is a *Long Blue Moan*?"

"God! You always ask the hard questions, don't you? I

mean *hoard*. It's too damn *hoard* to explain." He exhaled. "All I know is he *thought* he'd found it once . . . or twice. Maybe it was hidden in a piece of music, in the sound of a sad Jazz sax, or in another soul's eyes or smile or a heartbeat. But it was a lie, a mistake, a trick! It wasn't real, because if it was, it would have *sustained* him."

"Are you referring to contentment?"

"Yes—I mean contentment, and so much more, Doc. Maybe this is all too esoteric or too damn *ghetto* for *you* to understand. But that blue moan was something you earned. You earned it after searching for what felt like, forever. After all the beatdowns, break-ups, bad moves, setbacks, crushed feelings, and busted-up hearts, you *earned* it. You see, you had to be battered and kicked so hard it hurt in your gut . . . before you even *recognized* it. And once you had it, all the terrible shit, it just vanishes. You meet The One, and that person stimulates you, moves your senses, so deeply, that this *moan* would just come on like a vapor, and it was supposed to calm you—take all the craziness and make sense of it. It was sanctuary."

"But if I'm understanding you, then this Blue Moan is indeed a sensation of love and acceptance. Isn't that what we're all here in hopes of achieving?"

"Please. Tyrone was *nevuh* that simple, Baby-Doc. Of course he wanted those usual suspects from column A and B. But most of all, he wanted his entire flawed being flooded and freed by a sense of bliss. Don't you get it? Maybe you don't. Maybe nobody ever does.

"He wanted to moan out loud! To moan inside his own destiny. He held out for *years* at a time, seeking his divine soul mate. But all he ever ended up with, beyond the oh-so-rare fuck, and a few good moments, was to watch that so-called soul mate's essence dissolve and evaporate into a profound yawn of self-delusion."

"Interesting. However, David, even then, on those rarest

of occasions, perhaps, just perhaps, it was, for him, a delusion more *real* and more thrilling than that tangible moan could ever hope to be."

"Yeah. Whatever, Doc. In reality, I think he was asking for the impossible. But it never stopped him from wanting or searching for that Long Blue Moan."

Later that evening, as David lay in bed, he pulled out one of Ty's journals, and he flipped it open, not knowing what he'd find. But what he found was the secret, which Ty had kept hidden away from him for years, and until, Face Depina rambled a twisted version of it, and which would only later would Tyrone would confirm.

Inside the darkened glass booth, he switched on a red lamp. Face Depina looked even hotter bathed in red light. He dropped his jock. His piece pitched up—tall, tan, and lovely as its owner. He sat in the chair and he lead my head down, down . . .

"Suck me off, if you can!" he challenged me.

Yes, *naked* was Face Depina's color. Still, there was always that shadiness about him. So, I reached into my wallet, pulled out a Trojan. He protested about how he was "clean" as if I'd somehow insulted his manhood. I didn't care. Hell, didn't he know there are diseases out there, and some of them are deadly?

I rolled the rubber down his lengthy span. Then, in a New York minute, he grabbed my chin and fed me his warm, raging manhood . . . He rose from the chair and he bucked and he tried like hell to choke me.

"I knew you dug me back in school. I could tell," Face said with an almost sickening hubris. He pushed me against the desk. Then, all at once, his moist lips locked upon me and mine. "Wait! Wait! Don't you want me to put a rubber on?" I asked.

But he didn't seem to care. Like some reckless predator, he

was all over me, twisting, throttling, smacking my ass, lashing my my lips with, his lips, his mouth, his tongue, and then his throat. I never imagined one man could be so sexual. He was rough and vigorous, full of heat and slobber and rushing breaths.

It felt so hot and forbidden, and like something from a erotic dream, but, then, HE, Face Depina, told me that HE wanted to be *done*. *I couldn't believe it.*

His hands sailed down my belly. He grabbed my limb and jerked it into a stubborn hardness "Get up!" he said. "I want you to fuck me, Ty."

That night was thick with surprises. But I couldn't quite fathom this one.

He was violently erect, and at first, he laid face-up, his back on the table.

But looking directly at the beauty of Face Depina, head-on, I would've arrived much too quickly, so he I ordered, "Turn around."

Face did as I told him. I slowly massaged the red-lighted slopes of a perfectly glazed ass. I could smell the excitement on the air. Depina tensed and taunted and began teasing the hell out of me, until every part of me was quaking at the sight of him.

Slowly, very slowly I descended inside him. It was beyond intense. It was more like a tight, knotted Cheerio of flesh opening for me. He groaned that groan of anguished pleasure. I began to ride him then, easing in and sliding out, giving him more and then more of my measure.

And still, he wanted even more.

I pierced him deeper slicing and sliding inside a warm and engulfing tightness, as he fully enclosed me. Like some deep and magnetic furnace, it seemed to will me, to pull me deeper into its heat. My God! Being inside Pascal "Face" Depina was like plunging one's dick into the eye of a storm, a crushing, rushing, twisting cyclone. It was exciting and it was havoc. It was freeing and it was dangerous.

All of his passion, his beauty, his mystery and all I didn't know about him, it all merged with the intensity of actually *being inside him,* and this sent me to my edge. I could *feel* his whole body trembling , flooding with this ecstatic wonder. I lunged and instantly I felt my shudder.

There was something almost seismic quivering in him ,and in me, and it was about to commence and set us both free..

He heaved and he raised his hips, and then he erupted like something wild and untamed. And the skeet of his bounty blasted and flew so high ling into the air. And for one silky-hot sticky moment of transference, I felt as if we'd connected.

I pulled back, then slammed, and I shook. The whole of my entirety shuddered deep inside of him, wet, moist and satisfied.

I can't believe it! I can NOT believe it! I just did Face Depina!

But then, all at once, he was back to being Face the Shaky, Face the Untrustworthy, and yes, Face the Liar.

He sighed and said, "Man, that was wild, baby. Real wild. I guess I brought out that wild boy in you." He laughed, and then his aspect turned and it shifted from the humor in the moment. "But, don't go fallin' in love with me or anything, 'cause you know I ain't like you, right? I mean. I ain't gay. So you *need* to keep this shit between us. All right?" he said, his green eyes staring back at me in complete and utter seriousness. "This was just one of them experiments. You know, like, this is just an *actin'* exercise for me."

And something very strange had just happened. It was a kind of murder . . . a murder of a good moment. I'd heard him. I'd watched those pretty, lying green eyes trying to convey some truth that he knew and I knew was the height of mendaciousness. But it was all sort of like *waking up* from a dream, where everything sits in its own quiet haze and nothing is quite yet real.

"I mean, it felt all right. Don't be hurt. Can't say I was really all *into* it. But—"

And I said ,"What? Come on now, Face! This is me, Ty! You don't need to bullshit *me* with this whole I'm-that-tough-hard-*straight*-street-cat trip of yours anymore. You give head, man. And you take it up the ass, man. Last time I checked, that makes you pretty damn *gay,* man!" I fumed.

But he gave me some spiel, some bullshit about being up for a role as a gay man, and how he needed to KNOW what it was like. Why? Because, he was no "fly-by-night" and he was serious about his "craft."

It was to laugh.

I just stared back at this *actor,* this supposed thespian, and for the first time since I'd known him, Face didn't seem so damn pretty anymore. *Who was he, really?* Maybe I should've felt clowned again. But the laugh, this time, was on him. I wanted Face to know *I knew* for sure now that Pascal Ornate "Face" Depina was *not* legit.

"Acting?" I said. "Nah. Pascal, trust me on this: you were never *that* good. Yeah, sure, maybe sucking dick, once, might be an experiment. But what we just did here, and the way you kept demanding *more, well that* just makes you another deluded faggot! You think you played me? No, bruh. Ya played yourself!"

"Come on, Ty! I picked YOU outta all the guys I coulda picked, 'cause I knew you'd keep it quiet. So don't feel used. You enjoyed it. I know you did!" Face blustered as I walked away. "Yo! Just keep it between us, and don't be all mad at me, brotha! Hey! Ain't you never heard of *The Method*?"

"Whatever's clever, *sista!* You played yourself, but whatever's clever," I said, heading back into the room filled with men who knew, who acknowledged, and who embraced what they truly were.

I doubt if we're real friends now. It certainly wasn't a Long Blue Moan Moment. But one night, in a DJ booth, lit by a single red light, we shared this thing, this animal thing between us. And now we both know the truth. He can deny to his dying day, but I know and he knows, and that's all that really matters in the end.

"Bastards! Oh. My. GOD!" David fumed. And in a fit of righteous, furious, bitter, and wasted anger, David hurled the book across the room. The journals were becoming more and more battle-scarred by David's fits of anger over what he'd read in them.

David had always perceived something shared between Tyrone and Facey. But he never thought it would sink so low, or as common as sex.

Strange, even years later, after reading about the deception, it still troubled David that the two people he'd loved most in this whole wide world had betrayed him.

But more than this, from reading the account of fateful night, he recognized in Face Depina the same degree of self-hatred and denial he realized in a young Raul Medina. Hopefully Victor's son would know a better ending.

It was just a few pages later in the same journal that David would read the following:

These nights I wake up, cold. I am cold, where hands and fingers have prowled and patrolled my skin. I am cold with no desire to transfer heat or even relief or some fleeting pleasure. I am cold where lips have been. I am frigid where teeth have bitten. I am cold, where lonely souls, like me, have profited from dreams of sweat and heat and cum.

I remember one time, one night, one man stroked my mind, so deep, so completely. He rubbed his dick on my cerebral cortex. I squirted fifteen feet ahead of me.

Then, I passed out cold.

Now, men are passing out, dead. Now, beauty is rotting all around me. Now, flesh is decomposing in these streets with familiar names.

Now the hotness of once young, robust flesh is cold and

rotting. Where are the angels now? I've been calling on them. But they won't answer me.

Where the essence of perfection once reigned, I now see only scars. My hands are afraid now; afraid to prowl these lands of new fruit, too terrified of its deadly pulp. I am afraid to explore, to trust in these bodies and lands I once adored. I want more, more than moments of pleasure. I want time! I want to find and measure love by loyalty, by devotion, and yes, by fidelity. I am seeking a cure for this fear. I just want dreams that glow in the dark, and not This Thing—this cold and nightmarish thing that patrols the skin of my heart.

CHAPTER EIGHTEEN

BLACK MEN WITH DESIGNS

The disease had taken on yet another victim in the parade of people David knew and had counted on being there. This time, it was his assistant designer, Patrick. Patrick LeRoy was a talented artiste who possessed rebellious spirit similar to David's. They'd clicked instantly, and much of David's vision merged with Patrick's own unique flair for design and style. David knew that day was coming. He knew it by the absences, and the times Patrick would somehow manage to arrive late, looking horrible, and withered, with only his love of fashion to keep him alive.

There was so much going on and going wrong in David's life, and yet the grieving was done, and the business had to go on. It was what Patrick would have wanted.

For two weeks there had been a series of interviews and referrals followed by more interviews, and deadline brewing, and still no one seemed fit.

Enter the newness: Rodney. His name was Rodney Stansfield. He was a promising neophyte designer. He arrived in David's salon with portfolio in hand, and with the presence of a young, tight Sidney Poitier. There was a shiny black panther alive in his stride, and steely look of purpose mixed with ambition in his eyes. David's gaydar was clearly on the fritz with this one. There were no outwardly signs, no telltale gestures. There was only the naked fact that Rodney Stansfield was one "fierce-ass designer!"

This Rodney, whoever, and whatever he was, proved himself to be an excellent student of fashion history.

"Your look, your sense of style and detail is fucking brilliant, man. Seriously. I'm impressed with your eye," David said.

"Thank you," Rod said proudly. "I went to Parsons School of Design. I've studied the classic black-and and-white films from the '30s and '40s. Adrian, that designer was a God. He really knew how to make every actress he touched into an earthly goddess."

"Yes. I agree completely. Adrian was a bad mofo, squared! He gave Joan Crawford her grace."

"And . . . those legendary shoulders," Rodney said.

"What do you dream to be, my young Black designer?" David asked.

This question was crucial to anyone David took under his wing, because if they responded with some ass-kissing reply like: "I wanna be the next David Richmond," he'd clearly see through their bullshit. David was a fervent fan of Bette Davis. He'd seen her movie *All About Eve* so many times that he could quote it, verbatim. Bette played Margo Channing, a successful, well-respected, but rapidly aging actress. In comes poor mousy Anne Baxter, "Eve," kissing Margo's mad famous ass, wanting to do, be, to become and then take everything Margo had: her career, her fame, and including even her man. David was already a successful *Margo*. He didn't want or need an "*Eve*" in his life.

Rodney's answer to David inquiry was, "That glamour people like Adrian, Edith Head, and others gave to White women, I want to do that for Black women, and Black men.

We are an inherently glamorous people. We make a fashion statement whenever we head out the door. But glamour costs . . . so the *real thing* evades most of us. I want to give us glamour, affordable, stylish, make-you-wanna-smack you-mama glamour."

"Good answer, Rodney Stansfield!"

David liked his reply, his sensibility, his sense of purpose and ambition, and so he was hired.

In the days and weeks that followed, Rodney would become David's good eye, the youthful eye, the one that saw the styles on the street, sweetened and tweaked them in a way that made them fresher and newer. Rodney deeply admired David's fashion sense and his talent as well.

And though David no longer cared or even wondered what Rodney's sexuality was, he advised him to at the very least "be extremely gay-friendly around our clients."

Rodney laughed. "David? Do you really think you have to *tell* me that, man? I know what side of the cornbread is buttered, pa."

"No. I don't think you do, man. In this business, one of the few businesses that embraces gays and the culture, it's almost mandatory to be gay. People expect it. It's a safer zone when women can parade around half-naked if they know they won't be groped, or hit on inappropriately.

"Got you. So, you want me to *be* gay?"

"No. Be *yourself!* But *gay* it up a little. Flirt a bit, and be open to the vibes of others. I'm not saying you have be *turned-out*, or even whore yourself out just to get over. That would be wrong. But it would help you in this biz to get in touch with your sensitive, more femme side."

"My 'more femme side'?"

"Yes. And *please*, don't give me no 'I'm man, all man with a workin penis' spiel. Because, every man on this planet *has* a femme side. Most just try their damndest to *hide* it."

Yes, some hide it. Many did. But not Rodney. He was authentically himself—Rodney. A natural man, with a natural, non-stereotypical way about him.

If only David had boldly asked the question, "Rodney, are you gay?" ' Rodney would had have simply said, "Actually, I prefer the term *Same Gender Loving.*"

Weeks later, after lunches and nights spent working overtime on near-brilliant designs and the tediousness of deadlines, David and Rodney had become a working unit, a greased machine, a force of synergy. They were completing each other's thoughts and sentences, agreeing and disagreeing like men, and not two vogue-conscious bitches.

And yet, Rodney's six-three, two hundred and twenty-pound physical appeal was never lost on David. In David Richmond's sexual career, he'd always held a yen for the lure of Latino men. Rico Rivera, was his first, and all his future choices followed suit. Tyrone would quiz him sometimes, because it seemed that David was dismissing the down and True Brothas, in favor of the papi flava.

"I love my brothas to death. They can be so hard and tough and beautifully rough. But me being me, I see it threatens the insecure and weak ones. It ain't like I've forsaken them, but so many times my brothas have forsaken me. So, I crossed the street into El Barrio, where the gatos are naturally macho, so darkly beautiful, and ain't afraid to let that mad, sultry freak side flow."

And Ty answered, "Oh. Say no mo'."

But in David's eyes, Rodney was really quite exquisite, and becoming even more so by the days and nights. His dark, smooth-as-Korean-silk skin would catch his own fluorescence under the lights. His hands were like two hugely elegant black spiders, dusted with traces of hair. He was twenty-seven, at the apex of his allure, and in the prime of his heat. It would have been easy for him to have snared most any woman or man he desired. But he didn't lead with his sex, nor his sexuality. He went to the gym regularly each morning before heading in to work. His nights were not spent clubbing in Chelsea or dancing wildly in the village. Instead he was engaged in fits of new creativity, sketching, and planning the next collection.

David would advise and try to coax him out into the world of mingling and NYC nightlife, to dabble with the fashion fixtures, and grin inside the lights of the glitterati. When it was strictly for business purposes, sometimes he'd acquiesce. But Rodney was best in smaller, more intimate settings.

It was under such an ambiance while he was suppering David that the truth came out.

"You've worked with me for over six months, and so I think it's time you should know, I'm HIV-positive," David said, sipping his lime and club soda, studying Rodney's reaction.

"Oh, damn, man." Rodney's face nearly fell in his fettuccini. "God. I'm so, so sorry. I didn't know. I mean, I had no idea. Are you . . . are you ok?"

"Some days, I'm fine. Others, not so fine. It's a helluva tricky virus. It plays violent ping-pong with my insides . . . and wreaks havoc on my emotions. But I'm telling you, not for your sympathy or your concern, though I appreciate it. I am letting you know this because, on bad days, I may not feeling up to coming in, and it's those times I'll be depending on you most, Rodney."

"I feel kinda honored, brotha," Rodney said sadly, carefully perusing David's face, and deciding what to say next.

Damn, David. Just Damn, man! Do I tell you MY truth now? Do I tell you that I can see myself falling for you? Do I say that you're all I think about, and how at night, I lie awake thinking of ways to please you? What do I say? What should I say?

What he said was, "Do you have someone? Someone in your life, who can take care of you, and see you through this?"

"Oh, I can and have been taking care of myself. I had someone. He was wonderful, but he's gone now."

"Your lover?"

"No. Better than that. A *bestest* friend."

"I see."

"No. It's doubtful that you do, because we haven't discussed our personal stuff. I sometimes wonder why . . . The best friend I lost, he didn't die from this thing I have nesting inside me. He didn't have it. There are *other* ways for us to die, you know."

"Yes. I know."

There are many ways to die. I'm dying right now, right here in front of you, David. Can't you see? I'm dying because you're telling me you're sick. I'm dying that I can't say or do anything to help you, or to stop it. I'm dying because your words are killing a piece of me, right here at this table.

"I also had a dutiful lover, until recently," David reflected on Victor. "Oh . . . he was a good, sexy, decent man. I love him. But I wanted *better* for him than this thing. So, one day, I felt strong enough to set him free."

Would you, could you see yourself with someone else, David? Would . . . I do?

Rodney was feeling a plethora of things all at once. So much so, that if what he felt were designer rags, they would stretch the entirety of Seventh Avenue.

"This is been a night of uneasy confessions, hasn't it? So, I guess it's my turn," Rodney began.

"Oh? Look at me. Ever the fashionista! Am I starting a new trend here?" David joked.

"Do you realize how little you *know about me*, besides my talent at the salon?"

"Actually, don't be too surprised, but I've checked you out, your creds, your background. Typical work-related stuff."

"Well, did all that checking reveal my status, or my orientation? Doubtful, because I've always played that pretty close to the vest."

"Ummm . . . yes, I've noticed."

"It's not a sham, David. No smoke and mirrors, no pretense needed. I'm a Black man who happens to prefer the company of *other Black men*. I'm selective. I don't like nor do I relate to the word *gay*. That's an affectation, the White man's invention. It has its roots in a White male political movement, or else it's something wholly sexual. Well, I'm more than just sex, or someone else's definition of me. If I had to define myself, I'd say I'm SGL: Same Gender Loving."

And so . . . that night had just become a bit more intriguing.

David smiled. And though it had been years since he'd last lit a cigarette, he suddenly felt this mad, overwhelming need for a smoke.

"And as important as it was for us to have had this conversation, I don't want it to change the respect I have for you, David."

"Oh, it won't, pa. I promise. I'm glad you told me. I'd quietly hoped you were, but what you do and *who* you do, it was your business, until you made it mine."

"I'll confess something else: I've been feeling you for quite some time, man. You are so fuckin' brilliant at what you do. But in the months we've spent together, I've discovered that you're even more brilliant at *being* you. Please, don't ever change that! And please, please, don't change your opinion of me!"

"We fit, Roddy Rod. We have the same goals, the same dreams . . . the same . . ."

Rodney's large hand stroked David's smaller hand. They gazed inside each other's eyes.

"The same urge to kiss each other?" Rodney smiled.

Later that night at David's apartment:

Rodney placed the softest of kisses on David's sex-parched lips. He maneuvered his hand across David's shoulder and he ever so slowly lowered down to David's tiny waist. The Richmond Behind, The David Derriere was damn-near legend for its supple, rich, copper skin, and its sleek, fit dance-informed roundness. Rodney's hands became magnetized to it. It had been so long since a *Black* hand had touched him there, and there, and Oh, GOD, *there!* David immediately became accutely aware of his own body again: its pulses, its pressure points, its peaks and its palpitations.

When this strong Black man, this man without armor, without subterfuge, without societal rules or terrible health news removed his clothes, David, the designer, suddenly wished he were a sculptor who possessed the hands of Michelangelo. The exquisitely molded chest, the stones along Rodney's belly, and the long chocolate porcelain thighs with erotic etchings in them, this all made David crazy with excitement.

And when Rodney made love to him, David felt as if he was finding his own mind, his own pace and rhythm again. He knew the places where to taste him, where to touch him, and how long to taste and touch him there. Rodney even knew that secret place where his tears were manufactured, and he made them rain down David's cheek.

His organ plunged deeply between David's tightened

dancer's thighs, and the sensation felt welcome and warm and wilder than wild. He wasn't afraid to kiss David, and he kissed him like he *meant* it. He kissed him as if he wanted to leave this tattoo there. He kissed him as if he were determined to *be remembered.*

With the right person, the right body, the right souls commingling, *outer*-course could be just as deep and real and as spiritually intimate as any fit of intercourse could ever dream of being. The slick, hard, electric sweep of dick on dick frottage brought on a sense of huffing, puffing unity.

He moved with the gentleness of a careful lover mixed with the driving purpose of a rutting beast. David was HIV-positive, and Rodney was not, and yet there was nothing vaguely vanilla in this moist and torrid activity. This was chocolate and caramel, merging as one sweeping, grinding, living, breathing, sweating, pulsing, pushing, sliding, gliding entity.

And when Rodney's breaths charged and his whole body tensed, he sprayed his gift, and David arrived soon after it . . . And they gasped and panted against each other's hot skin, the two of them knew the humbling humidity of being *safe* . . . and of being men.

CHAPTER NINETEEN

PAPAS IN A YOUNG MAN'S EYES

The following morning, as David gazed inside his bathroom mirror, he wondered: had he *cheated* again? Had he betrayed Victor by making love and actually *enjoying* it with another man? Back in his old wild days, such a question would not have fazed him, nor would it have ever crossed David's mind. But this was now, and so he *wondered*.

Had Rodney, this cool, new and improved shot of adrenaline, provided David with the Long Blue Moan of Tyrone's dreams of compatibility? Perhaps not, but the brother did provide David with a Long White Gush.

However, no matter Rodney's skills and talents in and out of bed, he wasn't about to become David's lover. David wasn't searching for a new one, and so it didn't feel right to continually ask Rodney to stay the night. Rodney, thinking they'd shared some special connection, began to feel just a little rejected.

David was still thinking, still dreaming, still wondering about Victor. At first, he'd wanted a clean break, and so he'd purposely removed all of Victor's photographs from sight.

But the more time passed, his aching heart longed to gaze upon that handsome weathered face again. So, he removed his favorite photo from its storage and placed it on his bedroom table. He'd sometimes study it and welcomed the memories of Victor's strong Latino countenance, the powerful jawline, the dark velvet eyes, and how the subtly masculine features aligned to render him classically handsome.

"David. Can I see you tonight?" Rodney asked as they entered the salon elevator after a hard day's design. David wanted to say no. But Rodney slid his fine chocolate hand around his waist, and something in David weakened.

"That's not very professional, Roddy Rod."

"Damn that! The work day's over, and I'm aiming to get reeeeeeeeal personal with you," he whispered softly inside David's ear.

And so, they made their way to David's apartment. And so they kissed and slide their fabulous clothes away. And they made it to the bed, and they did those slick hot things they did, and when it was over, Rodney sighed noticed the photograph of that handsome older Latin man peering back at him from the night table.

"Who *is* that?" He'd asked this with a trace of jealously, and to David's attentive ear, just perhaps a little malice.

"It's Victor. My papa."

"Your *papa*? Your father? I didn't know you were *mixed*."

Again, there was a certain odor of discontent attached to the inquiry.

David laughed, and said "No, Rodney. My *papa*. My former lover. You can't be *that* dense, can you?"

"Oh. Well, he sure don't *look* black to me!"

"That's only because he's not."

"Oh. I get it. So, you *slipped*. It's ok. I can forgive that. White cats be all over me, like, like white on ermine. But I let them *know*, straight up, I am *not* down with the politics of the swirl."

"Hold up. Back it up! Rewind! Excuse *you*, Rodney, but you can *forgive* what, exactly?"

"Oh, I mean, I won't hold it against you for bypassing a brother for some other . . . whatever he is."

David sensed there was about to be some problem, some new issue ahead. His mind recalled the past conversations they'd had, and how Rodney always said he wanted to design for the *Black* customer, and to give *Black people* glamour, and just how *pro*-BLACK Rodney's sensibilities were. This Black consciousness in him didn't bother David in the least . . . but what *had* become suddenly bothersome was Rodney's blatant judgment of *David's personal* choices.

"Ummm . . . just so you know, he's Puerto Rican and Venezuelan. And he's not the first, the second, or even the third Latin man I've been with. In fact, I can count on *one* hand the Black men I've ever been with."

"Damn! Really? And *why* is that? We Brothas ain't *good* enough for you?" Rodney asked in a huff.

"Some? No. They ain't good enough. Some of them wanted me to be harder, or as least as hard as *they pretended* to be. See, I like realness. But mostly, it's because I sense they ain't about *loving* themselves enough to let someone else love them *back*. From what I experienced, some just got too much hate in them. Hate, for the White man, or the yellow man, or the brown man, or the red man, or the fuckin' boogie man, so much fuckin' hate that they can't seem to let that shit go, and be *a-for-real Black man!*"

"So you don't date brothas, huh? So, in other words, I guess I should feel *lucky*, then. Is that it?"

"You should feel a sense of grace that you enjoyed me, and I enjoyed you, and the color of our skin had little to do with it."

"Look, David. I like you. I *really* do. But your perception of what Black is or ain't, it's totally *whack*, brotha. Yeah, you can date who you choose, but when you date *exclusively out-*

side of your own race, I feel like there's some kinda . . ." He paused.

"What? Finish your damn sentence, Rodney P. Newton, my Black Panther-esque brotha!"

"It's some kinda self-hating, or self-denying, or self-*something* that you might wanna look into further."

"Thought I told you, bruh. I *love* me. I truly do. I love me just the way I am. And if more *brothers* loved me *for* me . . . then they'd be no problem. But you see, many brothas can't love me because they don't love, won't love, can't love, or refuse to love *the me* inside of themselves. So, maybe, you might wanna look further into the WHY of that, my *brotha*."

David looked at his watch and decided to give the usual Davy excuse, only with an edge.

"Damn! Don't you just *hate it* when a perfectly good screw leads to a perfectly *fucked-up* conversation? It makes me feel, all . . . I don't know . . . cheap . . . and used. Goodnight, Rodney. See you at work, bright and early."

For Rodney, David's dating outside of his race was the breaking point, the stalemate, the death, and the *coup de gras* on any further romantic entanglement. It was a shame, because he'd thought for a moment, David might've been *the one* for him.

And now, the line had been drawn and crossed, and he only hoped he could still endure a close working relationship with both maturity and the utmost of professionalism.

Two Weeks Later

David eyes were still attracted to those rare and beautiful things. At one time, he collected beautiful things. Or maybe they collected him. Time stands still when we gaze at beauty and it looks back at us with recognition in its eyes.

They were two Boricuas who boarded the subway on West Twenty-seventh Street, just outside of David's old alma mater F. I. T. When David first saw them, he thought, *Hmmm . . . two young, dark, trendy papis, with manicured brows and matching Caesar haircuts.* Their baggy jeans hung decidedly hung low beneath their boyishly thin waistlines.

The taller of the two wore Timberlands, and the other wore the appropriate Jordans. They seemed like typical New York kids—very cool, very much a part of the scenery. They didn't do anything to elicit David's attention, except to merely exist in their own youthful exuberance.

For a moment their faces and clothes shifted, and memory stifled the present. They became two completely other people, and one of those people was David. He remembered being that young once. He suddenly remembered as if it were yesterday.

David had always been frighteningly accurate at assigning the proper ages to faces. From their outward appearance, David reasoned they were barely eighteen. Barely eighteen. He began to drink them in, slyly, curiously. He sensed something almost palpable in the glances they exchanged. He could feel this *thing*, this quietly seismic vibration emitting as they displayed a certain comfort with each other. Most anyone else who saw them might have assumed they were good friends. *Yes, good friends, homeboys*, David thought. He had good friends, once.

His thinking mind began to remember his own good friends. Their smiling faces flooded his mind. He could see them, hear them laughing and happy again. Memory stifled the present.

David let the moment pass.

But before long, his gaze drifted back to the two kids sitting together. Maybe he should've brought something to read, a crossword puzzle, a fashion magazine, anything to kill the time. But he hadn't, and so he became ensconced in the two of them, shooting each other the most furtive of glances. His mind suddenly grew very active inside this causal act of idle people-watching. Yes.

His senses were still perceptive . . . but more than this, his instincts became overly active. He couldn't seem to shut off the fact that there was indeed some *thing* between the two of them. Perhaps the others couldn't see it or read it, but now David could read and see the subtext under their silent chins.

On the surface, they appeared to be nothing more than two young papis with manicured brows, matching Caesar haircuts, and jeans hanging decidedly hung low beneath their boyishly thin waistlines. But David knew, there was something *more*. He suddenly *recognized* that like many of the new breed of gay men, these two were *unclockable*.

David sensed such a strong and obvious urgency between them. It was something nearly combustible, as if they might burst or bust or self-destruct if they did not touch or show their feelings.

And then, he watched them as they slouched down in their seats. They stared, they grinned with a trace of a more sensual suggestion, a silent exchange written within the language of their eyes. It was then, to David's delight and surprise, that he saw them, stealing kisses . . .

Yes! I knew it! David's mind rejoiced, and he smiled just a little. They were kissing. Not lewdly, but sweet, so sweetly that David just sat there, secretly aching for them. How beautiful and how courageous they were. He began to take a strange parental *pride* in them, and yet a part of him felt envious, too.

He wondered then, *Where do Black men feel free to kiss? Is it only anonymously, in Greenwich Village bars? Is it only safe and accepted in the dark? Where have I experienced my best and most potent and passionate of kisses? Damn! Where and when-have I felt most free? Was it in the coolest, dimmest of clubs or rooms of secret ceremonies where penises were measured for Manhood Quotients, and positions were bartered like flea market notions?!*

Unfortunately, many times, the answer was a sad and unfulfilled, yes.

David wondered, *Why do so few Black men feel motivated to kiss?*

Where was that affection, that naked necessity to kiss because to do so would *fill* the emptiness? What were we so afraid of? Wasn't kissing *needed?* How many Black men did he know who kissed as if they might burst, bust, or self-destruct if they didn't openly show their fierce Love for each other?

CHAPTER TWENTY

COULD *YOU* BE MY KINDRED?

Business at the salon was booming. David was doing a final fitting on one of his original designs, and this, as always, was meticulous work. He was on his knees, inspecting the hem of a soon-to-be expensive pair of trousers. The model seemed perfectly satisfied, but not David.

"I'm not *loving* my work today. Stand straight, please! You see that? The way it falls? They should be kissing the vamp of the shoe, not *crowding* it. Damn it! Why can't I get this right!"

He was looking in the mirror, dissatisfied with his art. Then his eyes started to go a little hazy, in a sort of daydream mode . . . and *that* was when IT happened.

There, inside that mirror, he thought he saw something . . . a vision appeared in the background. It was strange and young and gangly, yet oddly beautiful to David's eye. But he knew it wasn't real. It was *far too Impossible* to *be Real*. Yet, for a moment, time stood still, and that vision was vivid and so brilliantly *alive*, David found himself smiling. He rose from his knees.

The vision passed by.

He wanted to go, to run after it, to follow it, to call out to it! He had to do something before the reverie of that moment all but disappeared.

"David! David!" Rodney called out. "So, do we shorten it another eighth of an inch?"

The sound and reality of Rodney's voice disturbed him, drew him away from the loveliness of that wonderful reverie.

Damn it! I am going crazy? Is this what crazy feels like?

Suddenly David walked, then ran away from the fitting, the work, the vision. All the voices and all the questions would go unanswered that day.

Was it the meds? Was it the AZT? David wondered and he worried. Was there something, some ingredient in them that caused these hallucinations?

When he returned home, David was haunted by a conversation he'd had with Tyrone years before. Though, at the time, it felt more like a confrontation, the subject was about "ghosts."

"Ty? Who were you just talkin' to? Please tell me you were on the phone, and not buggin' the fuck out." David, key in hand, had stopped by to drop off a shirt he'd designed.

"No, David. I was just talkin' to Trick."

"*Trick?* You mean Browny's brother Trick? . . . *Dead* Trick?

Ty immediately regretted his confession.

"Hold on. I'm gonna have to sit down for this one."

"I never told you how tight we were."

"So, tell it."

And with that invitation, Ty began to reveal to David, the story of his relationship with Trick and Trick's ghost. Through it all, Ty kept looking around as if waiting for some word from Trick, or for permission from the cosmos to speak.

"We shared this energy. We still do. A spiritual connection that makes me think we probably walked this earth together before. I *knew* him before I even knew him, and when I met him it was *home*. I know it sounds crazy, and if it is, I've been crazy for years. But *Trick is here*. See, we were on this road together, a short-lived but very cool Electric Avenue, I know he's left the physical plane. But a part of him remains . . . here. And I can feel it."

It all *sounded* perfectly *sound* to Ty.

"Ty, I love you. Even if you crazy as a shit-house rat, I'll still love yo' crazy, rabid ass. But this is scarier than Madam Zoreena's parlor that Halloween night she made fire in her hand. Is he here right now?" David asked incredulously.

"I feel him over there by the chair. I feel the vibrato of him laughin'. He knows you don't believe me."

"That chair right there, by the window? What he look like? Is he still Black as tar? No disrespect. Or is he White, and all see-through?"

" Just for the record: no one likes a wise-ass fag. He's not Casper, David. He's not some murky ectoplasm movie ghost."

"Then . . . what is he?"

"He's like a shadow or a flicker of light. His voice is in my head, like I'm imagining it, but it's his voice. Sometimes, not so much anymore, his face will flicker inside a shadow. He's different from how he is in my dreams. In my dreams he's whole and fully Tricked out. Here, he's just pieces of light, wisdom, comfort, counsel, and sometimes, just company. And *stop* looking at me like I'm illin'! I'm not crazy."

"Well, let's not talk about this shit anymore, 'kay?" David said.

And so they didn't.

Ghosts, like memories, were making their rounds again.

Sometimes, strange characters appear and reappear in our lives, as if they had been sent to loiter there. Maybe they are ghosts. Maybe they are Gifts.

Maybe they *are* Angels.

They come with this emotional terrain we find ourselves passing through—and even when they prove to be flesh and blood, bone and heart, some part of us realizes this place is *not* their own.

David just received some very sad news. It had become his tragic duty to report it to the other young men at the center. Before he did, he wanted to tell them something else. Something lasting and real.

"Do you know how beautiful you are? Do you possibly have any idea? Has anyone told you, you are rare, special, and *blessed* spirits? I'm being very real here."

He scanned the room of Black and Brown faces, some scarred by Karposi's sarcoma, others thin, withered, and aging, though most were not yet even thirty years old.

"Well, if they haven't, I'm here to tell you, you are all *beautiful* to me," he began. Yet after this preamble, his voice took a decidedly less gracious tone.

"The more I see and hear in this place, the more frustrated I become. Each time I come here, I hope and pray for the strength just to make it through. I think you should know, if don't already, Quincy died yesterday."

The mouths of several young men opened inhaled in loud and unthinkable gasps.

"He was twenty-nine years old." David held back a sniffle, and a tear in his left eye blurred his vision. "So, I ask you . . . who'll be next? Quincy seemed pretty damn healthy when he sat in this room, just two weeks ago. He managed to laugh and he even cracked a joke or two. He was doing . . . very fine . . . and he seemed to be in a good place. And now, he's . . . *gone*. This isn't a game, people. This isn't a fuckin' game," he repeatedly sadly.

"The more I see in the streets, in the clubs, the baths, the parks, and beyond, the more I realize this phenomenon is *eating* us *alive*. Aren't you tired of it, yet? I am. I'm so fuckin' tired of it, I could spit fire! HIV is not even mildly cute or trendy. Trends come and go, and this thing ain't goin' nowhere! I'm older than most of you, but not by much. But I can hardly remember a time when this *thing* didn't have a stranglehold on our community.

"I used to think it was a conspiracy against people like me. I looked around at who among us was contracting it, and for the most part, they all looked like *me*. I was convinced there was a war going on, and that war was being waged against gay, bisexual, Black and Brown men.

"Then, as the numbers began to lessen and fewer and fewer of our White brethren were becoming infected, I was screaming, 'BUT *IT'S STILL AFTER ME AND MINE, DAMN IT!*' Suddenly it was becoming this exclusively Black and Brown thing. But if this was or is some conspiracy, then we, all of us must be pretty damned *stupid*, don't you think? I mean HIV is a disease of opportunity, isn't it? By now you'd have to be mildly retarded not to understand how you can and can not contract it, right? Then why the fuck is this disease *still* spreading? Why are we still fucking without fear, and without condoms? Why have we learned nothing from the ones who lived fast and died young before us? Why have we not paid *attention*? And why have we not become more proactive? Are we really *that* suicidal?

"So, what are you *doing* to save your own lives? Whatever it is, it's not enough!

"Sure, there are medicines, and new hip medications, but don't you dare kid yourselves! They ain't no cure. At best, they can give you more time, maybe help preserve the quality of life. But half of those infected aren't even given access to these meds. Where's the *justice* is that, huh? Now, I'm not here because I'm *paid* to be, and I don't get off on whining and complaining or pointing the finger. I just want to *save* some *lives*, damn it! Whether we are dealing with a conspiracy by our government, or a conspiracy of assholes and dunces, *we* are clearly the prey. My only hope is that we start looking for solutions to this screaming epidemic, instead of looking for someone else to blame.

"I know some of you here will see me as some preacher telling you to repent and change your ways. Wrong! I'd be the last person on this planet to judge a single one of you. Trust me! I've been in that place where some of you find yourselves right now. I *know* how hard it is. I have the scars to prove it.

"I was never anybody's crusader. I was a dancer. I was a for-real, classically trained, disciplined, dancing cat, from ballet, modern, tap, jazz, you name it, and I've done it, to death. I've appeared in numerous shows you've all probably heard of, and no, I'm not bragging. I tell you this to say, I've traveled all over the country and parts of the world, and I've had unprotected sex in all of them. I've lived many of my dreams, and fell short of achieving some other ones. I tell you this because I thought I was young and beautiful, and thereby *invincible*. It's a very high and arrogant feeling to think of yourself as immortal. Sex was easy and love was hard. I trusted providence to be my dance partner.

"Meanwhile, I saw people—good, and real and fabulous people—I knew and loved, getting sick, growing skinnier and fading around me. But you know what? I was still alive, still David Donatello Richmond, and damn it, I wasn't gonna let death or fear or nothing stop my show!

"The most beautiful, talented, creative people on this freaking planet died! And me? I just kept on dancing on the outskirts of death. Nope. It won't get me! Why? Because I was arrogant enough to think I had to be one of God's *favorites*. I must've been. I was still getting my freak on, regularly, and I felt fine as wine.

"Now, I don't care how many scared first-timers, or jaded whores I'm speaking to here, I feel pretty safe in saying I'll bet I've had more sex than every single one of you. I am not proud. I lived to fuck and be fucked. Well, guess the fuck what? My luck with the fuck, and all my fuckin' luck ran the fuck out, my boys and girls!

I don't regret my past life. What I DO regret is not loving and not ***respecting myself*** enough to care about the temple of my *self*. Now. I'm positive."

Just as he made that raw and truthful pronouncement, David eyes searched those in attendance, and then, they widened when saw *him*. That vision, it was in the room, again. The one from his salon, the one he'd seen in the mirror, the same vision he wanted to run to, and call out its naked name. That vision stood up, looked David dead in the eye, and David suddenly idled. He heard his heart beating quickly, felt the blood pumping through his own veins.

This vision possessed the face of the best friend David would ever know. That vision was the spitting image, height and size of *Tyrone Hunter*.

Only now, that vision opened its mouth, the same mouth with the familiar lips that seemed begging to be kissed. It opened its mouth and it spoke. It had a question for David, and David grabbed hold to the edge of the desk and silently *prayed* for his sanity. He prayed that if he'd indeed lost his sanity, please God, in one last act of dignity, *please don't let me faint*.

"You say you've had more sex than anyone in this room. Maybe that's true. But, after a while, didn't you—I mean, didn't it all begin to feel . . . a little empty?"

It seemed like a question Tyrone would have posed, and for a minute it appeared that Tyrone had.

David was too busy trying to catch his breath to maintain his bearings. Did the others *see* it, *hear* it, too? Was this person really standing there, shooting words from his mouth? Were they too witnessing this event?

The room full of the faces all stared at David now. They were waiting for him to *say* something, do something. Moments passed, and David waited and he kept breathing deeply. He stared at the vision, expecting for it to vanish, or to suddenly sprout wings, to gravitate toward him, to journey him to a place of blinding White Light. But the vanishing never occurred, the wings never sprouted, and the White Light never appeared.

Another presence, a different young man in the room echoed the same question the vision had posed to David.

"Yeah. That must've felt a little empty if all you're about is the sex, and the nut . . ."

"The nothingness . . ." the vision finished.

It was all just a little too eerie now. That too would have been something *Tyrone* would had said to him. David thought it best not to run, or faint, or slide away inside some waiting insanity. Instead, it was best to breathe and challenge the invasion of this specter in the room.

"Yes," David began. "Sex is . . ." *Breathe, David. You can do this!*

Slowly, he found the will, and he forced himself to continue. "Sex without some real feeling attached, yes, it did begin to feel empty."

"Then why even do it? Why fall into that trap? You could've always masturbated. It least it's sex with someone you *love*. Or didn't you even *love* yourself?" the vision asked.

"Hey! Look, damn it!" *Breathe, David. Just breathe!* "Please don't judge me! I know all of us has felt empty at one time or another. It's a lonely feeling, being isolated, feeling unwanted and misunderstood. That feeling can leave you with a wicked hunger, not just in your genitals . . . but in your very *soul*! But you're told that you and that hunger and those feelings are wrong . . . and that it's sinful. You're told that you and your need to love *who* you love, in your own way, is ungodly. My father was a Holy-roller Baptist minister. Imagine that kind of torture weighing down my spirit."

Suddenly, David felt the need to testify before this specter with a younger Tyrone's face. His words became a kind of purging. He needed that vision to see and to *understand* him in an almost primal way. He didn't care that the room was filled with twenty-three other hurting people. His words were *intended* for this particular face.

"No matter what I did in my career, or how well I did it, I was still a useless, no good and sinful faggot. To many people, my name was *not* David. I was just '*that li'l faggot who dances on Broadway*.' I don't know. Sometimes I think, maybe that's my *Indian* name. But the size and sweep and breadth of my heart, *that* was not even a consideration. To hear them tell it, God Himself hated me! This is what I was told and what I lived with daily, nightly. That degree of emotional misery leaves a void in you. The void can be huge, and you think just maybe something physical, someone present, someone who knows the lonely taste of it can help you—help you fill that vacancy. Even in the most intimate act, for a few forgettable moments, you want to believe you'll be healed. I was so desperate back then. I needed to feel something close, and if only temporarily. And that, that's my story," he said.

It was time to go. As the room was emptying and others were putting on their coats, David, still unsure, still wondering if the young man real or just a mirage, asked, "Young brother. You, with the question, what's your name, son?"

The young man, looked directly in David's eyes and said, "My name is Kindred. You know—like *spirits*?"

And then he slipped on his hoodie over his head, and walked out of the door.

Had the angels sent him?

That night David dreamed of him. They two of them were inside some room. It was full of life and people and movement. As the dream became clearer, he realized they were seated in a busy classroom. In this vision, David was speaking with Tyrone. "Come out of your shell!" he kept repeating until finally he was screaming it. But the Tyrone in his dream placed his head upon his desk, and he appeared to be weeping. David touched his shoulder, and said, "I'll show you how to live again." But when the Ty in his dreams raised his head, it wasn't Tyrone anymore. It was *Kindred*.

Suddenly David awakened in a sweat.

He wanted to believe that this young man called Kindred was sent to him as a gift, from Tyrone. Maybe it was *his chance* to do their friendship over again. Maybe he could use this time to right a few wrongs. But even if this wasn't the reality, David desperately needed to *believe* it to be.

CHAPTER TWENTY-ONE

Sometimes Madness Wears A Familiar Face

When Kindred appeared, as he was apt to do at David's showroom, he said he was a student, looking for work.

"I'm very talented, man. I can fix things. I'm good with my hands. But I'll be honest with you—I don't know much about fashion."

Hmmmm . . . Neither did Tyrone.

"What I'm really good at is writing. I want to be writer."

Hmmmm . . . so was Tyrone.

David decided to take him to lunch.

"If you want to write, I know a few people who might be able to help. You'll have to *show* me your work, though. I don't want to put my *semi*-good name on the line, and speak highly about what you can do, if you can't "walk the talk."

"Ok. I understand. Thank you, David. I will show you what I've done."

"Coolness, Kindred. Coolness."

After that initial lunch date, David found himself staring at him on the street as they walked. It felt as if he were walking inside a dream. David's eyes were engaged in quizzical search for real and concrete things. His vision dragged the ground in hopes of seeing Kindred's shadow walking beside his own. He was both pleased and a bit unnerved to find Kindred did indeed cast his own. For moment, in a trick of sunlight, he thought he'd perceived a third shadow, a flash in a sun-drenched window. Was it Tyrone?

If it was Ty, David wasn't afraid.

In a getting-to-know-you conversation, he asked Kindred, " So, when did you *know*?"

"Know what?"

"Oh, baby. Don't be cagey with me! You *know* what I mean . . ."

"No. I don't. I'm not a mind reader, David. If you wnat to ask me something, just make it plain."

"Okay. All right, damn it! When did you know you were hetero-free? I mean, there had to be signs, right?"

"Signs?" he asked, scrunching up his face.

"Are you telling me you're *not a Friend of Dorothy's*?"

"Dorothy, who?" a confused Kindred asked.

David laughed. "Well isn't it queer?"

When One Door Of Happiness Closes, Another Opens; But Often We Look At The Closed Door And We Don't See The One Which Has Opened For Us.

David laughed. "I sit here looking at you, and it's like a dream. I can't even begin to tell you much you remind of Ty. I mean, damn! It's like I'm staring right at him, the *younger* him. And it's not scary or otherworldly so much as it is comforting."

"Tyrone, huh? They say everyone has a double somewhere. Tell me about mine. Tell me about your friend, Tyrone."

"Tell you? I'm not sure I could." David sighed. "I mean, there's so much I could say. But I'm sure I'll only . . ."

"Bore me? No. You won't. I promise," Kindred said.

David sighed again. He looked at Kindred, who resembled Tyrone so much to him, it almost felt like he'd be telling Tyrone all about Tyrone.

David smiled slowly and thought back to that Golden Time; and even God felt young again.

"Now that I think about it, we were kind of like these remarkable teens. Everyone said so. Ty, Facey, Browny and me, we were each unique in a way that made us fit, at least, when we sang. When our voices were raised in sweet music, seemed like no one and nothing could stop us.

"Tyrone was one of The Sensitives. Maybe he was a born introvert, but I did my best to try and change him, to ease away some of that tortured stuff. When you're a dancer, you're also a body-actor. You had to be observant—and you keep observing until it becomes a reliable muscle. People tell you the most intriguing stories and even their secrets, when they're not speaking, when they're just moving. And from day one, though Ty was *the writer*, I became the most observant student of the others."

"So, what did you observe about Tyrone?" Kindred asked.

"Ty? He was a kind and very gentle spirit. And he was a little afraid of letting people see him as anything else *but* kind and gentle. Of course, like everyone, he had a dark side. But he was better at *hiding* it than most players, or actors, or anyone else I ever met. Being *slightly* wicked, I tried my best to tap into his sleeping darkness. I did it—at first—for shits and giggles. Then, I did it to remind him that he was human, and thus, *not* perfect. While I'd strive for utter perfection on stage . . . in real life, I celebrated my imperfections. I will be the first person to tell you, 'I'm fucked up.' It is so freeing to admit that in yourself. I'd like to think that little of me and my fucked-upness rubbed off on him. And maybe a little piece of him made me *better*, li'l calmer. Not much, but a li'l."

"I think it did," Kindred smiled.

"When Tyrone spoke, he looked you dead in the eyes, and made you consider things. He was smart, but he wasn't so wise. He usually told you the truth of what he thought, unless he thought you were too fragile to take it."

"Could *you* take it, David?"

"Me? Take the truth? Please! Bring it on! I'd much rather someone to slaughter me with The Truth, than tickle my ass with the kindness of a lie. I was then, and always remained, wired to pick up the gist of bullshit.

"I see. I got that impression about you," Kindred smiled.

"Hey, I'm not saying I haven't been fooled before, but maybe I needed to be fooled."

The way David spoke those words, it was as if he were allowing the possibility of Kindred to be an *illusion*, and if he was, David would be ok with that. He stared into Kindred's eyes, and he spoke of Ty, as if to put Kindred or Ty's *ghost* on notice.

"People can only play you if *you let* them. But if you look them deeply in the eye, you can see their art, see the wheels spinning, watch the gestures. You can develop a talent for spotting the truth from the lies. Me? I've hung tight with the beautiful, the real, the flawed people . . . and those plug-ugly imposters."

Kindred said, "I think I know what you mean. Even as a kid, I watched people very carefully. And the one thing I've learned is, people want to put on their best face. But when you watch them when they don't *know* you're watching them, people can be a very revealing, and maybe little sad."

"Exactly!"

"That's why I want to be a writer," Kindred said. "I feel like I need to recite people, from inside out, to make them clearer for the world."

"Wow. Even that felt like something Ty would say. Maybe . . . just maybe you *are* his younger, more idealistic ghost."

David laughed, and then his face became weighted in concern. It occurred to him that maybe the idea of being Ty's or anyone's ghost was very disturbing to Kindred. David wanted to apologize. But he didn't, because a part if him *wanted* Kindred to *be* just that: Tyrone's second visitation on earth.

"So you wanna be a writer. Well, from what I've seen, writers are like these eternal teenagers, emotionally. No matter their age—they can take themselves wa-a-a-ay too seriously."

"Was Ty like that?"

"Oh, God yes! He took everything to heart. It was like he refused to get tough. Like being tough would damage his art."

"So, you thought he was weak?"

"Now, did I ever say that? No. I didn't think of him as weak. He'd been through a lot of stuff, and survived much of it. Was he a crier, or a wuss? No. But Ty could be hurt very easily, and try his level best *not* to show it. Maybe that's why he became a writer. He had so much he wouldn't express with tears, so he cried on paper. He loved carefully, but he loved hard. And he had an even harder time *forgiving* people if they disappointed him."

"Sounds . . . pretty uptight to me."

"Well, he didn't exactly have a stick up his ass, because frankly, he didn't like much of ANYTHING up his ass, but he was a little too stiff and mannered, and people saw that as arrogance, conceit, or privilege."

"I get that sometimes. People think I'm 'bourgie.' I'm not 'Black enough' for them. But to me, Blackness is a construction. My Black might be different than yours, or someone else's, but it's plenty Black enough for me. I don't do what most folks my age do, and I'd rather be alone than at a mindless party, with mindless people, saying and doing mindless things."

"Shit kid! You're only young once, and that youth is even more abbreviated if you're gay. So why waste it all being so damn dour and serious? Why not just *be* young and gay?

"Ummmm . . . David? Who says, I'm *gay*. Please, don't go confusing things, man."

"Oh. I'm sorry. It wasn't an accusation. But I'm rarely wrong about these things."

"It seems like you want me to BE Tyrone Hunter. I can't be. He's *dead*, remember? And even if you think we *look* alike, or want similar things out of life, I'm *not him*, David!"

"Understood," David replied, biting down on his bottom lip, sadly.

"My name is *Kindred*, not Tyrone. Do you *get* it now?"

"I get it. I do. Damn, you must really think I'm some crazy queen right now, don't you?"

"No. I don't. I think you miss your friend. I think you miss him inside your whole soul."

"You got that right," David replied, as he quickly wiped away a tear.

"I don't need to know Ty's entire life story today. It's not boring me at all. But it's too painful for you. I can see that now. I'm sorry, David. I guess I just wanted to know a part of his essence, and why you shared the kind of friendship you did," Kindred said earnestly.

It occurred to David that maybe one telling thing, an incident from their earlier life, would define who Tyrone Hunter was, and what would ultimately *become* of him.

"I'll tell you something real and true about Ty," he began.

"Ok. But only if you want to."

"Please. This is more for me than you. See, I believe a person is alive as long as you speak their name."

"Maybe that's true, at least in part. Nice to think so, anyway."

"See, Ty had a trick brow. A wrinkled frown would claim his forehead whenever he was thinking too much, or when he was angry, or when he was just being Ty. This was one of those things that kept him from being one of the truly handsome, at least physically.

"Anyway, it was Halloween. We were in our senior year. Just to get into the spirit of things, I took my young Ty to see Madame Zoreena. This woman was my guide, my guru, my girl in all things spiritual. Now, Madame Zoreena, she could be extremely mystical, with those dark liquid eyes and long, gray, flowing hair. She was black and something else mixed with it—part-Native-American and part-*witch*, maybe. She wasn't exactly a *pretty* woman either, and she could be more than just a little intense. But I trusted her with my life. I believed in her, and she always told me the *truth*.

"Ok . . ."

"So, when Madame Zoreena took a long look my long-faced furrowed-brow friend, she saw it as a serious flaw, and crossed herself, two times."

"What?" Kindred asked, furrowing his own brow.

"Yes, she did. To her, it was a kind 'curse.' With God as my witness, she said to Tyrone, " 'Young man . . . you need sit down and ask you mama what her worries were, and just what the problem was way back when, son.'

"Ty looked at her all quizzically and he furrowed his damn brow even more. Cocking his head, he asked, 'Problem? What do you mean by that?'

"Madame Zoreena said, 'Your mama, boy. She was all kinds of worried, and I do mean worried *plenty*, back when you were nesting in her belly, because son, all that worry, it sure enough shows on your face.' "

Kindred laughed. David laughed shortly after. It was their first real full laugh together.

"Oh, it was so hilaaaarrrrrious. Trust! I laughed my ass off. Ty, he just looked all hurt-up and confused."

"I can only imagine."

"But Madame Zoreena *wasn't* busting on him. She was my spiritualist, and the woman didn't have a humorous bone in her body. So she wasn't playin' the dozens, or being disrespectful to his mother. She was simply READING him."

"Ok. Reading him. I got you."

"So there was my boy, all perplexed and hurt-up, and growing even more pissed because I was laughing at him. Ty didn't want to come to that East Harlem parlor in the first place. So, he was leery of her and her mystical ways from the jump. Fact is—the woman just called 'em as she saw 'em. She probably saw or *foresaw* a lot more than she'd ever tell him or me or anyone."

"Really? She was *that* accurate?"

"To a tee. So, as we sat, she lit a candle for us, and she began to read Tyrone's untrusting and most dubious palm."

" 'You're going to make a lot of money, son,' she told him. 'More money than you'll know what to do with. You'll do some good things with it. But money won't change you, and it won't make you happy. That part's entirely up to *you*. There *is* such a thing as FREEWILL, you know.' "

"She grinned when she'd said that, like a gentle witch dispensing her wisdom and shit.

'There was a young girl, very pretty. I see you laughing with her, and it's summer. Not here in the city. Someplace else. Peaceful. She's a little older, wiser. But she loves you. She really loves you. You love her too. But you saw her as a sister. Didn't you? Well, there was that one time, that one night, when you didn't see her that way. Remember?"

"Ty shrugged his shoulder, like he didn't have a clue of what she was talking about."

Kindred began to fidget a little. Was it the subject of sex, or even the allusion to it which made him suddenly ill-at-ease? David wondered about this, but he didn't let on.

And then Kindred felt bold enough to ask, "But didn't you tell me that . . . Ty was . . ."

"Family? Yes. Ty liked men. But we all, well, *some* of us, slip sometime. Strange. But I never asked him about that one he saw as a 'sister.' What I did notice was *before* he shrugged it off, Ty had nodded vaguely, but uncomfortably, almost as if he was starting to *believe* Madame Zoreena's words. It seemed to me that Ty was afraid to look her in the eye. And that was weird," David recalled. "Because Ty always looked people in the eye."

"And you . . . what did you do, David?" Kindred asked.

"Me? I just sat there, resting in that knowledge that she was right. But, *then*, all of the sudden, those dark crazy liquid eyes went in back of her head. There is a cry in her throat. It started out real low, like a quiet humming . . . But soon it became this high-pitched, *crazy sound*. And I just knew . . . I mean, I KNEW she was *seeing* something—something in the future; something *we* couldn't see. Whatever that thing was, it made her shiver violently. She could be a *very scurry lady*, Madame Zoreena, most especially when she shivered like that when she caught a glimpse of *the future*."

"Stop! I've heard enough. You're trying to scare me, David."

But David would not stop. "Boy! You ain't seen or heard nothing yet! Because it was then that her head began to revolve on her neck and shoulders, first slowly, then faster. I'd seen her do that before. But what happened *next*, well, it should've made a *believer* out of Ty, because in the middle of her revolving head trick, the woman dropped Ty's hand like a hot rock. She held out both her palms, and SCREAMED. . . . And then, I swear to GOD—I saw FIRE!

"What?" Kindred asked in disbelief.

"Fire, I say! Real, hot, flickering fire! Bright orange, blazing red and this fiery glow was shooting out of this woman's palms! Oh Lawd! Talk about scared and yet hypnotized at the same time. The fire only lasted a second or two. The flame went all gold and faded into blue and smoke. I looked at Ty. He looked at me. I knew after seeing *this* he had to believe. But he rolled his eyes and frowned on me."

"If that's true, then it's pretty deep."

"Oh. It's true. And there was fire in Tyrone Hunter's future. Blue flames *did mean something*, especially when they shoot from a person's palm! That shit ain't normal, but it was *real*. And I'd never forget it."

"Neither would I."

"It didn't matter what we'd just seen in Madam Zoreena's parlor, though, because when we left, Ty still wasn't convinced."

" 'Man, the woman probably worked in a carnival. A sideshow circus tent, or something," he said in that dismissive Tyrone Hunter tone of his.

" 'But Ty . . . you saw it, didn't you? You saw that fire, right?' "

" 'It was a trick, David. It's just something she uses to scare people. Please. Don't you go believing in magic, or in tricks, Duch,' " Ty warned me as we were walking down West 110th Street. Oh trust, I did believe in magic—a few cute tricks, too. And I was very *sure* of my faith in Madame Zoreena.

" 'This New York City, Duch. It's full of charlatans and bullshit artists. What's next? Maybe you'll wanna go on to Forty-second Street and try our luck playing Three Card Monty? Don't be a sucker!'

" 'Hey. But next to dancing, being a *sucker* in the next best thing I do.' I winked.

Ty shrugged that Hunter shrug.

"It was then, right there in that moment, I began to see Ty differently. That furrowed brow became more noticeable than ever. Maybe it *was* his curse. A part of me also felt like I should *worry* about him, to look out for his welfare. It made me feel almost *maternal* towards him. That was the day I started calling him "Baby-Boy." He hated it, of course, and was quick to remind me he was older than me—which he was—by five months and seventeen days. But fuck it. He was "Baby-Boy" now, and for a good reason.

"I remembered what Zoreena said about 'happiness' and 'freewill.' Seemed to me, like this should've been very clear to him. I mean it was evident as The Empire State shooting over the skyline that she was saying, '*Happiness is a choice.*'

"Still, I recall how Ty shrugged his shoulders and brushed it all away. Here she was, trying to her *mystical* best to guide him, steer him toward a brighter future. And there he was, disrespecting her words of advice, making faces, and furrowing that brow and shit. It was as if her words were medicine, some vile castor oil, and he couldn't stand the taste of it."

There were beads of nervous sweat coating Kindred's forehead.

David noticed. "Madame Zoreena was never—and I do mean NEVER—wrong, baby. Not about *anything*. And as I live my life, I've seen that all things *do* come to pass."

CHAPTER TWENTY-TWO

INSANITY IS JUST A FLIP AWAY

The quaintness of Doctor Horowtiz's Village office had the look and feel of someone's country home. The western art, the geraniums, the books lined neatly in their mahogany cases, even the pale blue walls seemed designed to elicit comfort, as opposed to the sterile confines of the average mental help professional. For David it was all a trick, a ruse, a slick and subtle con to make his patients feel the comfort of home. And home was where most people felt free enough to speak with loosened tongues.

"Doc, I know for the last few weeks I've come here to moan and groan in your ear. It's been a *moaning* season for me. First there was Ty's passing, and Browny's published lies, and that Hunter witch, and the trial. Then came me ending it with Victor. That was a *rough* one. And just last week, young *Quincy* died. I tried not to lose my objectivity, but he was such a sweet, misfortunate soul. I came to care so much for him. At night, I even prayed for him. I wanted something better to come his way, because he *deserved* so much better than what he was given. Losing him so unexpectedly it, it's crushed my spirit, once again."

"I imagine it would, David."

"But just when things seem their bleakest, I met someone, and it feels like this small but beautiful miracle. Or maybe it's favor from God. But I feel so oddly lifted by his presence. It's like I can finally breathe and enjoy this chapter of my life."

"So. Are we in *love* again, David?"

"C'mon now, Doc! I don't fall in love *every* week– well, not anymore. And no, I'm not IN love, not in the romantic way. That would be very sick and très twisted, even for yours truly."

"Why?"

"Because, he looks *exactly* like Ty to me. I mean, the Ty I knew when we were young and foolish and full of dreams."

"Really?" The doctor exhaled. "And he's real? Flesh and blood? Not some dream or illusion?"

"No. He's real. Very real. And I don't think I *like* your *tone*, Baby-Doc."

"David, for a long time, you sat here telling me how you've seen Tyrone in the faces and postures and strides of others, how you thought you saw him on the street. So, it's perfectly normal to ask about the legitimacy of this latest sighting, isn't it?"

"Well, leave it to *you* to bring up *all* my past stuff. Oh, that's right. That's what you're *paid* to do, correct? To be honest, there has been a part of me that questions his realness. But he's not a ghost. He's not a figment of my imagination. He's real. God, *please* let him BE Real!"

"So, you're not so sure?"

"Nothing in this life is certain anymore. I mean, maybe Ty *didn't really* die in Africa. Maybe he was just hideously scarred. Maybe he had surgery to restore him to his younger self. Maybe he has amnesia now, but his spirit somehow led him back to New York, and to me."

"David? Do *you believe* any of what you're saying to me?"

"No. Not really." David lowered his head, despondedly. When he raised it again, he was wearing a very hopeful smile. "I'm speaking of miracles, and uncertainty, and how anything and *everything* is possible. Isn't it Doc?"

The doctor looked at David with a glance that could only be read as disappointment. It was always one step forward, and ten steps back with David. Hadn't all their time together, all the things they discussed and sometimes resolved made him a more stable person?

"When I look at him, it's impossible not to think of Ty, but I TRY, I honestly *try* to see him as his own individual. But it's hard, because it's almost like he's the embodiment of Tyrone's second coming. He's very strange, though. He's almost *too mannered*, and it's like he's not of this time and place. But the odd thing is, unlike Ty, I don't have this overwhelming need, this urge to try to *corrupt* him."

"Well, that's a good thing, isn't it?"

"Not wanting to change people, to make them over into what we'd like and dream they can be? Yes. It's a good thing. I see it as a sign of me evolving. Maybe we're supposed to give up *some* fights. Some fights are useless. Maybe there's a *grace* in that realization."

"Grace is very important to you, isn't it David?

"*Grace* is everything. It's why we're here on the planet in hopes of achieving. Isn't that somewhere in the pages of all these books you'd been reading?"

"What about people like Fasion Brown? You no longer investing in his makeover? No longer wanting him to change?"

David refused to talk about Browny, or say his name, so he chose to speak in *general* terms. "I know I once wanted *certain* people to be a certain way. But, even then, it wasn't all about me. I wanted that for THEM . . . for their own happiness and sense of self. I do wish people could be who they are and *all* that they are, and some do manage that feat, while others always seem to fail so miserably."

"Yes. They do. Self-actualization, while desired, isn't such an easy place to get to, David."

"Really, Doc? Tell me about it." David chuckled, just a little.

"So, this new friend, the one with Ty's face, if you see no need to change or to reinvent him into Ty's likeness, then that is indeed a good thing."

"Yes. Not to get all *Jennifer Holiday* about it, but, 'I'm ch-a-a-ann-ging,'" David sang. Then he stopped to deliver another wonder-filled tidbit. "Oh. I haven't told you the *best* part, Baby Doc. And this oughta kill any thought you might hold that *Kindred* isn't real . . ."

"'Kindred? 'Oh. Is that your new friend's name? How very . . . ummmm . . . interesting."

"Yes. Isn't it just? Well, Kindred wants to be a serious writer. He's shown me some of his poetry, his articles, his stuff. The kid is very, very good. Again, it's just another strangely *Ty-like* quality. He's very sensitive, and very much IN the moment. After reading what he'd written, we've discussed the possibility of him doing a book. A biography on me, on Ty, on Facey, and yes, even that dreaded *other* one. I mean . . . the *real* story about Da Elixir, and the years after we disbanded. I figure, who knows how long I have left here, and if someone is going to tell my story, and our story, shouldn't it be someone I *trust*, and someone who's objective?"

"So, you *trust* this Kindred?"

"Oh yes. God yes! Well, I do trust him far more than I do that deluded Brown Bastard! And when you think about it, the time we came into prominence, and then the hope, the youthful ambition, the innocence, the sex, the decadence, the greed, the dawning of this strange disease, there *must* be a story there. Don't you think?"

"It doesn't matter what I think, David. What do *you* think?"

"You're right. It doesn't matter what *you* think. I know you're sitting there, deciding in your own quietly analytical way that I've lost what's left of my mind. I know by the way you question me that you doubt that Kindred even exists. Well, maybe he doesn't. Maybe this is all just more bullshit from me. Maybe my mind's playing with ghosts, and maybe you or someone should have me committed. And I'm only half-joking here, because if any of this ain't real, then I have indeed flipped that final script into insanity."

When David left Horowitz's office, he walked through Washington Square Park. His head was full of Ty memories, Ty conversations, and Ty impressions. He'd taken to carrying some of Ty's journals with him most everywhere. They were like carrying a little piece of Tyrone Hunter inside his knapsack. He sat on a bench, and he watched the activity of life moving, playing, running, laughing, strolling, loving all around him. From some reason his eyes settled on a homeless man with a tin can his toes dirtied by asphalt, sticking out like the heads of turtles from the tips of his ragged sandals. David went into his backpack, and flipped opened a page in Ty's journal.

Ty wrote:

Sometimes, when I look inside the eyes of my people, I see a hunger there. It is a palpable and vulnerable hunger. It only shows in those few reckless seconds when we forget ourselves and relinquish our guards. The masks we wear to hide our desire, our dissatisfaction, our rage, our hunger, those masks are compulsory. They are essential, necessary accoutrements in this city. We sometimes gag our mouths to muffle our screams. We sometimes jazz our bodies with junk and dreams. Without them, without the belief in their possibilities, we might die, slowly; die before we sound our terrible screams loud enough blow out 200 million eardrums. But we won't just die, damn it! We will not meet our demise before we strike, before we blind our prey with the razor-sharp light of a thousand Egyptian suns. Why, you ask? Because damn it—we are so hungry, so tired, so sick and divided. And we've been angry and muffled into silence for too damned long!

You will never see us sweat, never know when we are most upset, yet the most violent implosion might be in full effect. Do not stare at us too deeply. This hunger in our eyes might just cut you to the quick. Beware of this hunger in my people. You are one who put it there. You'll receive no other warnings but this: Beware!"

It was a very dark collection of words and thoughts and ideas. David couldn't decide just who Ty was talking about. Was it the rage of Black people, gay people, the disaffected people in the city? This hunger Ty wrote of, David saw it in that homeless man's eyes. And he even recognized a hunger of his own, a hunger for love, for understanding in his soul, and a hunger for the simple delight of company.

Was he *so hungry* for company that *he'd* devised a new Tyrone from the ravages of his broken heart and from the loneliest corners of his own imagination?

Did Kindred *really* exist? Was he only a manifestation? He seemed so real to David, so tangible, and so like Ty. But if he didn't exist, it was indeed a disguise within his own mind, then that hunger inside of David would become sad and dangerous thing. And like Tyrone had warned, the world outside David Richmond's eyes had better "BEWARE!"

Why? Because sometimes insanity really *was* just a flip or the blink of an eyelash away.

CHAPTER TWENTY-THREE

A Tricky Little Dance Called Truth

Gradually David had begun to make Ty's haunted apartment his own. The once gold walls were painted a racy red, because red was the color of fire and the spirit of energy. There were portraits and pictures of famed Black dancers, and a large print of David leaping in mid-air. Yet, the traces of his friend hadn't all disappeared. Some of Tyrone's African masks, his busts, and antifacts remained, along with a few previous photographs and kente cloth remnants; but there were new rugs on the floor, and an ambience of exuberance, and not the staid dreariness of Ty's previous life.

Kindred had dropped by David's apartment with plans for the two of them to venture out for an afternoon of skating. It had been David's idea. It was once something David and Ty had delighted in, and if David and Kindred were going to write this book together, they needed to spend time doing Ty/David things to help revive the memories.

But when Kindred arrived, David's leg was bothering him again. It amazed him how getting older affected those parts of his body he'd once placed the most faith in, especially when he was younger and more than a li'l *spry*.

Not a single day or night went by that he didn't recall that magic-turned-maddening summer. The *Summer of My Great Fall*, he called it.

"David, you're walking very funny, man," Kindred said.

"No. I'm *not* walking funny! I'm gay, damn it, and this my sashay, so act like you know!"

"Seriously, what's going on with you? I can tell something's wrong."

"Nothing, kid. I've just grown old, sick and decrepit in New York City."

Kindred just looked at him, in that slightly irritated Tyrone-like way. "If you're looking for pity, I'm not holding that party. If you'd rather not go out, it's ok. We can stay here. Or if you want to be alone, I'll go. But please don't tell me nothing's wrong, David. I know that's a lie."

"Ok, Kid-with-Ty's face. Or ghost of Ty, or Kindred, or whatever your REAL name is . . . you asked. So, I'll tell."

Kindred walked in and took a seat, next to a photograph of David and Ty. The irony was not lost on David that he'd be finally telling the truth to *both* those haunting images of Tyrone.

"It's all very long-ago in a painful past life. But every good injury deserves a decent war story. People expect that, and my story's no different. When it happened to me, I saw a need to be *inventive*. I had to recreate a face-saving scenario to shield the embarrassing truth of the incident."

"So, you lied?"

"Oh, I've fibbed and *sugar-coated* about few things in my time, but this was the only *real lie* I ever told Tyrone. I needed to, because sometimes the truth is just too damn painful. Well, I'll tell you. The truth was this . . . This is the TRUTH:

"I'd been dabbling, as was my way, with a handsome

young papi named Hector. Aye Caramba! Hector. He was tall, dark, hot as a jalapeno. Hector the hefty and oh-so-heroically hung."

" 'Ummm . . . too much information, David. But continue . . ."

"We met at one of my fave spots, Esuelita's on West Thirty-ninth and Eighth Avenue. It was then, and still remains, a hot papi-shopper's paradise.

"Hector could dance his thick ass off, and of course, so could I. Oh, baby! We scorched the floor that night; a hot night of hot music, hot striptease and hotter lights. Somehow we fit, we clicked, we kicked it, and we were soon happily humping in Hempstead."

"Wow. That was quick. Not judging you, man. Just an observation."

"Well, Kindred, I really hope you *don't* judge me, ever. But I'm only gonna tell you the truth . . . and I expect the *same* from you. Anyway, Hector and I were engaged in a freaky fit of sexual inventiveness on a spiral staircase. It was all so good, so hot, so right. I mean *muy caliente*, baby! But then, the friction became too intense, so intense, so powerfully in*tense*, that I, the dancer, put on this earth *to* dance, lost my prized sense of balance, and took a nasty header downward. AYYYYYYYEEEEEEEE! ! ! ! ! !"

"Oh, my God!" Kindred exclaimed.

"Yes. Oh, my God, Jesus, Mary and Joseph!" David recalled sadly. "That fall, that treacherous fall . . . that loud, long, lingering fall, it broke my left leg, in three places! That loud, long, lingering pain-wrenching fucking fall, ended my soon-to-be fuckin' stellar dancing career!

"Needless to say, I lapsed into a deep despair from which I would never, and will never completely recover. The emergency room was bedlam, and I was its head banshee. I screamed, I cried, I bemoaned and bellowed to the tragedy of it all. I was a mad and muttering mess. I wanted sympathy. I wanted some understanding. I wanted my *mama*, but she was long gone. I *needed* someone to understand. I needed my best friend, my confidant, my heart's other half. 'Where is T-y-y-y-y-y-y-y-y-y-y-y?' I cried."

"Ty, of course. You needed Ty." Kindred nodded.

"Yes, I did. But then, when the pain took a pause, when I was able to call him to tell him this terrible heart-shattering news, I realized, I COULDN'T tell Tyrone Hunter THE TRUTH."

"But why not? I don't understand, David. You say he was your best friend."

"Back then I thought Tyrone would only look at me, shake his head, shoot me the foul brow, and see me as some frivolously foolish fag foiled and fucked-up by his own fucking faggotry! Maybe he would never SAY it, but he'd think it the rest of his life. He'd wrinkle that fuckin' furrow of a brow and just kill me, slaughter me with its silent judgment."

"I see."

"So, I wondered, how would I *work* this? How, in this scary, crazy, stupid, mad, fuckin' unfair world would I tell my best friend that my career was DEAD? Dead, because I was careless, and I didn't cherish my art! Shit! As much as I hurt, and I hurt to my core."

"Why? I don't get it?" Kindred said.

"Well, it was how we meet, being two young artists, with dreams. It was what *bonded* us, what challenged us to be the very best we could ever be. He was the writer, penning his art, and I was the dancer, defining mine with my body. Maybe you have to *be* an artist to understand this. But it was what we were put here for. It was the *best thing* in us, and about us, and it connected us forever.

"I see. I do understand that."

"And so, that day, *I'd killed my* Art. I'd stopped *cherishing it* long enough to say 'fuck it,' literally. And the death of this thing in me, this beautiful thing I did with my art, it would have hurt Ty even more than it was killing me."

David paused, took a breath as he remembered the caginess of his own past actions.

"And so I, being blessed with a wonderfully creative mind, wove a tedious tale of a 'particularly treacherous step,' a leap I was trying to perfect that, in the end, that went all kinds and dimensions of 'horribly wrong.' Yes, it was a dirty-nasty-filthy lie, but at least then I could hold my head up high, and earn some much-needed sympathy."

"That's intense, David. Even for you. I mean, I still think you should have told him, and if he *was* the good friend you believed him to be, yes, he would've been angry at you. But in the end, you would've understood. Bad things happen to good people sometimes."

"Please, let me *finish*, kid! So, it was there, laid up in a cast from my swollen ankle up to my lovely, if promiscuous hip, I recited that revamped piece fictional bullshit to Tyrone. And trust me, the words were breaking BOTH our hearts."

David stared at the floor then. He stared at the picture of he and Ty. Only, Ty's image seemed to be mocking him, so he turned quickly away from it. Then he tried to look into Kindred's eyes. But it was too difficult for him to peer at Kindred's face and not *see Tyrone* staring back again.

"Ty gave such *great hugs*. He embraced and almost healed your spirit, your whole damn spirit with his hug. If I'd had any doubt that this boy was my BESTEST friend, that day, he stepped up and proved it to me. Love is a verb. *Please, remember* I said that: Love is a *verb*.

"Ty held me so tight inside that hospital bed, it was like he tried to adsorb my pain, to take it all into his own body, and somehow free ME from it."

"Wow. Good hug," Kindred said, as if almost envious of David, and he wished that he too could had known the power of Tyrone's deepest embrace.

"Great hug. And together, he and I, we sniffed, and we sobbed and we cried such bitter tears to the death of my long-standing dream. It was killing me: the hugs, the tears, THE LIE.

"That, was the only REAL LIE I would ever tell Tyrone Hunter—and I felt so fuckin' broken by it! I thought I'd found in Ty, that one person I could tell anything, no matter how crazy or sick or unflattering, and know it would be guarded from judgment. But I just didn't *trust* him with my ugly truth. Maybe the line of trust had its own invisible limit—invisible, until you crossed it."

And Kindred looked upon David with a mix of pity and envy.

"I don't have a best friend. I have people I know that I tell some things to. But if I had a best friend, I'd consider it a *blessing*. Tyrone was your Blessing, and maybe you didn't *see* that at the time."

"I suspected it then. But fear of rejection and judgment can make some people, even me, do less than honest things. I know now Tyrone *was* my blessing. And I should have told him. And I didn't. But, it all came out a few years later, because one day, I said something I knew, something that he'd kept from me. And when I said it, it was accustation. And when he told me he knew about my leg, it was . . ."

"What? Judgment?" Kindred asked.

"No. Not that. It was like this silent secret he'd held because he loved me too much to confront me about it."

"This man, Tyrone Hunter. He was a very special person. I wish I'd known him."

"Special. Maybe. But flawed and fucked up, too. Trust. I hope I'm not painting a picture of Ty The Saint. He wasn't. Tyrone had his *own dirt*, and he was keeping it close to his dingy little vest. And a very *unfashionable* little vest it was, because, after all those years, he'd never told *me* about it. And so, the tally in the naked honesty count was about even.

Ty had lied to me by omission, and I'd lied to him by creation. But the fact remained: my dance, my dream, my reason for being was done."

"This is all so sad, David. But that's the most tragic part of all," Kindred commiserated.

"That was a low, lowly low, abysmal period. I'm not very good with depression. When I get dark, it happens so seldom, that things turn inward. I become susceptible to all sorts of psychosis and vile, un-Davy-like shit. My train . . . it was lost. It roamed from station to station, john to filthy john, trying to soothe my inner affliction.

"And without singeing your young impressionable ears with my past scandalous behavior, I'll just say: sometimes all I could do was look into my cracked, stained mirror and cry those Why-did-I-ever-lay-down-with-this-musty-moody-macho-mad-motherfucker Blues.

"I purposely avoided Ty. I reasoned that Tyrone Hunter had ways of saying shit, without saying anything at all. Maybe he didn't judge me with words. But I knew his silences, and I was *way* too familiar with that brooding, disapproving trick-eyebrow of his. I figured he'd just quietly *moralize* everything to fuckin' death, just like my father, when his ass was in no way perfect!"

"Of course, he wasn't. No one is," Kindred stated.

"During my extended affair with disappearance, oddly enough, it seemed my absence sent Tyrone into writing mode. Maybe my tragedy or his loneliness, or both, made him find his *deeper* Art. Here. Read it and weep," David said, as he handed Kindred one in the series of Ty's journals. "Please, read it out loud."

Tyrone's Journal Read:

When I witness someone's brilliance, I am transformed. A part of me becomes a smaller thing, realizing I'm in the company of Greatness. It's like standing before some tall, lofty building and being diminished beneath its massive shadow. David's talent is a massive thing. Watching him dance is to watch brilliance in motion. I know whatever talent I possess dims when he is in the room. His sun eclipses my moon. He is my friend, my Homeboy, my Hero, and unquestionably, finest artist I know. David is blessed with that magic something. It puts the balls in ballet, and the 'azz in Jazz. It makes him taller, wider, and endlessly more sexy than the rest of us. When David dances, he becomes a different kind of beast. He is a glorious animal of movement from his arms and legs, to his neck to his back to his toes. Seeing that animal go to work is a thing to behold. It has always made me so fucking proud just to know him. Now, this! I just don't know who he'll be now, or what will become of him without the joy of dance.

When Kindred looked up from reading that passage, he saw David was crying. Weeping silently, and yet wildly. David thought back to that painful day and wished he could erase Hector and sex on spiral staircases completely from his orbit.

David had always known he was good. First, his mother praised him. She'd told him he was "blessed by God," and she made him *believe* it. Soon after, his dance teachers, though hard on him, they too praised his wondrous application and his flawless technique. Fellow students secretly worshiped him, and his friends were all in awe of him. Yes, David knew Ty *appreciated* his gift. Ty would often tell him, and he *meant* it.

What made this so much worse was that David never knew just how *much* Ty *respected* his talent, not really, not until the day he'd first read those words. And to know his tragedy was a lie, a convenient tale that he'd hatched for his own self-protection, it still broke his heart.

"How would Tyrone have felt if he'd known what really caused my career's suicide, back then? His sonnet would have been a tirade to his freakish friend David, the so-called *artist*, who risked a bright and promising career for a few mindless minutes of bliss."

"Maybe. Maybe not. You knew him. I didn't. But the person who wrote those words *loved* you, David. He deeply admired what you could do, but he LOVED YOU!"

"He believed the story his ears received. He believed in my lie, and so, he deeply grieved for me. How terrible! How tragic! How gullible!" David sniffed. "Ty did not place his trust in very many people. Those he did trust, they were Special. I was *special*. And being special, Ty arrogantly believed he *knew* me, and he did. But how many of us truly *know* a person, inside and out, Kindred?"

"I don't know. You have to trust that some will love us, regardless of what ugly, deceitful thing we've done."

Those words he said, they seemed more personally directed *at* Kindred, himself, than to David.

"He knew my heart, yes. But Ty wasn't schooled in the tricks of my mind. He had no knowledge of my potential for bullshit and deception, at least when it came to him."

"Everyone has that potential, I guess. Maybe you shouldn't beat up on yourself so much for being human."

"Are *you human*, Kindred? Are you *really* human, my young friend with Tyrone's face?"

"Deeply, naively so," Kindred said. And that was all he said.

After a month or so of meeting and talking about Ty, David, the group, and their past, David began to really trust and depend upon Kindred. How could someone who wore Tyrone's younger face *not* be trusted?

He took Kindred to dinner and a show at Café Wha. It was a lively vibe on a lively night, and David was feeling very happy and very much alive. And then, after the live musical performance, David made a ceremony of handing Kindred Ty's prized journals. The first stack of them would give a clear indication of what treasures remained untapped and unread. They were wrapped in shiny blue foil, with a purple ribbon binding them. It was a gift from the heart, and David wanted Kindred to see the purpose behind it.

Kindred was both stunned and deeply appreciative to receive this gift. He was also a little afraid of it. He knew the importance of such a large gesture. He also feared some of the things he might read, and he felt overwhelmed by David's expectations of *him* as a writer. Most of all, he was beginning to really like David, and the last thing he wanted to do was to hurt him. Maybe he wasn't up to the task of making a story, a full and enlightening book from those remnants, ruminations, and reminiscences of the past.

He thought about the way things were playing themselves out, and how close he and David had become. It was almost as if this was *destined* to be.

Yet, a look, a grave look of concern washed over Kindred's brow, and noting it, David said, "Don't worry. You'll do fine. I trust you, baby."

"I know you do. Thank you for that," Kindred uttered sincerely.

"Now, I was there, but I couldn't be everyplace at once," David said. "They'll be other people you'll read about. People like Facey Depina. Ty didn't *understand* him the way I did. In fact, I doubt if anyone understood him but me. The thing I don't want to see is for him to be portrayed as an empty pretty boy. That's what *Ty* saw. But I saw *more*. I *knew* more," David said mysteriously, as if he held the *real* secret to Face Depina.

"I understand."

"I was deeply in love with Facey, you know? But it was *my* love alone. In the end, I know he loved me, too. But it was different than what I'd carried around inside my chest, since, well, since forever."

"I don't know if I can write about love and make it real, David. I don't think I've ever been in love with anyone."

"Nonsense! Maybe you just haven't found your Long Blue Moan, yet. No. Don't ask me what that is. It's all in the journals. In fact, *love* is all in the pages of those journals. Love isn't perfect, and it's not supposed to be. But it was something Ty and I shared. It's love that has me living in *his* haunted apartment, and love that made him leave *me* his estate. It's love that makes me want to be *tender* with those memories. And my memories of Facey are very precious to me too. I have pictures, such beautiful pictures of him. If you look at them long and hard enough, you'll *see* what was lovable about him. But you'll also need to speak with Bliss."

"Bliss?"

"Yes. Bliss Santana. She loved him too. Loved him madly. Still does, sad woman."

The idea of speaking to or meeting with anyone else but David was another cause for concern in Kindred.

"What *is it* with you? I mentioned Bliss, and your face just fell."

"Can't we just keep this between us, just you, me and the journals, David?"

"Well, we could, but it wouldn't be the most *objective* point of view. And that's why speaking to Bliss is needed. And Lawd help us, you'll also need to talk to Faison . . . umm, the Brown Bastard as well. I'll hate it with a passion, but it's unavoidable. He was a member of Da Elixir."

"Ummm . . . David," Kindred hedged, as he scratched his head the same way Ty used to do, when he was stressed. "I'm sorry. I'm really, really sorry. But I don't think I can *do* this. I don't know these people, and they don't know me. Knowing *you* has been enough. That's all I ever wanted . . . to know *you* . . . and Ty."

He slowly slid the journals across the table and back into David's grasp.

"Thanks for the dinner and the show. Goodnight."

And with that, Kindred rose and left the café, leaving David dumbfounded, hurt, and more than a little curious.

David's mouth was still agape. He didn't know what to make of this scene. He needed to examine the sequence of events and identify how and why things went so wrong, so quickly. Had he done something, said something wrong? No. David hadn't. But something was keeping Kindred *away* from the others. What?

In the midst of the room's swirling activity, the laughter, the talk, the energy, the sound of New York grew and mounted and reached a screaming cacophony in his skull.

David sat at the table and he pondered what had just occurred.

A man on stage blew a horn, and the sound of that horn became a moan. And the sound of that moan began to haunt David slowly.

What had he *said?* He'd only asked that Kindred meet with Bliss and Browny, and then, the climate inside that room grew colder. David had perceived it. And now, that damned *ghost feeling,* it was happening again. Maybe Kindred didn't want to meet with Bliss or Browny, because perhaps they wouldn't or couldn't *see* him. Maybe *only David* could see him. Was Kindred real or just another hopeful illusion? Was he something David's fragile mind conjured up from a need so strong to reconnect with Tyrone, and to the past again?

The more he thought about this, the more cause for alarm sounded with his soul's place.

He wondered, *Why doesn't Kindred ever want his picture taken?* He wondered why had they only met at David's job, or David/Ty's apartment, and why was it always just the *two* of them . . .

Was he really going crazy? Just when life was beginning to make sense again, was David finally falling through that trapdoor of reason and straight into the snake pits of insanity?

CHAPTER TWENTY-FOUR

IF CRAZY WERE A COMPETITION

For David, it was time to see a new face, a different face, a face that didn't resemble Ty, or his shrink, or the boys in the session. He wanted and needed the presence of someone ultimately feminine. He wanted his mother, but she too was so long gone that she wasn't even a ghost. He needed a voice, a face, some lucid sense of humor. And suddenly, he thought about Bliss Santana.

Her apartment was, in its typically New York Upper Westside way, elegant. The building and some of the furnishings had been featured in *Architectural Digest*. The rooms were large and the high ceilings were spacious enough to produce an echo. There books, lots of books, and photographs with the swells, the actors and playwrights, the high-heeled boys of New York's theatrical circles. There was even a piano. The motif was art deco, like something out of Hollywood in the 1940s. Bliss was not trying to put on a show; she simply like to lived in an air of manicured luxury.

"I needed to see you, Bliss. It's been ages. How you been, girl?"

"Since the show closed, I been mulling over my next project," Bliss said matter-of-factly. David knew that 'next project-speak' all too well. Bliss was yet another unemployed New York actor.

"What's going on with you, baby?"

"Well, I may be just going crazy."

"Oh. Really? Been there. Done that. Got that crisp, sterile, Bellevue T-shirt to show for it."

"See? That's why I like talking to you. You don't judge me. You *get* crazy! I need to be around people, people who GET crazy. Please, tell me this: Is there some sign, some warning for when that shit actually starts happening?"

Bliss looked at him. She gazed at David deeply in his eyes.

"Well, you don't have the *crazy eyes*, yet. No glazed eyeballs swimming in a sea of white. So, I think, you're all right, baby."

"Seriously?"

"Damn. You sound *disappointed*."

"I guess I just wanted and needed a good crazy bitch's opinion."

"Well, you just got it. And I'm a crazy bitch from way back. Just ask Pascal."

"God, I wish I could," David said in a hopeful tone.

"You know, I can say his name now, and not lose my breath, or fall into some strange delusional sadness anymore. God! I wonder when that stopped happening? Maybe it was today."

"I think of him every day of my life. I'm sure I always will. And it's so rare that the people we went to school with still linger through our days."

"You mean, like Ty?"

"Exactly like Ty. God! If I think of Facey every day, and trust me, I do . . . then I must think of Ty every five fuckin' minutes."

"I miss Tyrone sooooo much. That was my Honey Boy. He was such a calming influence on me, even at my craziest. And those eyes of his. People always made such a big thing over *Pascal's* eyes. Yes, they were green and lovely and played such brilliant games with the light. But Tyrone Hunter's eyes, God! There was a *real soul* behind them. They accepted me. I *miss* the understanding that lived so deep inside those eyes. So, yes. I think of Tyrone often, too," Bliss confessed.

"Well it's Tyrone, and not being able to shake him that's making me slowly lose my mind, Bliss."

"Missing someone isn't a mental illness, baby. It if was, we'd all be committed to sterile rooms with padded walls. Trust me."

"Well what if missing them brings them *back* from the dead? What then, huh?"

"Then, I'd say you're pretty damn lucky, especially if it's *Ty* back from the dead."

David held his head. "You don't understand, Bliss. Listen to me, mami. For months, I'd been *seeing* Ty. Not really Ty, but people reminding me of him. It was everywhere I went. And then, one magically scary crazy day, I meet someone who could *be* the reincarnation of him. I mean, the younger Ty, to a tee! He even wants to be a writer."

"Really?" Bliss asked, her voice raised in intrigue.

"Yes. Really. It's incredible. But maybe it's just a little *too* incredible. I think he may be a ghost. I think I may have imagined him. But he's *so real*, Bliss. I swear, he's so real. And I wanted *you* to meet him to talk with him, to *see the Ty* in him. But when I told him this, he bolted. I haven't seen or heard from him since. And that leads me to believe I've imagined him. And if I did, well . . ."

"Then . . . you're *crazy*? No. Not crazy, David. Lonely for Ty? Desperate to see a piece of him in others? Maybe. But not crazy. And who knows, maybe this person really does exist. Maybe he's just painfully shy or something."

"Yeah. Maybe."

"Well tell me this: do you FEEL like you're losing your mind, most times?"

"Most times I feel like I'm dreaming. I dream a lot. Good shit, horrible shit. Sometimes even *hopeful* shit."

"Well, damn you for dreaming so hopefully!" She laughed in that husky rich Santana laughter. "Listen to me now. You're *not* crazy, David. Besides, I really don't see *you* going for quietly insane trip. You're waaaaay too much of ham of that weeping willow in a corner bullshit. You'd be opting for the raving, rabid, foaming-at-the-mouth shit-house-rat genre of *madness*! Okay?"

"Thanks, Miss Blissy."

"It's funny though," Bliss pondered. "Because I have some very real *dreams* about losing *my* mind. It's such a hard thing to do, just to remain sane sometimes."

"Tell me about it!"

"Imagine it: I am wile and running naked through the streets of Gotham, wearing only my tightest black thong, and my fave rhinestone tiara, Krazy-glued to my skull. Oh no, the tiara shall *not* be moved!"

David laughed.

"I'll babble the prerequisite 'Michelangelo' as I zoom, tits flopping wildly through the Village for a bit. This, of course, is my preamble run, before my *real* sprint into craziness truly commences, and by then, all bets are off, baby!

"My high, crazy voice will pitch in a siren, a madwoman's howl at an ear-splitting decibel. I'ma be W-I-L-E! Ya heard me? I'ma be runnin' with a scream so loud on my lips, they'd hear it all the way in Hoboken, and parts of Jersey City. Trust! I'ma tear up some shit too, cause some shit needs some tearing up. I'ma bust up a few ritzy store windows—and sound the clanging alarm to a jewelry store or two. I'ma go on the most wicked of rampages not seen since the gangsters of the '30s. I'ma Bonnie Parker 'em. I'ma be a moll and a gangsta of m-a-a-d love, running and scoopin' up homeless men, boy whores and riffraff, grabbing hipsters and derelicts. I'ma be kissing babies and strangers, grabbing grand dames and bussin' 'em passionately on the lips. Oh, my crazy will be very dangerous!"

"Actually, it sounds like fun. Can I come?" David chuckled. It felt good to chuckle.

"Please. I don't do duets. You'll have to manifest on your *own* damn crazy, baby. Tell me, what's your idea of going off?"

David thought about it, as he often did, and he didn't freely share such thoughts with anyone outside the confines of Dr. Horowitz's office. But with Bliss, he felt he could.

"Well, much like you, I'll be running around naked, manhood flopping in the New York breeze, screaming: 'I'm not sick. This world is sick!' I'd dare any homophobic cop to come at me and try to tame my mad ass down! I'ma turn around fuck 'em up, show 'em how little black fags with holy-roller daddies learned to fight to the death, even when our fists are bloodied. And of course, eventually, this craziness would have to be harnessed. A mad black semi-famous faggot, running amok? Even the decadence of New York City could not afford the inappropriateness of all that, and so, the net would be a must. Yes, a net— and I ain't talkin' 'bout no Ms. Funnicello!"

"Yes, a net would be a *must* for you!" Bliss howled. And it felt so good to howl again.

"And the men in white coats would speedily arrive in a snow-white low-rider. They come to cart my madness away. All of them would be staggeringly handsome papas, with noticeable bulges, all the while clutching those requisite nets. I'll be too busy grinding my mad, yet still risqué nakedness against their piping-hot crotches, before they wrestle me into my custom-tucked straightjacket, direct from Bloomie's fall collection, of course."

"Oh, but course," Bliss concurred.

Then the light of David's giddy mood darkened with some slow internal shade, as he said, "But lately, I've been thinking, maybe crazy isn't quite so colorful or half that dramatic. Maybe crazy is a quiet place, full of water, and wind and rain. And the wind inside my head cries in a sad and prolonged moan."

Just then, Tyra, Bliss's daughter entered the room, and asked, "Mommy? Can I have some cereal? Pleeeeeeeeeeeeeeeeease?" She smiled and batted her light green eyes at David.

"Well, since you said the *magic* word, the answer is yes. But first, say hello to my friend, David."

"Well, Hello, Miss Tyra. You sure are a pretty girl," David said, his mouth fixed in a slow smile, and eyes beginning to hold back tears.

"Thank you, Mr. David. You want some cereal, too?"

"No, thank you. But you enjoy it, ok?"

She stared at him, as children do, as if trying to decide if she liked him. "I will, Mr. David."

And for some odd reason, she skipped over to the couch where he was sitting. She wrapped her little arms around him and softly kissed his cheek.

A surprised David sighed, "Thank you, Ms. Tyra. You don't know how *much* I needed that."

"Now, get out of here, ya little flirt!" Bliss teased.

And Tyra waved good-bye to David, and she skipped merrily away.

"My God. Oh, my God!" David exclaimed.

"Yes. I know," Bliss nodded.

"No. I don't think you do. I was like HE just kissed my cheek. Like HE let her know, that crazy or not, it was okay to . . . *love* me."

The tear that David had somehow managed to keep suspended suddenly fell.

CHAPTER TWENTY-FIVE

HE COULD ONLY PLAY THIS SCENE ONCE

Film is a haunting medium. The one film in which Face Depina had received his most glowing of notices was playing on the IFC cable channel. For those who knew and loved those people who act, it was a kind of hurting thrill to see them so active, so riveting and so beautiful, and so alive again. Film is a haunting medium. No doubt the family and friends of people who've passed on feel a certain irony in watching those dead loved ones alive and emoting in color, for the world to see. It was no different for David or for Bliss to watch Face Depina. Film was a haunting medium.

As it happened, his daughter was becoming more and more curious about him. Bliss kept a black and white photograph of she and Face on her dressing table. That very day, Tyra bounded into the den, carrying the picture behind her back and smiling mischievously.

"What's that you're holding, baby girl?"

"This!" she said, producing the framed photograph.

Bliss was suddenly startled by that picture and its memory.

"You look pretty. Mommy . . . tell me about my daddy."

Bliss sighed and mentally counted to ten. Earlier, she'd overheard an conversation Tyra had with one of her playmates.

"Where's your daddy at?" the little girl had asked.

"In the picture," Tyra had replied as she continued coloring in her book.

"No. Where is he at right now? At work?"

"No. He's in heaven," Tyra answered, matter-of-factly.

"Heaven? For real? How do *you* know?"

" 'Cause my mommy told me. And my mommy never lies."

Bliss was so proud of Tyra in that moment. She'd tried to never lie to her child about anything, including the frequent check-ups, the nasty medicines, and the time spent away from school.

She'd told her daughter, "You have a virus . . . a bad virus, and it makes you tired and you'll feel sick sometimes. But you're strong, and you'll get better. The doctors said so, and I promise you this. And mommy never lies to her baby girl, right?"

And now, Tyra was asking for more truths; truths about the father she never knew. She handed Bliss the picture and snuggled up beside her on the bed.

"Well, as you see here, he was a very, very handsome man. Everyone thought so. He was as handsome as a shining prince."

"So you were a princess, Mommy?"

"Umm . . . I thought you knew. I still *am*, baby girl."

Tyra smiled, and Bliss felt her heart grow full at the sight.

"And when he smiled, just like you're smiling now, oh, he made me . . . so happy. And he was very tall."

"Even taller than you, Mommy?

"Yes," Bliss chuckled sadly. "Even taller than me."

"What else you got?" Tyra asked, pulling on her mother's blouse.

Bliss chose her words carefully.

"Well, he liked to *play* pretend. He was an actor, just like mommy."

"Did he love you . . . *this* much?" Tyra opened her little arms as wide as a four-year-old child possibly could.

Bliss paused and looked inside her daughter's inquisitive eyes. Out of the mouths of babes often come the deepest of inquires; the kind that make even educated adults ponder. It was a painful question, a question she herself never knew the real answer to.

"He loved me . . . as *big* . . . as he could, baby girl."

"And did he love *me* too?"

"Oh, he would if he saw you. You look just like him. And knowing *your* daddy, that would make him very, very happy."

Later in the day, Bliss called David.

"Hey baby. The film is on tonight. Are you planning to watch it?"

"Yes. God yes! I loved that performance. Well, maybe 'loved' isn't the right word. But he showed the world what he was capable of in it."

"I know."

Film was a haunting medium.

"He was so . . . in his element, and such a commanding presence in that film. And when that scene comes on where he grieves his mother, oh my God! People have gotten *Oscars* for lesser work. That was a triumphant performance. Very real. Very Facey."

"Yes. I know . . . and I was thinking, maybe I'd let Tyra see it now. She's so curious lately. She's seen loads of pictures of him, but she has no memory of his voice, or the way he moved, and anything concentrate to say, 'That's *him*! That's my daddy. Isn't he something?' And I *want* that for her. I really want her to *know* the *best* in him. What do you think?"

"Me? You're asking me? I really don't know, Bliss. I mean, wouldn't seeing him so alive, make her think he IS alive? I don't know, so I'm just asking."

"She understands her daddy's in a place where he can't come back. But seeing him alive on a screen, it might be confusing to her, too. You're right. I don't know what to do."

"Maybe you could ask her if she'd like to see her daddy, when he was here, and doing his job of playing pretend," David suggested.

"Yes. Good idea. I'll do that. Thanks, David. So, how are you, baby?"

"Oh, I'm hangin' in, mami. You know how I do."

"Hey, ummm . . . would you like to see the film over here?"

"Nah. I like my own quiet time with Facey. That movie always makes me a little sad, and I want wanna be sobbing my ass off over there. I have my own sobbing place here. Ok?"

"Ok, baby. Take care. Bye-bye."

"Good-bye, Bliss."

Film *was* a haunting medium . . . and for some, it was more haunting than others. David knew the back-story to that film better than Bliss or anyone now.

Pascal "Face" Depina's mother Mattie had died being birth to him. For the sin of breathing air, Pascal's father Alphonse would never forgive him. His very existence was the cause of his mother's death, and so the father had no use for him, or the memory he induced. The elder Depina dropped the boy off at his sister's apartment, and he proceeded to slowly commit suicide by way of drugs, drink, and treacherous chemistry.

As a child, little Pascal had been bounced like an unwanted kickball from place to hard-luck place. He never had a real foundation or any sense of permanence. Being exceedingly pretty drew others to him, but the child learned never to rely on anything, or *anyone*, or any feeling hanging around and existing for the long run. All friends, family, lovers—people in general—had expiration dates.

And so, with that history and other darker episodes, he would become an actor.

In the film, Face Depina had some tough scenes, one of them requiring extreme emotional pyrotechnics.

When he'd arrived in Los Angeles, though closeted, Depina was already an addict. He'd been trying to wean himself away from heroin's seductive teat, but the pain coiled up inside him, weakening his charm, making him nauseous, difficult, and withdrawn. A day without smack was a day too long and distressing. What he needed was a little speedball, just to take off the edge . . . *Just one*, he thought, *and I can do this shit.*

When he strode back onto the set, his eyes were green windows, cracked by the telltale vandals of coke and smack. He stood with legs heavy as rocks, calling upon his inner strength, willing his brain into focus.

Sometimes all a man has left to *trust* are his bones. He trusts them to guide him, push him forth, and suddenly he's walking, talking, putting on his own Personality Light Show, until no one knows he's a crumbling fraud. Face did this to remarkable effect. Most *functioning* junkies did.

In that pivotal scene, the *lying* character he played had come home to find his mother dead; murdered in her front yard.

It was a hard scene to depict. The script required a degree of depth, emotional surrender, and yes, real tears. And so, seeing this mother figure lying there, her lifeless body stilled by *his* lie, a lie he'd told to a group of vicious hoods, he began to cry. He stooped and he roared and he slobbered in loud, savage, guttural grunts. He raged and wailed, he babbled in smears of snotty chatter. He cried and screeched, and he lamented the most brilliant tears a half-black, bisexual, closeted junkie had ever dared to cry, on-screen.

But was it *acting* or was it something closer to a public breakdown?

Those sounds he made, those rants, howls, and caws of the heart and soul, they were *outside of human*. He was more authentic than Brando, Pacino, Dean, or Denzel. Few men ever had the balls to reveal *that kind* of emotive intimacy.

He could only play that scene once. Luckily once was more than enough.

"Cut! Beautiful, Facey! Just beautiful. That's a print!"

But the wild tears didn't stop for Face. Every crippled feature in his aspect darkened, reddened, and wept. He crawled into a small fetal ball, and wept uncontrollably.

Witnessing this very real breakdown, and fearing for Face's sanity, a co-star ran over and tried to provide a comforting arm. But Face didn't want to be touched. How dare he or any of those others Hollywood motherfuckers touch him! He swung his arms wildly and he howled, "GET YOUR MOTHERFUCKIN' . . . . HANDS OFF ME! YOU AIN'T . . . YOU AIN'T . . . YOU AIN'T . . . MY DADDY!"

From deep within, he found the strength to rise from the floor and then he bounded away from the set.

In an attempt to lighten the atmosphere, the Assistant Director shouted to the crew, "Oh! Those fuckin' New *Yawk* actors!"

But this was not acting, New York or otherwise. This was Face Depina's Blue Moan, personified. This was the unleashing of a long, restrained and primal cry.

Face Depina was, at his core, a user. In rare and coldly sober interludes, even *he* knew that. Only, this time, he'd used and abused his tender, unformed memory of the mother he'd never cried for. But this one particular act of using burned like a branding iron. How does a boy, or a man, any *real man* recover from that?

Yet for that fit of naked emotion, the film critics loved him.

Six months later, Pascal "Face" Depina received an Independent Spirit Award Nomination for Best Supporting Actor.

Film is a haunting medium.

Faison Brown was lying in bed, clicking his remote when he stumbled upon that movie. It sickened him to see Face Depina's mug again, yet something *compelled* him to keep on watching. He'd never saw this movie before. It was the flick everyone else always talked about. Maybe he wasn't such a bad actor after all. The camera loved him, even when he was at his most pitiful. If Browny were being honest with himself, he would have to admit that it was a good movie, and that "Face Depina rocked that shit, yo!"

Juanita came in from just finishing her night shift, and there she saw Browny, her "Honey Bear" lying in bed, on the verge of tears.

"Baby, what wrong with you?"she asked. "Did, did somebody die?"

Browny couldn't seem to tell her, it was the friendship that had died. Maybe it was stillborn before it ever began. But the man on that TV screen moved him, made him wonder about what could have been.

"I know that ain't that Face Depina on my TV!"

"Yup," Browny sniffled. "That's that bastard."

And because it was nearing that key scene, the part where Face broke down and sobbed so uncontrollably, she too became riveted.

"See? Now *that's* how he woulda cried if I hadda kicked his punk ass!"

Browny looked her and smiled sadly. "That's because you Bonnie . . . and I'm Clyde, yo."

"You got that right," she said, pushing him over and lying next to him.

The weight of the bed shifted violently.

"Damn. He really is *bitchin' up*, ain't he?" she noted.

"Yup. Fo *real*, yo."

"I remember that day I paid him a visit. He was all strung out on that shit, and talkin' shit. I had to put him in his place. Funny . . . I always knew he was a bitch . . . but . . ."

"Shhhh, baby. Just watch, yo!" Browny said.

Juanita felt like smacking him *hoard* him upside the head for shushing her like that, but then she noticed that Browny was in some sort of trance just watching that face. For a moment it concerned her a bit. She thought she'd saw a trace of a sad love affair playing in her husband's eyes. And she wondered to herself: *Was he funny for that Face Depina, too?*

The final scene was freeze frame of Face Depina's long, lanky body leaning against a post of his dead mother's home. He was smoking a cigarette and looking forlornly into the sunset.

Powerful image. Film is a haunting medium.

Browny could not control his tears.

"Look at cha. You's snifflin' like a li'l thug bitch, yo!" Juanita laughed.

Browny didn't. It was a history thing.

CHAPTER TWENTY-SIX

EVEN PUNK BITCHES HAVE THEIR STORIES

That night after watching Face Depina be brilliant, for David, a distraction was needed. He wanted to go out. More than this, he wanted to find someone, some tall, light-skinned, mixed boy with green eyes and a mysterious grin standing in the shadows of his ambiguity. David wanted to pick him up and have to dangerous sex with him, and he didn't care what his name was.

It was a retrospective reaction to a retro kind of emotion. He missed his friends; his most beautiful friends. Some days were bearable, and some nights just weren't.

So he went out, and he walked along the pier, where thin, willowy wisps of boys leaned like antennas in the wind. There were so many of them, loitering, littering, looking for someone, anyone to pay them some attention. They leaned and posed in skin-tight jeans and smiled or screamed with their eyes. He watched the slow parade of men; men walking, men in cars, men in Jeeps, each of them hard and patrolling the scene. Loneliness was a question mark, and horniness, an exclamation that raged so erect in a dark front seat. It was a sad thing to see, the bartering, the poses, the doors opening and closing, and the heads of boys, slowly descending.

This scene saddened David, and he was beginning to leave, and then, a lone pair of green eyes clung to him. Those eyes were like pale bright green lights on an abandoned street with no name. His skin was like something brand new, so smooth and golden. David mused on just how many days or weeks or months of nights it would take for that gold to be tarnished.

Thank God for the power of silence! This young, golden Adonis on the pier nodded. And then, without speaking, David took him home.

And David turned off the lights. And he laid naked and perfectly still beside him. And he embraced and held tight this smooth-skinned young phantom with the eyes like pretty green lights.

The following day, David had an appointment with Dr. Horowitz.

"I'm not proud, Baby-Doc. But I picked up someone, or maybe he picked up me."

"David?" The doctor paused, realizing judging David or anyone was not a part of his professional demeanor. "Were you . . . careful?"

"Careful? I thought you knew! There's nothing 'careful' in picking up strangers. If you'll recall, it was my tendency for picking up pretty-boy strangers that led me to this pale blue room."

David closed his eyes and remembered that night, that vicious night when the savages came out to play:

Three Years Earlier

David was dressed in drag after having appeared in a stage show. It was New Year's Eve. The theatre was closing.

He'd no time go and change into his street clothes. He thought, just for the hell of it, he'd have some fun anyway. He stepped into a drag bar. It didn't take very long before he'd garnered someone's attention. Soon a drink was delivered his way, thanks to a cute brown boy with a persuasive rap and deeply compassionate Latino eyes. The boy spent a part of the evening flirting shamelessly with David. There was no pretense. No matter the time and expertise in hair and make-up to affect the look of Audrey Hepburn, he knew David was a male. He said he wanted to take David home.

But as soon as they left the bar, the boy said something coarsely homophobic and cruel. Davd felt a chill, and he knew something was not right. The boy said it again, and David was just about address it, to read and correct him.

But, just then, a group of hard boys streamed out of the alleyway across the street.

David turned. He was surrounded by six diabolical Brown and Black faces. He knew he'd been set up. A quick flood of panic rushed over him. But drag or no drag, he refused to go out like a sucker.

"Oh. So, you brought your boys, huh? Afraid you couldn't handle a soft, unsuspecting faggot by your lonesome? All right, Julio, Raul, whatever the fuck your names are . . . c'mon, bring it!"

But what they'd brought was a tire iron.

"Ya like suckin' pipe, faggot? Well, suck on this!"

With a blunt ram, someone yanked the scarf at the back of David's neck and everything turned black. Strange how in that state of semi-consciousness, David's mind and body recorded every assault—the quick slam of a boot on his back, the taunts of "Take pipe, motherfuckin' ass-bandit," the stun of fist after fist, kick after kick hammering his flesh. They had no mercy for a dress-wearing, sashaying faggot on the prowl. They were trying their best to crucify him.

With malicious intent, they dragged him into the darkness of that sociopathic alley. With no one to see, they continued their battery.

They did it for fun, for shits and giggles. They did it because they knew they could. David was no longer fighting back. David *could no longer* fight back. It didn't matter to them. A swift and sudden kick to his mouth knocked out two teeth. But how *many* kicks would it take? How many times would that iron need to rise and plummet down, rise and pummel down, rise and plummet down before David could close his eyes and no longer *feel* anything? He wondered this as he lay there, semiconscious. He lay there, waiting, just waiting for a neon sign from God.

Is God in this alley? his hurting skull questioned. *God? Do you see this?* The loneliness of his head wondered this, as the warm river of blood trickled, then gushed down, seeping through Audrey's little black dress.

The final humiliation came as the young thug from the bar ripped into *Ms. Davina's* purse, found a bright pink lipstick, and scribbled on David's bleeding forehead: FAG!

Then they ran away hyena-style, laughing, howling into the cruel Manhattan night.

"David, were you *careful*?" Horowitz repeated.

"I see. You think I had *sex* with him. I didn't. I could've. I wanted to . . . for a minute. But then, I don't know, something else happened. In my old age, I've become this pathetically sad Blanche Dubois. But it wasn't *the kindness of strangers* I wanted. I think what I needed was *recognition.* I wanted someone to know what *a prize* it was to be in my company. Not in my ass, and not on my dick, but in my essence. And so, it felt right to just lay there with him, and listen to his young, tender heartbeat. And so, that's what we did, and that's all we did. Surely I was the easiest two hundred bucks that beautiful kid ever made."

Dr. Horowitz was relieved.

"Was his boy a substitute, David?"

"Well, they're *all* substitutes for something or someone, aren't they, Doc?"

"Perhaps you're right. But who was this one subbing for? Ty? Carlos? Victor? Face? Or maybe Kindred?" the doctor wondered out loud.

David felt insulted to his core. Hadn't he already *told* Horowitz he wasn't trying to engage in a *physical* relationship with Tyronc's double? David was sure he's told him this, but perhaps he hadn't. Perhaps he was having those memory failings again. And maybe Crazy was becoming his new best friend.

"I'm sure the boy from last night thought I was this pathetically sad and crazy queen. But the joke's on him, because maybe only the *crazy* part was true."

"You feeling vulnerable again?"

"Well, that depends, Doc. Did you wake up suddenly feeling like maybe you'd have *blue* eyes and a *balding* head, today?" David chuckled. "Vulnerability is a part of my DNA, man. Doesn't make me a punk. It just makes me open to everything and anything . . . even to the idea that Kindred might be a ghost."

"So, you think he's a ghost now?"

"I always thought it. But then he did things to convince me that he wasn't. Like having the ability to be touched. Like casting a real shadow on the pavement. So I had to allow for the possibility that he was real."

"And how do you feel now, David?"

"Right now, I'm imagining myself going mad. I mean, it's bound to happen, so what am I saving it for? The trial is over. I won. I think I wanna go mad now. I've earned it. And not your average textbook case, either. That run-of-the-mill rage of an *unstable* soul on the fritz just wouldn't do for me."

"Well, maybe what you're talking about is rage."

"Call it whatever the hell you want. But my form of insanity will be one of those urban events, something *Eyewitness*

News, Fox5, CBS, CNN and all the news networks will cover. After all, I *was* quasi-famous, once. And you *know* how the media folk just love to see a washed-up celebrity on the fritz. Add Black, male, and gay to the equation, and I might have to save crazy; delay my fit for one of those network *sweeps* or something."

"Uh, David. You keep making this sound like you're looking forward to it. You have a successful fashion business. You have trust funds and a corporation to run and oversee. Would this be the *best* time to schedule your dance with insanity?" the doctor asked, only half-kidding.

"*Damn* that. When I think of all the shit I've been through and still going through . . . lesser men would have flipped that switch years ago. The fact that I haven't yet, it must amuse people, people like you, Doc. Of this I'm quite sure."

Maybe the delay stemmed from being a lifelong dancer of minuscule renown, and as such, he'd always tried to keep his body in tune, his mind sound, and his emotions limber. It was all about self-discipline. And David Richmond was nothing, if not resourceful. People can say, will say, and had said more than a few harsh and scandalous things about him. But anyone who *knew him* will tell you, David Donatello Richmond was as resourceful as the fiercest feline, a hard-core alley cat from the darkest depths of the Bowery, and that cat had at least six lives left.

And so, in lieu of giving in to the demons, instead of going buck-wild, balls-to-the-wall-fuck-it-all-and-fuck-the-world insane, David decided, as one of his final hurrahs, he would rent a little theatre in the village and put on a one man show.

A theatre on Sullivan Street:

It was as if the creative spirit once so alive in Tyrone had shape-shifted and somehow transmogrified to him, and

David crafted a performance piece called: from *From Fag To Man, The Journey*.

When he took to the stage, his face was fully made-up. He was dressed in red feather boa, wore fire-red boxing trunks, a boxing glove on his left hand, and lace glove on the right. And for footwear, he rocked a pair of six-inch sparkly red pumps. To the naked eye, David *looked* quite deranged. And that was the whole idea; the method to his madness.

The following is an excerpt from his performance:

"Perhaps a bit of my bio is needed here. My name is David. David Richmond. I'm a thirty-four-year-old man who God or nature or both conspired to make Black and Talented, Beautiful, and Gay. And before you poke me with the sharp end of your judgment stick, it may just behoove you to know this:

"I can box. I have boxed. I can fight. I have fought. I've been hit. I've gotten up. I've been bloodied. I've been kicked. I've been dogged, doubted, spat and shat upon. And yes, I've gotten back up. I've had a marathon of fists, real and figurative fists, flurries of furious fists punching, hitting, cutting, jabbing, stabbing, tagging, landing, connecting, stunning and dizzying me. And I've gotten up. With shaky legs, with wobbling knees, with both eyes blackened, with a face swollen the size of Waco, Texas, I have fought back, and I've won, dammit!

"I am a fighter. I've kicked ass and taken the names of the best of them. Realize, beneath my deceptively petite physique and this lovely copper exterior there lives and beats the heart of a serious ass-kicker. I've had to be. It was necessary, because I been bold enough, real enough to be *me*, without shame or apologies. So please, don't fuck with me, because chances are, these days, I won't be in the mood to be fucked with! Get it? Got it? Good."

* * *

And that was just the intro to his one-man show. His idea was to deliver all the decadent goods, straight-no-chaser, no edit, no filter. But the goal was to reach people, gay people, Black people, White people, Brown people, people with penises, and even the vagina-people. He wanted to reach them with his humanity.

"These meds are murda. They fuck with my mind, my heart, my decisions, my soul, my vision, and even my *fashion* sense. One day, thinkin I was too cute, I rocked this off-the-rack scarf, this sharp-ass scarf that turned to be *poly-me-ester* and swore the motherfucka was silk! So trust me, AZT ain't no joke. I mean, what kinda shit takes away your natural, God-given fag *aesthetic*? It's gotta be some powerful shit, right? But it's slowly gypping me into believing my life has a sense of *quality*.

"Yeah, I've got the virus, ya'll. You know me: always down with the *latest* trend! Lately, I've even been rockin' the latest in purple sores. And trust, purple may have used to be my *best* color, but this new shade? It's hideous.

"But you also need to know this: I'm nobody's quitter, so you'd be foolish to count me out. Let me say for the record: I've been through the thick of some terrible, soul-robbing shit, and I'm still here. I bet I already know what you think. You're thinking, aww shit! This is just another played-out fag's sad-ass memoir. Wrong! Sorry. *ANNNNNT*! You get the big Jeopardy buzzer on that one, baby.

"If you're looking for some soft swish-cheese, limp-wristed, *Judy*-gets-me variety of flamer, then keep looking elsewhere! Trust. Judy *nevuh* got *me*. And as far as a Liza/Babs/Diana-worshiping devotee, well—that fag ain't me. I hold nothing against my flaming brethren. I love my nieces to pieces, but you see, there are several stages to faggotry. I've already *done* my flamboyant act. Did you happen to see me? I was the cat in the bright pink tutu. Oh, I danced my ass off in that one, people. I truly did. Hell, I've played that merry role for most of my damn career.

"That was *Stage One*. I was not, repeat *not*, being fake, fraudulent nor phony with my shit. In fact, I was most *legit* with mine. But it was just at a different time and place in my ever-evolving journey in becoming David.

"Ah! Yes! *Stage One*. Somebody, please, cue the club music!"

Sylvester's, "*You Make Me Feel Mighty Real*" blasted the place.

"I must admit, some of it was wildly fabu and mad fun, too. I *was* the party, baby. I was the freak dance and the music, the whistle, the holler, the sweat, and the heat of the grind. And I was a bloody mess. I was that fool, hyped on booze and ecstasy. I portrayed that freak in my fly and most *f-a-a-a-aabulous* drag. That was me—the fun one, with the full glass of the best freakin' champagne. *Moet* for me, and all the queens with me! Somebody, *holla!*

"Believe me, I've known my share of hollas . . . and mornings of screaming yellow suns, complete with some snoring morning-breath bastards whose names I never knew, and their resumes didn't matter."

The music abruptly stopped.

"But then came the crash—that dreaded *Stage Two*. It goes a li'l sump-m like this:

"You wake up beside some groggy morning-after *regret*. You hate yourself so much it *hurts* in a place where you weren't even *fucked*. Maybe you'd been careless with your emotions so damn long you'd forgotten other people possessed them. Maybe you disappointed that one person you loved better than you loved yourself. Oops! Excuse you! You've just betrayed the one who most respected the best in you, who loved and *trusted* and believed in *you*. Not just in your mythic fabulousness—but in the buck-ass-nekkid YOU, dammit! Maybe you thought you were so cool and so damn slick with your shit that you wouldn't possibly get caught. But then you *did* get caught. Shame on you! A pox on you and all the people in your little glass backroom!

"Or, say it goes *another* way, and you don't actually get busted, but *you* still *know* you're full of shit. So, maybe the one you've disappointed and cheated most was *you*.

"Through that sinking, sick emptiness deep inside your gut, you realize you've helped deconstruct and detonate your own demise. Yes, these towers of lies we create do fall apart, sometimes. But don't blame the mayor. Don't even bother trying to sue the city! You, *you* were the architect, baby. When this shit happens—and it *will* happen, if you really wanna get real and honest with *you*, you *know* some serious *self*-inspection is due. That's what happened to me, yours truly. This becomes your introduction to *Stage Two*. Time to ask myself, the hard questions:

"Who am I, really? *Why* do I feel so damn *empty?* What's it gonna take to make me whole and happy to be nappy? Is it some new med? Then, where can I get it, and how quickly? Please, doctor, please, quick, write me a freakin' scrip! I swear fo God, I'll try not to OD on that good shit—honest. Why am I so damn empty? What's really gonna fill me up, when sex doesn't do it anymore? What's it gonna take, David Donatello Richmond? Will it be Love? Real *Love*? Is it God? Do you even know?

"Damn that fucking *Stage Two* of my Faggotry! It is a mad rough and painful bitch, and it doesn't have any answers, only more fucking tests and quizzes and questions. But, you know what? It's *necessary* . . . because if you don't do some *personal investigation* as to why you're still here, and what it all means, then you're nothing but just another useless fag without meaning.

"I'm opting for *meaning* now.

"Tonight, you happen to be meeting me while deeply ensconced in my *Stage Three*. Yes, this is my Third Act, people. Unfortunately, for the true-blue party freaks, I'm not half the fag, excuse me, the homosexual I used to be. I sought therapy to get some answers, some clarity, and resolutions to my past behavior, with the utmost temerity. Please notice, I said resolution, *not* absolution. Why? Because this is my life to live in every color of the rainbow. And I've done it in pinks, and purple, in jade and chartreuse, in reds and orange, and yellow, and blue shades, too. It's MY life, dammit! I regret nothing I've done. Life is for living, and for learning, and for *learning to love!* It's for stumbling, and for falling and for getting the fuck-up. Well, I'm UP! I'm *up*, and I'm conscious, dammit! And I dare a motherfucker anywhere to *try* and knock me down again!"

The crowded applauded wildly.

Opening night of David's show was a sell-out. He had invited most everyone he knew: Bliss, Zaire, Adeva, Rodney, the dancers he'd met on the road, his friends in drag, and Kindred, and yes, even Browny with Juanita rolled through.

And because of his Tyrone connection, even a few backers came through the premises. They loved the message, the fire, and the bravery of his performance. They were so enchanted by David's delivery that there was talk of bringing it to a bigger house and mounting an off-Broadway production.

David couldn't believe it. He thought after all the times he'd longed to dance on a Broadway stage, now just maybe *acting* upon an off-Broadway one, it would become his Third Act.

CHAPTER TWENTY-SEVEN

CHAOS AT THE AFTER-PARTY

David hadn't seen Kindred since the vanishing. But for him to show up there, where there were actually people, it was a milestone in the annals of mental health for David Richmond. People could see him and know that Kindred wasn't a figment of David's once lonely imagination. There were so many faces from David's many lives gathered in that room. But the one face he'd never expected, yet was endlessly happy to gaze upon was Victor's. He grabbed David's hand, and he didn't let it go for the rest of the night. He looked in David's eyes and *knew* the love was still there, and that it really never left. It was a look in the eyes and a meeting of the heart simultaneously. David's play had pretty much spelled out what Victor had known all along: David was acting brave, being brave instead being True to his heart.

Rodney was beaming with pride and it wasn't only from viewing, feeling and relating to David's show. After the success of the latest fashion line, he'd just received wonderful news. A house, a well-known designer house in Paris, wanted *him* as their next new wunderkind.

"God! That's, that's crazy! Wow! Congratulations, Roddy Rod!"

"Can you believe it, man? A Black man, designing at a couture house in Paris?"

"Yes, I can, Black man. You're an innovator at what you do. Hell, they'll be lucky to have you! I'll miss you, though. Miss you something awful, 'cause you made *me* look good."

"Stop the madness, David! You *are* good! I'ma miss you too, man." Rodney hugged him tightly, and then, he shook Victor's hand.

"A Black militant fashion designer in Paris. God help him!" David said as Rodney walked away. "And I'll give him two months before he's walking around the Champs Elysees with a *White* Parisian boyfriend on his arm." David laughed. "So much for being *true* to the game!" He chuckled.

There were others actively engaged in being *untrue* that night as well.

On this night, Bliss Santana finally met Kindred:

"Oh my God! Oh, my God! It's true! We all *thought* David was having a little hallucination, but my God, you *do* resemble Ty!" She touched his face gently. "And you're not a ghost!" She smiled. She liked him instantly.

Browny, however, who no one had invited, but who'd shown up anyway, well, his reaction to the circumstances was a different bag of snakes entirely.

"Yo, fool! I thought you stopped dressin in drag, yo!"

Because this was such an important night, a night of memories and longtime reunions, David decided he could be civil.

"Well, Browny, you know what they say: You can take the drag away, but as long as there's a tiara, a fag's gonna play."

"See, yo. If I'd said that shit, you woulda prolly hit me."

"You're right. I probably woulda. But not tonight. Where's Juanita?"

"Oh, she's up in here somewhere. Prolly at the buffet table," he joked as he looked around the room and spotted her. But his expression was not one of pleasure in the least. "She's over there in the corner, talking to that boy who look like Ty. What's his story , yo?"

"Oh. That's Kindred. He's my newest friend. And you'll want to meet him, I'm sure. He's writing *my biography*, from high school, Da Elixir, my life and loves, and all that good trashy stuff."

"Writing? You mean, like a book?"

"Yes, Browny. Like a book. Only, this will be a much more *truthful* one." David winked, still holding Victor's hand.

Suddenly, Browny saw RED . . . Bright! Blazing! FI-YAH-ENGINE RED! ! !

"What the motherfuck? You stopped MY book from selling so you could write your own? Yo! What kinda fucked up shit is that?"

"Breeeeathe, Browny! Browny, breeeeeeeathe! First of all, get your facts *straight*, girlfriend! I didn't put a stop on that book. That was . . . well, someone else. I had *nothing* to do with it. So, please, don't get it twisted!"

But Browny couldn't or wouldn't hear anything else. He cut a mad path over in the direction of that new author, the young 'mugfucka' who would be writing a new book. He was determined to rap to this new cat with Tyrone's old face.

"Oh boy." David sighed. "This could get very ugly, very quickly. Security?"

"Why, Puppy?" Victor asked.

"I didn't invite that Brown Bastard to the play, nor this party. And if he thinks he's gonna roll through with his ghetto ass and set it off up in here, well, I got news for him!"

"You calm down! He's outta here if there's trouble. Promise. Let's see if Kindred can handle him."

"But Papa, Kindred is *way* too kind. He's such a calm and

gentle soul. He's a sensitive spirit, even more so than Ty, if that's possible. I've never once even heard him swear. Not once! He's in this whole other league of beings, and certainly not a species of dunces like Browny."

As David and Victor looked on, Juanita stopped speaking to Kindred as Browny started throwing his animated hands in the air. Kindred just looked embarrassed. Browny kept on emoting, and Juanita was getting in between them. Kindred still hadn't said a word. People were looking in that direction now. Browny was showing out, talking loud and drawing a crowd. Juanita was trying to talk him down. Kindred nodded his head. He was wearing that Tyrone look then. It had claimed his forehead. David felt scared for him. He and Victor headed over. They saw an angry Browny push Kindred. And he pushed him again. And then . . . BAM!

A hush came over the crowd.

By the time David and Victor arrived, Browny was on the floor, out cold.

Kindred, had just *hit* him, to borrow the Depina version of the word: HOARD!

CHAPTER TWENTY-EIGHT

A MOST ENLIGHTENING 'BLUR'

That night Browny arrived at his homestead hotter than Hades. His ego was singed, and his nose and his mouth were slightly battered too.

"The nerve of that motherfuckin' new-jack punk!" he spat, dabbing a tissue to his bloody lip.

Well that new-jack just jacked yo ass, didn't he? Juanita wanted to say. If Browny weren't her husband, her man, her "Clyde," even she would have busted her side, laughing at him. But Juanita didn't say anything. Though she knew the only *punk* in the room proved to be Browny himself, she wasn't about to say it. No. She could be sensitive to her Clyde's shortcomings. What was needed most was some TLC and iodine. The iodine came first.

Browny sat on the edge of their bed, sulking and brooding and being Browny, on bruised. Juanita sat beside him. She softly kissed his cheek and applied a moist cotton ball to the bruised and bloody nose. Browny sucked his teeth, partially in pain, partially in embarrassment, but mostly in anger. No man wanted to be punked like that *in public*, much less in front of his *woman*.

She then began to massage his shoulders, and she slowly but surely eased his tensions away. Juanita and Browny . . . Browny and Juanita. People always thought they were a crazy mismatch, but Browny would be the first to say, "Y'all brothas just don't know, yo!"

For him, there was nothing more *soothing*, more down-home-comforting than making love to a large woman, a Sista of size, of heft, of girth. Her touch that night, as it did so often, proved to be enough to keep him earthbound. That night, Juanita's body provided him with a warm and cushy place to fall.

Her breasts weren't just bigger than his head (and Browny had quite the dome), her breasts were nearly gargantuan.. When he was in prison, he'd had these wildest of horny dreams starring nothing less than: *Titties! Titties! Titties!* From the very jump, he was obsessed with Juanita's big ole beginning-to-sag-some titties. And through the years, though they may have sagged even more, they never lost one ounce of their massive mammary allure.

Making love to Juanita, he could feel himself imploding into *all* of her. And to sink so deeply inside her was to be enclosed in soft, warm, spicy folds of love. Her hugs were his security, her kisses his insurance, and her sex and what she could do with it became his magic.

At 48DD, her titties were her *femalian* prize. She didn't possess the biggest, most roundest of asses, because God didn't Bless most women with both those assets. Yes, "that shit is w-iiiiiiiide, no doubt!" Browny would say of it. Yet for all its wideness, it lacked that black woman's massive bubble appeal.

Juanita's lack of "duh ass-ness" didn't matter much. She was rich with authentic sista flava, she was loyal, and best of all, she was real. He loved to hold her less-than-bubble ass when they fucked. And when the ghetto romantic in him was about to bust, he would sigh, "Lawd woman, roll dat big ass over here . . .

c'mon, slide it over, so I can hit right, yo!" this became Juanita's horny love song.

And together they sang, and clapped and rubbed and *wheezed*, and danced their way into funky, sweaty ecstacy.

And when it was over, a calmer Browny emerged. Yet, even *that version* of Browny wanted to kick that Kindred person's ass.

Kindred, once again, became a quick disruptive ghost in the night, and he promptly disappeared. For days he remained out of sight after The Bloodied Browny Incident, Part Duex—which is how David began to refer to it .

However, David's triumphant stage show and his star turn under the lights didn't go unnoticed by too many people from his past life.

"Hello, David Richmond. Congratulations on the play, man. Somewhere, I know Tyrone must be smiling," the voice on the other end of the phone said to him.

David thought he knew that voice. Surely, he'd heard it before. It was clear and distinctly masculine. It wore a touch of intelligence and none of the slight nasally merry tone in which most of his friends spoke. Yes, he'd heard it before, but that voice was never pleasant to him. The more he thought, the clearer it became who the owner of that voice was in his ear. Still, he had to ask.

"To whom am I speaking?"

There was a pause, a hesitation on the line.

And then he said it. "It's Blur, David. Blur Antonelli."

The Lord sure did work in mysterious ways, or maybe He just L-o-o-o-v-e-d nothing more than to keep testing David Richmond. David was trying his best to adapt a New Attitude, but Life kept making it hard. His patience, his will just kept on being tested with more of, as he would put it, "those-bullshit-oriented, need-to-get-they-asses-kicked type people." He detested those people's existence in his orbit. And in David's eyes, Blur was one of those people.

Ironically, David, who had been reading Ty's journals even more intensely during and after the trial, just the night before, had come across Blur's name.

Think of a thing and that thing *will* appear. And now *that thing* was on the other end of the line. David was determined to keep the conversation short, in much the same way as Blur had done all those times before whenever David called Tyrone and Blur would answer. He'd been nasty toward David because David knew who and *what* Blur really was.

"Thanks for the congrats, Blur. Much appreciated. Have a nice safe life. Good-bye." *Click.*

And that was that.

David thought, as he always did when it came to the subject of Blur, *Blur Antonelli. Apt moniker. Blur: hazy, unclear, obscure, not sure. Repeat, not sure. And Antonelli? Please! I told Ty long ago, check the name, brotha. That damn name says it all: anti-nelly.*

Blur was as Beautiful and beige, as he was deceptive and ambitious.

He'd taken Ty on a carnal ride through some dizzy little Disney World of his own design, and Ty believed he'd seen stars.

The blue light on his shoulder was the moon's glow, and it cast a spell the color of desire. What is this quiet fire in him. He stared at me, and I wondered: what do I make of those flashing eyes, giving me the signal to go forward? I am a student of yellow lights. I know only to proceed with caution. But this blue moon stains his shoulder, and my gaze moves like slow traffic across his chest. And then they venture beyond, to that risqué place where he takes my imagination and builds this tower that rises high and so stiffly from my lap."

Or so Tyrone was inspired to write of Blur Antonelli. Personally, David had never liked him, and the feeling was entirely mutual back then. But what can you do when your best friend is dizzy, and thinks he found his equilibrium in another man? You wait, with your arms open wide to catch him, when there comes that inevitable fall.

As Tyrone recalled in his journal:

Sometimes you just know when Destiny's in the building. He walked into the office as if he planned to own the place one day. Our eyes locked tighter than his chestnut shoulder-length dreads. My God! I was thunderstruck. Not since that sad day I first laid eyes on Face Depina had I seen a more staggering arrangement of beige and green architecture. Black and Italian features made my eyes cling in awe of what lush beauty two races could accomplish together. True, his skin was not my preferred cup of rich hot chocolate, yet I was sinking inside its soft taupe shade.

His hazel-green eyes pierced so deeply inside my core. Suddenly, my emotions were falling, tumbling, and sliding around like these clumsy acrobats, and I found myself wondering, *Who are you? Are you here for me? Could you be The One?*

"Tyrone. I'd like you to meet Blur. Blur Antonelli," my Editor Jim Bronstein said.

And just looking at Blur, I thought, *Well, hello! He's flawless. Not very tall, is he? Maybe Trick's height. Diz-zaamn, you's a fine boy! God! Is there a mind behind all that fineness? If there is, I might just relax my rules about fallin' in dig with you pretty boys. Please don't open your mouth and squawk like a fool, 'cause I'm feelin' you.*

Suddenly, I wanted desperately to be seen as cool, calm, mellow, and better dressed. Most of all, I just wanted the boy to open his mouth, form correct words, and let something memorable flow the fuck out.

"Well hey, Tyrone!" Blur said, shaking my hand rigorously, with this trace of genuine excitement in his voice.

"I read four papers every morning. But honestly, man, your column makes my day. Great stuff. It's perspicacious and consistently poignant. I digs, man. I digs."

And so, the world blurred around me. I mean this quite literally. This was one of those surreal moments in time, when the world moves in slow-motion. Meeting him was like some *West Side Story* kind of thing. My vision went hazy, then clear again. Yes, it was so *clear* he was put here for me to meet, to fall in love with, to sing happy songs with, and then fade to black. But even movies are temporary escapes.

Physically, I liked his look, the dreadlocks, the gold-green eyes, and I even liked his size. But mostly, I was falling in love with his mind. Keen mind. Educated, street-smart, and self-elevated, there were so many dreams in him and in those eyes. I thought we could dream them together. The lawyer and the journalist—maybe we could forge our own crusade in this city, and hell—even make a difference in the world.

Damn! I was such a delusional teenaged girl. David, if you're reading this, you KNOW how I always HATED it when gay men referred to themselves as 'girls'. But with Blur, I *got* it——that Golden Girlish Wonder of Such Beautiful Possibilities. I wasn't myself in those first few days, or weeks, or even months.

I was this embarrassment, a giddy *little girl* seeing only this dreamy swirl of kismet. I wanted to skip to myloo! Yes, damn it, I said it. Imagine me—Tyrone Hunter—skipping anywhere—let alone down the concrete and cobblestones of this freaking city, 'looking for fun and Feelin' Grooooveeeeee!' Now ain't that some kind of love? Well, it had to be love or some serious form of an undiagnosed insanity!

It was Blur and I, taking our time, sniffin' each other out, and liking the aroma in what we found. Blur and me, me and Blur, taking in a Yankees game and cappuccinos in Café Wha. Blur and I, courting, sparking, cavorting, and making woo. That's the Golden Time, you know? That's the foolishly free, gaga-giddy interlude, where everything they do is lovely and hot and oh so brand new. You're not even yourself. You're some new fool, so infatuated of this love, that you've become an enamored student of them. But you gladly, madly partake in this course. You see only what you *want* to see on the blackboard, and everything they write before your eyes is magical, bee-U-tee-FULL!"

And David thought, *Beautiful? Beautiful, Ty? Only if you're blind, and a got-damn girlish fool! His taking you to a Times Square strip show, THAT should have been your first clue, yo! Yes, he was far more cerebral and devious in his pursuit. Yes, so what if he was only scoping out the place for slick drug deals to report back to the commissioner! He was already showing you his ambitious trump card, when he should've been showing his hard-on for you!*

Poor Ty, so needing to be in deep love with an illusion! Poor prick. Those smart ones seem to fall the hardest, every time.

Antonelli's idea of loving Tyrone excluded any open display of that love. Blur Antonelli had no intentions of being *himself* in public, and even less desire to be Tyrone's overtly gay lover. While he bided his time, and said the right lines, he was not willing to form a genuine commitment. He came to resent and then despise that sense of *freedom* in Ty. There would be no parades for him, no holding hands, or open shows of affection. Blur was not about to spoil his chances of being a political mover and shaker, simply for the love of dick.

Sex was something to be done in the darkness. Sex with men was something was ashamed of even liking. Love was something only men and women shared in the daylight. Men with men should never put their business in the street.

It wasn't that Tyrone Hunter was a flamer—or a wild boy by nature. But when in love, Ty believed in the naked joy of snatching love, showing love, singing and writing songs about love—not stifling or hiding it like some dirty little perverted secret.

When Blur broke Ty's heart, as he inevitably did, it was always in a way that revealed his own self-hatred.

Blur did not *like* David. In fact, Blur could not *stand* him. David embodied everything Blur hated in himself: the movement, the intonations, the rapier wit and the hyper lust, the indiscriminate sex.

David, to his credit, saw beyond Blur's light-skinned physical beauty and into the heart of his darkness.

Days later, as if Ty or some other fickle angel of fate had planned it, David would see Blur on the subway. Maybe David was in his own world, and too much in his head to notice there were posters of Blur all over the city.

With Blur, Tyrone had once dreamed in color of a love, of mutual community service, of Black and beautiful righteousness, and the quiet hissing of Westchester lawns.

Now, there Antonelli stood in the subway, shaking the hands of potential voters. He was running for something again. He was always running for something, and at the same time always running *away* from something.

"I hope I have your vote as your next city councilman."

When their eyes met, David turned his head. He wanted the power of Barbara Eden's genie to *blink* the sight of Blur away. He'd never forgiven him for breaking Ty's heart, and for trying to break his best friend's spirit. For this, David

Richmond hated Blur Antonelli with the blazing intensity of a thousand white-hot Egyptian suns.

The last time their eyes met, it was at Ty's funeral. David wondered what the hell Blur was even doing there. If David only had the power of speech that day, he would have cursed him out, most viciously.

He'd heard rumors that Blur's disappearance from Ty's life was due to the shooting of Face Depina. But that one thing seemed to have no correlation to the other. It was only after a little research that David happened upon the most interesting fact that Blur's mentally-deranged sister was in an asylum. Her crime, a hushed act of violence that culminated on the night Face was shot.

Was Blur being noble, or wholly self-motivated to pull up stakes years earlier, leaving Ty and their relationship in mysterious tatters?

"David?" Blur called out.

Oh no! That bastard's heading this way, David thought, as sure enough, indeed, *the bastard* was.

Ever the politico, he stretched out his hand, and David felt tempted to spit, to hock a very slimy loogy in it. But instead of expectorate, he simply looked at Blur as if Antonelli were a lunatic.

"I know. And I'm not here to court your vote. How are you, David?"

"As if you care? Please, sir. Be *gone*," David advised with a turn of the wrist.

"I'd like to speak with you. Not here, and not now."

"Of course not. Careful! People are taking your picture. And I'm pretty sure those fotogs *aren't* from any *gay* rags."

"Okay. Granted, just maybe I deserved that."

"You deserve a *lot* of things. But I don't play God. I leave that job to you politicians," David snapped.

"I'd like talk to you . . . about Tyrone. I loved him too, you know," he whispered in a deliberate hush.

"Only, not enough to hold his fuckin' hand, or shout it from the rooftops, right?" David inquired, rolling his eyes and crossing his indignant legs.

"David . . . Haven't you ever, just once, regretted something so much, that it haunted you every day of your life?"

Oh. Gawd! He's good. Going for the emotional, are we? Those damn politicos are always so fuckin' smooth with the words.

David was nobody's cold-hearted snake, though he did audition for a role in Paula Abdul's video. No, he was not cold-hearted, nor a snake at all, but if he came close to venomously hating anyone, that bite was reserved for one Blur Antonelli. But if Blur, like David, held a deep love for Ty, even in his own closeted way, then David could give in, just a little.

However, this meeting would only be on *David's* terms. They would meet, at *David's insistence* in broad daylight. David was going to make the bastard sweat, and hopefully as uncomfortable as possible. He thought it best to meet at Le Swan, a known and very popular gay restaurant.

To David's surprise, he agreed. And for sheer balls alone, Mr. Blur Antonelli garnered four, ok five Cool Points from David Richmond.

When David arrived, Blur was already there, and seated at a not-so-discreet table. He didn't look like the Blur Ty had originally fallen for, as now he was sans bohemian chic dreadlocks and jeans, and the things that made him once seem cool and approachable. Now he appeared all tight and businesslike. Now he was manicured and wore a sensible Caesar cut, and his suit was something from the Stick-Up-The-Ass Collection at Barney's.

"David. You came. I'm glad. Please, sit down."

"I'm here. I hope it's not a waste of my time."

"I wanted you know a few things. It's important to me that you do. First and foremost, I need you to understand

and to know I never once stopped loving Tyrone. He was, and probably always will be the love of my life."

"Oh, really?" David asked dubiously.

"Really," he said. His eyes were possessed by a keen kind of seriousness. Either he'd become a very skilled politician, or David was actually beginning to *believe* him.

"He wasn't very hard to love, was he? Ty. All warm and attentive, and present and caring. I loved him, deeply. I just met him at time when I wasn't ready to *be* who I wanted to be. I was fighting my own demons, and biggest one wasn't my sexuality. It was my ambition."

"I gathered that," David said, as the waiter placed a glass of water before him.

"You don't understand where I come from, and I'm not about to make any excuses. I just needed to be someone who made a difference. Ty and I shared that trait. But there were so many other obstacles in the way; and some of those, I actually *loved*. Like my sister, Bina. I was young and caring for her, and trying to get her out that state-ran institution, and back into the world."

"Yes. But when Ty tried to help her, you went all kinds of ugly on him! You broke his heart, and tried diminish all the good he wanted to do, on her behalf."

"I don't . . . you see, I didn't want anyone messing with her mind, and . . . well, she trusted so few people. I was her guardian. I *had* to look out for her. Sometimes I failed at that, and it tore me up inside. Sure, maybe I was overprotective at times. I was all she had. All she could depend on. And if you think I was a bastard, that behavior had a lot to do with what had happened to her. Every big brother wants to look out for his baby sister. That's just the way I am with Bina. But what you don't know, and neither did Ty, was your friend, that bastard Face Depina . . ."

"Facey? What? What does Facey have to do with any of that?"

"Your good friend . . . Face fuckin' Depina . . . he saw her out with her college friends one night, and he paid her some attention, and being a young, naive girl with problems, she was very flattered. Maybe she was lost in the romance of what she imagined he was. And so he took her home, and . . . he put his slimy fuckin' hands all over her. And even when she said no, he violently assaulted her. He ripped at her dress, and he . . . he . . . *raped* her!"

"What? No! No, that's impossible. That wasn't in his nature! Not Facey!"

"Oh it's true. *Trust me* on this. Maybe he was high and didn't consider it rape, when a young girl thinks she wants to be loved, and then realized sex had nothing to do with love. Maybe he was kinky. Maybe it was some kind of thrill for him. Maybe he was not used to women saying 'stop!' And she said STOP! She cried STOP! And he didn't stop. And he ruined her."

"This is all too much for me to grasp, Blur."

"You? Imagine poor Bina, seeing that face of the man who didn't just take, but snatched her virginity. Imagine seeing that face on billboards and magazine covers, on newsstands and on TV. Imagine her reliving that night over and over, and nothing was being done for *her*! Where was the justice? Where was the fuckin' justice, man?"

David noticed him wringing his large anguished hands. But way too much information was coming at him all at once.

Facey? My Facey, a rapist?

"He was still living this high life. He was King of the City, and Bina was crouched so low and for so long inside a dark and frightening place."

He took a deep breath, and then, he whispered in a dry voice, "David, that night at Zebra Den, that night Depina was shot . . . my sister pulled the trigger."

David's mouth, and then his entire aspect fell.

"God!" David said, and it was all he could say. "God!" He was angry and confused and sad and suddenly . . . *informed.*

That day, staring back at Blur, David had received the answer to a haunting question he thought he'd never know.

And suddenly he didn't have to say anything else. David understood then, the sequence of events that followed:Blur picking a fight with Ty, and then his sudden departure from the city, leaving Ty to forever wonder why. The D.A.'s mysteriously hushing of the case. He even understood the strangeness of Face and how he'd never bothered pursuing it any further.

Who was Blur Antonelli, really? Was he just a flawed man protecting his unstable sister? Did he have to make his own *Sophie's Choice*, deciding who he'd loved most, and who he'd show his allegiance to—and thus, Ty was left behind?

"Funny isn't it?"

"What's funny?" David asked.

"Seems you can't swing a dead cat without hitting someone in this town that Face Depina didn't leave burned or scarred in some way."

CHAPTER TWENTY-NINE

FORGIVENESS, THY NAME IS "BLISS"

She saw him again, and it was like stepping back in time to when she was first famous. Her mind drifted back to all the soirees, all the fabulous parties, all the fans, the cameras, the lights, the golden days, the fast nights, and the slick men, who in spite of herself, Bliss Santana always liked.

"Claud! Oh no!"

He turned. He was him. Some of those long ago Models of the Moment survived the glitz and their cocaine diets, and really did live on, after the others had become cliches, tabloid jokes, or had died before their time. Such a surviving male mannequin was Claudio Conte. He was, to a degree, Face Depina's confidant. Claudio was many things to many people. For Bliss Santana, he'd been her friend, her dealer, and her rival for the time and close affections of Pascal "Face" Depina. It was she who had introduced them so many years ago.

And now, there stood Claudio on Fifty-ninth Street, looking as Italiano chic as she'd always remembered him, in a pearl-gray sharkskin suit, a black polo shirt, and black Italian sandals. He still had the most beautiful feet she'd ever seen on a man.

"Oh, my God! My *Blissness*!" he gasped upon seeing her.

In the mid '80s, Claudio's image helped put *fab* in fabulous, but he stepped as if he were the anointed Crown Prince of Coolsville, with his slicked back black hair graying at the temples and that long aquiline nose, which gave him the bearing of a proud Sicilian eagle. Instantly Bliss noted that he'd retained his allure, and was still the coolness du jour, very much the hunk for a cat in his late-forties, or was it mid-fifties? But then . . . who *knew* for sure just how old Claudio really was? She doubted if even Face Depina knew the truth to that enigma.

"Lay one on me, mami!"

She kissed him hard and long, her arms wrapped tightly around him. A stranger passing by would have thought they were lovers. Claudio kissed with mutual passion, and held onto her equally tight, and the feeling inside him felt warm.

"I was wondering when we'd run into each other again. You, being in New York, and being a former *GQ* royalty of this place." He chuckled.

Bliss pulled away, and pushed him "Fuckin' bastard! You could've called me, yanno! Lord knows I've no idea where to reach you anymore!"

"I didn't know where you were staying. I emailed your old address, but that was changed. Hell, I even tried to get tickets for the show, and it was sold the hell out. I figured, Bliss is back, and too damn big for me these days. Truthfully, my *feelings* were kinda hurt."

Bliss folded her arms, looked at him. "See? This is why *you* never made it as an actor. Your audience is supposed to *believe* and BUY the bullshit!" She gave him a look that could kill most men. And Claudio waited for her expression to change. It didn't . . . so finally he said, "Ok. I suck as a human being. Granted. But I'm still the sexiest man-bitch you ever knew."

Bliss grinned, and said, "You were the second *most* sexiest man-bitch, dammit! Let's not forget Pascal, the King."

"God. I was wondering if it was cool to bring him up. I'm glad you did. It wouldn't feel right if one of us didn't. I miss the hell outta Facey," Claudio said in all earnestness.

"You really were his best friend, you know."

"Ya think? Well, that David person always gave me a run for my money."

"Oh, David, yes. But there was a boyhood history with David. You, you were his first real adult hang. He even told me once, 'You know who I wanna be like? Claudio Conte. That's one cool, smooth-ass mofo.' I knew he looked up to you, and the things you did in your career. But wanting to *be* you? That totally shocked me. It also told me how much he cared about you."

"I kinda wish he was, like me, I mean. Then, maybe he'd still be here."

"C'mon, Claud. Walk with me. I've so much to tell you and show you. In fact . . ." Bliss reached into her bag, and pulled her wallet full of snaps of Tyra.

"Oh. My God. It's HIM. Dammit! That's him in a little female form."

"Ya think?"

"They don't come any more beautiful. What a mug. And those eyes. I smell a future heartbreaker."

"Tell me about it. Do you know, I get approached constantly by people telling me she should be a child model? Shit! The HELL with that! Not my kid!"

"Well, she has an aura about her, no doubt."

Over dinner and drinks at Tavern on The Green, Bliss and Claudio Conte sat and talked and reminisced. The high of seeing each other again, of missing the friendship they shared, and missing Facey in different degrees was a bonding thing indeed.

"You know the night I introduced you, and then you and I went into my bedroom? Pascal *thought* we were having sex." Bliss laughed.

"I remember that. What was he, tripping back then? We were gone for what? Three minutes, tops? Even as good as you looked that night, I've never been THAT quick. I think I'm insulted!" Claudio huffed.

"Yes. You *should* be. It didn't say much about your skills." Bliss teased. And she thought maybe, without meaning to, she could be perceived as *coming on* to him. "He was deeply insecure around other good-looking people, until he got to know them. But what about *you*, Bliss? How are you, really?"

"I'm fine. I have Tyra, and I feel *blessed* that she continues to do so well."

"Bliss?" he asked in a singsong tone, knowing they were close enough for her to be honest with him.

"Ok. Granted. I *do* get lonely sometimes, Claud," she admitted, and she bittered her face with a trace of regret. "And not just for *him* and Ty and the people I've lost from the old days. I get lonely for *me*, and the girl I used to be."

"Well, that girl is still a mad lovely woman as far as I can see," Claudio said, lighting a cigarette. His eyes probed her then, trying to read the sub-text beneath her chin, as if she were in a foreign movie. And what he read was this:

She's still beautiful, still vital, still a thousand complex, womanly things. She's still very much the Bliss I knew . . . and she has the virus. Damn Facey, for doing this to her! Damn him to hell!

He took her to his apartment. The place looked very much like Face Depina's old loft: the sparse touches of suede and leather, the tasteful display of art by Picasso and Monet, the African busts, and the nude black and white photographs of Claudio, in his prime, aligning the wall. It occurred to her that in his quest to "be like Claudio Conte," Face had stolen Claudio's tastes.

"White wine?" he asked.

"Sure, babe," she said.

Bliss already knew what could happen between then, if she let it, and if she wanted it to. Claudio knew of her condition, and he sensed what had been missing in her life. Bliss Santana had been celibate since she'd received the terrible news. A part of her felt as if the bloom was off her rose, and making love was something those other, *luckier* women got to do now.

And yet, there stood Claudio Conte, wanting her, still. He'd never stopped waiting her. He'd wanted her at twenty-three, when she was a fresh new actress on the scene. Bliss was something to see back then, a lovely green-eyed Latina ingénue, with flowing black gypsy hair, and just a trace of caramel in her skin. Oh, yes, he'd wanted her then. And when she'd become successful, and then, a wild New York party girl, he'd wanted her still. He'd wanted her when Face Depina had succeeded in stealing her heart while in her late twenties. And when Face Depina had broken that heart, he'd stood in silence, holding back his strongest desire to wipe her tears away. He wanted her at thirty-three. He wanted her at forty-three, and he would even her want if she lived to see fifty-three. Most of all, he wanted her *now*.

"I can't tell you how much I've missed you, Blissy," he said, handing her the white wine, and gently letting his hand touch hers.

She looked him in his eyes, and she smiled from the inside of them, and somehow he could still see it.

"I missed you too, Claud. I've missed so many things," she said.

He took her glass away. She stared back at him. He swayed toward her as if that apartment were his runway, and she, his most important client. "You don't have to miss a thing, baby," he said, licking the fullness of his bottom lip with a hunger she'd never known existed in him. He held her face in his hands, rubbing his forehead softly against her beauteous cheek, and then her neck. Bliss was losing her breath, and losing the need, losing her every desire to say, "No. Please. No!"

A touch to her left breast made that which had lain dormant suddenly rush in a wave beneath her skin. He planted his kiss there, and then down her belly, and then to the fine black nest of fur that had waited for so long to be kissed again, touched again, licked again, entered again.

She was a woman, yes, a woman living with a virus. But she was, at first, a *living* woman. Love held no ticking clock, no alarm bells, and no voice which howled "STOP!" At the peak of passion, being made love to brought only music, only light, only need, only desire, and that quick catch in her breath again. Being made love to held no death sentence.

He made her golden-brown thighs quiver like the last leaves stirring, then shivering in the autumn breeze, and then he gave the tears she'd held captive in her irises permission to fall.

He was pushing love into her, thrusting love inside her, making that love come alive again.

And she welcomed the girth, the length, the deep and sweeping motion of him. His manhood consumed her, made her knees weak, her mouth parched, her heart beat faster, and her spine strong again. He went deeper, and then deeper still to thrust, and push, and tap each place inside her left untapped, left unfucked, left uncherished, left unloved.

Something like a moan hummed between her inner thighs and it traveled and glided along the wild course of her, until it reached and raced and rose in her throat. And she cried out, "Oh, God! God! Yes!"

It was the howl of satisfaction mixed with the gush of gratitude.

And when it was over, in the silence that followed, they lay in bed, and thought of no one else, but *him*.

August 1994

In those final days, Face Depina was a man begging for relief, a reprieve from his demons, and there were too many to name. This was a man who'd known the depths of abject poverty, and the quick ascent to the glorious riches of fame. This was a man for whom beauty, sex, and drugs had become a declaration of his worth, and a ticking time bomb.

Bliss Santana was a recipient of it all, and now she too was cursed by the kiss of a beautiful boy.

It had been months since she'd last seen him. She'd heard things—terrible things—things about his crumbling looks, and his Olympian addiction. *Good for him!* she thought. Slow suicide should *not* be painless.

But there she was, in New York again, amid the players and the wildly fabulous heartbreakers, amid the lies and the liars, cheats and the cheaters of an Empire. She walked the streets unrecognized now. Perhaps this was a *good* thing. Once she was famous, and then she was infamous. Suddenly, she was invisible. Invisibility was better.

He'd called her hotel several times. Why? Why now? Wasn't it a little too late to appease his crimes?

She went to see Ty. She'd missed Ty; his steady presence, and that sweet passion pouring from his eyes.

As she stared at his easy smile and long, lean frame, she realized *he* would have been the far better choice, the better, healthier father to her child. Life was strange.

"Have you seen him yet?" Tyrone asked.

"No. Not sure I want to?" she replied solemnly.

But Tyrone knew. He knew it was a lie.

"We never were friends . . . not really. But I do feel sad for him . . ." Ty said. "Don't you?"

"Sad for him? Shit! I wanna *kill* him, and if I saw him now . . . I just might do it. I'm serious, Ty. I'm very serious. I've thought about it. I've laid in my bed late at night and thought of nothing else."

"Ummm, you mean seriously, diligently, *planned* it."

"Yes, damn it! Yes!"

Ty chuckled softly. "Join the club. That charter membership is strong. Almost everyone I know has some secret what if, some slick, homicidal revenge plan for him . . . well, everyone except for David."

"Maybe, in the end, we're measured by the impact we leave on the lives of other people. Some will love our asses, and others will hate us madly. But maybe the ones who hate us will remember us longer. And maybe that's the legacy he wants to leave us with. Ya think?" Bliss asked.

"Nah!" Ty answered. "Nah, Face wants to be loved and adored, but on *his* terms. David loves him, no matter what. David is the person I know who truly GETS the meaning of Love. Love has a long legacy as a fighter, Bliss."

"David! David! Always, David. I can't have a conversation with you without hearing his name."

"Hey, I could say the same thing about you and Face," Ty snapped back.

"Maybe. But the way you go on about this David person. I think just maybe, you're *in love* with him, Ty."

"Bite your tongue, *hoard*! I am not IN LOVE with him. I Love David in the purest way there is. I Love him because David *is* Love." Ty paused just long enough to realize the truth in that statement. "I wish I could love people as fiercely as he does. But I can't say the same thing about Face."

"You make me want to *know* David. I'll have to put it on my to-do list."

"That's right. After all these years, you two New York *divas* still haven't met. Well, you *should* know David. It's an experience, I'll say that much. And so is knowing Face, especially for some people, like you. So, maybe you should see him. See him, one last time—if he lets you. See him, and finally, just get it *all* said."

Bliss could sense a guru-like calm in Tyrone . . . a quality she not could sense or ever see in herself. She loved and envied it, in equal parts.

She kissed his cheek softly. "I *do* love you, Honey Boy."

As much as she loved him, she knew she could not truly ever *have* Tyrone. But she loved him just as much as she despised Face Depina now.

When in Atlanta, she could feel that hatred so strongly, sometimes it produced an odor. And she hated him with good reason. But in New York, the reek of that hatred slowly ceased, and the love she held so tight to, it became stronger. It reached that still-sentimental region of her heart, and it became more enduring than even the hate.

She noticed how few things had changed since she'd last called the city her home. People still discarded each other, still bumped into one another, and just kept going on their way, like over-determined brawlers in a desperate fight for space. She noticed how the energy waxed and waned and played games with sound as it merged with the swish of traffic, the chattering exchanges, and the rumblings underground.

Arriving back at her hotel, there were three more messages from Face Depina, each one more urgent, more desperate than the next. He wanted her help. Could she refuse to lend it now?

Even the sound of his voice reminded her of the pain he'd brought into her life.

The girls, the boys, the tricks, the drugs, the public embarrassments, the bullshit he passed off as Love. The gift he gave her and others was that one *cursed* gift that would tragically keep on giving.

And so she went to see him.

She was not ready for the sight of him. This couldn't be her Pascal "Face" Depina. He looked ghostly, ghastly, and a thousand morose things she never thought he'd be. This was once considered by many to be "The Prettiest Boy in NYC." Where was that boy now? Could he not have even managed a cameo?

They would argue like wild and sickly dogs that night, and Bliss Santana would cry such deep and bitter tears.

He told her he was sorry. He fell down on his knees, and he begged her to please *forgive* him. She told him she had. He didn't believe her. He wanted to kiss her, one last time. If he kissed her, then he would *know*.

"C'mon, baaaaabyyyyy," he drawled. "All this stuff between us, all this wasted, craaaaaaazy stuff. Remember Pascal and Bliss? Bliss and Pascal, those crazy kids. Huh? Remember us? That's history, but it's got *some* love in it. Don't it? Don't it, Bliss?"

Bliss shook her head quickly, and tried to look away as he held her tightly by the shoulders. He held onto her was if she was his last needle, and that her kiss would be his final fix.

"Kiss me, please. Please, Bliss! Show me, you can be better than all this shit. Kiss me."

She allowed him that one last thing . . . that three-second kiss on her lips; that cheap, dime-store closure to it all.

"Thank you," he whispered, a slow smile crossing his twitching face. "Thank you," he whispered again, knowing it would be the last affection passed between them.

When she left him that night, Pascal "Face" Depina was alive . . . but for how long? Bliss closed her eyes and imagined that the evening would end, as so many of his nights did, with him lying in his bathtub, and sticking a needle in his arm.

That very same night, Browny stood outside Depina's building. He'd come to even the score. He thought maybe Face would have *something* for him, or maybe he'd be so strung out, that Browny could procure a few expensive items from the apartment and call it homeboy justice. Then he'd seen Bliss enter and so he turned all chickenshit. But he didn't leave. Faison Brown was there, the whole time. He stood in the darkness, smoking a borrowed cigarette, watching Face's apartment and he figured something very dramatic had to be going down in that place.

And then, the next day, Face Depina was dead. Browny, being someone who'd always sucked at math, arrived at the *pissed Bliss + wasted Face = Murder* equation. He added it, poorly, and most, incorrectly.

Bliss had never once spoken of that night. After seeing him, she boarded the plane home.

A day later, Claudio Conte called her in Atlanta and he delivered the inevitable news: Face was dead. She appeared to be shocked, but not totally surprised. She appeared to be deeply saddened. But Bliss Santana was an actress, wasn't she?

What ever happened from the time Bliss entered that apartment until the wee hours after when she exited it was left to Faison Brown's speculation.

CHAPTER THIRTY

A GHOST STORY REVISITED

It would be an obsene understatment so say that Kindred didn't like Browny. He silently cursed the day, or was it the night, he'd ever laid eyes on that face.

Six Months Earlier, in a Harlem Bar Called The Lennox Lounge:

Browny was pissed, highly pissed, beyond pissed, exceeding the limits of his own fanatical pissosity.

He'd taken a years-long smoky toke of that strong shit, the hellish joint that is New York City, and the bitch turned around and stole his dreams composed of moody saxophone riffs, mixed with Afro-Blue operatics, prison bars, and vicious nightmares that flowed from the trash heaps of his soul.

Sometimes, in the Wee Small Hours, men in bars will affect this posture of last-chance Romeos or sad-eyed Sinatras, nappy King Coles, and old, graying Panthers. And the women didn't always treat them fine, because Harlem ain't

Broadway, nor Hollywood and Vine. It's just a rhythm place uptown where the people are beautiful and lively and striving, and yes, some are hungry, too. But inside that moody bar, Browny sat bluesing where wine spilled and gin and vodka flowed as youth slowly rotted with the atrophy of time. It was a place where people like him sat and drank their yesterdays slowly and drunkenly out of mind.

Browny was there with a glass of groggy spirits, drinking down every dream he ever had.

The book, which he had placed his every hope and every aspiration of a brighter, wealthier future was suddenly taken away. There would be no second printing, no more royalties, and no seeds placed into his Big Dream kitty. His publisher just abruptly cancelled it, and it was taken out of circulation. He asked why, what happened, what or who made this horrible dream-snatching incident occur? But his publisher remained mum. All he said was there were serious legal problems, and he was not willing to risk an expensive lawsuit and possibly losing his business because of Faison Brown's history of grudges.

Bliss Santana made it happen with a few well-placed phone calls. But Browny didn't know that. No. When Browny searched the Rolodex of his skull, one name above all others came into play: David Richmond. David hated that book. David hated the very idea of that book. And David had let that be known, in public. Surely, with Ty's money, David had more than motive, David had the *power* to make it all stop, cease, go POOF!

And so once again, in Browny perception, yet another member of Da Elixir had cheated him. Once again, he was poor and downhearted, and lost as to where he would go, or what to do, and left to wonder what would become of him and *his* dreams.

He was stewing and drinking, drinking and stewing, he was brooding and ready to kick someone's ass. And when he ordered his next drink, he saw something. He saw a Miracle. That Miracle played inside a face inside the barroom's mirror. Was he drunk? He hadn't had that many vodka tonics. Was he tripping? No. He hadn't really tripped in nearly two years. He didn't believe in ghosts, but when he tried to blink the vision away, it was still there. Still in that mirror, still looking remarkable real, and astonishingly like the dead Tyrone Hunter.

Maybe fate or God was at long last kissing Browny's dark cheek, and the cosmos was finally aligning in his favor.

"Yo! Yo, man. What's your last name? And would it by any chance be . . . Hunter?"

Kindred shook his head, no. But he'd recently been asked that question before.

In Browny's mind, the deeply uncanny resemblance was enough to even make *him* trip, so he could only have imagined what seeing Kindred would do to David.

David. Poor mentally, emotionally fragile David. If such a soul could be convinced that he was seeing a ghost, and that ghost told him to *do* things, things most would deem inane, then he'd have to be finally declared unstable, perhaps certifiably insane. In the madness of Browny's own brain, unstable people would need people looking out for them, and their money. Unstable people couldn't be responsible. They certainly could not be legally relied upon to handle such an impressively lucrative trust fund, or stock holdings, or a corporation, or those perennial new monies and such, could they?

Of course they couldn't, and so a plan was hatched that night. That night Browny made a new friend with a familiar face. By evening's end, he asked to have their picture taken. He would show that photo to her wife, Juanita, the only other person who knew the secret, his only other co-conspirator, of sorts.

And so went the plan . . .

Only Browny hadn't counted on the end result. He had no way of knowing that Kindred would be *charmed* by David, or that Kindred would come to love David in a way only a true *friend* would. Browny wanted David committed, and instead, Kindred *was committed* to his friendship with David.

And now, what was this new bullshit about Kindred writing a damn book about David, Ty, and the life and times of the boys from Da Elixir? That was not the plan! That was the ultimate betrayal in Browny's eyes. It was, unless *Kindred* had a plan of his own.

Maybe Browny should sing a whole damn aria now. Maybe he should tell David that Kindred was a fake, a phony, a fraud. If he couldn't get his hands on the trust fund monies, then at least he could inform David of Kindred's deception. Hey, maybe David would even be so grateful, he'd *reward* Browny in some way for his honesty. Stranger things had happened in New York City.

Two weeks after the showdown with Browny, Kindred appeared at The Center just as David was leaving.

"Hey you," he said.

"Hey you," David said. "Where you been, son?"

"Around. Thinking mostly."

"Thinking's good. I've been doing some of that myself."

"Makes your head hurt, doesn't it?"

"Doesn't it . . . just?"

"Your play, it was deep."

"Yes, well, I'm in my deep stage."

"Sorry about the party."

"I wasn't. My show needed another act."

"Busted my hand."

"Busted his ass, too."

"He deserved it."

"Who you telling?"

David noticed that he and Kindred were even developing

a rhythm together; a rhythm like he and Ty had once shared.

"David, remember how we met?"

"Of course. I do. I'll never forget it"

"You thought I was a ghost."

"Not just any ghost . . . Tyrone's ghost."

"Well, you know I'm not a ghost now, right?"

"Yes. Kindred. I know."

"I never set out to be anything more than your friend. I didn't have any motives, and I'm out to get you, or make you fall in love with me."

"I know that, baby. I couldn't. You look too much like Ty, and that would be practically incest! I've freaked quite a few ways in my time, but never nothing like . . ."

"Just listen, David. I want you to GET it, to understand what this is all about."

"Are you about to *confess* something?"

"I've wanted to for a long time now, but I didn't know how to approach you, or what to say."

"'Hello' is always a good start."

"Can we start again, David? I mean, like it's first time we ever met?"

"Go for it, kid."

"Hello. My name is Kindred. I'd like to get know you and Ty, too."

"Hello, Kindred. I'm David."

"Hey, David. In the beginning, I wanted to know all about you. But I didn't do it the right way. God, she told me this would be hard. But I didn't realize *how* hard."

"Who? Who told you it would be hard?"

"It doesn't matter, she's gone now. I came to meet my father for the first time. Only, I was a month too late. I stayed because I wanted to know who he was and what he was about. And *you* helped me do that."

"Wait, Kindred! You're talking in riddles again. Please, don't do that. What or who are you talking about?"

"God. I hate this, because when I say it, you won't believe me. And even if you do believe me, you'll question why I went about it this way."

"Just tell me, son," David said patiently.

"Do you remember that story you told me, about Ty and the mystic woman who made fire in her hand?"

David nodded. Of course he did.

"Remember, how she mentioned a girl who loved him, and who he loved, but only as . . ."

"As a sister . . . yes . . . except . . ."

"Except for one night. She *did* love him. And he loved her . . . back. He was so easy to love. At least that's what my mother always told me . . . about . . . my father."

"What?" he asked. David felt a mix of an oncoming faint, a sense of wonder, of disbelief, of happiness, and of betrayal. All at once, he had to sit. He sat on the curb of sidewalk on East Thirteenth Street. He looked at Kindred under the street light, and he *saw Tyrone!*

"She never told him. It was a summer theatre camp in Pennsylvania. He was fifteen, and she was seventeen. They became very close. She loved his mind. He wrote her poems. Beautiful poems. She showed them to me. She never told him, because she knew . . . well, she didn't think he'd ever *love her* the same way because . . . She knew . . ."

"He was gay, and young, and unformed . . . and a thousand other beautiful things."

"Anyway, when she was two months pregnant, she married a man who was her boyfriend. A man, who I thought was my father for most of my life."

"So, you're telling me, you're actually *factually* Tyrone Hunter's . . . *son?*" a still stunned David asked.

"Yes. I'm telling you what was told to *me* before my mother passed. And I couldn't believe it." A tear raced down

Kindred's cheek. "And then, I came here to see him, to meet him, to talk to him, and . . . he'd just *passed*. I felt like an orphan. I still do . . . only sadder, because I *never* knew the real truth of my life. Everyone who *could* tell me, who could fill in the blanks was . . ."

"Gone," David finished.

"My mother's name was Giselle. Giselle Parker, back then. Did Ty ever once mention her?" he asked in a hopeful voice, staring up at the stars over lower Manhattan.

"I don't think so. I think I would've remembered."

"Well, I'm not *lying* about it, David. And if it's a lie, then it's a lie my mother told me when she knew she was dying."

"I don't think you're lying. I just, I just don't know *what* to think. Ty didn't know about *any* of this." David held his head in his hand. Wild tears began to roll from his eyes. "And if he only *knew*, his life would have been so much richer, and more complete. He loved children. He *loved* children sooooo much. He'd gone to Africa to *save* children. Maybe if he *knew*, oh God! He wouldn't've gone there. He'd be here, with you, and me, and still alive! God! Oh God."

It was too *much* to process.

But that wasn't *all* of the story. The rest Kindred wondered if David could handle, much less forgive him for *his* part in the great deception.

"I'd been in the city for two months. I researched all I could find out about Ty, my father. I read about the group, the past. I read about his deep friendship with you. I found out where he lived, and I discovered that you lived there now. I saw you coming out of the building, and I wanted so badly to speak to you. But I was afraid to. I'd seen his picture. I knew he *had* to be my father. I looked like *him*. That made me happy, and it made me scared, too. I mean, what would people think or say when they saw me? And what would *you* think or say or do? I didn't want to freak you out. So I tried to follow you around the city. I wasn't stalking you. I swear!"

"I *saw* you!" David said in amazement. "I saw you, so many times. It must've been *you*, Kindred. You! And I thought I was losing my mind. I thought . . ."

"That I was a ghost."

"Yes. That you were a ghost."

"I'm sorry. I never wanted to hurt you. I just didn't know how to approach you and tell you who I was. I thought you'd think I was after something, his legacy, his money. And that would only cheapen all these things I was feeling."

"Well, there are tests to prove or disprove such things. If you are his son, you are his rightful heir. And I couldn't and wouldn't ever deny you that."

"There's more, David."

"What Kindred? What?"

"I've been here, feeling lost, feeling defeated, feeling like I missed out on knowing my father, and . . . then . . . one night, I wandered into this bar. I was wondering where I should go, and what I would do, or if I should just leave New York, and then . . . I saw him."

"Who?"

"Faison Brown."

"Oh God."

"He wanted me to get close to you. He wanted me to make you think I was Ty, back from the grave, haunting you. He wanted you to go crazy, and to be declared insane, and somehow, he thought he'd get his hands on Ty's money, through me, because I could prove I was a Hunter heir."

"God. This just keeps getting better."

"David, I *never* agreed to do his dirt. Honestly. I never liked him, and I could smell nothing greed all over him. So, I never planned to do his bidding. I only let him THINK I would. I just saw this as a way to stay in touch with you, and to get to know *my father* through you. That's all I ever wanted. And I still do. I didn't do half the things *he wanted* me to do, or say the crazy things he asked me to. I couldn't. I hope you know, I wouldn't!"

"Oh I can imagine. So, he didn't haunt me in my sleep, or jump out any closet going 'BOO!' But you *lied* to me, Kindred."

"No. I just didn't tell you *everything*. But I always planned to . . . I mean, I meant to . . . and I was going to, in time, and in my own way. I swear it, David!"

"You lied. And now, I know the truth." David rose from the curb. "I always told you the truth. And you lied. You lied to me . . . and if you *knew me* at all, you'd know didn't ever have to." David began to walk away.

"David, please. I just needed *you* to understand. This was so hard for me!" Kindred said, tagging behind him.

"You lied. You were in *cahoots* with Browny. Browny, of all fuckin' people! And he tried to *destroy my sanity* . . . over money? That's . . . that's just *evil*. Evil! Don't you *get* it? It's really kind of creepy to walk around thinking you *know* a person—when in fact, beneath it all, there lives this sick and twisted individual, some emotional assassin, lying in wait to strike at any given moment—whatever the cost. That was Browny. And now, that's become *you*, Kindred."

"No. I'm not. That's some whole other person, not me! David, please. You don't understand. I love, and I respect you, man. I've got to make it right. Just let me try to make it right again!" Kindred touched his shoulder, and David kept walking away. He thought maybe Kindred made a better ghost, because now even his touch felt *cold* to him.

"Please, don't follow me home," David said. "I'm done talking to you for the night."

CHAPTER THIRTY-ONE

COULD YOU BE LOVED?

Kindred wondered if he'd ever get the chance to make things right with David again. It hurt his heart deeply that David saw the things he'd omitted to tell him as a betrayal. Maybe it was.

Didn't David get it? Didn't he realize Kindred felt lost and alone, with one secret to depend upon, to keep him from losing his own mind? Kindred had no sense of self anymore. It had abandoned him the sad day he'd discovered that the people he'd loved and trusted most in this world had kept the truth and the facts of his own life away from him.

Maybe David was too hurt to understand. But David Richmond had given him his father back. Some gifts are indeed forever, and for that alone, Kindred would be eternally grateful.

Since David had also given the journals back to Kindred on the night of the play's opening, Kindred now had become a fast student of Tyrone . . . the man, the father he never knew.

It was an eerie experience for him to read his words, and

to know what the future held in store for Tyrone Hunter. But reading about him made Kindred begin to understand that caring part of his nature.

In the midst of losing friends in the life, losing lovers, losing his bearings, Ty had become haunted by his inability to find a lasting *spiritual* center. It had worn him down. He'd spent his life attempting to create *better in his self*, in others, and to write or sing, to photograph, or carve something beautiful out of the pain of existence. But he grew tired of trying to show the world his scars, and its scars. It was time to concentrate on the business of healing them.

It had been building . . . forming, erecting and becoming taller in his mind, this Higher Calling, this second level to being a human being.

The metamorphosis had begun in November of '91, with his first trip to Africa. Something in Africa, in that time he'd spent wiping the sweltering foreheads of dying children, that humbling experience had resonated so profoundly in him.

And how he wished Bliss hadn't lied about Tyra being his child. Though he'd forgiven her in the end, it left a raised scar on the complexion of his future.

Tyrone wrote:

I feel as if I have a bigger purpose. If my friends are dead or dying, and I'm still here, there must be another reason for it. God! I wish I had a child. I could give him or her so much. And they, in turn, could teach me so much. If it's in The Creator's Plan for me to ever find someone *real* to love, maybe we could adopt us a child to love. Maybe I could impregnate a willing lesbian friend. Maybe I could father a child of my own. Wouldn't that be something! Maybe, *just maybe*.

Life is full of fucking maybes.

Kindred, the unknown son of the man who so desperately wanted children of his own, cried a bittersweet tear.

"But I'm here, Ty . . . Dad . . . what do I call you now? I'm here. Can you see me? I wish I could meet you, talk to you, love you. I'm everything you wanted. I'm your child. I'm your son, dad. I'm here, and you're gone."

Ty dreamed of children, but children were alone and dying on a dying continent. Disease and famine were ravaging both coasts and rocking the interior. Imani, Ty's African friend, wrote him such troubling letters from the sadness and insanity Liberia.

> Dear Ty,
>
> I write you tonight with a heavy heart. Inside the capital of Monrovia this conflict has already claimed over one hundred fifty thousand lives. I believe there are even more. Today a baby was born in my hands. Tonight a child died in my arms. So many others are losing their way. Mothers, fathers lie dying beside their children. But Ty, though people are barely holdin' on, some are holding to survival, even in the hot and dry faces of death. I see them, and I am humbled. Even through famine and disease and the guns of rebel factions, these people, my people of the sun, are striving to survive!

It was a dawning of an epiphany. In the final analysis, even staring into the eyes of death, the best of us strive for some kind of existence with dignity.

There had to be *something* Ty could do.

And so, Tyrone decided to once again plan a trek to Africa. He approached several publishers, editors and producers about embarking on a photojournalistic project on Africa's children. He was promptly rejected. Ty didn't care. Fuck them! He was strong-willed and independent. He went on his own.

Tyrone left for the Motherland with the intent to do better by the world.

He'd tried to snatch a piece of Joy in giving Art, giving Love, giving concern, giving hugs, giving money, and then, in giving food, in giving comfort, in giving hope to others. And he died, abruptly, never fully realizing that joy in himself.

The events in David's life were beginning to make sense and yet becoming crazier in the twisted sort of sense that they made.

On top of this, Jose, that lean, delicate-looking Blatino boy, Jose who was all of twenty-four, and a former hustler, had passed away. He was the rebel in the room. He needed cold cash. He tricked. He made no apologies. And in the end, AIDS ravaged him. AIDS was the cruelest trick of all.

DAVID, In Dr. Horowitz's Office:

"I thought of Ty today. But what *else* is new? Thinking of Ty and missing him, that's just what I do. I thought of him because, I saw that young couple again. The two Boricuas I'd seen before on the subway into lower Manhattan, the ones who were barely eighteen, and whose true sexuality was *unclockable* to all, except for me. You know, Doc, maybe they're coming into a *better* world than the one I'm leaving behind. Just maybe this one will be a New World of Infinite Possibilities. A world beyond fear and lies, and deception, a world where there's just naked honesty.

"Victor's son, Raul . . . the one who hates me, well, guess what? He's just another closeted self-hating young man who refuses to come to grips with his reality.

"Are you sure, David . . . or is this just speculation?"

"Oh, trust me. I've seen things I wasn't supposed to see. He's a secret friend of Dorothy's. I know this. Victor doesn't. It's not my secret to reveal. But I feel like the Rauls and even the Kindreds of this world have to step up and be men, men of integrity. Life gets *better* when you live it in honesty."

"I quite agree."

"So, seeing those two Boricuas, they still give me hope, Doc. Could it be a world where young men with men, and women with women could kiss freely and lovingly, and hold hands without fear? Maybe. Or maybe I'ma madman poet, waxing all madly and romantic and shit. But wasn't it mad lovely to dream so?"

"Yes. David. It is a lovely thought."

"But what about the rest of us? What were *we* so afraid of? Isn't kissing needed? Isn't realness and affection desired and needed, by any means necessary?"

"Of course it is. But many people will tell themselves, and even convince themselves, that there's less hurt when there's no investment of affection. It takes bravery to love, David."

"Maybe. Maybe it does. I don't know many of us who kiss as if we might burst, or bust, or self-destruct if they didn't openly show their fierce Love for each other. That saddens me, Baby-Doc. That saddens the shit outta me. Damn it! Just to be REAL with another human being, with no pretense, without guile, without buster or bullshit, just REAL . . . that has to be even better than a Long Blue Moan. That was surely a long and Liberating Moan."

In those last months, he'd never been a witness to so much hope. He saw it in his relationship with the boys at the center, and he realized it most of all in Kindred. That *hope* was keeping David alive!

And in the end, Kindred had lied, and so maybe David's hope was a lie. But at least he had Victor. Victor would never desert him, even when *hope* had.

But hope was still needed, and it was David's job to project it, especially to the young men at The Center.

* * *

David Addressing the Men at The Center

"I know some of you will hear this and think I'm some sick and corny mofo. But you know what I hope? I hope tonight, in someplace where men meet and dance and grind, I hope that someone is *lucky* enough, *blessed* enough to find another soul who's in it for *real*. I hope beyond the alcohol, and the ecstasy, the cruising eyes, hard-ons, and all the lusty sighs, I hope someone who's out there, wanting love, needing love, who knows how to love, and is willing to *be* loved, finds them that piece of Love, tonight.

"Now I know some people walk through life, too damn cool to care, like *love* is the last thing they're looking for. They'll swear up, down, and sideways it's the very last thing they want. Bullshit! Who the hell do you think you're foolin? Not me! I'm here to tell you, anyone who says that is a liar. They are straight-up frontin', you hear me? You know that song by Bob Marley, 'Could You Be Loved?' I always liked that song. I could wind my hips real slick to that one. It sounds like a simple title, doesn't it? '*Could You Be Loved*? 'Well, there was nothing simple about Mr. Marley. And take it from me, there's nothing simple about the meaning of that song. Not everyone *can be* loved. Maybe that's because they really don't know how, and maybe, they were never *shown* how to love. That's sad. Maybe, the one time they let themselves be loved, that one time they *allowed* it—some foul shit happened, feces occurred, and their heart was broken in the process.

"Take it from me, the human heart does get smashed to smithereens. And that's so tragic. Boo-hoo! Tough shit. If that *one time* did you in, and you've had it, called it quits, hardened your heart against the idea and the beauty and the reality of real love, I'll feel s-o-o-o-o sorry for you," David told his counseling group.

"Please don't be cowards, people! If you don't love somebody and no one gets a chance to *see your heart*, and love you for it, then you've wasted your time here. No one on the planet will even *miss* your sad, loveless ass once you're gone.

"So, could *you* be loved? Ya damn right! I can. Hell. I have been. Takes some work to learn to love and let yourselves *be* loved. But once you find the bearings and balls to, damn it! Love, like you mean it! Love like it's the last day! Love as if you might burst or bust or self-destruct if you didn't get to touch the soul of that person! That's it. That's all. Meeting over. Be safe. Be loved. Goodnight."

There was a single tear glistening in David left eye. Somehow, it remained there, refusing to fall, until the last person had left the room. Then, it made the slowest trail down his cheek. He wiped it away, quickly.

CHAPTER THIRTY-TWO

REVELATIONS IN A STORM

Two Weeks Later
Dr Horowitz's office:

"We live in a city of fictions, Doc. We exist in these little cubicles of steel and metal and brick with our secrets and our lies, and our tongue-kissing jaws of terror. To avoid them, we dance to rhythms . . . so many rhythms. There are always crazy rhythms in this city . . . and crazy rhythms in me. They hiss and moan, and rumble and beep, but even I can't always dance to their urgency.

"The best of us, the actors in us, put on our best face, and we walk that atmospheric strut of *survivors*. Some of us walk so coolly, we learn to ignore the sights and sounds around us, even the suffering ones. We dash pass those troubled souls like we're selfishly going for our own Olympic gold.

"But me? I never wanted to be one of *those* people. Ty *taught* me to a better a listener. When I hear that sound of suffering or I see it in the flesh, God help me—I have to react.

"I talk about Love a lot. I can now, because I know the

power of it. It is a fierce thing. A madly fierce and scary thing indeed."

David sighed the final sigh he'd ever sigh inside that office.

"Well, Doc. I wanted to say thank you, old chum. Thank you for your patience in listening and for trying to unravel this riddle of me. But I'm done. Won't say I'm completely cured, but this is it for me. You won't have li'l David Richmond to kick around and analyze anymore."

"Well, it's been an adventure in . . . something, I'll say that much . . . and off the record: I'll miss you, David."

"Of course you will, Baby-Doc. Hell, you'll soon discover that I'm . . . I'm a very *missable* cat! Bon soir."

Conversation with the man in the mirror:

Right now, in this hour of reflection and revelation, I must tell you this: I feel like such a fuckin' fraud. I have been. I've spoken of love, my endless love for Ty and my ardor for Facey, and I made it sound so black and white. Love *ain't* black and white. There's a whole mess of colors, a rainbow of gray with so many shades between.

When I love people, *deeply* love them, I hate like Hell to see them in pain. I mean, there's so much fuckin' pain out there, so much, and I've known my share of it . . . trust me. It's always been my way to try to shake people out of pain, with a laugh, a face, with a retort, or a gay witticism, with a comment that reminds them, and me, that life is this crazy, ridiculous dream. Sometimes, I did it with kiss on the cheek or a hug from the soul, and for a while, things actually *appeared* better. That was my role. I did it more for *me* . . . than for them.

You see, I've always been one of those hypersensitive boys. You cut yourself, and watch me bleed. You vomit, my stomach hurts, and I double over in pain. If you come to experience some dark, some gut-wrenching heart ache . . . then just watch mine . . . as it slowly breaks.

Facey. God, I *loved* that boy. But he wasn't perfect. He did a lot of things—cruel, harsh, foul, and hurtful things—simply because he could.

Maybe this world gives the Beautiful Ones a special ticket. But it's what they DO with it that makes all the difference. Facey used his ticket to ride through life on the heady octane of fierce and fabulousness. He never tried very hard to impress, or to endear himself to you. Someone long ago must've made him think, even when the world turned ugly, his physical beauty was all that really mattered. And so he worked it, like a whore. He'd dazzle and blind and trick you with it. He'd charm and tease and he'd play and use you, and eventually he'd destroy you with it, because a part of him secretly resented your reaction to him, to IT.

Beautiful People are often the most tragic. Sometimes they forget that tedious work involved in beautifying the soul. And Facey, he was one of those quietly damaged people. Only, he managed to hide it with his full-bodied beauty mark. Oh, poor Facey.

You need to understand. I loved him long before he was the Face Depina of magazine covers, and that tortured mulatto man-child of independent flicks. I loved him during the height of his utter butter celebrity. And, I loved him wildly after it. And in the end, when it all came crashing down and he was suffering from the disease of his own bad choices—well—he wasn't alone. As long as there was a David, he wasn't alone.

I would never have let him go through all that terrible pain alone.

I don't know how much time I have left. But time is not measured in years or days or even hours. Time is now. And now is the time for my last confession.

* * *

Picture it. August** 7, **1994:

It was raining very hard that night. I was restless. The boom and crack of thunder and lighting made it difficult to sleep. Then, the phone rang and the sound alone scared me shitless. It was a very late, 4:17AM.

I answered. It was Facey. He'd never called me that *late* before. We hadn't spoken in so long. I was happy to hear from him. And I was scared to be hearing from him. I used to be his fix-it man. The one he'd turned to in small emergencies. But he rarely called me when he was in deep trouble, or deeply troubled.

This was not a call, a shout-out or "how you been?" This was Facey's final cry for help. No smoky veil, no cool, slow drawl, and no hipster speak. He'd given them all up. He'd surrendered all his masks and pretenses to his wounded inner child. I knew that child by its naked first name. His name was Pascal. And that night, he was his self, the essential Pascal Depina again. Me, being so in-tuned to him, I could hear Pascal's pain. Oh, but that night beyond hearing it in his voice, I could decipher it in all the things he didn't, or wouldn't or couldn't seem to say. I think I heard his *heart* breaking.

"Davy. My favorite queer. How you doin, baby? You all right? I just called to say, h-e-e-e-ey."

"H-e-e-e-ey, Facey. Hey. It's late, baby. You okay?"

Of course I knew he wasn't. His silence after the question said so such. It was my turn, my cue in the dialogue. My turn to ask . . .

"What's wrong?"

"What's right?" He chuckled for a short second. It was the saddest show of gallows humor I'd ever heard.

"Where are you, Facey?"

"Out of my mind."

"Oh. I've been there," I said.

"No. You haven't, Davy. Not really."

He was quiet for a long time. I think he wanted to *say* something. But then I thought maybe he'd nodded away. I sat up in bed and tried to listen to see if he was still breathing. He was, though his breaths sounded so shallow to my ear.

"Facey? Face, wake up! Are you there? Can you hear me?"

"Hear you, Davy. Love you, Davy. *Need* you. Wanna . . . show you how much. Come see me."

Come see him? I could not believe the simplicity or that largeness of those three little words: "*Come see me.*"

By then, he was not letting *anyone* see him. The theatre of his glamorous facade had closed its green neon-lit door. I'd heard rumors of how "bad" he looked, how he wouldn't let anyone in, and how he was living this hermetic existence. But he'd just said "Love you, Davy" and it was *my music*. I hadn't prompted it by being silly or stroking his ego. It just flowed the fuck out, like, like breath itself!

He'd just invited me, David, his "favorite queer" to come where all the others were no longer accepted. I felt honored. I felt *scared*.

God! The thoughts I had that night. I remember being fifteen. I remember being the best dancer in school. I remember how a dancing kid's heart became so full of rhythms—when the auditorium door opened, and there stood this minor god in the flesh . . . Pascal Depina! I remembered how brilliantly *Beautiful, Magnetic, and Troubled* he was. I remembered falling in love inside that moment—in love, with a boy full of sharp angles and green-eyed mischief. I remembered delighting in his chameleon-like skin and how everything just seemed to come alive when he smiled.

Even after he left our little singing group and we'd disbanded, those times when he'd publicly disrespected me, and even after all the nameless heart-fracturing shit, fate intervened. Somehow, one night in the Village, we'd found each other on a Lafayette Street, and he was so *glad* to see me.

He'd added me to his menagerie long ago. I'd been one of his inside homeboys, one of his collectibles. There was once a small army of us then. Men and some women who Facey saw something in, a talent, a quality he could use or exploit to his selfish advantage. Maybe it was strange and just a little of pitiful to feel so *honored* that he wanted to use me one more time.

I went to see my baby, my Facey that night, unprepared for who or what might await me. And yet I prayed the world would finally be his, mine, ours.

But it wasn't Face or Facey or even Pascal who cracked open that door and let me inside.

Physically, I couldn't see or even recognize the *real him* anymore. His once-gorgeous face was only a mask of bones. His beautiful body was just a long, thin ghost. Yet I knew a time, not so long ago, when that face and body belonged to a god. The ghost of that god stared back at me that night. I kissed the highest of those bones on the cheek. I hugged that body tightly. I whispered, "It's all right."

I suddenly felt very weak. Hugging him, I could feel only shaking bones and a strained weakness between each and every one of them. That weakness had somehow infiltrated *me*, now. But I needed to be strong for both of us, because I was holding and sharing his disease.

When he pulled away, I wanted to see, I needed to see his eyes again. I always loved his eyes best. There were so many things in his old face to love. But those shards of green light brightening when he looked at me . . . they were my love's food.

The room was dark, and whatever light was diffused from the storm both outside and inside of in that loft.

The little beige boy voice came out and said, "We gotta do something about me, Davy."

I loved it when he said "we," because he rarely ever said it. He lived in a *Me, Myself, and I* world. He was alone, even when he was in a crowd and everyone wanted him. He was his best when alone. Maybe we all are. I felt that. Now he was saying "we" to me. *We*, dammit! It was his final flirt, and my secret love note.

"We gotta do something about me, Davy," he repeated, and I noticed his jittering.

He wasn't speaking about the prospect of me styling his thinning hair, or of me finding just the right outfit for him to wear to an event or fashionable affair. He wasn't asking for makeup, or a tip, or a lesson in just what cleverly-cool thing say at some fabulous downtown soiree.

Our telepathy was working very keenly that night.

I was trying not to cry. But if a tear sneaked from the corner of my eye inside that darkened room, I prayed he couldn't see it. I wanted to be my most stalwart, for him.

"We gotta do something about where I'm going, baby. See, I hurt . . . . all the time. You *know* about hurt, right? You know about hurting when it twists from inside you, when it feels like . . . glass and gravel in your veins?

Sadly, I nodded, yes.

"Well, I hurt that way all the time, every day, every night. Man, I hurt so bad and so much and so many people . . . I can't even tell you. And I don't want to hurt *this bad* . . . not like this. Not anymore. I just can't do it."

"Then, we'll just have to get you some *help*, baby. The best clinic, best doctors. We can do it *right* this time. But you gotta *fight*, Facey. Fight with me! If you've forgotten how, then let me teach you."

"I'm too tired for fightin'. Can't do it no more. Been fightin' for years. I thought you *knew* that!"

And with Facey, yes. I knew plenty.

When your mother dies giving birth to your star, and your father never forgives it and wants nothing more to do with you, when you're a pretty child and all people want is to touch you in bad places, places that should be sacred, and when you're betrayed and raped on birthday, maybe a part of your soul . . . just . . . stops . . . fighting. Maybe the only fight left waging is the war to *forget.* And so, you try to forget. You try to numb the pain, the rage, this misunderstanding within your fucking fucked-up existence in whatever way you can. That was his history. That was his endless fight.

"Tired of fightin', Davy . . . That's why . . ." His voice trailed off.

"That's why, what?" I asked him desperately.

"That's why, I thought you came here . . . I need you. Damn it! Help me! Make it stop!" he whisperd.

If he could never be my Lover, then at least I could be that one thing he'd never had and always needed—a *brother*. In that moment, he became my brother. I adopted him into my heart that night—his last night on earth. I loved him that deeply, and so completely, I would have done whatever he needed of me, whatever had to be done. I would never let him go through all that terrible pain alone. But what did he *want*?

He looked at the floor and then at the storm in the window as a violent blade of lightning struck outside. There was lightning in that room, and a storm inside of him.

"What is it?" I asked again

He mustered up the final finesse, his last ounce of seduction, and then he whispered *it* in my ear.

No. NO! How dare him! NO! Never! I can not believe he called me here, in that driving New York City rain, to do this thing! No!

He touched my face so softly. A green and bronze butterfly landed on my skin, and for a split second, I saw his eyes. My God! Those eyes. Inside them, I saw the reason why. I never imagined staring into those beautiful eyes, and seeing no light, no living, no fire left inside them. I'd never seen such pain and suffering, such living death.

He left me and staggered off to the bathroom to prepare himself. I stood there wondering if I should, or if I could, if I had the courage to do this one *last* thing.

It was the first time I'd ever seen him naked, and I had not thought of sex. Naked, he was once, sex, personified. Naked was once his best, most brilliant color. Not anymore. Naked, he'd become this long and weeping sadness in the flesh.

I drew the water high in his tub, just the way he'd always liked it. He wanted music, but not just any music would do. He wanted a particular song . . . "Running To Stand Still," a song by the group U2.

"Step out a driving rain, maybe,

Run from the darkness in the night . . . ."

I'd listened to those words with him before. They were morose to me back then. That night, each word, each pause, every aching syllable seemed composed to break my soul in two. Bono was a dark genius. That song had to be written for a junkie's desperation. There was a cruel poetry in that song— and it could have been my Facey's anthem.

"Tell me, Davy. Tell me what you'll say," he whispered, as slow and shaking. He placed his long, frail, ravaged body into the tub, leaning on me as he did.

"I'm creative," I sniffed. "I'll, I'll . . . just create."

"No! Tell me! Tell me, what you'll say, about me . . ."

He was raging, sweating, and so impatient with me. I felt that storm, and it was rolling up in *my* eyes.

His needle was prepared and poised. His arm was a valley of collapsed arteries, but I managed to find his one goodenough vein. I was strangely surprised at how steady my grip had become that night. Maybe it was my gift, a gift of calm and of grace.

"I'll say, 'once, there was this gorgeous, gorgeous time, when we were all living our dreams . . .' "

"Ni-c-c-c-c-c-e . . ." he sighed. Suddenly, he drew a sharp breath, and then, as he exhaled . . . this gentle, sighing, placid expression had came over him. At last, this thing I'd always known down deep, this beautiful tortured thing . . . now wore a look of peace. It slowly drifted over every aspect of his being and settled into his face. His eyes no longer looked terrified.

In that final jerk of quiet, he sighed, "D-a-a-a-vid. Love."

He drew that breath in an upward motion, defining the moment that will forever live and breathe within the youngest, most loving part of me.

"D-a-a-a-vid. Love. . . ." The inhaled breath, it froze there, lingering in the space between us. It was as if he and it marveled at the idea of what would come after it. Death. Maybe it was beautiful.

I hope so.

I think, that look he gave me, maybe it was *gratitude*.

The pain and raging and the anguish he'd known for so long, it was all over then. Finally, it was finished. Done. Completed in a needle's prick.

I'd like to believe he really *did* love me. But even more than that, I'd like believe there was for him, at least somewhere in his soul, there came a Long Blue Moan in the end. Maybe it felt like some kind of liberation.

My Facey was gone.

I'd done what he'd first asked, then begged me to do. Now, ain't that love? I try to tell anyone who'll listen: Love is a *verb*, damn it! A motherfuckin' verb!

"I love you." People say it all fucking time, but how many

of us actually do one damn thing to *prove* it? I *did* love him. I did, and I showed, I manifested, and demonstrated that love until the very end. This was my final gift of love to him. Now ain't that love?

See, he couldn't make it a suicide. What would people say or think of him? That he quit . . . gave into his weakness? No! Not my Facey! He deserved a little dignity. An O. D. was better. A little trace of mystery was better still.

I didn't feel like some malicious criminal piece of shit as I wiped my fingerprints from the needle, placed it inside his hand. I didn't feel as if I sinned some unforgivable sin. All I'd done was to finally ease his motherfuckin' pain. And *that's* the way I want him to remember *me*. David—the one person in the whole crazy, beautiful, ugly-hideous world who put an end to his suffering once and forever.

I took one final look at him. My Facey—peaceful at last.

Don't you dare point your judgement stick at me! I didn't feel as if I've done anything wrong back then. I still don't, even now. I guess in the end, The Creator will be my judge.

CHAPTER THIRTY-THREE

NO TEARS PLEASE

Spring 1997

David was growing weaker and more listless by the day. That merciless time clock was ticking, ticking away at the quality of his remaining days and nights. He was still putting up a fight, but so much of that fight was gone.

He could only prolong the inevitable for so long. David had one more earthly wish. He wanted so desperately to have that one wish fulfilled.

"Baby. I have to go to City Center. It's a must! Trust me, I can and *will* go alone, if I have to . . . but I'd rather have you come with me. I know it isn't your favorite thing to do, but it would mean so much to me."

"What is it, Puppy?"

"I *have* see The Alvin Ailey Dance Troupe. Ms. Judith Jamison will be expecting me. And ya don't wanna piss off Ms. Judith."

"Oh boy. The things you put me through, Puppy,"

Victor sighed.

"Well, I'm worth it, right? Right? RIGHT?"

"You're worth everything and anything. I love you."

"I know. I just needed to hear you say it."

"Won't it make you . . . sad?"

"Sad? How so?"

"To see those dancers spinning and flying the way you used to do?"

"No. God no! It will make me *dream*, Papa. If I couldn't make it on *that* stage, at least I can still *feel* the thrill of the dream."

"My Puppy. You are such a *pig* . . . a show-off. I'll have to handcuff you to the chair, so you don't run on stage."

"A *pig?* A pig, señor? Did the man just call *me*, a pig? Ummm . . . I think you mean, a HAM, Papa! I'm a *ham*, dammit! You didn't even *know* me in my *pig* days. So? You'll come with me?"

"Of course. Whatever you want, Puppy."

To see those magnificent dancers move the charged air around them, and to see them virtually command the stage was a supernatural thrill for David. This was his every dream, personified.

Even as a child he knew and had memorized every move to the routine for the classic Ailey piece "Revelations." It was performed to the tune "Right On, Be Free!" by The Voices of East Harlem. He sat transfixed, refusing to even blink. As he watched it, he held Victor's hand tightly, and his heart, it didn't just beat faster, it leaped, it spun, and it *danced!* Yes, he *did* want to run, to charge, to soar upon that stage, and become the *Danseur Noble* . . . to *Tour en l'Air! Sauté! Jeté* and end in his own *Variation.*

"Right On! Be *Free*," indeed!

It was a stellar time at City Center. He'd seen them. He'd felt them. And for one moment inside his own imagination, he'd *become* one of them. And this, for him, it was something beyond beautiful. It was lovely. Mad lovely.

And now, David could die happy.

Tyrone's Last Entry About David

Today, I am no longer David's mother. I've given up the gig. Besides, he never put in an application for another Moms. I'm sorry I've wasted so many fucking years misusing our friendship. He might've stopped boxing long ago, but David remains my Champion. I think I realized that again today. Today, I saw him at Wigstock, rocking the crowd in his big, hyper-blond-atomic-Afro wig, dancing to "I Will Survive." It was like he didn't have one sad bone in his entire body.

Later, as I watched him, falling safe and contented inside Victor's arms, I wondered: Why am I worrying? David's fine. All HIV-positive queens should be so fine. He's got a good man who's big in the pants.

Yes, every now and then when those crazy eyes of his get weird and teary, I'll ask him if he's ok. But he tells me those tears are because he's "happy!" I have to believe he is, because he looks so much like that queer copper kid I used to know at fifteen, when all the world's stages were just ahead of him. So I'm not gonna worry about his mercurial ass anymore. The Duchess is happy. Bravo! You go, Baby-Boy! Snatch joy!"

DAVID:

Can you keep a secret? Come closer. My secret is this: I'm not a well man. Hell, I may already be dead as you read these words. If so, whatever you believe in, please, without getting all Dionne Warwick about it, please, say a prayer for me.

The leading cause of death in HIV-positives in those last few years had been liver failure. Liver failure was not an AIDS-defining disease in any way. It was however, an acknowledged side effect of protease inhibitors, of which David had been taking in massive daily doses, for years.

"NO TEARS, PLEASE!"

That was what he'd asked to be handwritten on a sign next to the number on his door. Most of his visitors tried their best to comply. Steely queens do indeed have their inner strengths. Victor had forbid the entrance of anyone and everyone with the tendency to display fits of emotional histronics. Those with the penchant for overblown theatrics were to be banished. There would be only meaningful words and wonderful remembrances, no dramatic good-byes, no hysterical wailing at David's bedside. His life had already been filled by more enough of that, thank you.

Rodney came. Nothing could have stopped him, not even delayed planes from Paris, and not even the completion of that first couture collection bearing his name.

He sat by the bed for hours, and when David awakened, Rodney smiled and said, "I love you, brotha David. Because of you, I *am!*"

Of course, Bliss Santana came to see him. Bliss wiped the sweat from his forehead, and she brought her communion crucifix. Her lasped Catholicism notwithstanding, she placed her rosary in his frail little hand, and she said her prayers for him. And the torrent of tears she'd held for David, and for herself, would be delayed tears, cried on some other colorless day.

Adeva came. And instead of wildly affected behavior and fits of drag queen hysterics, she brought that huge hyper-blonde-atomic-Afro wig David had once performed in at Wigstock. She wanted him to wear it. She wanted him to remember what strength and bravery it took to be beautiful and bawdy and outrageous again.

And then, one sunny afternoon, too much amazement, Faison Brown showed up at Harlem Hospital. Juanita had convinced him to go and to pay his respects. She even accompanied him there to make sure he went and didn't turn chicken-shit. Victor didn't know what to make of his appearance there.

But Juanita said, "My baby *always* had love for David. He might not admit it. And he did some bad things, and just plain wrong stuff, for the wrong reasons, but . . . I know this. Brothas don't go from boys to men, deal with what they went through together, and survive it without *Love*."

Browny entered the room, and the shock of seeing David that way, it made him place his hand over his mouth. But then he realized that reaction wasn't right, and bordered on the offensive, and so he tried to revert back to being Browny.

David seemed to rally, just a little, when he saw him.

"Hey, fool."

"H-e-e-e-e-ey." David sighed through a very tired smile.

"Damn. I didn't wanna roll through here, yo. Juanita made me, tho. I didn't wanna."

"Got ya."

"Nah. No, you don't, David. I mean, I didn't wanna be seeing you laid up here all sick, and have to walk around here for the rest MY days, rememberin' *seeing* you sick. I cant take that shit. I had enough. Too painful, yo."

"So . . . it's still all about you . . . and *your pain*, isn't it?"

"Well, that's all I got."

"Nah. You got a wife that loves your crazy ass. Don't know why, but she do."

"Yeah. That's 'cause I be puttin it ON that fat ass, errrr-e night, yo!"

"Well, so . . . you got two big things to cling to. Juanita's fat ass, and . . . your old sob sad stories."

"Watch it, yo! This ain't high school mo more. I'm sure I can kick your sissy ass now!"

"Don't underestimate me." David's breathing was shallow. "Just . . . just let me speak. You never got to grab . . . the brass ring, did you, Browny? You . . . . didn't sing . . . that great solo in the show. Boo-hoo . . . Poor Browny. Your brother was . . . murdered before you could prove . . . he was *wrong* about you . . . and your talent. Nobody ever gave you . . . a decent chance to shine, right?"

"Right."

"Maybe . . . you never gave yourself, a chance . . . *a real fighter's* chance. You quit so easily, Browny. Always did. Then . . . you waste your whole fuckin' *life* talkin bout what you *coulda* done, what you *woulda* did. I've heard it . . . all . . . before. I'm sick . . . with it, Browny."

"So. What you sayin', David?"

"You ever . . . asked yourself: Do I . . . have the power . . . to make this shit . . . stop happenin to me? Huh? Bigger Question . . . comin' atcha: Will *you* ever make it . . . stop?"

"I ain't God, David," Browny sniffed. "Yo, I'm just . . . unlucky, I guess."

"Breathe . . . . Listen . . . . Please . . . just listen to me, poor prick! You . . . listenin?"

"Yup."

"A whole lot of foul . . . fucked up things . . . happen to people in their lives . . . BUT THOSE THINGS ARE NOT . . . YOUR LIFE! Some of us DIE . . . in those moments. . . . we freeze . . . inside those terrible . . . moments . . . and we never fully recover . . . never finish walkin' . . . never finish working. You want it bad enough, then you pray . . . and you work your Black ass off for it. Life don't give you shit you don't *earn*. That's what we're . . . supposed to be doing . . . right now . . . Earning . . . the lives we get . . . livin' and workin for the better moment."

"That ain't never worked for me, David. You know that, yo!"

"Just let GO . . . of that thing that held you . . . down. LET GO! They ain't never been helpful . . . or healthy, Browny! Shit will knock you . . . down and sometimes, yes . . . even knock you out . . . BUT YOU GET UP! Get up! Get the fuck . . . up! Damn it!"

Browny, with his tears in his eyes, and his hands clasped in a useless prayer said to David, "I'll try. Just for you Davy, I'll try."

"Fuck that . . . just for . . . Davy shit! I won't *be* here . . . to see it. Just do it . . . dammit! Do it . . . for you! For Faison!"

Browny nodded his head very quickly.

"Now . . . get over here and . . . knock me . . . a kiss. You know . . . you always . . . wanted to."

Browny slowly moved toward the bed in which David lay. He thought of everything they'd been through from the time they were sixteen and seventeen. Maybe he was a *better* man for having known the likes of David and Ty. Maybe. Just maybe.

A single tear fell from his right eye and it landed on the white of David's pillow case.

"Yo . . . I ain't no fag, tho," he said, as his lips landed softly on David's forehead.

"No," David grinned slowly, as he reached up to touch Browny's cheek. "But that's only . . . because . . . we . . . wouldn't *have* you, yo."

AIDS is not a pretty disease. Young men do not go easily, nor gently into that long goodnight. A large blue sore had appeared on his neck, and other lesions dotted his face, forehead, and his chest. David weighed all of eighty-three pounds. His hair, what was left of it, had gone surprisingly gray. He looked like his father now. He *hated* that shit.

When he could, David managed to smile at Victor. But it was a sad smile. Victor could feel that storm in him. It was as if there was some raging, screaming wind inside of him, and yet David refused to let it rain. Crying was too easy. Fighting was harder. David's fight inspired Victor to do the same. And so, he saved the tears and put the grief that he was slowly losing David on layaway.

When Kindred appeared at his bedside, David was pleased to see him. In the weeks following his confession to David, there had been no more conversations between them. David did however, transfer the power of attorney to him, and all of Tyrone's worldly goods now belonged to Kindred, Ty's only son.

And because he wanted to appease for all the wrongs and all the perceived wrongs he'd done, David even transferred some Internet stocks into a personal portfolio expressly for *Faison* and Juanita Brown.

He'd been engaged in cleaning his slate. The fashion business would be left to Victor, and run by Victor's nephew. Bliss Santana too was not forgotten. Maybe there would be a cure for HIV in her lifetime, but whether or not that panacea ever came to be, her daughter, young Tyra Renee Depina Santana was assured of a college education.

He needed one more thing from Kindred, the man with Tyrone's face. Though speech and coherency had become unreliable phantoms, as Kindred grasped David's hand tightly, David managed to say, "Please. Read . . . read it . . . to me."

And so, for a friend, Kindred opened the journal beside David's bed. It was bookmarked to the special place, and he began to read Tyrone's last words . . .

Ty's FINAL JOURNAL, IN THE VERY LAST ENTRY:

Life. Does it really have a plot? Would it make a decent flick? Does every existence on this planet have an expressed purpose? I'd like to think the answer is, yes . . . and hopefully, sooner or later, we all begin realize it. But is any life supposed to follow some a linear theme from point *A* to *B* to *C*?

No. I don't think so.

Maybe we earthlings simply move unknowingly through

one event, one dilemma, one triumph, one tragedy, one love, one disappointment, one joy, one drama, one heartbreak, and one memorable adventure after another.

I don't know much, but this is what I've concluded, David: We're born into these roguish skins to feel these feelings and share them with a few souls, to laugh and cry, and dance and sing, and bitch and moan, and then one day, it's over.

Life. None of us will get out of it alive. So, the best of us move through it with courage and some assemblage of dignity. Me? I tried. God knows I've tried. But sometimes, I failed. For that I'm sorry, truly sorry. But I wouldn't give anything for the journey. I have no doubt, your journey be gentler and far more colorful than my own.

We all have a story, some terrible, joyful, wonderful, woeful, transcendent story inside us, and how we handle it, this becomes our legacy. But, hey, what about the moments, David? Shouldn't they count for something?

I can tell you, I enjoyed sharing so many Good Moments with you, my friend. We sure had ourselves a whole mess of them, didn't we? I've loved you, admired you, been amazed and confounded, worshiped and hated you, but most of all, I've thanked God for you!

So, that's it. That's all.

No book, no story, no plot, just a journey through Love. But I defy any author to write a better, more joyous, more difficult, more mysterious, more complex, and more worthwhile story than that, my friend.

I love you, David Donatello Richmond. That's it. That's all. That's EVERYTHING.

Ty.

For Kindred to have read those words, it was for David as if Tyrone was standing right there, mouthing those words to him. What a gift! *What a gift!*

Through this clash and clamor of his last days, David

knew now, a sweet and complacent calm. He realized, beyond fear, there was a Grace in the acceptance of his fate. And with the conclusion of his fight, came this inner knowledge that there was something *more* awaiting him in the end. Morphine was the only drug of choice now. The numbing was needed.

As he lay there in that hospital bed, tubes shooting out of him making him resemble "some sickly octo-pussy boy," even when in pain, David wore what was now his best outfit: a strange unmovable gaze, which to some, looked almost peaceful. Perhaps he was looking forward to seeing his beloved mother, his Facey, his Carlos, his Ty, and all of his wicked best friends again.

Disease may have claimed his body, but something far more *rapturous* was claiming his soul. Though his physicans assumed it was *pain* making David weep, little did they know, those tears David cried were the tears of snatched joy!

When the end came, his eyes shot wide open. From his mouth emanated a harsh noise. He sounded as if he were choking. He sat up and gasped in a loud and audible inhalation of breath. But then, David fell back inside his bed. That harsh intake of air, the fearful noise of it descended, and in its place there came a long, slow and cathartic moan.

The journey was ending.

He closed his eyes slowly, and he surrendered to it.

In his head, on his skin, and then right before his eyes, there came the softly nostalgic golden- light of an Indian summer once remembered. David appeared to smile just a little. He closed his eyes and thought of Tyrone.

Peace was bright light. *Yes*—such soft tones of laughter and lumunious plains of Light. It was then David Richmond muttered in a high and angelic song, and in the lyric of his voice it sounded like he said: "Tyrone . . ."

* * *

And so, the city would go on without him, without them. The city would continue being the same rhythmic, tough, and steely bitch as it ever was. It would still continue to scream and freak its concrete skin, continue to sex, sip its martinis, giggle high and naughtily, smoke its furtive alley cigarettes. The City would continue to break apart about a million hearts, daily.

After all, this was New York City, with its rogue Romeos and its sorrowful addicts, its oxygen thieves, and its dying poets.

"Tyronnnnne . . ."

About the Author

L.M. Ross is a New York writer and a poet of immense musicality. His work, which has appeared in over 270 magazines, journals and anthologies echoes the best of lyric writers, and yet contains brutal slashes of honesty.

His novels include the haunting, *Manhood . . . The Longest Moan*, a story of youthful ambition, maturing success and heartbreaking disappointment, and Ross' latest work *The Moanin' After* is the sequel, and a deep, wistful, brave and harrowing account of a handful of New York denizens seeking to find their wings after the winds of flight have been taken away by absence, disease and death.

But more than pure story, *The Moanin' After sings* with a poetic music inherent in the writing. It is like a jazz movement and a Blues suite mingling with memory, life and tension as Ross' uniquely poetic voice sings throughout the narrative. Its main characters are David Richmond, a former dancer, seeking to find the legs in which to walk through life with bravery and dignity. Faison Brown, a bruised and angry soul desperately trying to snatch at the last remnants of fame and success. Bliss Santana, a single mother, cursed by a past love and determined to live in the shaky present without stigma or regret. And then, there is Kindred, who is either the spirit of purity personified, or the ghostly return of the beloved Tyrone Hunter.

These characters glide the book's journey over the years, as the reader comes to care for, root for, cry for . . . and despise.

The Moanin' After is a character study about people you will know, recognize and feel from the inside out. With themes of success, love, loss, deep loneliness, anger and hard- edged rage, ***The Moanin' After*** is about choices and their sometime brutal consequences, it's about secrets and lies and the way they can so slyly determine the shape of the future.